THE DUZY

HOUSE

OF

MOURNING

THE DUZY
HOUSE
OF
MOURNING

a novel

KA HANCOCK

www.kahancock.com

Manufactured in the United States of America

ISBN 978-1-7923-9999-2
ISBN 979-8-3507-0854-7 (ebook)
ISBN 979-8-3507-1668-9 (Hard cover)

KAMAKI
PRESS

Dedication

To Daughters...who become Mothers...who then understand the need for Forgiveness.

Acknowledgements

Mark, then, now, and always, I love you. Thank you for doing life with me! I'm especially indebted to you for your unfailing expertise in all things technological. You are my rockstar!

To my daughters who read each word—several times—and gushed forth kindly. Hilary, Abby, and Whitney, thank you for being stellar critics and awesome women. And to Shawn, deepest gratitude for always believing! I adore you all!

For reading the many drafts of this ever-evolving work and offering such generous and inspired insight—I thank my crew Dorothy Keddington, LuAnn Anderson, and Carol Warburton. No writer could have better friends!

True and honest thanks to Lauren McKenna. You changed my life as a writer. I grieved when you left Simon & Schuster.

To Emily Poole, you are magic. Thank you!

And finally, all my love to my sweet mama, Joyce Lloyd.

prologue

She was still in the grip of a contraction when the truck hit them. The force of it slid them to the curb, then tipped their car onto two tires where they teetered before the full weight crashed down on top of them. Slowly and somehow unfiltered, she captured what could not possibly be happening, frame by frame. She watched the inside of their car bend in on itself, and on them, glass and steel giving way under the load. The love of her life groaned a torturous "Noooo" as he was crushed against her, then into her. She heard their bones break and her head crack, felt sensation in her legs evaporate and breath gush from her chest. And she felt the warm wet of blood run across her face, but she didn't know if it was hers or his.

Her husband was holding her hand when he died, and she was a mere breath behind him when she felt it. The woman couldn't fathom it—this tiny kick, this gentle quiver in the midst of unimaginable destruction. Death was next to her holding her hand. Life was still beating inside what was left of her.

And in that instant, she was granted the unthinkable: a choice.

one

I prefer to work on the dead in privacy. I like a little Chopin on in the background, sometimes Liszt or Gershwin, and once in a while, Gaga, or, frequently, Norah. I like all my tools within easy reach so I don't lose focus looking for anything. And I like the door shut. In theory, this is an indication that I want to be left alone with my deceased. Sadly, my ideal methods mean little to my grandfather, and I work for him. Poppy is very hands-on. So even though I like to work uninterrupted, I am frequently interrupted.

I'm the one who prepares their final face—the last face the world will see. I fill their mouth with just enough of whatever is called for to plump out their sunken cheeks and place a guard along their gums if they have no teeth. I glue their eyelids shut over caps that are stand-ins for fallen eyeballs and clip their nose hair. The same goes for ear hair and errant tufts from eyebrows and upper lips. When needed, I use wax, sometimes putty, to fill holes caused by trauma. When everything is plumped and spackled, glued and clipped, I spray foundation over all of it to mask any discoloration. If I've done a good job, I'm left with a very clean slate ready for transformation.

If I'm lucky, I have a feel for who this person was before they crossed my path, meaning I've had a peek at them through the eyes of someone who knew them. Sometimes that's not possible; sometimes, the only one available is a dispassionate lawyer with power of attorney or a nursing-home orderly with nothing much to offer. But I take what I can get, hoping it will translate into enough intuition for me to create a memorable goodbye.

As the haunting notes of Chopin's Nocturne in E-flat faded into silence, I gulped the last of my warm Dr. Pepper and wearily scrutinized the sleeping canvas before me. It had already been a long day, and it was far from over. "So, Miss Ashley Pierce," I said to the dead woman. "Who exactly were you?"

I took in the short round body, the enviably thick hair that seemed prematurely threaded with gray, her short neck and flattened features. The paperwork said she was a thirty-three-year-old female with Downs Syndrome who'd died of a respiratory infection complicated by asthma. She'd arrived unaccompanied late yesterday, although someone from her family was expected tonight. Apparently, the Pierces were in the midst of an extraordinary situation given that the timing of Ashley's unexpected demise coincided with the rupture of her mother's appendix. Mr. Pierce was in China trying to get back to deal with these two crises, and as a result, our consult had been delayed. So, with nothing formal to go on in the way of preparing my deceased, I had simply washed and embalmed her. Ashley had a sweet face that spoke of innate happiness, and I'd formed her mouth into the almost-smile it seemed naturally accustomed to. I brushed her clean hair, then put her back in the fridge.

Next, I pulled out Julian Broadhead. Poppy and I had put him back together two nights ago, and his family had finally dropped off his suit. The fifty-two-year-old's car had been slammed into on the turnpike by a kid texting his girlfriend. He'd been a shattered mess when he arrived, but all of that would be hidden beneath this dark blue gabardine.

I was just knotting his bright red tie when my grandfather poked his head in. "Janny?" he asked. "Can you come up?"

I checked the clock on the wall. "Can you give me a few more minutes? I'm almost done here."

Poppy pushed open the door. "I wish I could. I'm fielding two visitations, and the Pierce family has shown up. Actually, they've been waiting, and I can't get to them. Please come now and do the consult. There's no one else available. It's the brother and his wife—I think it's his wife—and they're getting a little frustrated."

His serious expression told me it wasn't a request. Tess was still in Las Vegas, Calvin was handling a collection, and I knew that my grandmother was in a consultation of her own. "Okay, let me just change."

We all do triple-duty around here, but in addition to pinch-hitting wherever we're needed, my Aunt Tess and I do all the embalming. Initial consults are my least favorite task, but I'm not called upon to do them often.

"Thank you, January," my grandfather said with a weary, knowing nod. "They're in the coffin room. Grandy is using her office."

"I'll be right up."

"Good girl, *Kochanie*," he winked, using the familiar Polish endearment.

In our tiny, attached washroom, I pulled off the scrub top I wore over my black tank, washed my hands, and slipped out of my draw-string bottoms and into the black pencil skirt that had been hanging on the back of the door. I then ran my fingers through my dark blond hair, checked my teeth, and put on some lip-gloss. It was 7:40, and I'd been at it over twelve hours; thankfully, I didn't think I looked it. I traded my Nike Airs for the red pumps I'd worn down this morning and checked the package in the mirror on the door as I tucked a gray shirt in at my waist. Pushing a belligerent curl behind my ear, I left a pants-less Julian reposing to my favorite of Frédéric's etudes. Then I walked up the tiled hallway to the elevator.

I grew up here in my grandparents' mortuary, in Wallington, New Jersey. Officially, it's the Duzinski Funeral Chapel, but I have affectionately coined it the Duzy House of Mourning. Since I was twelve, I've done odd jobs that included buffing and filing and painting dead fingernails, tweezing, waxing, occasional hair washing, and helping Tess drape and casket our decedents. Today, ten years later, I've graduated from mortuary school and am now versed in all elements of the funeral process. This is why I keep street clothes hanging in the washroom and dress shoes in the corner of my embalming theater.

The elevator never came, which was no surprise, so I took the stairs to the main floor and walked out to the other side of this business's split personality. Downstairs, we dealt with the mechanics of death: repairing and preserving, draining fluids, pumping in chemicals—impersonal, utilitarian. In contrast, the main floor was soft, a place of reflection, whispers, and tempered grief. That was all my grandmother. Diana Merlyn Duzinski—proprietor, quality-control maven, and frequent hand-arranger—insisted on quietude up here so that emotions could flow without censure. And this evening there was a lot of that emotion in the people navigating between our two chapels. It was a busy night here at the Duzy House of Mourning.

I walked down the hall to our coffin room, which is tucked into an alcove off the chapel hall across from Grandy's office. We call it that because, aside from being a very nice consultation room, it has the added function of housing our casket collection. We keep them behind a wall of heavy drapes that part with the touch of a button found next to the light switch. It's very impressive, but at the moment I hoped they were not on display—it can be quite unsettling for loved ones to be alone and surrounded by burial options.

I took a breath and pushed open the door. Thankfully our merchandise was hidden from view and the room was in consultation mode: soft lamp light, large desk, two sofas separated by a coffee table, and a nice-looking couple gazing up at me. She was a striking brunette wearing glasses that made her look smart; he, too was good-looking—very good-looking, in fact—with intense green eyes that were the definition of sad.

"Sorry to keep you waiting," I said, approaching.

He stood. "No problem." He was around twenty-five—maybe a little older—wearing jeans, a white button-down, and a beige sports coat. The woman, in sleeveless yellow, didn't stand.

I reached across the coffee table to the man's outstretched hand. "I'm January Duzinski."

"I'm Tyson Pierce. This is my friend, Brynn Duncan." The woman lifted an eyebrow, but I don't think it was meant for me.

"It's nice to meet you."

"Mmm, I think my sister is here," the man said.

"Would that be Ashley?" I said, sitting down across from them.

Tyson Pierce nodded, sat back down, and looked honestly exhausted.

The woman looked over at him, then stroked his arm in a very tender way.

"I'm so sorry," I said. "And I understand your mother is in the midst of quite a—"

"Oh, it's such a mess," the Duncan woman interrupted. "Ty's dad is traveling. His mom just had surgery, his brother is out of town…This poor guy has had a lot to deal with—haven't you, honey?"

Tyson Pierce looked the slightest bit annoyed at her rambling as he stared at me.

"And we've been waiting quite a while," she continued. "Do you know how much longer it will be?"

"For what?" I said, confused.

"We're supposed to meet with a funeral director," she said a bit sharply.

"Ah. That would be me."

"Oh," she said, lips parting. "I thought… I thought we'd be meeting with… someone…" She shrugged. "I guess… sorry."

I turned to Tyson Pierce. "I'm actually a mortician here. And I've been taking care of your sister."

His eyes widened, then he cleared his throat. "So, Ash has…. Has she been embalmed? Is that what you do?"

"It is," I nodded. "And she has."

"Can I see her?"

"Oh, I don't know, Ty…" the girl noised, her tone discouraging.

"Of course," I said over her.

"But maybe we could chat for a moment first. It would help me if I knew a little something about her."

"Like what?"

"Maybe just something about her personality. What she was like. If I can, I'd like to capture some of that as I prepare her."

"Oh," he said thoughtfully. "That would actually be nice." He swallowed. "That would be nice."

"Were the two of you close?"

He hesitated, and again the woman found his shoulder. "I'd like to think so," he said. "But… I mean, not really. She pretty much adored me, but I wasn't a great brother, not to her."

"Oh, Ty. You were a wonderful brother," Brynn cloyed.

He ignored her, and the look on his face rather broke my heart. He swallowed. "I'm sorry. This wasn't supposed to happen," he said softly.

"I know. I'm sorry," I said.

He cleared his throat. "I don't really know what I'm doing here. My dad sent me over because he's flying in from Beijing to be with my mom, who's still in the hospital. I'm supposed to get her on the phone, if that's okay—she has questions." He shook his head, took out his phone. "This is all a little out of my realm. What do you need from me? Do I need to pick out a casket, bring Ash some clothes, pay you? I don't know anything about funerals. I don't know what to do."

"It's okay. You're doing fine," I said calmly, calmer than I felt. "No one is ever really ready when this happens."

"And I'm right here," chirped Brynn Duncan, who had now threaded her hand into his.

Tyson Pierce sighed, cleared his throat, again. "Do you have some water?"

"I do," I said. "Water? Or I have a Coke?"

"Oh, I could use a Coke if you've got one."

I glanced at Ms. Duncan, but she held up a hand, declining my offer.

"I'll be right back."

I took our temperamental elevator to the third floor—which is where we live—and hurried into the kitchen where my great-grandmother was playing solitaire at the table. She looked up at me and smiled. "Hello, my Janny," she said.

"Hey, Babi. You're up late. Is that my cell?"

"Yes. Is ringing, so I answer. Was Jasmine. I am warming the milk when she call. She say to call her when you can."

"Thanks," I said, pocketing my phone, which had been charging near the toaster. Then I grabbed two Cokes from the fridge and planted a kiss on the head of my little Polish Babka. "Must run," I said. "Busy night with the dead."

I headed back down the hall but stopped abruptly, thinking of Tyson Pierce and what was not supposed to have happened and turned back to the kitchen. My great-grandmother is ninety-four—tomorrow—with hair so white it belongs on an angel. She's tiny, has lived a life no one should live, and always has a smile for me. For more than twenty-two years, she has been my truest champion—one of them, anyway. As I re-entered the kitchen, she looked up at me and grinned again, her eyes disappearing into a web of deep wrinkles. "Forgot something, Kochanie?"

"Yes, Babi." I rinsed her favorite mug from among the still-dirty dishes in the dishwasher, then poured the simmering milk into it. Babi's mug was chipped, and I set it down backward so she'd have the smooth edge facing her. Her craggy little hand found my face and patted. "Thank you, my Janny."

"Do you want me to help you back to bed?" I asked.

"No, no. I am lucky winning the cards. You go. Busy night with the dead."

"Yes. Busy night." Again, I kissed her head. "See you tomorrow, Babi."

When I walked back into the coffin room, I found Ashley Pierce's brother and his girlfriend studying a painting on the wall. It was an oil of a tulip field. Very vibrant, yet very soothing.

"My grandmother painted that from a photo she took in Holland many years ago," I said. "She told me she'd never seen a more beautiful sight—tulips as far as she could see. The next day, all the flowers had been cut and the bulbs were being harvested. She said there were mountains and mountains of tulips."

"That's awesome," said Brynn.

"Is she still alive?" Tyson asked.

"Yes. She and my grandfather own this place."

"Oh, I didn't mean to assume. My grandmother died last year, so…" he shrugged. "I hate death."

"Of course you do, honey," the Duncan girl simpered, squeezing his arm.

I looked at him looking at me and handed him the Coke.

"Thanks," he said. "I don't know what's wrong with me. It's just been a really long day."

"I'm sure," I said, standing close enough to him that I had to look slightly up to meet his eyes. They were green and intense. I felt another set of eyes on me as well, but I didn't look at Brynn Duncan.

"So, what do I need to do?" Tyson Pierce asked.

"Well, we should probably discuss your plans for burial. Is your sister to be buried or cremated?"

"Buried," Brynn said before Tyson could get the word out. "She'll be next to their grandparents at Crest Haven, the memorial park. Do you know it?"

"Of course. It's very pretty there."

"She loved the whole idea of parks," Tyson said. "You probably know this, but she was Downs—she had Downs Syndrome, so in many ways she was just a big kid." He nodded as his gaze slid away from me. "She loved parks."

"Well, then I can't think of a better place than Crest Haven."

Brynn Duncan got a call then. From the bowels of her purse, the theme song from CSI erupted. She beelined to the sofa where she dug through her bag until she found her phone. Swiping her screen, she said, "Oh, I have to take this," and walked out, cheerily greeting whoever was on the other end.

That left me alone with Tyson Pierce, who looked both annoyed and relieved as he glanced at me.

I smiled. "Do you feel like you could pick out a casket? Or has your family made plans for that already?"

"We haven't done anything. Nobody saw this coming."

"Okay. Well, let me show you what we have," I said, walking to the wall. "This room actually doubles as our retail space." I pushed the magic button, and as the draperies parted, the bay behind them lit up to illuminate our selection.

Tyson Pierce looked sincerely impressed and the tiniest bit appalled. "Wow," he breathed.

"It's a little overwhelming," I agreed. "But it makes the selection process easy, if you want to go this route. There are other choices out there, but these are what we offer." Tyson followed me into the bay where our collection of ten caskets was arranged in a horseshoe. Our assortment of urns lined the back wall.

Tyson stopped at the first casket, looked over at me, then ran his hand across the back of his neck. "I should call my mom."

"Okay. But maybe we could narrow it down first."

He looked at me. "What do you mean?"

"Well, was Ashley…was she a girly girl, or more of a tomboy?"

My question seemed to focus him. He even smiled—through a threat of tears. "She was all girl. My sister was a Barbie doll trapped in a…" he shrugged. "Just trapped. She was all girl."

"Okay. Then let's eliminate these." I waved away the stained solid wood choices as well as a shiny grey metallic coffin. That left four decidedly more feminine options: a pale pink, highly glossed metallic; a pale lavender-blue steel; a hardwood painted brilliant white; and a navy-blue metallic with a fussy pink lining. Tyson further narrowed the field to the navy and the blue-lavender. That's when he got his mother on the phone.

As they video chatted and he showed her the options he'd settled on, I answered questions on cost, but mostly I felt like an eavesdropper. I nodded appropriately when his questioning gaze met mine, needing encouragement, but basically, he was doing fine

Finally, there was a soft knock at the door, and when my grandmother walked in—Brynn Duncan at her heels—I was actually relieved—consultations are her wheelhouse. "How are we doing in here?" Grandy said. "Anything I can help with?"

"Tyson," I said. "This is my grandmother, Diana Duzinski. Grandy, this is Tyson Pierce, and his mother is on the phone with him. And it looks like you've met Ms. Duncan."

"I have," she smiled at the woman in yellow. "And I am so sorry for your loss," she offered, approaching our client with utter ease, her hand held out. Tall, slim, put-together in a dark suit, her reading glasses resting in her short gray hair, my grandmother was the picture of maternal professionalism. "And, goodness, Mrs. Pierce. I understand you're recovering from surgery and your husband is traveling," Grandy said, addressing the phone. "Please know that whatever we can do to make this as easy as possible for your family…we are at your disposal. There is no rush."

Brynn had again resumed her rightful place by Tyson's side. "You okay, sweetie?" I heard her whisper.

"Thank you, so much," Tyson's mother voiced from the tinny speaker in his phone. "I think we've decided on a casket, and Ty will be back tomorrow with a dress. My husband and I should be by tomorrow night."

"That will be just fine," Grandy said. "In the meantime, I can assure you that January here will be taking very good care of your daughter."

More tears and a squeaky "thank you" emanated from the phone, then Tyson told his mother he'd see her soon and disconnected the call.

Grandy didn't miss a beat. "Goodness, there is a lot on your plate, Mr. Pierce. How are you managing?"

He breathed in deeply and let it out. He looked at me. "I'm doing okay. January has been a big help."

It got just the tiniest bit awkward then because he wouldn't let go of my eyes. I didn't really know what to say with him standing there looking suddenly so tender in his grief, his girlfriend like a tumor growing out of his side. "Thank you," I managed, then cleared my throat. "I need to get back," I said. "But it was lovely to meet you, Tyson…Brynn. Grandy can help with your questions about what comes next."

Tyson looked at Grandy, then back at me. "Okay. Well…thank you," he said. "Thanks again for your help, January."

"My pleasure." I smiled.

When I got back downstairs, I told Miss Ashley Pierce that I'd met her very cute brother and that she'd been holding out on me.

***

I was just filling in Ashley's thin eyebrows when I heard a soft knock, and Grandy peered in. "Janny," she said. "Mr. Pierce would like to see his sister. Is it okay?"

"Sure, give me just a second."

There was a sheet pulled up to the woman's thick neck, and I'd run a curling iron through the ends of her long hair. She looked nice, though it would have been less unsettling if she'd been dressed and casketed. But I *had* promised him.

Not all mortuaries allow for viewing during prep, but Poppy has always been very open to each family's individual needs. He thinks early viewing can help the grief process, so we honor requests like this whenever we can. And tonight, I could. I pulled the curtain separating my workspace from the rest of the embalming theater and opened the door. Tyson seemed the slightest bit reluctant to enter. Brynn was not with him, and I didn't ask why. I looked at him; he looked at me. Then I smiled as Grandy slipped out.

"It's okay," I said. "She's just Ashley." I took his elbow and led him into the room. I'd seen Grandy do this dozens of times, and no one had ever rejected her offer to hold onto them as they viewed their deceased loved one for the first time. Tyson Pierce was no exception, and I felt him tremble slightly against me.

"I can't believe it," he said in a small voice.

"Are you all right?"

A breath shuddered out of him as he gazed down at his sister. Then he moved closer and leaned in. "Ash," he said softly. "What are you doin'? What are we supposed to do now?" He stared at her for a long time, sniffing back emotion; as he did, I saw him get used to what he was seeing. Finally, he looked over at me with moist eyes. "She looks really nice. You did all this? This is what you do?"

I nodded.

"She looks pretty. She looks like *her*."

"Thank you."

"You wanted to know something about her," he rasped.

"Whatever you'd like to tell me."

He looked back down at her. "She always had bows in her hair. Always. Does that count?"

"Absolutely."

"They looked ridiculous, but she loved them, and Mom loved her, so she always had a bow in her hair." Pulling out his phone, Tyson scanned through the pictures until he found what he was looking for and then showed me: a round little face, small upturned eyes, big smile, hair parted on the side with a large red bow holding it off her face. "That's pretty recent," he told me.

I leaned in to take a closer look. "Could you email me a copy of that?" I asked.

"Sure. Where should I send it?"

I gave him my email address, and as he stowed his phone, I asked him to tell me more about Ashley.

He looked down at her. "She loved to watch *Dancing with the Stars*. She loved getting dressed up. She loved to eat—everything, but mostly candy, especially those big Life Savers; she always had a handful of those in her pocket. And she sang all the time. She had a terrible voice, but she didn't know it. Of course, I had to tease her about it. She called me stupid—said I didn't understand her talent." He chuckled. "But that girl could *not* sing."

This made me smile. "What is your favorite memory?"

He thought about this. "She came to all my games—soccer, football, baseball—mostly because my mom did. But Ash hated the thought that I might get hurt, so she was very...tense—and loud.

When I was in Little League, I lived in terror that she would throw a fit if I was tackled on the field." He shook his head, remembering. "She was very excitable, and it embarrassed me. I used to hate that she was there. I could be a real brat."

I looked at him. Oh, how I could relate!

He sighed. "But every kid should have such a cheerleader." This last part wobbled out on a little sob of emotion. He shook his head. "Sorry."

"Don't be," I said. "My grandfather says tears are just wet memories."

Tyson looked at me and pushed the heel of his hand into his eye. "Wet memories. I like that."

I smiled because I didn't know what else to do.

"Thank you for this. For all of it, I mean. This was tougher than I thought it would be. I don't know what I thought it would be, but you made it...*almost nice*," he said.

"I'm glad I could help." I turned the light out on Tyson's sleeping sister, and we walked down the hall to the elevator.

"Do your parents work here, too?" Tyson asked.

"No," I said to the floor. "My father used to...a long time ago. But now it's just me."

I could feel his eyes on me, but he didn't ask any more questions, and I was grateful.

Upstairs, Brynn was on the sofa doing something on her phone. As we approached, she quickly stowed it and got to her feet. The yellow dress was short, and her tan legs were long. She was very pretty. As she reclaimed possession of Tyson, I heard her ask, "You okay, honey? Was it awful?"

Tyson looked at me, then away. "No. It was nice, actually. I'm glad I got to see her."

As I showed them out, Tyson Pierce hung back a few steps. "I think I know the dress I'm supposed to bring tomorrow," he said. "Will you be here?"

"I'll be here," I told him. "But if I'm not available, you can just leave it with my grandmother."

He smiled, held my gaze. "Thanks again, January," he said as Brynn tugged him toward the parking lot.

two

There were still a few people milling through our halls when Tyson Pierce and his girlfriend left. I sighed, watching them leave. It had been a long, long day.

Grandy was chatting with a weeping woman near the chapel while Poppy sat on one of the sofas in our lobby. As I walked past him, he eyed me with weariness and mimed piano fingers—his way of requesting I play him a song. I knew he was just waiting to lock up, and since his day had been longer than mine, of course I complied.

There are three pianos on this floor—an upright in each chapel, and a baby grand in the lobby. The space around the baby grand is rather vast, designed for mingling and quiet conversation. Seating is sprinkled throughout the area, and the acoustics are stellar, so the music carries softly, soothingly through the halls. I'm nothing if not an obedient granddaughter, so I walked over and sat down. Lucas King's brilliant "Quiet's Theme" immediately came to mind. I knew it by heart from drowning myself in it, and my finger memory was even better than that, so within seconds it was effortlessly flowing out of me. And after a day like this, to be able to just sit and make that soft loveliness emanate from these keys felt better than a full body massage.

My mother had played *gloriously*, so I come by my love of the piano honestly—that's what Poppy says. I've never heard her play, but legend has it my father fell in love with her at a Chopin competition where she took first prize. Clearly, she must have been amazing. She went to Juilliard for a semester in high school and that's no easy feat.

Across the room, my grandfather was smiling, his lips parted in trance-like appreciation. He was pouring it on, and it made me chuckle. Still, he looked every inch the funeral director that he was, silvering hair, white goatee, and black suit—very distinguished, if a little sleepy at the moment. He winked at me.

My dad had been his only son—the only son of an only son named after his father, my grandfather, Stasio Tanek Duzinski. Stasio is my Poppy; Tanek, which means immortal in Polish, was my dad. I never met him, but I've seen pictures.

"Oh, I do love this piece," my grandmother said as she sat down on the bench next to me.

I smiled. "Finally finished?"

"I certainly hope so," she said, sighing appreciatively as I repeated the refrain. "Lovely, Janny. Just lovely."

I bumped her shoulder with mine in acknowledgment of the compliment.

Across the room, my grandfather was ushering out an elderly couple, the last of the stragglers. He gave the woman a hug and shook the man's hand, nodding with patient interest at whatever the gentleman was saying.

"That man was made for the death business," I said as I played.

"Yes, he was," Grandy agreed. "But I'm going to kill him if he doesn't let me hire an evening director."

"I'll help you."

She sighed again. "I am so done with this day, January. Let's go up."

I let the final chords echo into silence then lifted my hands from the keys. The peaceful arrangement had been a soothing nod to the end of this busy day. I shut the fallboard and pushed in the bench while Grandy went over to talk to Poppy. I heard him say he'd be up soon, which undoubtedly meant another couple of hours. She kissed him and it made me smile. My grandmother is taller than my Poppy by a couple of inches, and she has no compunction about wearing her heels, which extends that distance. He doesn't seem to mind a bit. He adores her— sometimes from his tiptoes—exactly as she is.

I walked over to them. "Poppy, what do you need me to do so we can lock up?"

"Get to bed," he said. "Calvin will have two in the fridge for you when you wake up in the morning. At least. He's on his way back now from Little Saints Hospital, and I just got a call from Sisters of Charity Care Center. I'll wait for him, and then I'll be up."

I leaned over and kissed his cheek. "One funeral tomorrow? Or two?"

"Just Julian Broadhead in the afternoon. The other's a graveside that Calvin will handle."

Grandy reached over and straightened Poppy's tie. "I'll give you an hour, old man, then you'd better be in my bed."

He looked at me and shook his head. "I wish that meant what it sounded like."

My grandmother gave him a look. "How do you know it doesn't?" she winked, taking my hand.

I sighed. "Don't mind me."

Grandy laughed. "We're going up. One hour, Stas. I mean it."

He saluted, and we walked down the hall, me internally lamenting the fact that my grandparents had been married almost fifty years and still got naked with each other, whereas the only naked men in my life were dead. Worse still, that was kind of okay with me.

"What?" Grandy asked.

"Nothing." I wearily smiled as I pushed the button to summon our unpredictable elevator—it was original to the building and had a mind of its own.

My grandfather had bought our building years ago, when it was a decrepit apartment complex on the verge of being overtaken by rats, if you believe Grandy. The only thing he'd kept was the main elevator. He'd torn out all the walls upstairs separating the tiny apartments, all except for my great-grandmother's because she refused to move. Our entire home had then been redesigned around Babi's original rooms. We live on the third floor, and our decedents are prepared in the basement. The chapels and offices are on the first floor, and the second floor is all storage. Everything—all the inventory and supplies needed to run a mortuary *and* a family—is kept on the second floor, between our home and our business. But it's also a bit of a hoarder's paradise because my grandfather is averse to throwing anything away. That floor houses everything from old furniture and camping equipment to chemicals and canned goods from Costco. There is also a room for

Babka's pinwheels, a labor of love inspired by her family who died at Birkenau.

Two elevators traverse the three stories. One opens directly into the tiled entry just off our living room, and one opens into the laundry room. You can also get to the third floor through the garage and take the stairs to the kitchen, or there is a set of stairs outside that serves as a fire escape. I usually take the garage stairs, but that night we were still waiting for the elevator.

"What a day!" Grandy groaned when it finally arrived. "Thank you for your help with Mr. Pierce. How did he do seeing his sister?"

"It was a little tough on him."

"He was very nice, I thought," Grandy said. "He thought you were nice, too."

I deadpanned my grandmother. "That's because I *am* nice."

"Yes, you are," she smiled. "Now, you remember we're taking Babka to lunch tomorrow for her birthday?"

"I do," I said. "But I'm not sure how much time I'll have. I may have to meet you there. Where are we going?"

Grandy eyed me. "She wants to go to Potomac Manor so Claire can be part of the celebration."

I nodded. "That makes sense."

The elevator opened up into the laundry room, and Grandy smiled wearily as we stepped out. "I know it's not the most convenient, but I hope you can make it, Janny. It's been weeks since you've seen your mother."

"I know."

"She misses you."

"I know."

"And the staff there, of course, have arranged a private lunch for us on the patio at Rahela's request. Nothing like planning your own birthday. Your Babka is a stinker."

"I'll do my best," I said, knowing bodies in the fridge gave me a ready excuse to bail.

My grandmother palmed my chin, which made it impossible for me to miss the concern in her eyes. But since that was typically her response to my lack of enthusiasm for seeing my mother, I was used to it. She kissed my nose. "Sleep well, my love," she said, then walked down the hall.

"You, too," I whispered.

I walked into my room and into a mess of clutter—boxes and bags and piles of clothes, as well as stacks of books and music. It looked like a place ready to be vacated, which it had been for the past three and a half weeks since the furnished apartment I was planning to lease had fallen through. I was now on a waiting list. A couple of them, in fact. But despite its current condition, this room still felt like home. And truth be told, it was going to be hard to leave. I'd slept in here every night since I was a baby—well, except for a few months after the fire. I was just four, or almost four, when that happened, but I still remember how before that, Claire used to sit in a chair by the window and watch me sleep. That memory is part of this room…is part of me.

My mother was always broken, her face not pretty, her walk not smooth. To wake up behind the bars of my crib and see her there would have frightened me, I'm sure, if I hadn't always known her to be that way. But she was disfigured like Grandy was tall and I was little. It's just who she was, who she'd always been, familiar to me in every way. And I remember that when I napped, she sat in the chair in the corner and watched over me.

The fact that Claire *was* my mother was intelligence given to me from the beginning; no one had ever kept that from me. But it was just a label—a label that didn't carry any actual primordial meaning, because Grandy was my imprint. Grandy was my parent. From my first awareness, she had been the primal source of my security and belonging. Claire was a nice bonus, an additional someone who loved me, as evidenced by her keeping vigil over me while I slept. To me, I had a mother (Claire). And I had a *Mother* (Grandy).

I never knew my parents, either one of them, really. But there are many pictures, from *before*. One sits on my nightstand. I see it every day, even if I don't always look at it. It was taken at their wedding: a beautiful bride and groom looking idyllic for the camera. In the picture, Claire is exploding with laughter, and my father cannot take his eyes off her. They're gorgeous. They're dancing, so they're holding each other very close, and you can clearly see their love. It permeates the photo. They're my parents, and I came from them, but they are essentially strangers to me.

My father died the night I was born, and my mother, who was hurt in just about every way a person *could* be hurt, was expected to die that night as well. There is a plastic bin downstairs full of her memorabilia. In it there is a newspaper, the headline of which reads: *New Year's 2001 Ushers in its First Fatality as Well as its First Birth, Both in the Same Family.* The drunk died, too, but he didn't make the headline.

My mother did survive, but she was never whole again—not anywhere near. She sustained a traumatic head injury and was in a coma for a long time, and then in a rehab hospital. It took almost a year for her to come home. I never knew the lovely face in the pictures. I have only ever known the one that is arranged all wrong, with a pallet of scars, a glass eye, and a smile that lifts only on one side. She claps a lot and blinks her yeses and nos because she is nonverbal. She makes sounds, but they are not words. Before I was born, she played the piano, and danced with the love of her life, my father. Now she limps and doesn't speak and moves very slowly.

And she used to watch me sleep.

Until the fire.

I have only fragments of that awful night—the faulty impressions of a four-year-old—but those have rather fossilized in me. Trauma does that, apparently. What I remember most is that I couldn't breathe—that has always stayed with me—like drowning in smoke. And not just drowning but being held down to drown by a tremendous weight crushing me. I couldn't move or breathe because Claire was on top of me. I'm twenty-two years old, and that memory is still rich in unyielding detail, even if everything else that happened is less clear.

The fire destroyed my room, the living room and part of Claire's room. Babka's room was strangely untouched, while my grandparents' closet went up in smoke. But nobody died *that* night, thankfully.

During the four months that our home and mortuary underwent massive repairs, we stayed with Aunt Margaret, Grandy's sister. But not Claire. Claire had to go live at Potomac Manor, which, in more of my faulty kid-reasoning, was because she started the fire.

But my mother had nothing to do with the fire—of course, she didn't—that was just the way I connected the dots as a traumatized little girl. It was defective wiring in a restored building, factual details that meant nothing to a four-year-old. I'd been trapped under my mother while flames danced everywhere around me. There was no room for logic, not when I honestly believed at the time that Claire had tried to hurt me, not *save* me, which is exactly what she had done.

My grandparents tried desperately to help me. They took me to counseling, to play therapy, to clergy. They soothed me through my relentless nightmares. But nothing worked. I was deathly afraid of Claire. And in that irrational state, I could not comprehend how everyone else could continue to love her. It made no sense that we would visit her, that Grandy and Poppy would take her presents, and talk and laugh and love her like nothing had happened.

Me? I recoiled. I acted out. I couldn't tolerate being around her. I pushed her away for a long, long time and I hurt her terribly. I know I did.

I don't push her away anymore. But I'm not close to her, and I don't know how to be, so I avoid spending time with her.

It's awkward and troubling. My feelings for my mother are very complicated.

three

I set my alarm for 5:45 but was awake and staring at the ceiling long before it went off, the July sunrise well underway and filling my room with light. Two bodies in the fridge made for a short night, and if I was going to make it to Babka's lunch, I had to get one out of the way before I left. I turned on the radio and jumped in the shower. Then listening to the news, I dressed in a white tee and jeans because it was easy to throw scrubs on over them. No reported shootings, which was good news—they're messy. There had been a raid on a party where the designer drug Pink was said to have been responsible for two deaths. Hmmm, it didn't say where. The day was going to be hot, and the Jackals had lost in a blowout...again.

"Well, of course they did," I told my reflection as I inspected my face. My skin looked decent, so I just did my eyes, which, in my opinion, were my best feature—kind of green-gray with good brows. I toweled my shoulder-length hair and sprayed it with product so it could dry in its natural waves. Then at 6:15, I made my way downstairs with an English muffin and a Pepsi—the breakfast of champions.

As promised, there were two in the fridge: The first was Milo Bitters, a ninety-year-old veteran, wasted and gaunt with a sweet face; second was a girl about fifteen who looked completely healthy. My heart sank as I picked up her paperwork. Teagan Lowe had overdosed. Toxicology was pending, but synthetic opiod found at the premises, and "Pink" was the suspected culprit: "A raid on a party where Pink was said to have been responsible for two deaths." I blew out a breath recalling the news. Kids were the hardest for me, next to babies, but

I'd choose working on them any day over dealing with their family and friends.

When a kid dies, it's an event. The unfinished life of someone young brings stunned people out of the woodwork. They take refuge in each other's introspection and feelings of guilt. And there's always an air of incredulity. Teagan Lowe would have started her sophomore year at Bonaventure High next month. Today she should have been heading to the mall or her job, to flirting and laughter. Instead, she'd overdosed on the latest and greatest.

I pulled the girl out of the cooler and slid her onto my work surface. "What did you do to yourself, m'dear?" I asked as I cut away her clothing. She was tiny, compact, with no bruises that I could see. She had mild rigor in her limbs, which I massaged, and rings on every finger, which I removed and bagged.

Her long hair was dirty, her forehead broken out, and the black polish on her nails was chipped. She had extraordinarily long eyelashes caked with mascara. I got to work.

***

It was almost eleven when Poppy knocked on my door and walked in, the knock a perfunctory exercise only. I looked up at him and then at the clock and couldn't believe how the morning had flown. I'd washed Teagan's hair, sewn her jaw shut, and cleaned every inch of her body. I was just shaping her mouth as Poppy sidled up next to me. Kids were hard on him, too, especially this kind. He shook his head. "Parents due anytime," he said. "They'll want to see her."

"I'll put her in the receiving room."

"She looks nice, Janny. Innocent. I think that will help."

"I'll dry her hair. Give me ten minutes."

He looked at me and smiled sadly, and I knew what he was thinking. And he knew I knew. "I love you, too, Poppy," I said.

"Mind reader," he murmured as he walked out.

When I was in high school, two kids I knew died of heroin overdoses a week apart. It sent a chill though our community and, in particular, my grandparents, who were raising me with parenting tools from the sixties. After those deaths, we'd had another lengthy conversation that elicited another promise from me never to do drugs. I'd promised. Again.

They'd been afraid for me and *of* me since I'd scared them so terribly on my sixteenth birthday. But I'd never done anything since. And I wouldn't. Because of me, dead kids and their heartbroken parents have always sparked in Poppy tremendous reflection on my preciousness. It's a bit overblown, in my opinion, but understandable given the loss of my father—I am ever aware that my importance to them is completely framed by his absence.

I'd just finished combing Teagan's freshly washed hair over her shoulders when Poppy texted me that he was on his way down with her parents. I wheeled her into the small room across the hall that we use when it's available—it's easier on families than our embalming suite. Then I steeled myself for their emotion. But as they walked in, Poppy informed me that I was needed upstairs.

I expressed my sincere condolences to the grief-stricken Lowes and left them to their daughter. On my way down the hall, I ducked into the washroom and peeled off my scrubs.

Tyson Pierce was waiting in the lobby when I got off the elevator, and I was surprised to see him. When he saw me, he stood up and smiled. He was in cargo shorts and a dark tee, and I thought he looked a little better than he had last night, or maybe I just thought so because he was unaccompanied. "Hi," I said.

"Hi. I...I brought this." He handed me a blush-colored dress that reminded me of something a bridesmaid would wear. It was draped in dry cleaner's plastic, and hanging with it was a large, rather frilly headband. "My mom said this was Ash's favorite."

I held it up. "She'll look pretty in this."

He glanced at my clothes. "Casual Friday? Or are you off today?"

I looked down at my jeans. "Little of both," I said.

He nodded. "Well...you look good." Then he reddened. I might have, too. He cleared his throat. "Um, is that everything you need?" he asked, jutting his chin at the dress I was holding.

"I think so. Thanks for getting it to me."

"I'd better go," he said. "My mom's coming home this afternoon, and we're out of milk. Apparently."

"How is she?"

"Her doctors don't want her to leave the hospital yet. But she promised to stay in a wheelchair, so, you know, that'll be interesting."

I frowned. "Terrible timing."

"Yeah."

Behind us, the elevator opened, and I turned to see my Babka totter out, leaning heavily on her walker. She was wearing a red pantsuit and sunglasses, and I suddenly felt very underdressed for her luncheon.

"Janny, there are you be. You are driving with us?"

"Hey, Birthday Girl. Channeling our inner Hillary Clinton, are we?" She either didn't hear me or ignored me as she made her way toward us. "Babi, this is Tyson Pierce," I said. "We're doing his sister's funeral. Tyson, this is my Babka—that's Polish for great-grandmother. She's ninety-four today, and we are off to celebrate."

"Well, happy birthday, ma'am," he smiled. "And she's crazy. You're much prettier than Hillary Clinton."

She wagged her bony finger at him. "You, I like." She then moved closer and looked up into his eyes. "I am wary sorry for loss of your loss."

"Thank you," he said softly.

Babka studied him for a beat. "Your sister in wary good hands with my Janny."

He looked at me. "Yes. I think she is."

I lifted my brows and offered an embarrassed smile.

Thankfully his phone rang. He glanced at it, then cleared his throat. "I…I'd better go. It's my dad." He looked at me. "Thanks again," he said softly. Then he walked out.

"Such nice young man, this Tyson Pierce," my Babka said.

"He is nice," I said watching him get into his car.

She looked at me. "So. You not like my this outfit?"

I laughed. "What do you mean? I love your outfit."

***

As it turned out, I drove separately to Potomac Manor, using the excuse of finishing up with Teagan Lowe. It wasn't a lie. But I did prefer my own transportation so I could leave when I needed to.

The care center where Mom lives is in Glen Ridge, about twenty minutes from Duzy House in light traffic. I was twenty minutes late, so when I got there, Harry Golding—the chubby, toupeed owner and operator of PM—directed me to the patio where our little luncheon party was already seated.

"Thank you, Harry."

"Very nice to see you, Miss January. It's been a while."

"I know it has," I said.

He winked at me knowingly. "Well, you're here now, and Claire will be thrilled. Enjoy."

I smiled stiffly, as I turned down the hall toward the patio.

Our luncheon could have been featured on the cover of a magazine: lovely table set with fine china—because that was how the Manor did things like this—a centerpiece of balloons and an ancient birthday girl at the head of the table wearing a crown in her white hair. Babi looked in her element. Everyone was laughing. My Aunt Tess had said something hilarious, and her husband Zander was kind of shouting over everyone to explain what she meant. Something to do with the vacation-slash-business trip they were just back from. Claire, too, was making her indecipherable noises.

My mother was wearing her lopsided smile, of course, and I watched as Grandy, who was sitting next to her, tenderly pushed a strand of hair off Claire's face. Grandy loved my mom—they all did—and Claire knew it. We were her whole world. Her own unforgivably awful parents had had nothing to do with her since she'd married my dad. As a result, the Winstons were rarely mentioned in our home; the last time had been a little over a year ago, when my complete stranger of a grandfather died. So, we were it, this little gathering. My family was Claire's family.

As I stood there in the doorway leading to the patio, my mother spotted me, and the side of her face that functioned filled with joy. It was the same every time, a response reserved solely for me. Undeserved in every way.

I put on my smile and walked out. Claire immediately struggled to get up from her chair to greet me, so she was my first stop. I steeled myself as her thin arms came around me and pulled me into a vice-like embrace—she's much stronger than she looks. I gently patted her bony back. When I pulled away, there was a tear in her good eye. "Hi, Mom," I said. "It's been a while."

She patted my face as she always did, affection pouring from her disjointed expression. My mother adored me, whether I was worthy of it or not.

"You made it, dear one!" my Babi exclaimed, reaching over to squeeze my wrist.

I let go of Claire and bent to kiss my Babka's angel head. "Happy birthday, Babi."

She kissed my hand.

"Nice of you to join us," my aunt teased as I took the vacant seat between her and my grandfather.

"Backatcha. How was Sin City?"

"Grueling for Zan, and I was sick the whole time. But I did manage to win a twenty-three-dollar jackpot on the nickel slots."

I laughed. "You alerted the IRS, I assume?" I caught Zander's eye and smiled. "Welcome home. How was it?"

"I hate everything about Vegas," he said. "But the conference was good. As good as a stuffy group of ocularists can make it," he qualified.

Zander is the maker extraordinaire of artificial eyes. He's who fitted my mother with her prosthesis, which is how he met and fell in love with my prickly aunt. He is a gem and has always been beyond kind to me.

Under the table, Poppy reached for my hand and squeezed. "Nice to see you, Janny."

I squeezed back. "How did it go with the Lowes?"

"Oh, you know…They're taking it very hard. But they were pleased with how nice their daughter looked. So, well done, *Serce*." He nodded his approval. "At least we could give them that."

"Ma'am? Would you like dressing on your salad?" a caterer asked, placing a wedge of lettuce rimmed with cherry tomatoes in front of me.

I looked up at her. "Ranch, please. On the side."

I glanced around the table to find the only eye on me was my mother's. I offered a tiny wave, and she lifted a stiff little hand in return. Her dark hair was shorter than the last time I'd been there, her bangs no longer hiding the thick scar on her forehead. And was she thinner? How could she be forty-six? She looked like a little girl.

"Janny?" My grandfather elbowed me as he passed me the rolls. "You okay?"

"Yes," I said, my attention reclaimed. "I'm fine, why?" I took a roll and passed the basket to my aunt and hoped I'd sounded breezy and convincing.

Thankfully Babka was very chatty on her big day, which made her the welcome focus. Throughout lunch, she regaled us with her favorite birthday memories, and at ninety-four, she had quite a few. There was the time when Poppy was about sixteen and working for the mortician in the basement. He had given Babi a set of pearls that were unclaimed by a woman's family who'd had her cremated. "I never did wore them," she laughed. "Not once."

Poppy shook his head. "They were perfectly good pearls, Mama."

Then there was the talent show Tess and Tanek had put on for her when they were little, broke, and thus highly resourceful. Babi's recollection was that my father had been ten or eleven and Tess five or six. My dad had dressed Tess up in a clown wig and striped pajamas, and painted her lips bright red. He'd then proceeded to introduce her as his dummy and himself as the ventriloquist. He apparently mumble-sang "You Are My Sunshine" as Tess mouthed the words.

My aunt was rolling her eyes. "Every time he pinched my neck, I was supposed to open my mouth, but I couldn't stop laughing."

"It was bad," Poppy snorted.

"It was adorable," Grandy countered.

"Never this I will forgot," Babi said, obviously touched by the memory.

It was lovely to hear my father spoken of with such joy since conversations about him still sometimes sparked tears.

"One of my best rememberings was birthday Clairy taked me to lunch." She leaned toward my mother and smiled. "You remember, Kochanie? The stroller?"

Claire smiled and touched her own face. She did that all the time, but I was never sure it meant anything.

"It was one day, such long ago," Babi continued, now looking at me. "After we have lunch, she ask me to shop for with her a gift for our Tanek—our special days are only few apart. I was younger then and could walk the good, so I say yes, of course. Most delightful time. We went to Bergen Mall—remember, Clairy? Is called something else now, but we go to Paramus and have a day. So much treat for me to have this girl to myself."

As I watched my mother, she seemed to access something of this memory in the rubble of her damaged brain. This always surprised me with things that happened before the accident. "What did she buy?" I blurted. "For my dad?"

Babka laughed. "You think I am too old to remember. But I'm not tell you yet. No, I first tell you how lovely was your mother this day. Always is she lovely, but something wary different about her this day, some big happiness trying to come out. Then suddenly, my Clairy laughed. 'I know what I get to my Tanek,' she singed. 'I know perfect thing! I buy stroller. Will be surprise way to say my love he will to be a father.'"

"What?" I coughed.

Babka giggled. "So excited!" She turned again to my mother. "I still your face can see, all lighted up with the happy. You were pregnant and full of the joy, and you share it to first me."

My mother smiled but seemed a little lost.

Babka patted her knee, then she looked back at us. "She swored to me keep her secret because we both know she should not have telled me before she telled Tanek. I promised this, but my heart is exploding."

"I never knew that," said Grandy, a bit miffed. "Rahe, I can't believe you didn't tell me!"

Babi shrugged. "I make promise. Such happy day, this. Such happy birthday to me." She smiled over at my mother who looked to have a tear in her eye.

"I do remember the stroller, though," Grandy said. She turned to Claire. "Tan called us over later that night, after we'd celebrated his birthday. We were in our pajamas and thought there was an emergency." She smiled at my mom. "My kind of emergency."

"What happened?" I asked.

Grandy had gotten misty-eyed and couldn't speak, so Poppy jumped in. "We drove over to their house in a panic, is what happened. But they just smiled, both of them, and sent us upstairs. There was a room by their bedroom—a little room they had told us when they moved in would someday be a nursery. Remember, Di? *Someday* be a nursery."

Grandy nodded, still misty. And next to her, Claire was now nodding, too, and smiling her odd smile, and I wondered about this like I always did because, again, this memory was from before and....

"So...what happened?" I pressed.

"Well," Grandy said. "There was a big sign on that door that said Someday is December 30th. And the stroller was sitting inside that empty room with a big bouquet of white balloons tied to it."

Poppy nodded and looked like he would cry. And then I looked over at Claire to catch undeniable *dawning* fill her face. I leaned into my grandfather. "Do you really believe she remembers that? In her warzone of a brain?"

Poppy looked at me. "I hope she does...It seems like she does."

I couldn't fathom her remembering *anything* that had happened before her brain was ruined. But suddenly that small detail was secondary to my unexpected emotion. In my whole life, I'd never imagined my newly pregnant mother excited to tell my dad she was going to have *me*. And it certainly had never crossed my mind that they might have been beyond excited to tell Grandy and Poppy.

"Janny?" my grandmother said, yanking me from my thoughts.

I looked at her, surfacing.

"Can you help Claire? She needs something from her room."

"Ummm, sure." I pulled myself together, and as my mother got to her feet my tricky grandmother winked at me and said, "Thank you, sweetheart."

"Of course," I said. Then Claire and I walked slowly back into the building—slowly because that's how Claire does everything. We walked around the corner and through the foyer to room 13, my mom clinging to my hand and me rather desperate to fill the silence.

I cleared my throat. "Do you really remember that stroller, Mom?" I finally managed.

She nodded, quite vehemently, smiling.

I studied her as we walked. She smiled a lot, and nodded a lot, but this? "Mom, really?"

She looked over at me and blinked her yes.

I swallowed. "Was...was Dad...was he happy? About me?"

She stopped, so I stopped. Then she looked at me and touched her heart.

I stared at her. "Really? You remember that? That would have been twenty-three years ago—*before* the accident."

She blinked her emphatic yes and then patted my face as gently as she could muster.

"Wow, that's amazing…" I was still skeptical, but suddenly I wanted the details about that night: my dad's reaction, the look on his face, what he'd said to her, had he cried, had he laughed? Instead, I blew out a breath, flustered that all the particulars about that life-changing memory would forever be lost to me. I sighed, deflating a little. Then I patted her hand, and we continued down the hall in silence, the skepticism back because skepticism was easier.

My mother could not recognize letters or symbols, which meant she could not spell or read. This was because the injury to her brain had been profound in the left hemisphere—that's what I'd been told, anyway. Despite this, she comprehended the world around her and answered yes or no questions by blinking with what always seemed to be dependable accuracy. Now I was trying to recall if there had been other occasions when she'd seem to remember something from *before*. Before her accident. I couldn't. But then I'd spent so little time with her—or maybe it was that I just spent so little time paying attention to her—that I honestly did not know.

We arrived at door 13, which bore an engraved mail slot with *Claire Duzinski* written in block letters. To make the door extra recognizable to her, there was a big, framed picture of me hanging above the mail slot—graduation from mortuary school last year, honors ribbons, cap and gown, goofy grin on my face. There had always been a picture of me on her door, updated with every special occasion, piano recital, holiday, or for no reason at all. An outdated stack of these photos was in the bottom drawer of Mom's bureau—a timeline of my life that could have wallpapered her room.

She pushed open the door, and we walked into her home: a roomy studio equipped with a full-sized bed, two armchairs, a television, and a mini fridge, over which sat a small counter. There was a stereo system on the dresser and a shelf filled with CDs on the wall—mostly piano music, from Grieg and Rachmaninoff to Schumann and Lang Lang and everything in between. A big picture window looked out onto a courtyard and imbued the room with natural light. It was a cozy, personalized space, made more so by a new three-dimensional butterfly mural above her bed. It was made up of dozens of individual butterflies in bright blues, oranges, and yellows, a few in green, each pinned to the wall to form a huge swarm. She looked at me looking at it.

"Where did this come from?" I said. "It's beautiful."

Of course, she didn't answer—yes or no only.

"Did you make it?" I simplified.

Two blinks, which meant no.

I didn't know where to go from there, so I changed the subject. "What are we here for, Mom? What did you forget?"

Claire walked to her bureau and pulled open the top drawer where she retrieved a square box wrapped in tissue paper.

"Oh. Babi's birthday present. Of course."

She nodded, smiling. It was a Polish potbelly mug, I knew, because Grandy had ordered it online for her to give to Babka. Babi would love it, since hers was cracked and chipped and ancient, and I was mad that I hadn't thought of it myself.

As we shuffled our way back to the patio, my mother again slipped her stiff little hand into mine. I responded with a tepid return of affection. I love my mother; I do. I just wish I was better at it. The fact that I'm not is why I'm so uncomfortable around her.

four

When we got back, Harry Golding was lighting the candles on the cake. I was tempted to ask for my slice to go. Instead, I grudgingly sat down and joined in the off-key "Happy Birthday" that Harry led. I'm ashamed to admit that it was always like this—a point always came when I just wanted to get out of there, nervousness blooming in my gut and threatening to overpower me.

It started when I was a little girl.

My angst at having to spend time with my mother morphed into true aversion on my seventh birthday. Claire gave me a book—*The Velveteen Rabbit*. I threw it at her, and it made her cry. And I made her cry again when I wouldn't let her hug me. When she tried, I squirmed away, shrieking obnoxiously. I can still see myself doing that and it makes me sick to this day.

My Babka, who has always loved Claire with the purity of an angel, scolded me in searing fashion. I remember that clearly, because never in my life had she done such a thing. Babka had always been soft and wise, a place of complete safety. She'd never been harsh. Until then. Because of Claire.

My grandfather angrily swatted my butt—another first—and Grandy planted me in a chair facing the wall. In a stern, unyielding voice, she warned me not to make a sound. I complied out of sheer terror, my banishment from her affection nearly unbearable. On the way out that day, I got a sympathetic look from Harry Golding. He'd always been kind to me, and I remember begging him with my eyes to save me. He didn't.

I don't recall the ride home but I'm sure it, too, was unbearable. When we got there, I was told to go to my room and wait. I vividly remember the three most essential people to my existence glaring down at me, making it impossible to argue. Or plead.

In yet another moment of twisted kid-logic, I blamed Claire. This was all her fault. I was in this terrible mess because of *her*. I never wanted to see her again, and I felt my heart harden toward her even more as I sat on the edge of my bed awaiting punishment.

Soon my Babka walked in, followed by Grandy. "Janny," she said, looking in my eyes. "We have wary grown-up story to tell you. Are you enough big to hear it?"

I nodded, probably wide-eyed, probably unsure.

She reminded me of what I already knew—that I was Claire's daughter. She told me that Claire had once been a very pretty woman married to the tall smiling man whose picture was everywhere. I knew who they were because Babka had once drawn me a crude pedigree chart that explained who went where. My father was beneath my grandparents and next to him was the picture of Claire before she'd been hurt. And, of course, the picture of me underneath them had been placed there so I would always know I was theirs. And I understood this. In theory.

But that day, my behavior with Claire had prompted them to tell me more of the story. Somewhere in that lecture, my grandmother informed me that bad things happen in this world. "Wary, wary bad things, Kochanie," Babi echoed. They told me an awful accident had happened the night I was born. A crash with a big truck…My father had died. He was now with Jesus.

I knew he was with Jesus, but I'd never really been told how he got there. I remember feeling queasy at the details.

Grandy was crying when she took my hand. "Your mama…was hurt very badly, Janny."

"Wary, wary bad hurt," Babi repeated.

"Her head, her legs, her face, her eye—everything was hurt," Grandy elaborated. "But she did not die, Janny. She didn't go to Jesus like your dad." Grandy took hold of my face—I remembered that— and looked me in the eyes. "Who am I talking about, January?"

I swallowed. "Claire?"

She nodded. "Claire."

"She loves you so much, Kochanie," Babi said. "She has known such pain, such terrible pain. To add to it is cruelest thing you can do." She wagged her finger at me, something she seldom did. "You must never to be unkind to her again. You hear what I did tell you?"

I nodded, making a promise. But even as a child, I knew my motivation was far from pure. I'd felt bad hearing about what happened to Claire but being good—or *acting* good—had little to do with what my mother had gone through. No, I simply could not bear standing outside the circle of my family's grace. So, I was good, or I *acted* good. I became intentionally well-behaved because I couldn't live with their rejection. I was obedient, well-mannered, and never again was I overtly unkind to my mother.

But I never warmed to her. And they knew it.

The truth was I didn't know my mother, aside from what had happened to her. Add to that my own traumatic but faulty impressions and my horribly misguided rejection of her because of them, and there was *nothing* but distance between us.

So, I simply smiled my way through the time I spent with her. Then and now.

I smiled and ate cake as we celebrated my great-grandmother's birthday. And I was still smiling as Claire hugged me goodbye.

***

By the time I got back to Duzy House, I'd done what I usually do after seeing my mom: hoped I hadn't hurt her again, questioned my capacity to love her, felt bad about myself, and vowed to do better next time. And those feelings promised to linger through the afternoon because they always did.

When I walked in, Calvin was just finishing the paperwork on a collection he'd done after his graveside service. Our number-one assistant and go-to guy was dressed in his funeral uniform—black suit, black shirt, bolo tie, and black cowboy boots. He looked like a redneck gangster. He was in his late forties and balding, but the hair he lacked on top he made up for at the back, which he wore in a graying ponytail. He always wore a hat and tinted glasses, and he fancied himself quite the ladies' man, which he probably was considering his four divorces.

I couldn't see it, though. To me he was just Calvin, one of the few ever-present fixtures in my life, who always called me Cookie.

"Hey there, Cookie," he said, on cue. "Got a messy one here."

I glanced at the form he was filling out and recognized the logo from the Medical Examiner's office.

"Self-inflicted gunshot to the chest," Calvin said. "Sorry."

"Well, that's better than the face," I said, unzipping the bag containing our newest acquisition. The damage was extensive, and the gaping hole had been crudely packed by the medical examiner. But at least it wasn't oozing. The man, Jordan Rush, was young, maybe thirty-five, tattooed and wearing a wedding ring. I couldn't imagine what had gotten so bad that he'd aimed a gun at his heart and pulled the trigger. I zipped him back up and wheeled him into the fridge. He should have been assigned to Tess for later, but I was in the mood to stay distracted, so I added him to my list of priorities for the afternoon.

"You need me for anything, Cookie?" Calvin said.

I looked around. The fancy dress Tyson Pierce had dropped off was hanging on the back of the door. "In about twenty minutes, can you help me with a casket? I just need to get my gal dressed."

"You got it," he said. "I'll go out and wipe down the coach. Text me when you're ready."

"Thanks," I murmured, preoccupied.

"You okay, Cookie?"

"I'm fine. Short night, long day is all."

"I hear that," Calvin said as he walked out.

Ashley Pierce turned out to be a good salve on this afternoon of sobering reflection, which, of course, is the saving grace of my chosen vocation—and my almost vocation, for that matter. There's no backtalk from the dead, and there is no noise but my own when I'm playing the piano; I guess that's why I find irrational peace in these two favored pastimes. I even opened up to Ashley about Claire and the long-ago stroller tied with balloons from twenty-three years ago. Ashley seemed to find the whole thing as sadly just out of reach as I did.

Tyson's sister was a bit unwieldy, but I was still able to dress her by myself, which I did with care. I got the fancy dress in place, tucked it around her so it lay in nice folds, and loosely rested her chubby hands between her small breasts. I then texted Calvin to help me casket her.

In a moment, he wheeled the shiny navy Belmont the Pierces had chosen into my workspace. Then, with him at Ashley's head and me at her feet, we lifted the woman onto the soft bedding where I again smoothed the dress around her. Once everything was spread and straightened, her hair arranged down both shoulders and her sandals in place, I stood back to scrutinize Miss Ashley.

"You do fine work," said my cheerleader, peeling the cellophane from a big Life Saver and popping it in his mouth.

"Thanks," I said. "Hey. Do you have any more of those candies?"

He checked his pockets and handed me three. "If you want more, there's a big bag of them in the glove compartment of the hearse. Help yourself, Cookie."

"Thanks."

When I had Ashley Pierce arranged exactly right, hands glued together, lips glossed and locket clasped around her neck, Calvin helped me wheel her upstairs to the receiving room attached to the west chapel. The room was set up for the family viewing tonight, with space in the corner for the casket. We got Ashley situated, locked the wheels of the church truck, and straightened the drape that concealed the hardware. I opened the top half of the casket and again nestled the locket at the young woman's throat. She looked nice.

Calvin checked his watch. "I'm taking off now. Tell Stasio I'll be in early tomorrow."

"Big date?"

"The biggest," he said. "Meeting my lady's kids for the first time."

"Ooooh. Sounds serious."

"Might be, Cookie," he sighed. "We'll see."

"Well, good luck," I said, not optimistic—he'd met a lot of kids. "Thanks for your help."

After he left, I turned on the lamps, which cozied the room. As an afterthought, I ran upstairs for one of Grandy's fancy bowls, and I filled it with the stash of big Life Savers from the hearse. I left them on the coffee table.

***

I was just finishing my third embalming—the suicide, Jordan Rush—when Grandy came down to check on me. I'd known she would eventually. It was her way. She poked her head in and smiled. "How ya doing?"

I blew out a breath. "Good. Almost caught up."

She walked in. "Well, good. It's almost nine. But you know that's not what I meant."

I looked up at her and shook my head. "I'm fine, Grandy. I am. And as usual, I'm sorry I'm not better at that stuff."

"You did fine, sweetheart. I don't know what you're talking about," she lied.

I gave her a look then proceeded to remove the hose attached to Mr. Rush. After I packed his chest cavity, I stopped the hole in his thigh from leaking with a Trocar button, then pulled the sheet over my pinked-up decedent. "Tess owes me," I said, wheeling him back into the fridge.

"Which is just how you like it," Grandy chuckled.

"Exactly. How is your night going?"

"It's going. The Pierce's were very pleased. Nice people—very tender. Rahe sat with Mrs. Pierce for a good half-hour—your Babi has the touch."

"Yes, she does."

"Oh, the son—the man you helped the other night—he was looking for you."

I raised my eyebrows. "What did he want?"

"He wanted to thank you…for the Life Savers. Did you put one in his sister's hand?"

I smiled.

"Nice touch, Janny." My grandmother cleared her throat. "Honey, can you stop for a minute? I need to talk to you. Can you…stop?"

I turned from the sink and eyed her. "Is everything okay, Grandy?"

My typically direct grandmother seemed to mull, and it alarmed me. I rinsed my hands, dried them, and walked over to her. "You're making me nervous," I said. "What is it?"

"It's Rose, honey."

"Rose who?"

"Rose Winston. As in, your other grandmother."

"Okay. What about her?"

"She died this morning."

I looked at her, feeling nothing. "Oh," I said. "What happened?"

"I don't have any details. I just know it was sudden."

I lifted a shoulder. "Sooo, are we doing her service? Is that what you're getting at?"

"No. No. Heavens, no. I'm—her attorney called. He wants to talk to you."

"Me? Why?"

Grandy shook her head. "You now know exactly what I know."

"Is he here now?"

"No. He just called. He's coming Wednesday afternoon."

"Coming here. To talk to me. That sounds...strangely ominous."

"I thought so, too." Grandy seemed concerned.

We looked at each other for a thoughtful moment, then I asked, "Does Claire know?"

"Not yet. I just found out, and I think that news needs to be delivered in person."

"But Claire won't know her, will she...I mean has she even seen her mother since...." I shrugged. "Grandy, will she even care?"

"Oh, sweetheart, Rose was her mother. And Rose *wasn't* Stephen."

"Close enough."

My grandmother shook her head, then sighed. "When I think of how those people treated your mom.... And now their attorney wants to see you. I don't know January. I don't know what to think." She glanced at her watch and sighed. "I'd better get back upstairs. You okay, sweetie?"

"I'm fine."

I *said* I was fine, but I was actually a little disturbed. I'd never met my other grandparents. The only thing I really knew about them was how they felt about my father—that they had in fact disowned their only child, my mom, because she'd fallen in love with him, a proud *Polish* undertaker whom they'd deemed far, far beneath their daughter. I'd always found that so hard to believe, but it wasn't something we ever talked about, so I had few details. My Duzinski grandparents had adored their son, so naturally any reference to the people who'd detested him on such a spectacular level only caused them pain.

So much of my mother had been damaged by her brain injury. I hoped the worst of the memories of her parents were lost in that wreckage. But… after the other day, who really knew what Claire had access to?

five

I was still asleep Wednesday morning when my grandfather knocked on my door. "Janny? You up?"

I yawned. "Of course," I fibbed. "Come in, Poppy." I sat up and grabbed my phone, then squinted: 7:15. *I really need my own place.*

"Sorry to wake you," he said. "Is there any way you can be available at 8:30 to help Grandy? She has two consultations that might overlap, and we need a backup. I just sent Calvin to Our Lady of Emanuel for a collection—Tess will be in at 8:00 to start that one, then Calvin's got a home pickup. I've got the Pierce funeral and graveside. That leaves you, m'dear. What do you say?"

I swallowed a groan and kicked off the covers. "I'd better get up."

"Good answer. I'll see you downstairs."

I turned on the shower and jumped in while the water was still cold, the most effective way I knew to wake up fast. Then I dressed in a black pencil skirt, white blouse, and pink heels, then readied my head. Starting the day this way required some gearing up on my part. Consults were never going to be my favorite, but they weren't hard when the death had been anticipated, someone who'd been sick or was elderly and their passing was not a surprise. But if it was a child who'd died, of course that tended to be awful. And if it was a suicide…Then I remembered who I had in my fridge. *Jordan Rush.*

While I waited for my hair to dry, I went into the kitchen and popped some bread in the toaster and then finished my eyes—a little mascara and a tiny bit of liner, nothing dramatic. As I inspected my work in the hand mirror, Babka tottered in, her thin hair sleep-flattened on one side. She was holding the new mug my mother had given her for her birthday. "You're up early, Babi."

"Busy day, Kochanie. The girls are take for me to lunch for my celebrate, and I have much to do before they come."

The girls were Anka and Lydia from church, both older than Babka. "Do you want me to wash this out for you?" I said, taking the mug.

"Oh, thank you, my Janny. I desperate need tea."

"Coming right up."

Sitting down, she said, "You look wary pretty today."

"I do? Thanks. Just your basic consultation *ensemble*," I responded, rinsing her mug.

"And for meeting with attorney," she said. "Diana told me about Rose."

"Well, yes. There's that."

"Rose was…*interesting* woman we not speak of wary much."

"Much? Try *not at all*, Babi."

My great-grandmother sighed. "Always is best we not speak of this people. No good can come."

I buttered my toast and handed it to her, nodding absently. I'd heard some variation of this mantra my entire life. I popped in two more slices, and while the kettle came to a boil, I slipped down the hall to the den for the newspaper. Poppy's morning ritual was old school: a Montecristo Classic, a V8, and the newspaper; a cigar, two servings of vegetables, and absolutely no online world updates. "I like my information made of paper and ink," he always said. "Like God intended."

Back in the kitchen, with the hot water poured, the tea bags and honey within her reach, and the newspaper on the table opened to the obituaries, I buttered my toast—round two—and I kissed my Babi's head. "Have fun with the girls," I said.

"Have fun with the dead," she sighed. "And the attorney."

At about 8:15, I took the elevator to the basement. I wanted to check on Jordan Rush, just in case his family insisted on seeing him. I'd packed his chest and wrapped plastic around the man's torso to keep the crater he'd made there from seeping. It was still intact this morning, but I didn't want the Rushes to see any of that. So, since no usable clothes had accompanied him from the ME, I grabbed a set of blue scrubs we sometimes use for this very thing and quickly dressed him. When I'd finished, Jordan Rush looked like a napping, tattooed surgeon. I combed his clean dark hair off his shaved face and arranged his arms at his sides, then pulled a clean sheet up to his chin. And since my veteran, Milo Bitters, was set up in our little receiving room, I left Jordan in the middle of my work room with the partition pulled to hide the embalming equipment. Tess wasn't here yet, but she knew the drill. With any luck, the family wouldn't even ask to see him.

Upstairs was still quiet even though that was destined to change at any moment. I knew the viewing for Ashley Pierce was scheduled for ten o'clock, just before her funeral, but the family would be here long before that. I slipped into the west receiving room to make sure everything was in order. It had already been put back together after last night's gathering, and Ashley was in the corner, although her casket had been closed. Poppy liked to do that—button everything down for the night. I opened it, happy to see that Tyson's sister had not been disturbed. I double-checked that the locks on the church truck were still secure and then straightened the drapes surrounding it. Then placing my hand on Ashley's, I whispered, "It was lovely to meet you."

When I turned, a woman was standing in the doorway. She'd startled me, but I don't think it showed. "Hello," I said.

She walked toward me, slowly, gingerly. "You must be January."

"I am."

She nodded and looked past me to the deceased. "I'm Nicole Pierce. I wanted to thank you for taking such good care of my daughter. And my son—Ty was a little overwhelmed." The woman's eyes misted.

"It was my pleasure," I said.

"I know I'm early. I just…I just wanted one more moment with her by myself."

"Of course. Let me get you a chair." I retrieved one from the wall and placed it close to the casket, then helped Tyson's mother into it. I didn't tell her I knew she was supposed to be in a wheelchair. Once she was seated, she looked up at me and took my hand. "Thank you," she whispered. "The candy was the perfect touch."

I smiled. "You're more than welcome. Is there anything else I can do for you?"

She shook her head. "No. But could you shut the door?"

I did as she asked.

On the table just outside the chapel, I opened Ashley's guest book to a new page and straightened the stack of programs next to it. Then I made my way up the hall to where a family clearly belonging to Jordan Rush was speaking with Grandy. There was a man in biker chaps with a blue bandanna on his head, an older woman dressed similarly with steel-gray hair slicked off her weathered face, and a younger woman wearing black leather everything. All of them had tattoos and looked completely out of context in this setting. There was also a child, maybe ten, whose gender I couldn't be sure of, dressed in jeans and a chambray shirt. No tats. As I approached, they stopped talking and turned to me. Each wore the look of fresh grief.

"This is my granddaughter, January," Grandy said to them. Turning to me, "Janny, this is the Rush family: Brandon, Jordan's brother; his mother, Linda; and his wife, Jolene."

I made eye contact with each of them. "Nice to meet you," I said. "I'm very sorry it's under these circumstances."

Tears filled the younger woman's eyes and she nodded.

"And this is Wyatt," Grandy said, indicating the child. "Jordan's son."

He was a beautiful boy with long blond hair, a veritable sunbeam amid this dark and edgy family. I extended my hand. "Nice to meet you, Wyatt. Is that a violin?" I asked, taking in the battered case he was holding.

He nodded, shyly.

Brandon Rush cleared his throat. "Yeah, we'd like the kid to play a song at the funeral. Hopin' that'd be okay? He's real good, but he's a little nervous. Right, sport?"

Wyatt Rush looked at the floor.

"I think that would be lovely," Grandy said, eying the boy, then me. "Maybe while I speak with your family, January here could show you the chapel," she said to him. "You're welcome to practice in there if you'd like." She looked at me. "The Pierce funeral is in the West Chapel, but East is empty at the moment. How 'bout you take him down there?"

"Perfect," I said, relieved that I had escaped this consultation.

Grandy pointed the Rushes in the direction of the coffin room but hung back to speak to me. "This little guy needs some TLC," she said under her breath.

I nodded and whispered, "I pulled our deceased out of the fridge just in case they ask to see him. He looks okay—he's dressed, but keep the sheet up."

"Bless you, my child," Grandy said, squeezing my hand.

When I turned back to the little boy, he was staring at me. I don't think I'd ever seen a more forlorn look on a child. Suicide grief is like that, somehow more piercing, more suffocating than other grief. I wanted to hug him. Instead, I smiled sadly. "Soooo, would you like to see the chapel?"

"Sure," he shrugged.

"It's this way." As we walked down the hall, I asked him how long he'd been playing, indicating his violin.

"Since I was four," he said.

"Wow. And how old are you, now?"

"Nine."

"That's a lot of practice."

I got a small smile then as I pushed open the door to the chapel. Wyatt took it in, and I saw him swallow. When he looked up at me, his blue eyes were rheumy. "I'm so sorry about your dad," I said.

He swallowed again. "It's okay."

"My dad died, too," I told him. "It's never okay."

A tear slipped down his cheek, then, as he studied me. "Did your dad shoot himself, too?"

"No. A drunk man driving a big truck ran into him."

"Oh."

After a moment of heaviness, I asked him what he was going to play.

"My dad's favorite," he said.

"Would you like me to leave while you practice?"

Subtle alarm filled his eyes. "Can you stay?"

"Absolutely, I can."

I sat down on the back pew as Wyatt made his way to the front of the chapel. I watched him ready his violin, then stare at the floor for several seconds. Finally, he positioned his bow, inhaled, and slid it over the strings, filling the chapel with a bloom of beautiful sound. It was lovely and such a surprise, given his family, who didn't seem the type but had clearly found time in their assumed nomadic life to nurture his gift.

He was playing Leonard Cohen's "Hallelujah" impeccably, until he got emotional and lost his place. He broke my heart. When he suddenly stopped, shoulders trembling, I thought I would cry. I hadn't made a sound, but he became aware of me again and turned, embarrassed.

"That's…that was beautiful, Wyatt."

"I can't do it," he croaked. "I can't do it."

I walked toward him. "I understand completely. No one should have to perform at his father's funeral. That's too much to ask of anyone."

He sniffed. "He liked that song. My dad liked when I played it."

"I can see why. You're very, very good."

"No, I'm not," he said again. "I can't stop shaking. And I can't stop crying. I can't do it. I can't!"

"Maybe you'll just have to tell them that."

He looked at me as if that option had never occurred to him.

"But maybe for now, we could just play for your dad." I jutted my chin at the piano. "Do you mind?"

The boy rubbed his eyes with his sleeve. "I never did it with the piano."

"Would you like to try?" I said, sitting down on the bench.

"Ummmm…Okay. Who starts?"

"I'll start. You come in when you're ready."

"Do you have music?" he asked.

"I don't. Do you?"

He shook his head.

"What's your first note?"

"I start on C," he said.

I played the first chords of the classic introduction. When nothing happened, I played the beginning a second time. Then once more. That time the boy didn't hesitate. Again, angelic loveliness rose from his instrument. I adjusted to Wyatt's tempo and watched him get lost in the piece. It was seamless and from his heart, and even though pain saturated his innocent face, he did not cry. Until the end when he looked at me. Then his lip quivered.

"That was amazing, Wyatt," I said, fighting my own tears. "You're awesome."

His face colored a bit as he lowered his violin.

"You know what I think? I think whether you play at his funeral or not, your dad is already pleased. And so very proud of you."

He sniffed. "Really?"

"Absolutely."

After a moment, the little boy again lifted his violin. "Can we do it again?"

"Of course."

I glanced up then to find Tyson Pierce standing in the chapel doorway. He looked at me through wet eyes with what seemed a bit like awe. For a moment, we stayed locked in a gaze, and then he turned to something in the hall. Before he left, Tyson glanced back and gave me a sad smile, and I wondered how long he'd been watching me.

six

When I got downstairs later, there were two fresh deliveries, bagged and side-by-side. Tess was checking the paperwork, and Calvin was giving her the rundown as he added them to the whiteboard. According to the list, two more were ready for dressing and casketing. I unzipped one of the bags and found an elderly woman, puffy in the face, throat, and hands. "Anaphylaxis?" I asked.

"Yep," Calvin said over his shoulder. "She was given something bad at an urgent care facility. You'd think they could have reversed it. I predict a lawsuit in their future."

In the other bag was a woman who'd died of cancer. She had very thin hair and looked like she'd been sick for a while. I tagged them both and put them in the fridge.

"So how did it go meeting the kids?" I asked Calvin, wanting the scoop on his date.

He looked at me and rolled his eyes. "Don't ask, Cookie."

"Bad?"

"I thought she had big kids, you know, out of the house. Turns out they were kid kids. I'm way too old for that stuff. Which is a shame because I like her. A lot."

Tess, who'd been pretty quiet, started to cough. "I'll be right back," she said, hurrying out of the room. She didn't look good.

"Something I said?" Calvin asked.

"Undoubtedly," I teased.

Before he left, I threw a gown over my clothes and had Calvin help me dress and casket Milo Bitters. Our little veteran's wife had dropped off his World War II uniform. But Milo was so thin that the olive drab suit dwarfed him. I had to cut away a good six inches from the back and cinch the coat at the waist; when it still looked too big, I had to add quilt batting at the shoulders.

I was just knotting his tie when Babi walked in.

"There you are, Kochanie. I was look for you."

"Off to lunch?" I asked absently. "It's a little late."

"Might be early supper. The girls are get here 'ventually." She walked over to inspect my work. "Look at that sweet face," she said as she fingered the medals on Mr. Bitters' chest. "Bronze Star. Means was he brave and good." She patted him lightly with her little arthritic hand. "He looks wary nice, Janny. I do silver pinwheel for his name."

"I think that would please his wife."

She straightened and looked at me. "I make pinwheel for the Mrs. Pierce. She come tomorrow."

"Oh, I'm glad. I think she's having a very rough time."

"Yes. I see her upstairs. You come to plant with me the pinwheel tomorrow?"

"I can do that."

"You good girl, my Janny," she kissed two fingers and touched my wrist.

"Have fun with the girls," I said.

Tess walked back in just as Babka was walking out, and my great-grandmother looked at her. "You're sick, my poor lamb? I heared you in the bathroom. Go home. Janny can do the works."

Tess laughed, but not convincingly. "I ate something bad, Busha, but I'm okay now."

"Phew," I noised loudly, and only half joking.

Babi wagged a finger at me then patted Tess's cheek. "You need some seltzer water?"

"No, no, Busha. I'm fine."

"You are bad fibbing." She kissed my aunt's hand. "I go. Feel better, my girl. Janny, let my Tessa rest."

I fake-smiled as Babi walked out and was about to say something sarcastic to my aunt when I caught the look on her face. She was going to cry.

"Tess, what's wrong?"

My aunt looked up at the ceiling and shook her head.

"Tess?"

"Nothing is wrong!" she snarked.

"What kind of nothing…is wrong?"

She brought her hands to her mouth and slowly shook her head. "I'm pregnant."

I looked at her, shocked, and didn't breathe, not sure how to react. After a long pause, I played it safe and said nothing as I walked over to her. My lovely, haggard, greenish-tinged aunt looked at me and let go of a single tear. "I can't tell if you need me to be sorry or happy right now," I said.

"Me neither." There were more tears.

I rolled a stool over to her. "Sit down. Talk to me."

"What am I supposed to say?" she snapped.

I stepped back and eyed her. My aunt was a bit sick at the moment but still completely beautiful. She was cut from the same mold as my grandmother—tall, thin, big dark eyes, great skin. She had thick hair, but hers was dark like my dad's had been. In fact, she looked very much like the pictures of my father. "What's really the matter, Tess?"

"Did you not hear me, January? I'm pregnant."

"I heard you. Don't be a snot."

"I'm forty-one. *Forty-one*, January! And pregnant. What else is there to say?"

"Is that bad? What did Zander say?"

"I haven't told him. He's forty, you know. Almost forty. I can't imagine he'll be thrilled. This wasn't exactly part of our plan." She heaved a huge sigh and rubbed the back of her neck. "This wasn't supposed to happen."

The news caught up to me, and I giggled.

"What is so funny?"

"You're pregnant. I'm sorry, but I think that is so cool!"

She slumped. "Did you miss the forty-one part?"

"So? What's wrong with that? It's very celebrity. I think J-Lo was like forty when she had twins. Forty-one is nothing. It's cool."

"I don't know. I don't know, January."

"What are you so worried about?"

She stared at me. "So, so many things. That Zan won't be happy, that it will be born with three heads, that I won't know what I'm doing…" She finally breathed.

I pushed the hair out of her face and stared at her. "None of that is going to happen," I said. "You are going to have a perfect mini-you or mini-Zander, and you'll both slobber all over that baby every day, and you'll be a wonderful mom—forty-two or sixty."

"Really?"

"Really," I insisted. "You love babies."

She sniffed. "I do love babies."

"See!"

"And I'm good with babies."

"See!"

"I loved when you were a baby," she said absently.

"Well, there you go."

"I loved to just hold you all day long…" Tess bit her lip and was quiet for a beat.

"Really? Nothing better to do?" I teased.

She sniffed again. "Not really. I was kind of mourning the death of my brother." She glared, then immediately softened.

I swallowed. "Sorry," I grimaced. "The point is, obviously, that you love babies and now you're going to have one. Sounds like a win-win. And if it's a boy, I think you should name him Tanek."

She looked at me, and I watched tears fill her eyes and spill onto her cheeks. "I have to go," she said. "I have to tell Zan. I won't be long, I promise."

I glanced at the sink full of instruments then over her shoulder at the crowded whiteboard and sucked in a sigh. "*How* long, do you think?"

"Not long. And don't you dare tell anyone about this." She raked her hair back. "I'm sorry I'm such a mess."

"It's okay," I sighed. "You probably can't help it."

She fake-sneered but pulled me into a hard hug. Then she hurried out, and I was left to ponder the fact that, at twenty-two, I was finally going to be a cousin.

I filled the sink with soap and hot water, letting my mind wander. I was an only child/grandchild. I'd never even changed a diaper. That I'd been a pretty special baby came up every once in a while, but just like with Tess, I was usually late with the proper reverence.

What I knew about myself as a newborn was that, despite my dramatic entrance into the world, I had emerged from the womb relatively unscathed. I'd weighed in at six pounds even, and I'd had a lot of hair and a lot of personality, according to Poppy. But, naturally, all of that was pretty much eclipsed by the death of my dad and the shape my mom was in.

In the same box where Grandy keeps my mother's memorabilia and clippings of all the newspapers from that night, there is a diagram of Claire's head injuries. As I sanitized our embalming instruments, I thought of all the red arrows on that diagram, more on the left than on the right. The illustration had been drawn that terrible night in an effort to help my grandparents understand exactly what had happened to Claire's brain, the systems affected, and why she was expected to die. On that same paper is a little box outlining the Glasgow Coma Scale. My mother's score was marked as "gravely disabled," not the very lowest score because by some miracle she was breathing on her own. But given the gravity of her trauma and the lack of brain activity, Grandy told me her death had been considered imminent. Despite this, she'd hung on all night...and kept hanging on—no change, but she didn't die.

They kept me in the hospital for six days because I turned yellow and needed to be monitored. And apparently my grandparents and Tess rotated sitting with Claire and rocking me—I'd been told this many times and should have remembered when Tess mentioned it. They did this around the clock because they wanted to be there when Claire died. On the day I was to be released from the hospital, the nurse who had been taking care of me thought it would be nice to introduce me to my mother. Grandy said when she laid me down next to her and I whimpered, Claire's heart rate increased, and blips appeared on her EEG. Nothing major, but definite activity that hadn't been there since the accident.

From then on, they would place me next to her for an hour twice a day. It was a variation of co-bedding, which they did sometimes with premature twins when one was doing better than the other. Poppy or Grandy or Tess (one of them) would take me to the hospital every morning and every night to be with Claire. And one day when I was almost six months old, she opened her eyes and looked at me. Or so I'm told.

"Janny? Hello? Hello!"

"Poppy!" I jumped, dropping a measuring cup into the sink, causing a splash. "Sheesh! You scared me."

"What are you doing? I've been texting you."

I dried my hands and checked my phone. Sure enough, four texts from Poppy. "Sorry. What's going on?"

"Rose's attorney is here. He's waiting for you in the coffin room."

seven

The man was elderly, bald and bespectacled, and he had a white mustache. He wore a dark three-piece suit with a yellow tie, and when he stood, he leaned on a cane, which somehow made him seem very distinguished.

"Sorry to keep you waiting," I said as I walked into the coffin room. "I'm January Duzinski."

He smiled. "Thank you for meeting with me. I'm Oscar Thibodeau."

"Hi." I shook his extended hand. "How can I help you?"

He appraised me for an awkward moment, then shook his head. "I apologize for staring, but you look so much like your mother."

"You knew my mother?"

"Yes. Many years ago." He seemed preoccupied for a beat, then cleared his throat, "I'm so sorry to disrupt your day like this. But I have something important to discuss with you, and I'm afraid time is of the essence. Can we sit for a moment?"

There was an open briefcase on the coffee table. Glancing at it, I said, "Should I be nervous, Mr. Thibodeau?"

Still staring at me, he sat down on the sofa, so I sat on the one across from him, again glancing at the paraphernalia separating us.

He removed his glasses. "No. Not at all." He smiled. "But I can imagine you were surprised by my call."

"A little, yes."

"Well, that's understandable, but I think my visit here today might prove less anxiety-provoking than you anticipated." He replaced his glasses. "As you were probably informed, I'm here regarding your grandmother, Rose Winston—I'm the family's attorney. You do know who Rose is?"

"Of course. My grandmother said she died."

"Monday," he said. "And just so I don't assume anything, can you tell me what you know about her?"

"About Rose? Well…." I lifted a shoulder. "Truthfully, I don't know much. I never met her—and we rarely speak of the Winstons. So," I clarified, "I really only know that she and my grandfather rejected—disowned, I guess—my mom because she married my dad. Because of that…our family has never had anything to do with them. Does that help?"

He studied me for a moment, then nodded. "With all due respect, there was a bit more to the story than that. But unfortunately, you are essentially correct. I've been the Winstons' attorney for nearly forty years. My firm represents their business interests, but I personally have always overseen their private affairs as well. And in that position, I've been privy to many of the sadder aspects of their lives, so I am well aware of what happened there."

"So, you know about the accident?"

"Oh, yes. Tragic."

"And that even after my mother got hurt, her parents had nothing to do with her?"

"Well, they *have* paid for her care. And the living trust—the stipend that pays her monthly expenses—nothing will change in that regard."

I looked at him, taken aback. "I don't know anything about that. I'm sorry…"

"Well, it's really neither here nor there, I suppose. The point is her care has been and will continue to be taken care of—all of her expenses. Nothing in that regard will be altered."

I simply nodded because I had no idea what he was talking about.

"So…clearly, you've been left with a less-than-favorable impression of your grandmother?"

"All I know is what I've been told, Mr. Thibodeau: that everything pretty much fell apart between my mother and her parents when she married my dad."

He considered me. "That's an understatement, my dear. The Winstons were livid. And your grandfather died livid. You knew he died last year?"

"I did know that."

"Did you know him?"

"No."

"He was a dreadful man."

I suppressed my surprise. "That's pretty much what I've heard."

"He was a brilliant businessman but a rather loathsome human being—throwing money at problems notwithstanding. And he knew it. Were you aware that your grandfather stipulated in his will that there was to be no funeral for him?"

I shook my head. "No. That's rather...*unconventional*."

"Stephen arranged to have his death announced in *Forbes Magazine* and *The New York Times* the week after he died. I think he did that because he feared no one would attend his service, and I believe he was right. He had many enemies. Be grateful you didn't know him."

I looked at the well-dressed representative of my mother's terrible parents. "Okaayy." After an awkward breath, I cleared my throat. "So why exactly are you here, Mr. Thibodeau?"

He gazed at me over the rim of his glasses. "Well, January...I'm here because next week the process of dismantling your grandparents' estate will begin. Their art and furnishings will be sold at auction, their home will be put up for sale, and all the proceeds will be donated to the American Cancer Association—per your grandfather's wishes. He died of liver cancer. Not sure if you knew that."

"No, I didn't know that."

He studied me for another moment. "I was very fond of your mother, January," he said. "Claire was an exquisite talent and a truly beautiful soul."

"Thank you," I said. I didn't know a lot about my mother, but I did know she'd played the piano—*gloriously*, according to my grandparents. To hear her spoken of by this stranger like she had once been a real person with exquisite talent pierced me in a way I was not prepared for.

He smiled a sad smile. "You so remind me of her. And from what I've seen and heard, it's clear you've inherited a good portion of your mother's talent as well."

"I'm sorry?"

He nodded. "After Stephen died, Rose...and her attorney"—he smiled—"took in some wonderful piano performances. We especially enjoyed *Ravel in the Round.*" Oscar Thibodeau let that statement hang for a second. "You're very talented, my dear. Rose was truly impressed."

I narrowed my gaze. "I don't understand. She...she saw me perform?"

"A couple of times. You should do that more often..." He sighed. "Perform."

I looked at him. "I wish I had the time. Why didn't she say anything to me?"

"Oh, she wanted to. That's probably too little, too late, but I can tell you your grandmother very much wanted to get to know you. I think she thought she had all the time in the world to reach out to you again, but then Monday, quite unexpectedly...it was a brain aneurism."

"I'm sorry? What do you mean? Reach out to me *again?*"

Now the attorney looked surprised.

"What does that mean, Mr. Thibodeau?" I repeated. "*Again?*"

"My dear, the letter. The letter she sent you a few years ago."

I stared at him. "I never got a letter from her. I don't know what you're talking about."

"Well, that's strange. Are you sure?"

"I would remember a letter from Rose Winston," I assured him.

"Yes, I suppose you would," he said, looking hard at me. "I'm very sorry that you never received it. Rose was certain you weren't interested in meeting her and that was why you never responded. And that's why she was reluctant to approach you."

"I never got a letter," I said again, taking a second to process his words. I swallowed and met his eyes. "I'm not sure what she thought would happen, though. What she did to my mom was..." I shook my head, reactions colliding in me. "I can't see myself ever warming to her, to either one of my grandparents. Not then. Not now. But... I would like to know.... When did she send this letter?"

"I see," he said. "I'm not sure, several years ago, I think. But, no, I understand completely. And you are absolutely entitled to feel the way you do." His lips parted, as though he wanted to say more, and for a beat nothing came out. Then he sighed. "But if you ever change your mind and find yourself interested in knowing more about Rose, I think I could offer some perspective. We were friends a long time."

"Thank you," I said, awkwardly. "But I...I can't imagine why I would."

"Well, you never know."

I didn't know what else there was to say, so I checked my watch and scooted to the edge of the couch.

"Did you know, January, that for your mother's sixteenth birthday, her parents gave her a Steinway?"

I stopped mid-scoot. "An actual Steinway?"

"A concert grand. It is *beautiful*, as you can imagine. It hasn't been played since your mother left, but Rose has kept it tuned." He let that settle a moment, then continued. "*Technically*, that piano still belongs to your mother, and therefore it is not *technically* part of the Winston estate."

"What's going to happen to it?"

"Well, that's why I'm here, January. If you want it, it's yours. Having seen you perform, there's no question that you should have it."

I stared at him, dumbfounded. "I don't—what? A Steinway?"

He removed an envelope from the briefcase. "January, this is the address of your grandparents' home. It's a gated estate in Chestnut Hill, Pennsylvania, a suburb of Philly—about two hours from here."

"I...I don't understand."

"The code to the gate is there, and a key to the front door. Instructions on how to disable the alarm are listed on the back. My number is in there, as well." He slid the envelope across the table. "I think you ought to go to Philadelphia, my dear. Soon. Go, and take a look around."

I gaped at the envelope but didn't pick it up.

"While you're there," he said, "I'd recommend you spend some time in the room immediately right at the top of the front stairs. That was your mother's room. It, too, has stayed essentially untouched since the day she left."

I looked up at him and honestly wondered if I was dreaming.

He was not smiling. "January, as Rose's attorney, it's my legal opinion that anything in your mother's room is assumed to have belonged to her and is therefore not part of the estate." He looked hard at me. "And before it is sold or discarded, in a few days, I thought you might like to go through it."

"I...I don't know what to say."

"I knew the Winstons for a very long time. I knew Claire. She was an incredible young woman you've missed out on knowing. I'm here to tell you that if you've ever had any curiosity about your mother, I think some of it can be satisfied within the walls of that home and that room." He reached down and tapped the envelope. "As I said, you only have a few days, but you are welcome to anything you might want that belonged to her. Including the piano."

eight

After Oscar Thibodeau left, I got in my car and drove, feeling numb and bewildered. I had no real destination, but I had to get away from Duzy House and let everything settle.

If she'd been in town, I would have gone over to Jasmine's. But my best friend was working her way through a pharmacy degree at Rutgers over in New Brunswick, and she'd opted for summer classes. I hadn't seen her in weeks, but of course we kept in touch—sometimes several times a day.

I got in line at the So-Soda drive-thru on McNaughton. When it was my turn, I ordered a dirty Dr. Pepper, then found a place nearby to park in the shade.

I pulled out my phone and texted Jaz.

> Hey.
> > Who is this?
> Ha. Ha. Busy?
> > In a lecture on anabolic steroids and erectile dysfunction. Yawn.
> LOL. Sorry I never got back to you the other night.
> > You should be Jans! You are a sorry bff.
> Any time today? I need to talk.
> > Sorry, class then work, then class. What's up?
> Long story, mom's mom died, am now proud owner of a Steinway.
> > As in piano?
> Yup.
> > OMG and Sorry about Claire's mom.

Thx Jaz. Anyway, looks like I'm going to PA to check it out.
  When?
Not sure, I have a few days.
  This is big! You okay?
IDK
  I work tonight, tomorrow. Have no life! I'll call when I have a break.
I miss you Jaz! Forget big Pharma. Come home!
  OK. LOL

A moment later, Jasmine sent a picture of what took me a minute to identify as a diagram of a limp penis complete with shriveled up circulatory system. There was a caption—Tip of the day: stay clear of steroid-addicted body builders. You're welcome.

I almost laughed. Almost.

***

Tess never came back, so I had no choice but to dive into our workload, which was actually a good thing. I needed to stay busy at the moment—attorneys, Steinways, and dead grandmothers who'd written me letters I'd never received notwithstanding. I was exhausted when I finally quit for the night. But I'd gotten both of our new ladies embalmed, and by some miracle, nothing else had come in, so we were caught up. I'd already decided that tomorrow was all Tessa. Pregnant or not, forty-one and a basket case or not, future sixty-year-old mom of a demon teenager or not—my generosity was officially spent. That was my prevailing attitude when I walked into the kitchen at almost 9:30 to find my entire family chatting around the table—even Babka, whose bedtime would ordinarily have been hours ago. I eyed them and the box sitting in the middle of the table. "What's going on?"

My gaze landed on Tess, who smiled tiredly at me, and I knew then exactly what was happening. I sat down next to Poppy, who was in his pajamas and drinking coffee. He turned to me. "How far did you get, Janny?"

I looked at him, then at Tess, then back at him. "I finished both of them. I'd like a big fat raise, please."

He chuckled. "Good girl." But his eyes lingered on mine, and I knew he wanted to know about Oscar Thibodeau.

Turning to my aunt, I narrowed my eyes, "Sooo. What's the occasion?"

"My question exactly," Grandy piped. "For some reason, T and Z have brought us a cake…"

"At the exact time I was headed to bed!" Poppy bellowed with feigned annoyance.

"Stas, shh!" Grandy scolded, then turned to Tess. "Janny is here now, so can we open it? Finally?"

Once Tess nodded, Grandy stood and lifted the lid of the box. When her expression froze, we all stood and looked inside. It was a cake, a white layer cake cut in half and pulled apart. On one half was written Tess and on the other, Zander. Nestled between the two halves was a white cupcake on top of which was a little flag that said "Babycake arriving February 12." Grandy finally found her voice and screamed, "What? What? WHAT?" Then she and her daughter were happy-crying and dance-hugging in an explosion of joy. Poppy sat mute, but tears had filled his eyes. Babi didn't quite get it until I explained it to her, and then she just grinned and wagged her finger at my aunt, who was also crying. But the best tell was on Zander's beaming face—clearly, Tess's concerns about him had been unfounded.

Then it was nonstop laughter, hugs, and baby chatter, cake and milk and more cake, which turned out to be my dinner. Babi even had a bite before she shuffled over to kiss the top of Zander's head and rub her cheek against my aunt's. "Something bad to eat, eh? Shame for lie to old Busha," she smiled. "Such happy news for old womans. I go to bed now."

Before she left, Tess hugged me, hard. "Thanks for taking over today," she said. "I meant to come back, but we just couldn't stop talking."

"You're welcome. And congratulations, Tess. It *is* happy news."

She squeezed my hand. "I think it is." She sighed. "But I'll still be forty-two."

Zander was still grinning when they walked out. And then it was just me and my grandparents.

"Are you hungry?" Grandy sighed happily. "I saved you some chicken."

"No. Too much cake."

Poppy glanced at my barely touched slice and cleared his throat. "Are you okay, Janny? Tell us about the attorney."

I blew out a breath. "It was interesting," I told them, reaching into my pocket. "He gave me this." I slid the envelope with the key inside across the table.

"What is it?" Poppy said, picking it up.

"It's a key and instructions on how to get into Rose Winston's house. It seems there's a Steinway up for grabs. If I want it."

"What? Rose left you a Steinway?" Grandy coughed.

"No. She left her estate to the Cancer Association, or I guess that was Stephen. But apparently, anything that belonged to Mom isn't part of the estate and I can have it. That attorney said I have until next week to decide what I want to do."

"Oh, Janny," my grandmother breathed from behind her hands.

"They gave Mom a Steinway. For her sixteenth birthday, her parents gave her a *Steinway*. And now it's mine if I want it."

There was a momentary silence, then my grandmother reached over and placed her hand on mine. "Are you okay?"

The truth was I was still a little wobbly. It was partially Oscar Thibodeau, but it was also just what happened sometimes when my thoughts drifted to whom my broken mother had been before she was broken. *And she had played a Steinway.* "It's just a lot to take in," I said.

"I'm sure it is, sweetie."

I looked at them both. "He mentioned that the trust fund that pays Claire's bills won't be affected by any of this, and that I shouldn't worry…I didn't know what he meant. And I felt like maybe I should."

My grandparents looked at each other, then back at me.

"What bills? What trust fund?"

Grandy matter-of-factly opened her palms. "I guess it's never really come up, but that's good to know…that Rose's death won't impact Claire's trust fund. That's what pays for Potomac Manor."

"I didn't know that," I said.

"Why would you?" Grandy said, clearing the cake plates.

"I just…I thought *we* paid for it."

"Hardly, dear one. You may not have noticed, but I can barely get your grandfather to spring for an evening director. You do *not* want to know what it costs to keep Claire at Potomac Manor."

"Hmmm." I was about to ask how much, but when I caught the look on Poppy's face, I opted for something else entirely. "Mr. Thibodeau did say something else weird. He told me Rose had seen me perform—apparently, she's been *watching* me since Stephen died—and that she wanted to get to know me. Can you believe that? I think that's...*interesting* and a little creepy." I fought the urge to say "nice."

"What?" Grandy said, looking slightly horrified.

"And he told me she sent me a letter. I never got a letter. Did I, Grandy?"

My grandparents exchanged another look that answered my question, and I felt my throat tighten. "What?"

When neither of them said anything, I narrowed my eyes. "Tell me."

My grandmother sighed, caught. "She did send a letter. About six years ago."

"Six years ago? Why didn't you give it to me?"

She shook her head. "Janny..."

"We were afraid, January." Poppy blurted. "We were afraid that she would hurt you."

"Hurt me how? It was a letter."

"It was an invitation," Grandy said, wiping down the table. "One that you might have been tempted to accept."

"So.... You just didn't give it to me? That wasn't your call."

My grandmother stood, stiffening. "I beg your pardon, sweet pea," she said with crisp authority. "It was absolutely our call. I'm sorry that you're finding out about this after the fact. But looking back, I wouldn't have handled the situation any differently. You were sixteen and we were losing you, and Rose was...unpredictable. Maybe even dangerous, like Poppy said. It *was* my call—our call. And we'd do it again."

For a moment, I just stared at her vehemence, disregarding the "losing you" part—it had never been as bad as they'd thought. "Dangerous? What does that even mean?"

Poppy shook his head. "Blind hatred, bigoted hatred. That nonsense makes a person pretty damned dangerous, Janny. Rose and Stephen hated your father—"

Grandy corrected, "They *thought* they hated him; they didn't know him."

"Doesn't matter, Di. It made them very cruel," Poppy went on. "We didn't trust them."

"Why would they hate *me*?" I said, not even sure why I was arguing. "They didn't even know me."

"Because, January, they were the Winstons," Grandy said. "The *Winstons*. And you're a Duzinski, my love. Unforgivably Polish."

"You've said that before, but *that* cannot be the reason."

"Oh, but it was," she sighed. "Trust me, it was."

"They met your father one time," Poppy said. "Just one time. And then they threatened to disinherit your mom if she married him." He stared hard at me. "Rose Winston had no fondness whatsoever for this family. Nothing good could have come from you knowing about that letter."

I stared at my grandparents and sighed. "Well, I guess we'll never know." I was upset and not even sure why. Hadn't I told the attorney that I couldn't see myself ever excusing what my Winston grandparents had done? And wasn't that exactly what I would have had to do to let them into my life six years ago when I was being the brat of the century?

Grandy met my eyes with weary warmth, but Poppy remained unmoved. "You were not in a trustworthy place back then, January. We were never going to risk it."

I wanted to argue, but there was no point, so I opened the fridge and grabbed a bottle of water. "I'm tired. I'm going to bed," I said, and turned to leave.

"What about this?" My grandfather reclaimed my attention, holding up the key to Rose Winston's house.

I looked at it. "I guess I'm going to Chestnut Hill. Probably be the day after tomorrow. After the Rush funeral."

***

I took a long shower and tried to reconcile my thoughts. I decided I felt cheated somehow by the fact that my nasty grandmother had up and died, taking with her the possibility of my ever meeting her, which was ridiculous. She was probably just as horrible as I'd been told; she and my grandfather both. Certainly, their treatment of my mother had been unconscionable. And their treatment of my dad had been patently appalling. What kind of people actually did that? But Rose had secretly attended my performances? Was impressed with me? Did that mean proud? *Who was this woman?* It didn't matter! She'd rejected her only daughter because that daughter had fallen in love with my father. I should not be having these bizarre regrets!

I sat down on the edge of the bed to dry my hair, and as I did, my gaze fell to the photo on my nightstand. I picked it up. There was so much I did not know about them, about her. My mother had been an *"exquisite* talent." So much so that her parents had given her a Steinway. And now it was mine if I wanted it. It still didn't seem real.

There was a soft knock, and Grandy cracked my door open. "Janny?"

I looked over at her, "Hi, Grandy."

She made her way to me through the mess and glanced at the photo in my hands. "Still and forever one of the happiest days of my life," she said.

When I didn't respond, she handed me a yellowed envelope with my name on it and a Pennsylvania return address. "It sounds like a perfectly innocent note, Janny—I read it. But Rose wanted something. I'm sure there would have been a price."

I looked at her.

"I know you're upset about this, but I can live with that. I know that you know Poppy and I have always done what we thought was best for you."

"Of course, I do."

She kissed my forehead and walked out, leaving me with the letter written by my mother's dead mother. I stared at it for a long time, then lifted the single sheet of stationery from the envelope and unfolded it.

Dear January,

I'm sure you'll be surprised to hear from me, and I know it's possible you will not be happy about it after all his time. But I want you to know that I think of you every day, and especially every New Year's. This New Year's you had a birthday, a big one if turning sixteen is still as significant as it was in my day. I would like to meet you. I'd like to get to know you. You're probably thinking I've had all the time in the world to contact you, so why now? The answer to that question is mostly curiosity on my part, and I am making this request fully prepared to accept your refusal. I wouldn't blame you, and I won't make any other attempt to reach you. The ball is in your court, as they say. My address is 24 Moon Hollow Court, Chestnut Hill, P.A. You are welcome anytime. My email is ERW1000@ROHO.com if that is any easier for you. If you decide against contacting me, I will honor that. Either way, Happy (belated) Birthday.

Regards,
Your Grandmother, Rose Winston

I read it again, and I couldn't find the malice Grandy was so sure was there. Maybe I just didn't want to. All I could see was I'd had a grandmother, until yesterday, who had fleetingly wanted to know me, who had secretly watched me perform, and who had written me this letter.

I don't know why that humanized her in light of everything else I knew, but somehow it did.

nine

T he next morning was very busy. We'd received a woman who'd died as a result of a rowing accident on the Passaic River. There had been an unquestionable account of what happened, and she'd flatlined in the ER, so a medical examiner had not been involved. But she was messy, so Tess and I were working on her while Poppy dealt with the family. A tragedy like this is always very dynamic and tends to throw everything off. Emotions are ragged; people are raw and overwhelmed. Sometimes they come undone. Poppy is a master at creating calm, but it can still be draining.

In the midst of all this, Grandy had phoned down to say I was needed upstairs, which I dismissed since no one had told me about an appointment; I was up to my elbows in work as it was. But a few minutes later Babka called to remind me that I had agreed to accompany her and Nicole Pierce across the street to plant Ashley's pinwheel. I'd forgotten all about my promise to her. I left my frustrated aunt to fend for herself—she owed me for yesterday—and ducked into the washroom to slip back into the long sleeveless dress I'd worn downstairs today. I checked myself in the big mirror. Not bad. I hadn't slept well, but I didn't look it.

When I stepped out of the elevator, I was surprised to see Tyson Pierce sitting near the piano. He stood when he saw me, a look of relief bathing his features. His reaction was likely due to the group of people congregated in our lobby and the unchecked emotion vibrating from them. I knew this was the family of our rower, and indeed the sight was a bit overpowering. They were waiting for one of my grandparents, and thankfully just as I skirted around the gathering toward where Tyson stood, my grandfather stepped from his office. When I reached Tyson, he blew out a breath and glanced over my shoulder. "That looks like a few ruined days," he said.

I nodded, steering him toward the door. "It was an accident—those are always hard."

Tyson grimaced. "So sad."

"I know. Hey, I'm sorry I kept you waiting," I said. "I actually didn't know you were coming. I thought Babi said it was your mom. Is she—"

"I drove Mom here. She and your grandmother already went over."

"Oh."

"Yeah. I didn't realize the Pinwheel Garden was just across the street, so I told them to go on ahead and I'd wait for you. I hope that's okay?"

"Sure," I said, feeling a bit blindsided.

With that, we started across the street. It was a blue-sky late morning, warm but not unbearable, and there was a tiny breeze. And the fact that I was focused on the weather was evidence that I felt a bit awkward. Why did this feel awkward? Tyson Pierce was just a nice guy—and nice looking in his khakis and a white linen shirt. I was in a long orange dress and sandals, so we could have been going on a picnic—behind his girlfriend's back. Maybe it was that he was here in the first place, that he'd waited for me, or even that I'd seen him check me out as I accompanied Wyatt Rush on his violin. Or that he was this cute guy who I knew had abandoned his defenses to reveal some of himself to me—the way grief does. I was just being stupid, reading more into everything than I should. I finally broke the silence. "How did it go yesterday?"

"I think it went well," he said. "I'm no expert—I'm twenty-six and that was my first real funeral. My grandmother died last year, but I was sick and wasn't able to go, so it wasn't really *real*, if that makes sense. This was real. It was…hard. But nice, I guess. Sad. But nice. Very hard for my mom."

I nodded. "My grandfather says that the most exquisite pain for a parent is to outlive their child. He knows—he lost his son."

Tyson Pierce glanced over at me. "That's rough…and it makes sense. Ash was Mom's life. She was the first, and when she was born— you know, with Downs—Mom didn't want any more kids. But after about six years of begging, my dad finally convinced her to try again. Then my brother came, then me, and then my little sister. Well, Ava's not little, she just had a baby. But Ashley was Mom's…I don't know, *purpose.* Caring for her was a lot of work, but my mom sort of thrived on it."

"That's a huge loss for her. I'm so sorry," I said.

Tyson nodded. "Yeah, we're pretty worried about her."

We walked the rest of the way to the center of the common in clumsy silence, then Tyson said, "I've seen this park, but I never knew about a pinwheel garden."

"A lot of people don't," I told him as we passed a stone mausoleum with rippled windows. "It's in the Peace Garden, which is right over there." I pointed. "And the Pinwheel Garden is in the corner." We walked through a stone arch that was the official entrance to that quiet area of the park and entered—still without speaking—into a place rich with greenery and birdsong. Shade trees and benches for contemplation were scattered throughout the area, but there weren't too many people around.

"I had no idea," Tyson said on a quiet breath.

"I know. I love it here. I come here often to…*think deep things,*" I said dramatically.

"Like what?" he said, not smiling.

"Oh, you know—the mysteries of the universe…and my own life."

His eyes begged for details, but I just smiled. And then we heard it—the soft, erratic clicks.

"What is that?" he said.

"The chatter of angels. That's what my great-grandmother calls it," I said softly as we rounded the corner and came upon the source of the noise.

Tyson Pierce stopped. "Whoa. What is this?"

"This is the Pinwheel Garden."

He was a little open-mouthed as he took in the sight of hundreds of Mylar blooms spinning lazily in the breeze. They were all different colors and ranged in height from one to four feet, each catching the sun and reflecting it back with its own shimmer. In the midst of these, standing about six feet high, was a copper statue of a little boy holding a pinwheel to the sky.

"I...I've never...this is amazing," Tyson said.

"Can you believe this place, Ty?" interjected his tearful mother who had steered into view, my great-grandmother behind with her hand on the back of Nicole's motorized wheelchair.

"Hello, Mrs. Pierce," I said. "How are you feeling?"

"I'm okay," she said, looking around. "I think I could sit *here* all day."

"I sit here to *hear* my ones I love," Babi said. "They sing to old woman's heart."

"How lovely," Nicole rasped.

Tyson took them in again. "All of these are for people who are dead?"

I nodded. "Uh huh. We used to plant them on our roof, which is our backyard. But Babi petitioned the city council the summer after 9/11. New Jersey lost seven hundred forty-nine people that day, so Babka made seven hundred forty-nine silver pinwheels. She asked if she could plant them here in the Peace Garden on the first anniversary, and the city agreed. And now they get planted every year on the first of September and are up until the twentieth. In the meantime, she plants these." I jutted my chin. "From October until the 9/11s go up, everyone prepared at Duzy House gets a pinwheel."

"A *wiatraczek*," Babi corrected. "Is Polska for the wind collector."

"Right," I said. "And if they want to, they can plant it here. When it's time for the 9/11s, people come back for their pinwheels and help us trade them out for the memorial. It's kind of ceremonial—very cool, actually. There's a picnic, too."

Tyson looked at me like I was from another planet. "Unbelievable," he said.

"Why? Why pinwheels?" Nicole asked.

"Always I make for my little brother *wiatraczek*," Babi smiled. "He love them."

I looked at my great-grandmother. "She came here after the Holocaust," I explained. "She has a lot of terrible stories, but one bright spot was her little brother, Lubomir. She adored him."

Babi touched her heart.

"Cool name," Tyson offered.

"For means love of peace." Babi announced softly. "The war was wary terrible time. Lubomir was small boy, and when things wary bad and he get scared or sad, I make for him little *wiatraczek* to distract him. We made game. I make from scraps of paper or leaves and fasten to sticks he find—this part of game—always I have pin in bottom of my dress so I can to make *wiatraczek* for my Lubomir."

Nicole Pierce lightly touched my Babi's wrist. "So…your family was actually in the ghettos?"

"Not the ghettos, no—those were for the *Zydzi*—Jews. My family was Polskie…and Katolicki. But Hitler want all of Polska, so he destroy all the peoples. He destroy us just like the Jews. He shoot all the priests and burn the churches, kill the so many for being Polskie, and made many hundreds to go to work camps. My family go to Birkenau."

"Really?" she said.

"People don't remember that almost as many non-Jewish people died during that time as Jewish," I added. "We just don't hear about them. But Hitler was an equal-opportunity dictator."

Tyson stared at me, a bit awed. "What happened to them? Her family?"

I patted my Babka's hand. "They all died. All except my Babi."

"Not the little boy?" he asked in hopeful disbelief.

Nicole Pierce, too, met my eyes, nearly pleading for this to not be true.

"They killed all the children at Birkenau."

"Are you serious?" Tyson said, horrified.

"Most of them."

He stared back at the garden. "I'm so sorry."

"So, you…you make pinwheels because of your little brother?" Nicole asked tearfully.

"Yes. I do this for all of this peoples," Babi said. "Everyone lose a Lubomir, and each one should to be remembered."

I nodded. "This community understands better than most," I told Nicole, gazing out at the pinwheels chattering. "Lots of Polish ancestry here in Wallington. They know. A few years ago, the Mazurs—a prominent family in the community—honored her with that sculpture. That's her brother. But Babi says it really represents the innocence they all lost in that nightmare."

"I don't know what to say," Nicole Pierce whispered.

"I know."

"So, everyone in her family—they all have pinwheels?"

"They do. Her parents, her brothers, her best friend Tola—all died during the Holocaust. Later, after the war, she lost her husband, then more friends. My dad. They all have pinwheels."

"Your dad?" Tyson said.

I nodded but didn't look at him.

We were quiet then for a few moments, Tyson and his mother grappling, presumably, with the sad history of my family, my Babka and me with the tender meaning of this garden. Five hundred stems made of green PVC pipe had been inserted into the ground—the god-sent creation of an Eagle Scout. The pinwheel shafts slid down the small tubes, keeping everything stationary but the petals, which were then free to dance in the wind with no threat of blowing away. At the top of every tube was a notch for the nametag—two nametags, actually, as one tube was made to accommodate two pinwheels, and frequently had to.

The garden was pretty full right now, but there looked to be a vacant stem near the statue. I glanced over at Tyson and pointed it out. "That might be a good place," I offered. "Or there is probably some space around the far edge." He stood and guided his mother's wheelchair as close to the statue as he could get. They spoke quietly for a moment, then Nicole Pierce handed her son the pinwheel and dabbed away tears. Tyson looked at me, "What do I do?"

Babi hobbled over to comfort Mrs. Pierce, and I met Tyson at the edge of the garden, where he followed me into the blooms. We stopped near the empty stem. "Will this work?"

He looked over my shoulder at his mother, then nodded. "Perfect."

"It just goes in there, and then you pull out the tag."

Tyson Pierce bent down and gently placed the pinwheel in the tube, and I saw his hands tremble as he pulled his sister's nametag through the notch. He then gave one petal a little flick to get it going. It caught the breeze and began to spin and whisper.

When he finally stood up, he looked at me with moist eyes. "Thank you, January," he said. "Thank you so much for this."

"You're welcome."

For a moment he looked at me in a way that felt like something might be happening between us, and I had to drop my gaze because his had become so intense.

"I'm sorry about your dad," he said.

I glanced back up. "Thank you."

"You said he has a pinwheel in here?"

"He does. It's over here."

Tyson followed me to the back of the garden where a small cluster dedicated to those most precious to Babka was separated just slightly from the rest. Her parents and grandparents, her three brothers, and of course my great-grandfather—the love of her life. And my dad—the other great love of her life.

I tapped the quiet pinwheel, making it spin as Tyson leaned in to inspect the tag—*Beloved Tanek. 1972-2000.*

He looked at me. "2000? That's more than twenty years ago."

"Twenty-two," I said. "He died the night I was born."

"What? What happened?"

I shook my head. "My parents were on their way to the hospital to have me. There was a blizzard...and a drunk driver..."

I watched him swallow. Twice. "January, I'm so sorry. What about your mom?"

"She was hurt," I said. "Badly. But she didn't die."

He eyed me, poised for specifics that I did not offer.

"Is she okay?"

"No," I said with no explanation. Instead, I looked past him at my father's pinwheel, red and gold that turned deep blue at the edges.

After a moment that bulged with uncomfortable silence, Tyson finally said, "Tanek. I've never heard that name before."

"It means 'immortal' in Polish," I told him. "Which I think is very cool."

"That is cool."

I looked at him looking at me and cleared my throat. "We...*I* should probably get back," I managed to get out.

"Oh, right...right. Me, too. I need to get Mom home, then I probably should go to work."

I smiled. We walked out of the Peace Garden, several steps behind Babi and Tyson's mother as the sound of the angel chatter faded and finally disappeared into our silence. In truth, we didn't speak again until we had crossed the street, which was beyond awkward.

"I'm sorry," I finally said at the exact same moment he did.

We looked at each other. "Why are *you* sorry?" we also said in unison. It was funny, but we didn't laugh. Not really.

Tyson stared at me, looking very different from the grieving man I'd first met. He seemed somewhat commanding and genuinely attentive. "I'm sorry," he said again. "I made you uncomfortable back there, asking about your parents."

"No, no. It's just me…" I lifted a shoulder. "I'm never really sure what to say…"

He eyed me. "That must be——" He shook his head, grappling. "I can't even imagine losing my dad before I ever knew him."

"It's a lot to try to explain. I didn't know him, so I have nothing to miss really, but I miss having had the opportunity, if that makes sense. And then there's this constant reminder that it happened because of me, and that's a whole other thing."

Tyson slowed, so I slowed. "What does that mean?" he said with a surprised look.

I looked at him, surprised as well. "Nothing… Just that if it hadn't been for me, they wouldn't have been in the path of a drunk driver in the first place."

The expression on Tyson's face had turned almost comedic in its incredulity, and it made me swallow my words.

"What? That's ridiculous," he retorted. "You can't honestly blame yourself? I'm sorry, but that is completely ridiculous."

"I know that," I said, feeling diminished—and mad at myself for it.

"Well, I mean…it's not like you had any control, right?" he back-pedaled, attempting to soften his abruptness. "You weren't even born. So, you have to admit…."

I smiled tightly.

He closed his mouth and eyed me for a beat. "January, hey…."

I waved him off with a dismissive laugh. We'd reached the entrance to Duzy House, and I stepped ahead to hold the door open for Babka and the wheelchair she pushed conveying Nicole Pierce. Tyson's mother smiled up at me. "Thank you again, January. I wouldn't have missed that for anything."

"I'm so glad. It's one of my favorite places."

Poppy was waiting in the now quiet foyer with some papers for Mrs. Pierce, one of which I knew was a laminated copy of Ashley's obituary. It was the perfect time for me to leave. I turned to Tyson who was rather hovering at the edge of the circle, then looked again at Nicole Pierce. "I have to get back now, but it was lovely to work with your family. Good luck to you."

Nicole Pierce reached for my hand and squeezed. Tyson looked as though he had something to say but Poppy stepped in front of him to inform me in hushed tones that Tess had gone home sick and hadn't gotten too far with our rower. Behind me I heard Babi tell them: "My Janny work the too hard, I worry she forget to be young."

Nicole Pierce said, "She's such a lovely girl. I was so touched by how sweet she was with my Ashley."

"My Kochanie is good girl."

As I waited for the elevator, I heard Tyson say something about me playing a mean piano. "She was practicing with a little boy, and I listened in for a minute. I was blown away."

"She play the beautiful. Her *matka*—mama—used to play before Janny was borned. So beautiful…such gift to give her daughter."

"Does she still play, January's mother?" Nicole asked.

No! Don't talk about her! I mind-screamed punching the button again. *It's none of their business!*

"Oh, no. No. Claire had wary, wary bad accident. Never she did play again the piano. Only my Janny, now."

Thankfully the elevator arrived, and I walked in without looking back. As the doors closed, I sighed and leaned my head against the wall. If Tyson Pierce thought my feelings about the night of my birth were ridiculous, I could only imagine the party he'd have with the weirdness I'd had going on with my mom ever since.

I thought of Jasmine again, wishing I could just drive over to her house and unload. She was the one person who knew how complex I was, or thought I was, and loved me anyway. Her meth-addicted mother had walked out when Jaz was a baby. She used to always tell me that a broken mother was better than no mother at all.

We once got into a terrible fight because I 'd been whining about having to go see Claire. "Poor, pathetic you!" she'd yelled. "Poor pathetic you who has to go see your mother who loves you. You make me sick!" She'd then driven it home with words I've never forgotten. "She's damaged, January. So what? It has never stopped her from loving you. Not that you deserve it!" Jaz had glared at me so hard it hurt. "I have a mother somewhere on this planet who would trade me for an eight-ball," she'd sneered. "So, pardon me if I think you're insane. And a spoiled brat."

We'd been maybe thirteen. It had happened in Jasmine's kitchen. She'd been folding her father's underwear at the table. I remember how small I'd felt, how ashamed. I'd hated her until the next day— and she'd hated me back. But I'd never whined to her again. Not about going to see Claire.

ten

Downstairs was quiet and there was a note from Tess telling me she'd made little progress on our rower. She'd gotten her cleaned up, but not embalmed. She added that Calvin was doing a graveside and would be picking up stroke victim from Glen Brook Senior Care on his way back.

I sighed. I had been hoping to find a little piano time today. I'd been invited to perform at the Teterboro Harvest Chimes concert in September and had planned to grab some practice this afternoon. But it didn't look like that was going to happen—not with a trauma repair waiting, the dead piling up, and my aunt calling it quits at ten after one. Maybe I'd find time later.

This year the concert was dedicated to Chopin and Liszt, two of my favorites, so I was excited to be involved. My go-to piece was Liszt's "Liebestraum No. 3," but what I really wanted to do was Chopin's grueling "Fantaisie Impromptu." That piece was my secret passion, and technically it had always driven me rather mad with frustration. But as I pulled our rower out of the fridge a little annoyed at my plight, I suddenly realized that if I remembered to take my music, I could practice on my mother's Steinway.

***

Two hours later I'd made good progress and I was starving so I decided to head upstairs for an apple and a couple of Cokes. I was surprised to find the kitchen empty and wondered where everyone was. Babka's door was open just a crack, so I poked my head in to check on her. She was sitting on her bed reading her mail, and when she saw me, she dropped her letter and smiled. "Kochanie."

"Hey, Babi. Did you have lunch?"

"I just finish the leftover quiche from the yesterday. With the girls."

"Do you know where Poppy is?"

"He got call. Was going to eat with me, but…psh." She scooted over and patted the space she'd vacated. "Come for a moment and keep old womans some company."

"I shouldn't…Tess left, and Calvin's on his…well, maybe for a minute," I said, really in no hurry. I sat down next to her and pulled my feet up. When I leaned my head on her shoulder, she kissed it.

"How is my Janny?"

"Busy."

"Ba! You work the too hard."

"I should be working now! Look at me.."

She laughed. "I think this Tyson is nice boy."

"He's okay."

"He likes my January. I can tell this."

"He has a girlfriend."

"Ba."

I sighed. I should have left then. Calvin was probably back. But instead, I nestled in. I love Babi's room. I love the feel of it, the separateness of it. I always imagine the entire country of Poland distilled down to these walls. The space had been her original apartment when she and my great-grandfather had moved here, and years later when Poppy had bought the building, he'd reconfigured everything around her rooms. My *pradziadek* (great-grandfather) had carved the fireplace mantel, and the cracked mirror above it had come from somewhere near his family home in Olsztyn. It is a little like a circus mirror, so wavy it distorts your reflection.

On the windowsill are pictures of my Babka and Pradziadek on their wedding day. He had a shy smile and was very tall; my father had gotten his height from him. A faded rug covers the floor in front of the fireplace, and a small carved cross hangs above the mantel. On the back of Babi's ancient rocking chair is a lacey shawl like one her grandmother used to have. There is a lot of blue and white porcelain in here, distinctly Polish. Some of it is badly chipped, but Babka can tell you exactly where it came from and why it's important to her. A round wooden table and two bookshelves hold precious memorabilia and a lifetime chronicled in photographs.

Somewhere in this room there is a threadbare Star of David armband that was worn by her dearest friend Tola Pilch. A toy truck that belonged to her beloved Lubomir sits in a place of honor, missing all but one wheel. In the center of the table in a tiny basket rests a silver cufflink that is like one that belonged to her father. These things are priceless to my Babka.

I looked around for the box my father carved when he was a little boy and spotted it on the mantel. It was full of marbles. Babka had told me that at the beginning of every school year, he gave her one of his favorites so she could hold it and not miss him while he was away. She'd saved them all.

My gaze drifted to her nightstand where, amid a garden of photographs, was one of my father as that little boy. He was grinning widely to show off the loss of his front teeth. I picked it up and leaned again into Babka's neck. "How could anyone hate that face?"

"You speak of Rose?"

"How could she have disowned her only daughter for marrying him?" I said, still studying the picture. "I hate her."

"Then you are no better than she, my love. You never did to know Rose. And she did never to know your father. Always must to remember, true hate cannot be without true knowing, Janny."

"Maybe. But I still think what she did was unforgivable."

"It would seem. But we cannot see the world through Rose's eyes, so we are not good judges."

My great-grandmother reached across me to pick up a faded picture of a little girl and a lovely woman. "My *matka*, she was wary beautiful," she said, stroking the face in the photo. "My *ojciec* used to say he was envy of all the mans. When I was young girl, we were taken from our home. It was wary terrible, Janny. We were stay in crowded building for many days, and each day was filled with more not knowing. I was trust and hoped that good would come. But, Mama, she was not hope. She was crying all the time and give up. The day we evacuate, I thought we were be free, and going home, that it would be time of great rejoice and Mama could be happy again. But no.

"The soldiers they stormed in our rooms shouting and with their guns, pushing the old peoples, yelling to the childrens. They ordered us to the streets with our little possessions and shoot the anyone who moved too slow. So much chaos. When Papa fall, two mens beat him in his head with their guns, and when my brother Tadeuz tried to help, they shoot him in his face."

"Babi!" I gasped.

She shook her head. "I don't believe what I am seeing, Kochanie. I did not even know the sound of my own scream. I threw myself at this mens. I begged them stop. I pleaded. One of them looked at me in way that made my belly turn with fear, but…but also hope, too. I should be so shamed."

"Babi, why are you——"

"He say something to his friend, and they look to me strange, and one touch my face gentle while the other one kicked my *ojciec* into gutter like so much garbage. It was wary awful this, Janny. Never I will forgot."

I reached up to stroke her face and found it wet. "Let's not talk about this anymore."

"Hush, my girl. This is story you must to hear."

Her harsh tone, a true anomaly, made it impossible for me to argue.

Babi continued. "In short moment, I am between this mens, and they are taking me to where I not know. Were they let me to go? I was so afraid I could not think, but they were taking me from the train, and they did not to beat me. I am limp with relief, Janny, but if I would think, I would be shamed because of what they did just do to my papa and my brother. Yet I would be free? Could this be? One of them he smile to me, but it was wary bad smile, a smile I was too young to understand.

"Suddenly Mama was in our path. She did let her long hair down, and it was golden in the sun. Lovely. She was wear her green coat, which made her always like a flower in a sea of dust. Those mens saw her beautiful and smiled their bad smile at her. *What you want with a child?* she say in a voice I did not heared before in my life. *Let her go,* she say with no fear. *Take me. Take me instead,* she say. What she was doing, I could not know. But they threw me aside and my chance of escape gone—stealed from me by my own *matka*. I hate her in that moment, Janny. I hate her!"

I had never heard my Babka speak like this, and it was making me queasy.

"She yelled to me find Lubomir and not let him from my sights, but I just stand there. *Run, Rahel!* Mama yell. *Find him!* she shout as she go with this mens down the alley. The mens, they were laughing a wary bad laugh.

"I just stand there crying when someone pull me back into the peoples. *You're going to get shot, stupid girl!* they say. Who was it, I never know."

Babi was quiet for a beat, and I realized I was afraid to say anything.

"By some miracle," she said, shakily, "I find my Lubomir. I try to hide with him, but they drag us on train to hell. I am so angry to my mama, but hours after when finally we move to pass by that alley…" Babka's voice broke with her tears. "Janny, I see Mama's green coat and one of her shoes in that alley. But I never do see her again. Not ever."

"Babi…what?"

"When I was at Birkenau, I heared what those mens do to her. Awful things. And when they finish, they shoot her. They shoot my *matka* dead, Janny."

"No…"

Babka kissed the photograph she'd been holding. "I did not have true knowing, my Janny. I was flawed in my judging. I think I hate to her, but oh, how much I love to her," she said stroking the picture. "How I can thank to her, Kochanie, I never can know."

My heart was pounding with shame. "Babi, I'm so, so sorry."

Finally, she reached past me and put the picture back on her nightstand. She then turned her old, very tired, very wet eyes to mine. "Janny, I hate my *matka* when I think she stealed my chance to be free. When I know that she save my life with hers, everything change. You understood what I did tell you, my love?"

I nodded, wanting to bathe in her wisdom. She'd lost everyone, in the most horrific way, lived through the most horrific things at the hands of the most horrific people, and yet somehow here she was tutoring me in the soft lessons of understanding. "What do you do with all of the why's, Babi? Why did your mother have to die that way?

Your whole family? Why did my parents have to crash the night I was born? Why? Sometimes I'm so mad at God."

She patted my hand. "You must not shut your heart to Him, Janny," she said. "God is holder of all our pain. He hurts same as you."

"Oh, Babi." I sighed.

She turned my chin to her. "All love flows through God, January. Never forgot this."

"Doesn't really explain all the terrible things He lets happen, though, does it?"

She shook her head. "True is this, Kochanie. My journey is paved with this questions and still I have no the answers. I have only trust that God knows why. But I have came to know that even if terrible mans— or terrible chance—takes a life from us, those lives are not lost to Him—not your father, not my father. None are lost to God. I must to believe this or I cannot live, Janny."

She took my hand and brought it to her lips. "Kochanie, my peoples leave ashes of many millions human hearts. And I believe that God knows each one of them."

"Oh, Babi…."

"I tell you something I never told you before. I prayed to know this is true. Was many years ago I am ache with missing all my dead ones. And one night I dream of Birkenau, of the furnace rising up from hell. It was day my precious Lubomir was lost to me forever. All was lost. The childrens had been gathered and were being taken away. Lubomir was there, but he not see me. Never I will forgot that face. I shout for him until my throat bleeds, but my voice was lost in the pain of us all as we were watch the death-march of our little ones. I fall to my knees and wail to the empty heavens for God to turn, just this once, to hear me, to save for my Lubomir.

"This moment have I relived many, many times, Janny, and it was same in my dream. But when this time I drag my burning eyes up, I saw…I saw the night sky filled with angels, Janny. Angels. Angels carrying our babies to paradise. I saw them, January. It took many years, and many, many prayers, but I know now that on that…*dziki* night, our little loves walked in and out of hell and straight into God's embrace. I think they all did—my Lubomir, my Tola, my brothers Eryk and Tadeuz, Mama, Papa—all of this peoples. I must to believe this or I cannot to stop the hurt."

"You amaze me, Babi," I whispered through my swelling throat.

"Oh, my sweet one. I wish so I could share to you my peace," she said. "For you I would give this. But you must to find your own peace."

"How do I do that, Babi?"

She squeezed my hand with her ancient one. "You must to open your eyes, my Janny, and see bigger. See more…"

***

Babi's words stayed with me all afternoon, like sticky wisdom I couldn't peel off. Truthfully, I kind of hated how she'd always had a way of reaching that nether place in me that I preferred stay buried and unexplored. But she did have a way. I sighed and again tried to shake off my preoccupations as I clipped the last of the nose hairs from Jerome Toobin with whom I'd been discussing the situation. Then I stood back to admire my freshly embalmed handiwork. I was pleased. "Much better," I told him. "You look very handsome, my friend. Thanks for listening."

The eighty-eight-year-old man, who'd died of a massive stroke earlier today, was in great shape. He had a full head of white hair and matching beard, which I'd just trimmed, as well as a thick mustache. I hadn't seen any pictures yet, but he struck me as an ascot guy, an artist type who I imagined smoked a pipe and did okay with the ladies.

As I wheeled him into the fridge, my first phase of preservation complete, the phone rang, and I almost ignored it—it was 9:40 p.m., and I was done. I was tired and hungry and needed a shower. But I knew if I didn't answer, my cell would ring in the next ten seconds, so I answered. "Hey Poppy, what's up?"

"Oh, good, you *are* still there."

"I was just headed up. You barely caught me."

"Can you first stop by my office for a second?"

"Really?" I grimaced.

"It won't take long."

"I'm in scrubs."

"Not a problem. The viewing is long over, and no one's around."

When I stepped off the elevator a few minutes later, my grandfather was waiting to step on. He smiled. "You have a visitor waiting in my office."

"What? Who?"

"And Calvin is in Grandy's office finishing some paperwork. He'll lock up."

"Poppy, what's going on?"

My grandfather smiled as he stepped onto the elevator. "I believe it's an apology of some kind." He shrugged. I stared at him as the doors closed between us.

What?

My first thought was that Tess had come by feeling bad about leaving so early today, which would have been very out of character for my aunt—she rarely feels bad about anything, probably less so now that she's pregnant. Still, when I walked into the office, that's who I expected. Instead, there was Tyson Pierce looking a bit sheepish.

I swallowed, completely taken aback.

He stood. "Hi, January."

"Tyson. Hi, what are you doing here?"

"Hi," he tried again, chuckling uncomfortably.

I stared at him.

"Sorry. I'm a little nervous. Do you have a minute? I know it's late."

"Okay…What's going on?"

He took a breath and proceeded to rub the back of his neck, which gave me the chance to take him in. He was wearing dark slacks and a blue shirt, and he'd loosened his tie. I remembered that he'd had to go to work earlier today, and I suddenly wondered what he did.

"Look," he said, reclaiming my attention. "I just wanted to apologize. I was rude today, and I don't even know why. I didn't mean to be, it just came out wrong."

I looked at him, and his "that's ridiculous" flooded back into my head. "*Oh…*" I smiled, taken aback. I could see it had taken something for him to come here tonight, and it was hard not to be impressed by that. "Oh…Tyson, I…That's so sweet. I didn't give it another thought."

"Really?"

"Well, maybe a tiny thought." I smiled.

He smiled, too, and took a step toward me visibly relieved. "I'm so sorry. I'm glad it was just a tiny thought, because the truth is, you are a really interesting girl, and I'd like to get to know you…if I haven't blown it. All I could think to do—all day long—was to come here and see if there was any chance you'd let me make it up to you." He grinned, but it was a very nervous grin. "I know I'm probably dreaming here," he said. "You probably have a boyfriend, right? But I was just hoping you'd have lunch with me—just lunch," he quickly added. "Even if you're married, it's just lunch. You're not, though, are you? Married, I mean?"

I fought not to smile. "No," I said. I didn't tell him I was the queen of set-ups and first dates and evidently too picky for my own good, according to Jasmine.

He blew out a breath, relaxed a little, and I lost the battle. But just as quickly I unsmiled when a glasses-wearing brunette in a yellow dress walked her long legs through my mind. "Tyson, what are you doing? Don't *you* have a girlfriend?"

He groaned. "Nooo. No! I don't."

I cocked my head and lifted one brow, making myself a human question mark.

"I don't!" he insisted again. "Brynn thought…I guess she thought the death of my sister would be a good time to audition for the part, but she didn't get it."

I narrowed my eyes. "Does she know that?"

He nodded. "She knows. She's not happy about it, but she knows."

"Sounds a little messy."

"Not really," he said. "So, lunch?" Then it was awkwardly quiet for a few beats while he waited for me to answer.

I didn't. I didn't know what to say. It *was* just lunch. But there was this not-happy girl who'd lost out on the role of his girlfriend…and he *had* called me ridiculous.

"No answer…" He sighed. "That probably means I should go." He glanced at his watch. "Besides," he fake-chuckled. "Your grandfather said I only had five minutes—he's pretty intense for an old guy."

I laughed, just as fake. "He'll be thrilled that you think so."

We looked at each other for another awkward moment. He finally nodded. "Listen, I'll be at the Colonial Diner in Lyndhurst tomorrow at 11:45. No pressure, but if you can make it, that would be great. And if you don't come, I'll know I shredded my dignity for a good cause anyway, because"—he lifted a shoulder—"I am truly sorry."

I smiled.

"Night, January," Tyson said as he turned to leave.

"Wait—"

He looked back, steeled but hopeful.

"I need to play for a funeral tomorrow morning," I said. "Could we make it 12:15?"

He gave me a crooked—relieved—smile. "Absolutely. I'll see you then."

eleven

My goal the next day had been to leave for Chestnut Hill right after the Rush service. But now I'd be further delayed because I'd agreed to a quick lunch with Tyson Pierce, which I was simultaneously kind of dreading and kind of excited about. But the thought of it was a distraction I couldn't afford, and I was tempted to reschedule—I really did have enough on my plate today as it was. If he just hadn't been so sweet...and if I just hadn't been so touched by his apology. But it was just lunch—he'd made *that* perfectly clear.

I sighed for the hundredth time to clear my head. I had a rower to finish.

Heidi Simon was thirty-eight years old. She'd been a wife, a mom of three boys, an escrow officer, and an avid rower. She had also been very pretty until she was hit in the temple with an oar, knocked overboard, and drowned. She had short, dark hair, a good chunk of which had been severed from her scalp by the oar. This had also left a sizable gash in her deeply dented skull. But Tess had finished the wound repair early this morning which was now nicely firm. We were ready for wax.

When the filler was soft and malleable, I pressed it into the concave place above my deceased's left ear. I smoothed it with the heat of a blow dryer, and a few minutes later all evidence of her fatal blow was concealed beneath an industrial layer of base coat, and she was ready to make up. I glanced at the time. I had a little over an hour before the

Rush funeral at ten o'clock. I gathered my supplies, propped Heidi's head on a block, and started filling in what was missing.

As with most mortuaries, we had a drawer full of emergency hair: extensions, toupees, human hair wigs, all shades and lengths and textures. I borrowed a small fistful from a curly toupee and glued it to the bare spot behind the woman's temple. I added a bit more and combed her own hair over my reconstruction. Then I did her makeup, which was minimal. She was tanned and healthy and had lovely skin. Aside from camouflage and airbrushing, she required just a little mascara and brow work. At just before ten, she looked impressively natural. Tess would have to get her casketed when she got in—whenever that would be. I had to change and get upstairs to accompany Wyatt Rush in his "Hallelujah."

Jordan Rush's service had already started when I snuck in and sat down on the back row. It was an interesting gathering, not too large but very heartfelt. There were several bikers, outfitted in their unique regalia, others wore jeans, some were in suits, but they had all shown up to mourn. As for Jordan Rush, he was outfitted in the uniform of his life: levis, chaps, a black Harley Davidson tee, leather vest, sunglasses. His wife had wanted his arms bare to show off the tats he had been so proud of. He looked good, with no evidence of how he'd taken his life.

After a bandanna-clad friend, whose wiry beard was braided down the front of his chest, offered an impromptu life sketch, Jordan's mother read a very touching tribute. The officiator then announced Wyatt's number. The little boy stood, looking a bit unsure until I walked to the front of the chapel. He was in a pair of jeans and a white shirt with a cool little bow tie. When he saw me, he visibly relaxed. I sat down at the piano, and he gave me a timid nod. I played the introduction, and just as we'd practiced, Wyatt Rush came in when he was ready. He played flawlessly, and when he was done, there was not a dry eye in this mixed bag of grievers. He was such a beautiful child. I found myself worried about him, trying to imagine his life from here on.

When the service ended, I was already at the piano, so I played some soft postlude music as the chapel emptied. I was completely absorbed in my own thoughts—so much so that I was startled when Wyatt tapped my shoulder. He and his mother, Jolene, had hung back.

She was a weeping mess of leather, tattoos and untamed hair, her heartbreaking misery melting away all the hard edges of her. I stood, and she hugged me.

"Thank you," she whispered in my ear. "Just…just thank you."

"You're so welcome. It was a beautiful service." I looked at Wyatt, who was staring up at me, and palmed his chin. "And you were simply fabulous, sir," I said. "Your dad is undoubtedly very proud of you."

He didn't say anything, but his thin arms came around my waist. He squeezed me, then hurried out of the chapel after his mother, turning once with a small wave.

"Good luck, Wyatt," I said softly, but he didn't hear me
.

***

It was just after noon when I left for Lyndhurst, a ten-minute drive away, and I again felt a bit anxious to get this over with. First dates are extremely delicate—just ask me, I'm an expert on them—and lunch dates, in my opinion, are the first cousins to job interviews. But I did take some small comfort in knowing that this one was disguised as an apology, so not really a *date* date. Tyson Pierce was just a nice guy who seemed to like me—what little he knew about me. But did he really? He'd been more concerned about making amends than finding out if I even had a boyfriend, so how much, really, could he actually like me? And then there were all the long-legged women auditioning to be with him. Goodness, this was exhausting!

These were my thoughts as I sat in the parking lot of the Colonial Diner at 12:14. Tyson had just walked in. He looked good: dress pants, tie, white shirt sleeves rolled up, sunglasses. He had great style. And he was employed. And from an intact family, which in my limited experience made for the best men. Not always, of course, but usually.

I checked my face in the visor mirror and glossed my lips. I looked nice, too (thanks to the Rush funeral) in a sleeveless black dress and my go-to pink pumps. I had just enough of a tan to look healthy, and it was a good hair day. I got out of the car and walked into the bustling diner. I didn't see him at first, but I felt his eyes on me and then heard him call my name. When I saw him, the smile on his face suddenly made me happy. He was seated in a booth but stood as I walked to the table, not breaking eye contact. He looked me over and seemed to approve.

"Hi," he said as I sat.

"Hi."

"You look *great.*"

"Thanks. I'd love to say this was all for you, but this is my funeral-slash-work look."

He laughed.

The waitress appeared and handed us menus, rattled off the specials, and took our drink orders. Then we studied the lunch choices like they were national security headlines—well, at least I did. When I glanced up from my menu, Tyson was looking at me. He blew out a breath. "Hi. Thanks again for coming."

I laughed. "Hi to you, too. And you're welcome."

He shook his head. "I hate first dates."

I narrowed my gaze, teasingly. "So, this *is* a date?"

He laughed and his nervousness somehow calmed mine.

We both ordered cheeseburgers and decided to split a large order of fries. When the girl walked away, Tyson grinned.

"You thought I was a salad girl, right?"

"I did! I'm so glad you're not. I don't trust salad girls."

"No, they're very untrustworthy."

"Not that salads are bad," he qualified.

"No, you gotta love a good salad," I added.

Small talk. I hated it. Thankfully my phone buzzed. I grimaced. "Sorry, I'm kind of on the clock," I said, picking it up. But it was just a text message from Oscar Thibodeau:

> One other thing I forgot to mention, January. There is a portrait of your mother in the entry. I can't imagine that would be of interest to anyone but you. If you'd like that, please feel free to take it. Best, OT

"Are you okay?"

I looked up at Tyson. "Yeah. I just…I'm sorry, it's been a weird couple of days."

"Anything I can do?"

I sort of smiled. "It's just my life. It's a little complicated at the moment."

Tyson leaned onto his elbows. "I'm a captive audience if you need to unload."

"Careful what you offer," I laughed, shaking my head. "You're sweet, but it's nothing."

He sat back, and we were quiet for a minute. "I could apologize again to fill the silence, but I think that will make me sound too pathetic."

I smiled. "Please don't. You've apologized quite enough. Thanks for that, by the way."

He grinned and took a long draught from his Coke.

When the quiet again threatened, I said. "Soooo…where is work?"

"Trimming Law. Downtown."

"You're a lawyer?"

"No. I'm an accountant—a forensic accountant. Just getting some experience under my belt until a buddy of mine from Rutgers gets licensed. Then we'll start our own firm."

"That's awesome. What is a forensic accountant?" I asked, having never heard the term. "What do you do, exactly?"

"Study the numbers, make sure everything adds up right. If it doesn't, we investigate, get it all litigation-ready. FA's identify fraud in business."

"Oh. So, you work with a lot of cheaters?"

He chuckled. "The people who hire me work with the cheaters. I work with the numbers. I like it because numbers don't argue."

"I so get that! That's why I like working with the dead. They don't argue either."

"See! We have something in common," he said. "Sort of."

"I guess we do."

He leaned over his elbows. "Have you always wanted to do what you do? You know, work with dead people?"

I smiled and relaxed.

"I'm serious. You probably get that question a lot. I mean, how many girls actually *do* what you do? So, did you? Always know that's what you wanted?"

I lifted a shoulder. "I don't know. Maybe. I just grew up with it, so I'm not sure. I remember coming home from school as a little kid and going downstairs to find my grandfather. I'd sit in the corner and eat an orange and tell him all about my day while he worked on someone.

It was just part of who we were. It's just what we did. Do. And then, when I was about twelve, I started helping my aunt. My main job was fingernails. I clipped a lot of nails. Painted a lot of nails."

Tyson grinned.

"The dead are easy. The grieving can be bit more of a challenge for me."

"Really? But you're so good at it."

"I'm learning—but grieving people are Grandy's domain. I'm better at the mechanics. I learned all that from my grandfather. He has a reverence for this work that I have always found fascinating."

"So how old were you when you decided this was what you wanted to do?"

"Oh, maybe sixteen or seventeen. I'd gotten a headache at school and wanted to go home, so my grandfather picked me up. But he was driving the hearse, and when I got in, he said in his serious voice, 'January, exactly how sick are you?'"

I laughed and Tyson smiled.

"I told Poppy that I'd never dream of throwing up in his deluxe funeral coach—that hearse is his most prized possession. It cost over $120,000, so he's very protective." I smiled. "Anyway, he said 'Good, because I need your help.' That turned out to be my first *collection*."

"You picked up a body? What was that like?"

"Humbling," I said, playing with my straw. "It was a residence pick-up, which was why we were in the hearse—my grandfather thinks people do better when their loved ones are driven away in a Cadillac coach rather than the utility van. Which I'm sure they do." I shrugged. "We pulled up to the address, he turned off the engine, and we just sat there. And I said, 'What are we doing?' And he said, 'Getting ready.' Then he took my hands and said a little prayer that we wouldn't add to the pain already in that home. Short and sweet. Then he told me, 'It's imperative to enter a grieving home in the right frame of mind.' I never forgot that."

"You grandfather is amazing—a little scary—but he was very gentle to my family."

"He's one of the good ones."

Tyson nodded. "So, what was it like?"

"Sobering. I remember there was a dog whimpering, this beautiful golden lab. He was just whimpering, begging for someone to notice him. Dogs know."

"They do," Tyson agreed. "We have a dog—Roxy. She knew. She *knows* Ash is never coming back."

I frowned. "I'm so sorry. It must be so sad for them. This one had the saddest eyes—it broke my heart. He followed us to our deceased, who was in the bedroom. The girl was about my age, and her mom was brushing her long hair over the pillow and just quietly weeping."

Tyson leaned closer, listening intently.

"I was so uncomfortable, but my grandfather just kept patting my back—firmly—in a 'not now, my dear—this isn't about you' kind of way. So, I sucked it up. When the woman finally looked up at us, Poppy told her there was no rush. 'Whenever you're ready.' And we stood there for a long time because it took her a long time to be ready. She just kept brushing and brushing until finally her husband had to pry the brush out of her hand. That, for me, defined the moment. She looked up at him with such *disbelief.*"

"Oh, wow," Tyson said on an awed breath.

"I know," I said. "It was snowing when we got back outside, and I remember how it seemed completely fitting—sad, cold, wet, gray. But I think that's when I knew, even at sixteen, that death was in my future. It felt like a privilege, almost, to be part of it. That probably sounds weird."

"Not at all," Tyson said.

I chuckled. "My grandfather was worried about me, so he took me to Krause's on the way home and bought me some white chocolate pretzels. I *luuuv* those." I grinned. "That was quite a sight, I'm sure, the hearse pulling into that little parking lot, us running in for homemade candy while a body cooled on the deck in the back." I shook my head. "He probably asked anyone in earshot if they needed a ride—he does that."

Tyson laughed. "He sounds so cool."

"He thinks he is."

"And you never looked back? Career-wise? You just went for it."

"Oh, I look back all the time. I got a scholarship to Seton Hall, in music. I went for two semesters, but when I looked at my two *lives*, I saw more death than piano, so I went to mortuary school. I graduated last year. I could apply again for Seton if I wanted. I probably should. Somedays, I think I definitely should. But, you know…" I shrugged.

"I've never heard anyone play like you—I don't know how much better you could get. When I saw you with that little boy the other day…that…that was awesome."

I felt myself color. "Thank you. He *was* special." I lifted a shoulder, a bit uncomfortable and so grateful the waitress had shown up at our table. But the whole time she was setting down our plates and refilling our glasses, Tyson Peirce never let go of my eyes. When she said, "Will there be anything else?" it was me who looked up and spoke. "No. This is great. Thank you."

My lunch with Tyson Peirce lasted two and a half hours. Long enough that we ordered two desserts an hour apart. He wore me down with his sincere interest in my life. And he really wore me down when he opened up about himself. He was the youngest of four, played the guitar in a garage band with his brother and some buddies, had had what he thought was one serious relationship in college. But the girl had broken his heart by stealing his car. He laughed telling me about it. "My brother wrote a song about her called 'KeKe Keyed My Heart and Dad Blew a Gasket.' Her name was KeKe," he said. "She's Hawaiian."

"That's…really bad," I teased.

He told me that his little sister had just made him a brand-new uncle on Easter—a baby girl they'd named Piper Wilhelmina.

I told him about Tess and Zander and their cupcake announcement of the other night and my aunt's dramatic lament of being almost forty-two.

He told me there was office space in Hasbrouk Heights that would be the home of his business-to-be and how he'd been saving every penny to pay for the first year's lease.

I told him all about my grandfather, who had been just a kid when he'd come upon the mortician who lived in the basement of the building we lived in and the body the guy had spilled on the sidewalk in front of it. "Poppy said he helped the half-blind funeral director get the corpse inside and landed his first job."

Tyson laughed. He had a body story, too. "When I was in college," he said, "I worked for my uncle, who owns a moving company. We were hired by a family to clear out an apartment in Queens. I think it was the mom's mom who was going into a nursing home, or maybe she'd died. I can't remember, I just know we found a freezer full of frozen cats."

"Ewww," was my appalled response.

"I know!" he said. "Every cat she'd ever owned. Apparently."

It felt so good to laugh. Really laugh. And it was so unexpectedly easy being with him. Easier than I had imagined.

I learned that Tyson's parents called each other Homer and Marge, which made me giggle. And his dad had just been offered a permanent position in China. Tyson laughed when he told me what his mom's reaction had been. She'd said, "Have a good time, Homer. I hope you'll come home on holidays for conjugal visits." He shook his head. "That's when I said, 'Ewww!'" he laughed. "Needless to say, he won't be taking the job."

Tyson was especially interested in our home above Duzy House. I told him the whole story about how Poppy had kept Babi's rooms intact and built the rest of the house around them.

"That sounds incredible," he said. "I'd love to see it."

"I'd love to show it to you," I said, a little surprised at myself. But it was such a rush to be this comfortable with someone new that I couldn't help it. I smiled, and we were quiet for a minute. It was the perfect opening to leave, but Tyson's eyes on mine said he was in no hurry.

I blew out a breath and got serious. "I was a little weird yesterday when you asked about my mom. Obviously."

"Not weird. Private."

"Maybe." I looked at him, swallowed. "She's in a care center. She's been in a care center most of my life," I said. I let that statement hang there for a beat, and when he leaned forward, gaze glued to mine, I went for broke. "And her mother, my grandmother whom I never met, just died. And if you can believe it, I'm headed to her home in Chestnut Hill, Pennsylvania, this afternoon because, it seems, years ago, she gave my mother a Steinway…as in grand piano. And now it's mine, if I want it."

"Oh, wow," he said. "Are you okay?"

I was both surprised and touched that *that* was his question—*was* I okay? "I honestly don't know," I said. "It's a little overwhelming."

"You want to talk about it?"

I stared at him, almost completely sure that I didn't. But then I heard myself say, "How much time have you got?

twelve

It turns out that when someone drops the possibility of a Steinway in your lap, not to mention the associated history, it takes a bit of steeling to walk into that world and claim it.

Tyson Pierce actually kind of offered to come with me to Chestnut Hill, and I almost let him—not really, but he was about the nicest guy I'd met in a long time, and he asked. I was still surprised by that.

And he'd been so easy to talk to. I'd opened up about things I usually kept pretty guarded: the fire, my subsequent fear of my mother, the tangled ball of my feelings toward her. If he judged me harshly— if he judged me at all—I never felt it. I told him about Oscar Thibodeau and the grandmother I disliked so much yet still rather wished I'd known. I told him how that should bother me, given her terrible treatment of my mom, and the guilt I felt because it didn't. I told him I was a bit anxious about the task ahead—of walking into my mother's past. That's when he offered to come with me. We talked for way too long but left our annoyed waitress a twenty-eight-dollar tip— he had ten and a five, I pitched in a ten and three ones. When he walked me to my car, I thanked him for the therapy.

He'd looked at me intently. "I think you're all kinds of interesting. I'll listen anytime you want to talk."

That was me, freakishly interesting.

I was jolted from my reliving of it all by Google telling me to turn off the mainline in eight hundred yards. I was almost there.

I followed her directions through two lights and a left-hand turn. When I pulled up to an unmanned security booth, Google informed me that my destination was on the right. I rolled down my window and punched in the code the attorney had given me. A moment later the wrought-iron gate swung open, and I drove into a neighborhood comprised entirely of mansions. It was like another planet. I navigated slowly past pristine lawns, carved pillars, a driveway where two Escalades were parked. The third house on the right was partially hidden behind a brick wall, but as I got closer, I saw "Winston, 24 Moon Hollow Court" engraved on the side of an art nouveau mailbox.

The home was massive. Chestnut Hill was apparently the upper crust of the upper crust of the wealth pie. And my mother, who now lived in one room at a care center, had grown up here? At least it was a high-end care center. I pulled into the drive and killed the engine. Then I sat there feeling very strange, wondering at the strangeness that had brought me to this moment, to this home that belonged to people I'd never met, for a piano given to a mother I did not know. The situation seemed too bizarre to be my life.

I got out of the car and followed the footpath to the front door, and then I just stood there like I was lost. "I don't know if I can do this," I whispered. But I turned the key and stepped inside. My instructions were to lift a faux sconce found directly to the right of the front door, which revealed a small control panel. When I disabled the alarm, the lights came on, startling me. "Hello?" I called out, pretty sure I was alone, but not completely sure.

It felt beyond strange to be standing here. *Here.* "Hello?" I said again, glancing around. The entryway extended up two floors and was immense. From it radiated three halls and a winding staircase. According to Mr. Thibodeau, my mother's room was up those stairs. I turned slowly to take in the dome-like space and stopped short—stopped moving, stopped breathing—when I saw it. "Ohhh…"

It was hanging above an ornately carved entry table—a portrait of a girl who looked a lot like me. I felt my pulse ticking in my temple. This must be what Mr. Thibodeau had texted me about. I walked over and gazed up, overcome with foreign emotion. It was stunning. She was stunning. And as I stared up into my mother's beautiful, flawless face, I went a little weak. I was looking into the face of a mother I had never imagined, and there was a subtle smile in her eyes that seemed to say, "Well, hello, January—it's about time you got here." I stepped closer, lost in the moment and completely overwhelmed. I could never have dreamt her this lovely.

She was sitting at a piano that was only partially in the painting, wearing a red dress with long sleeves and a wide neckline that grazed her thin shoulders. Her dark hair was pulled back at the nape of her neck in a cluster of thick curls, a stray lock snaking past her jaw. At her throat was a ruby choker rendered in amazing detail. I couldn't make out the signature in the bottom corner, but the date was 1992, which made Claire about fifteen when it was painted. I'd seen pictures of my mother, a few, but none like this. This was lovely and painful, and for a long time I could not look away. Had Claire—my mother—really been that beautiful girl? Unexpected tears filled my eyes, and it was as though I was meeting her for the first time.

It felt very otherworldly to be gazed upon by this lovely—very lovely—ghost. They were all ghosts, and I was alone except for them: two deceased grandparents, and a silent mom who had not been in this house for the whole of my life.

I took some deep breaths and gathered myself. I was here. I was in the last place on earth I ever thought I'd be, and it was a little eerie, but certainly not so much that I wanted to leave.

The house was a bit like a maze; I slowly explored each tentacle-like hall, feeling like a trespasser, albeit an invited one. One hall led to the kitchen that, for its scale alone, could have been the heartbeat of a fine restaurant with its two double ovens and two refrigerators. Attached to it was a small breakfast room, which was infinitely more inviting. There was a round table with a single place setting at the ready but untouched. It looked so lonely. I pictured my grandmother sitting there all by herself and suddenly wondered where she'd died. Had it been here? Had she been alone in this massive house?

Down another wide hall, I passed an office, dark-paneled with lots of leather and a flat-screen TV on the wall. It was a commanding space, a masculine space, clearly the sanctuary of my dead grandfather. But unchanged? Never repurposed? Why? I didn't go in.

I passed a bathroom with gaudy gold fixtures and next to it, a guest room, equally opulent. Opulence was everywhere I looked—*in overdrive.*

At the end of yet another hall, I opened a set of double doors that revealed a room the size of which rivaled the foyer at Duzy House. It was magnificent. "Hello?" I tested again, before stepping inside.

I took in the enormous space that boasted bookshelves reaching to the ceiling. The furniture, overstuffed and plentiful, was richly shaded and soft to look at. Grandy would have loved the Persian rugs and the abstract art on the walls. In one corner was a large antique desk, the legs of which appeared to be gold-leafed. I walked across the room to approach it. The desk wasn't tidy, and it seemed to me Rose had probably been in the middle of something when she died. In another corner, behind glass, was a gleaming coat of arms, Goliath-sized and very unnerving. Tall French doors let in the early evening light and brought the outside in. I walked over and opened them onto a lovely, large covered patio that boasted thickly cushioned wicker sofas, and a huge yard, meticulously manicured. Between the two spaces—house and patio—there was room for a hundred people, at least, to mingle comfortably.

The entire set up was beautiful.

When I walked back into the room, I was now facing the opposite corner and the gift of all birthday gifts: the Steinway. It took my breath away.

It was indeed a concert grand, and it owned the room. Deep, rich ebony, the lid up, it practically dared you not to play it. I walked over and stroked the gleaming wood. It felt like gold and history against my fingertips. I'd played Steinways at my recitals, so I knew they were exquisite, the concert grand even more so. And the sound…nothing could compare. My long-time piano teacher, Nicholas Schaffer, had said all the greats deserved to be performed on an instrument of this quality. He'd always told me, "Don't strike a single key until you're ready, January. Sit down. Close your eyes. Breathe in the spirit of the composer. Pay homage to the genius." This, he'd emphasized, was how one released the *voice* of the instrument into the soul of the musician. He was an old man, and when I was younger, I'd thought he was quite dramatic. Now I understood what he meant completely. *Completely.*

I reverently lifted the fallboard and pressed the middle C. It was like a single drop of water-colored sound—rich in its center, fading at the edges. Pure and perfect pitch. I opened the piano bench and fingered through the sheet music I found there. When I came across Rachmaninoff's "Rhapsody on a Theme of Paganini," I couldn't help myself. I picked it up like it was a piece of delicate lace and sat down. The name written in the corner in faded ink: *Claire*.

My heart was beating so fast, too fast, and again I had the strangest feeling of otherworldliness, as if I were somewhere I had no right to be yet still belonged. The feeling overwhelmed me. I looked down to see that my hands were poised above the keys in the exact position hers would have been. She was here. In a way, she was right here. My mother, my intact mother, like a shadow. I breathed deeply, closed my eyes, and invoked Rachmaninoff. And then I was playing that glorious instrument—the touch no more resistant than water, the tone mad perfection. Sergei's music filled me, flowed out of me, and broke my heart with its beauty.

I knew these notes from hours of practice, but sitting here, *here*, playing *her* sheet music at *her* piano—not Claire's, not the Claire *I* knew, but a mother I'd never imagined—it was like I was trespassing on an apparition who'd trained these keys to the will of this masterpiece. My hands somehow managed the expansive reach with ease, and my phrasing was unbelievably polished. It was lovely and pure, and every chord was delicious to my ears in this room of acoustic perfection. For a moment I was utterly transported into the music, lifted into that nether realm where composer speaks to heart, inhabiting the same space that my mother had.

And then I stopped because I was crying, sobbing, and I didn't know what was happening to me. What *was* happening?

I lifted my hands abruptly, the sound dissolving into the open space. I shut the lid over the keys. I shouldn't be here. Not like this. I should be here with my mother, visiting my grandmother for the weekend. There should be warmth and laughter, sitting on the couch with our feet up, catching up on important events. It shouldn't be me here alone, a stranger in this house, my mother barred years ago, my grandmother dead. I let go of a sob, then swallowed back my agonizing sentimentality, and wiped my eyes.

When I could focus, my gaze landed on a picture that I recognized. My mother was in a cap and gown, and it caught my eye because I'd seen one like it at home. But that one had been taken with my dad, and they were kissing. She'd graduated from Yale, and the two of them had clearly been celebrating the milestone. But in this photo, Claire was holding a certificate, and she was beaming shyly at the decorated official who had handed it to her. She was beautiful. And just as I wondered what the award was, I spotted it in a rather gaudy gold frame nearby. The Overton Comprehensive Award for Musical Intelligence and Achievement—Yale University, May 24, 2000.

May 2000. My mother would have been pregnant with me. Barely.

There was a handwritten note taped to the back of the frame:

Mom and Dad,

Today, I stood before my peers, the product of an undeviating investment in my education. I am nothing if not the daughter of parents who committed themselves absolutely to my success. For that I am profoundly grateful. Since you were unable to attend my convocation, please accept this proof of my accomplishment as a token return on your venture.

Claire

My mother's parents didn't attend her graduation? From Yale? Unbelievable. Because I knew Grandy and Poppy would never create a barrier between us that would preclude their complete support—and celebration—of anything I ever did, this broke my heart for my mother. Still, it was obvious by the myriad memorabilia in this room that they were beyond proud of her. The entire library was its own world, big enough to hold a small recital, but made completely homey by all the pictures of my mom. It was a feast for the eyes filled with color, art, photographs, and books.

And trophies. So many trophies.

On the wall near the piano, I found a huge curio cabinet full of awards. It was an impressive display, glass shelves backlit and crammed with trophies, ribbons, and certificates. Each one had Claire's name on it. "She was an exquisite talent," the attorney had said. I'd known she could play, had played—my grandparents had told me this my whole life—but how had I not known the extent of her accomplishments?

Why had no one told me? Or had they, and I'd simply never let it sink in enough to care? Was I so completely detached that I really never imagined this life… *any* life could have been Claire's. But this room—this entire space—was a testament to her, a woman as far removed from the bent and broken Claire that I knew as could possibly be. That my mother, my mother, could have been this person left me breathless…and ashamed.

Claire had graduated from Yale. I'd known that, but now suddenly I knew it differently, somehow. I knew it in context. She had graduated summa cum laude and been awarded a distinctive recognition for her musical accomplishments. Now she couldn't speak, couldn't recognize the very notes she used to play that earned her that honor. I couldn't absorb it. I had a fair number of trophies of my own on a shelf at home, and I knew what they had cost me: Hours. Angst. Burnout. Unmitigated pain. I suddenly felt a strange wave of affinity for Claire. We had a corner of hellish beauty in common. How could that be? How could any of this be?

As I swept new tears from my face, another focal point of this room came into focus: the massive family portrait hanging over the fireplace was austere and commanding. I walked over to it, decidedly mesmerized. In this painting, everyone was young. My mom, in white, was a beautiful young girl, maybe ten years old. She wasn't smiling, but there was something of a restrained temperament in her expression. My grandparents were regal, imperious in black. The only color was Rose's blood-red lips and Stephen's matching tie. I stared at them, at my grandfather's high chin that made him look so judgmental, so severe, as if he were expecting to be disappointed. Rose had a similar expression, but she was quite lovely despite it. She was wearing pearls but no smile. No one was smiling.

I dropped onto an oversized ottoman, feeling tired and heavy, drained, actually. I looked around to take it all in again. This room was a showpiece, sophisticated and elegantly appointed, but I could feel little joy. It felt lonely and sterile and sad, like sad things had happened here. It felt the kind of cold that had nothing to do with temperature. My gaze moved once more to the fireplace and back to the portrait. There was no happiness there either, just a kind of ownership in my grandfather's eyes and polished resignation in Rose's.

And in my mother's a kind of portent nesting there as she sat firmly clutched between her parents.

thirteen

I'd been standing outside my mother's old bedroom for several minutes just staring at the double doors. They were carved and had beautiful silver handles that were a bit medieval in design. Medieval door handles? I was stalling.

I *was* stalling.

I wondered if it was because part of me actually wanted Claire to just stay the one-dimensional person I'd known my whole life. That was undoubtedly awful, but Claire, reduced to only her strangeness, was somehow manageable for me. What had caused that strangeness was a second-hand horror I avoided like pain, and whom she had been before was so removed from me that it was too distant to comprehend—or had been. Until I walked into this house.

"If you've ever had any curiosity about her, I think it can be answered within the walls of that home." That's what the attorney had said. And now my mother—Claire—was beginning to coalesce into an actual person. And what's more, I suddenly had faces to go with the parents who had hurt her so unforgivably.

It was too much. Part of me wanted to turn around and leave. Instead, I pushed open the doors to peer into a space shadowed in buttery warmth. I stepped in, holding my breath, and let the room gather around me. From the bed, which was soaked in a soft yellow light, to the twin bay windows, to the bookshelves, to the painting on the wall—peacefulness permeated this room. It was so unexpected that for a moment, I couldn't move. I simply drank it in.

As I walked in farther, I caught my reflection in an oversized floor mirror standing in the corner. It startled me for a second and reminded me again of how alone I was in this museum of a house. I blew out a calming breath and stepped closer. I looked tired, and a bit altered, too, which made sense to me.

The big mirror was a repository for random photos. They were tucked into the frame or taped to the glass, and I leaned in to get a better look. My eyes immediately misted. Images of my mother laughing, pulling faces, being silly with her friends—my mother in happy moments. She was beautiful and so buoyant, so full of life. This mirror was the Instagram account of her adolescence, snapshots of her girlhood frozen in time and seemingly untouched since.

I looked around. Everything in here seemed preserved, a kind of time capsule. Except in one of the bays. There the pillows were rumpled and an open book lay face down on the cushioned seat. It was the tiniest bit haunting and for a moment I wondered if my mother could really have been the last one to read there, the last one to be in this space. Somehow, I didn't think so. This room was too much of a sanctuary, too inviting, too soft. It would have been hard to stay out. I felt it, undeniably; surely my grandmother must have felt it, too.

According to what I'd been told, there hadn't been much to like about Rose Winston, but I thought of her standing in this room, so thick with memories and proof of life, and I imagined her filled with terrible regret. I wanted that to be true. I wanted her to have realized what she'd done and ached because of it. Such a waste. Her only daughter. And nothing to show for it but this shrine. As I was thinking these harsh thoughts, a picture on Claire's dresser caught my eye. It was a shot of Rose and my mom when Claire was a teenager. The photo had been taken outdoors, and Claire was holding a rake. They were both laughing so hard you could almost hear it. The smile transformed my grandmother, somehow tempering my harsh impression of her. She was lovely. So was my mother, and it took me a long time to stop imagining what had prompted that joyful moment. I suddenly wondered what Claire's reaction would be if I gave it to her. Would she know the faces in the photo. *Would she remember?* According to my grandparents, Claire probably knew more than we would ever realize.

Above the dresser was a large oil painting of a little girl with auburn pigtails. She was wearing denim overalls and playing a grand piano, her bare feet dangling from the bench. It was charming and unexpected, and in an instant, I knew that if I ever had a daughter, this would hang in her room. Something beautiful from her grandmother. I smiled at the thought, even as tears stung my eyes.

It was all so overwhelming.

As I turned to once more take it all in, my breath caught. On the wall above my mother's bed were dozens of paper butterflies. It was a pink and orange and blue swarm—probably at one time very bright but now faded. I swallowed. Just the other day, on Claire's wall at the care center, I'd seen almost an exact replica, only the butterflies were brighter, crisper. I'd just assumed it was a project someone had helped my mom create. If it was, it had been patterned after this faded three-dimensional mural of a memory, which would make it rather uncanny. If it wasn't just a memory, though, that meant it had to have come from Rose, which was even more unsettling. I sat down hard on the foot of the bed. Had Rose been visiting my mother? I was so confused.

As I mulled over that possibility, I looked around the space, reveling once more in the soft spirit of this amazing room. My mother had grown up in this room, and I again found it incredible to find myself here. My gaze landed on a thick leather-bound scrapbook sitting on the bench at the foot of her bed. I leaned over and pulled it onto my lap. It was full of sheet music, pictures, and notes, an apparent record of my mother's competitions dating back to the '80s. More ghosts. She'd written personal notes about each piece she'd ultimately performed, cues to help her remember things like double flats and time changes. On measures she'd struggled with, she had written little comments in red, bits of advice on how to approach the music, like "imagine emerging from a dream," or, "imagine jolting from a nightmare, being chased or chasing." Her notes were incredible, and I couldn't quite believe I was holding yellowed composition pages filled with my mother's musical thoughts. The musty paper smelled to me of both ink and genius.

On the far wall, twin bookcases took up the space between the mirror and one of the bay windows. They bulged with music books, sheet music, and novels—so many novels. There were classic works— the Brontë sisters, Jane Austen, and Shakespeare in leather-embossed covers, as well as later classics like *The Bell Jar*, Joan Didion's *Slouching Toward Bethlehem*, Orwell's *1984*. There were books about composers and musicians, Bernstein and Copland tucked between Beethoven and Debussy. The bottom shelf, however, held a different story—*hers*. Stuffed with a mash-up of different-sized books, some with loud covers, some thick, some thin, some leather, a couple just spiralbound notebooks, there must have been thirty journals, maybe more. The sight of them set my pulse racing. My mother's journals. A bit hesitantly, I pulled a yellow diary from the pack and opened to the first page.

> My birthday was fantastic! I wish I could turn 10 every day! Mom and Dad gave me money, but the best part was going to the Mutter Museum. I LOVED it soooo, so much. Some of the other kids got grossed out by the skulls and body stuff in bottles, but not me. It made me more sure than ever that I want to be a doctor or a science teacher. Or maybe just work at the Mutter. But probably not, since I want to figure out cures for things. And now I have enough money for a microscope! But Dad won't let me! He says my future is music and he doesn't want to hear any more nonsense. It's not nonsense! But just to be safe when I get my microscope, I will hide it at Monica's.

I never knew my mom wanted to be a doctor. I wonder how long that lasted.

I pulled a pink-zippered diary from the middle of the grouping and unzipped it. The book opened to a page made thicker by a note that had been taped there. The date was March 10, 1989.

> I thought I did a good job. Mrs. Elliott looked happy, and I can always tell if I've done bad because her eyes get squinty. But they weren't squinty, and she smiled when I walked off the stage. But Dad didn't say anything on the way home, and Mom hardly ever says anything, so I knew I

was in trouble. And then when I got up this morning, I found this note.

Claire—Your mother and I were so pleased that you had been invited to the Young Artist's Compendium—that's quite a coup for an almost twelve-year-old girl. We thought you were ready. Apparently, we were wrong. "Beside a Spring" is meant to evoke contentment—it requires a light touch. Only a novice would plough through the dénouement as you did. You embarrassed us all—not to mention Liszt. Clearly the ovation you received was obligatory, insincere accolades at best. Of course, Mrs. Elliott bears some responsibility for your overwrought performance, and she will be hearing from me! In the meantime, you will increase your practice by thirty minutes each day for the next month. The next time I hear this masterpiece, I expect perfection. Substandard may be acceptable to you, young lady, but it is not to me.

Dad

What? Really? I read the note again and felt my blood boil. But Claire followed up with this:

Dad can be mean and sometimes he makes me cry. But Mom told me that if I cried every time he was mean, I'd be crying my whole life, so I don't cry so much in front of him anymore. At school Mr. Tennerly told me something important—he said smart kids always remember they won't be kids forever. That's true. I'm already less of a kid than I was at my last birthday. So, I don't cry anymore. I just do what Dad tells me and grow up a little every day. But I'm sad about Mrs. Elliott. I like her. If Dad yells at her, she will probably want to stop being my teacher just like Mr. Rudd and Miss Marguerite did.

"He was a terrible man." That's what Oscar Thibodeau had said. "Be glad you didn't know him." I was glad. Clearly my grandfather was an equal-opportunity bully, making no exceptions for his family. But my mom had apparently just bided her time and grown up and hadn't let it crush her.

I laughed at the last entry:

> Today Dad yelled at me and Monica for walking on the new Persian rug, from Persia, made by Persians in Persia. I wanted to say, relax, daddio, it's a rug—we walk on rugs around here, that's what they're made for. Duh. I didn't, but I sort of laughed at his mad face, and now I am grounded from Monica for two weeks. Mon says Dad is crazy. It's true. But really, she has no idea.

She'd drawn a fancy rug with colored pencils and a big sign on it that said KEEP OFF THE RUG (unless you're Persian). I liked that little girl.

I closed the diary and looked for something a bit more contemporary. The last journal on the shelf was dated 1999, and the writing and the penmanship had grown up substantially.

So had the subject matter.

fourteen

The journal was leather-bound, vintage, and distressed, with her name stamped in the lower corner. In 1999 Claire would have been twenty-two years old, my age. I sat down on the bed feeling strangely conflicted about meeting my mother as a peer. It was bizarre, and I knew it was bizarre to feel this way, but the truth was I was more or less accustomed to the detachment I felt for this woman I didn't know. I was comfortable with that detachment.

I stared at the journal for a long time before I opened it.

September 20, 1999

I was not expected to win the Dabrowski. I was a last-minute qualifier, invited to participate when the prodigy from Croatia dropped out. This, I'm sure, would have rankled the preeminent Stanislaw Gustov, not to mention Mila Dubois, if they had been paying attention to anyone but themselves. But the former lovers were convinced that the contest, despite the other myriad talent slated to compete that night, was clearly between only the two of them, so I wasn't of any consequence...until I was.

It was Chopin's night. The best of the best. The Lincoln Center. Perfect acoustics. Great audience. New dress. Happy Mom (Dad was out of town). Extraordinarily fun. The way the competition worked was called random affiliation. When it was my turn, I sat down at the most delicious concert grand and a judge pulled two tiles from a golden urn on which were engraved two of Fredrick's masterpieces. I got to choose which to perform. I hit pay dirt when he pulled "Fantaisie Impromptu" and "Heroic Polonaise." I chose "Fantaisie" (of course!) and played it perfectly, making it to the second round where I pulled "Grand Valse Brillante." In the end, it was me and Stanislaw and "Etude 10/2." I actually couldn't believe I walked away with first place. Neither could he, but the man from Sweden was very gracious if a bit shocked. I may have giggled.

I was familiar with the Dabrowski Compendium. Kudos to Claire. And she'd played "Fantaisie"? My personal nemesis? And been awarded the top honor? Okay, that was cool.

September 22, 1999
Mom called this morning to tell me again that I'd looked nice on stage but that she liked my hair better up when I performed. Sigh. There is always a *but*. Per my award, she said, *well done,* so at least she was listening despite the distraction of my apparently awful mop. Dad was on his way home from Singapore, so he missed it, but he sent an email congratulating me. He also told me he was extremely excited for his upcoming birthday. Extremely excited to turn 60? Odd. Oh, who cares? I'm in New York until tomorrow. Will pick up the perfect dress, then Monica and I will head home for Dad's big birthday party—the one he's so weirdly excited for.

September 24, 1999 (3:38 am)
How could my life look so completely different than it did at this time yesterday? Or a better question might be:

can a 22 y/o Yale MMA Student really become an orphan this late in the game? That's what I've been asking myself for the last three hours, driving back to school in the middle of the night after what I think was a decree of divorcement issued by Dad when I did not agree to marry Denton Hyde. That run-on sentence looks as ridiculous on paper as it sounds said out loud. It's absurd. The whole thing is absurd. But even for a narcissist like Dad who has pulled some stunts in his day, attempting to arrange my marriage is a line I have to believe he never truly intended to create, let alone cross. But I'm almost positive that's exactly what happened, and I'm still stunned. And when I refused, my father looked me squarely in the eye and said: "If you leave without doing what I say, Claire, don't bother coming back." He said that to me, and I had to look around for signs that I wasn't walking around in a bad dream. It really happened. That was three hours ago. He said it. He said I had to make things right after embarrassing everyone—I'd embarrassed everyone by telling Denton no—and if I left without doing so, I was no longer welcome in his home. So, given my two choices, I turned my back on my ass of a father and my pathetic excuse of a mother, threw everything I could carry into a garbage bag, and left. I'm back at Yale now. I've replayed the entire evening too many times to count and it still doesn't seem real...

What? Wait, what? What had happened? It was almost dark, and I was completely swept up in what I was reading when I heard the chimes. The sound startled me, and I blew out a shaky breath as I set the journal down and gathered myself. I'd been hunched close to the light of a lamp at my mother's bedside. The rest of the room was drenched in creeping shadow. The chimes sounded again, followed by a hefty knock, and I suddenly became keenly aware of how alone I was. Turning lights on as I went, I made my way down to the front entry to be greeted by another insistent rap on the door.

Cautiously I opened it to find Oscar Thibodeau smiling at me from the dim porch. He seemed relieved to see me. My face, I'm sure, did not mirror his sentiment. "January," he said. "It looks like you found the place okay."

"I did. Should I not still be here? I'm sorry, I'll——"

"No. No, no, no. I'm not concerned about that," he said. "I was just thinking how overwhelming this might be for you."

His humanity surprised me, as did his casual clothes. He was not the lawyerly gentleman I'd met two days ago, but a decidedly less impressive elderly man wearing a tee shirt and plaid golf shorts and looking sincerely concerned about me.

"I'm all right," I said, fighting sudden emotion. "But thank you."

"With all due respect, my dear, you don't seem all right."

Caught, I swallowed.

"Can I come in?"

I was still on my side of the threshold, and he on his. I desperately wanted to talk to him, talk to someone, about what I'd just read, but it seemed imprudent to invite him in. I didn't know him. I swallowed again, torn.

"January, I think I can help you."

"You don't even know me."

"That's true," he said. "But I knew them. And they merit explanation."

I took in the bent old man. "I have mace...somewhere," I said wearily, trying to remember where my purse was. "And I'm not afraid to use it."

He arched a brow. "I have arthritis in every joint and a new, rather painful hip. I also have a key to this door."

I slumped, suddenly too tired and overwhelmed to care about anything. It didn't hurt that he could have let himself in. That he needed a cane was also a point in his favor. I opened the door, and Oscar Thibodeau smiled as he shuffled past me. He stopped in front of the portrait of my mom and gazed up. "She was an amazing girl, your mother."

I didn't say anything, but I did nod.

After a moment he turned to assess me. "How long have you been here, January?"

"I'm not sure. I got here about 4:45. What time is it?"

"It's almost eight. Have you had anything to eat?"

"I should probably go."

"Have you had anything to eat?" he asked again.

I stared at him. "I'm not really hungry," I lied.

"I don't believe you," he winked. "Come with me. I'm sure Rose's pantry is still nicely stocked. I'll make you an omelet while you tell me what you've been doing."

As resistant as I should have been to this strange old man waiting on me, I had to admit I was curious…and starving. I followed him to the kitchen, where it was clear Oscar Thibodeau knew his way around. He tucked a dishtowel into his waistband and pulled a skillet from the pantry. He handed me cheese to grate while he cracked eggs. Then I made toast as he set the massive bar with two place settings of fine china and stemware. In Rose's pantry he also found two bottles of wine, one red, one white, and I found linen napkins. He had me sit down as he scooped a gooey omelet onto my plate.

"This is lovely, Mr. Thibodeau. Thank you."

"Don't thank me yet," he said. "It's been a while since I cooked for anyone—hopefully you'll find it palatable. And it looks like Rosy has a nice Beaujolais Nouveau as well as an Alsatian Chablis—both pair nicely with eggs. Which can I pour for you?"

"I think I'd just like some water, if that's okay."

"Of course." He went to a fridge and came back with a green bottle of Pellegrino. I didn't really like sparkling water, but I thanked him anyway, and he sat down and poured himself a half-glass of the Beaujolais. He took a sip and sighed appreciatively while I shoved a forkful of ham and cheese deliciousness into my mouth and sighed the same way. "I guess I was hungrier than I thought."

The old man smiled.

"How did you know I'd be here, Mr. Thibodeau?"

"I got an alert from the security system and assumed it was you. Then I got thinking that being here might feel somewhat daunting, so I thought I'd make sure you were okay. Are you?"

"I'm fine," I said. But the words were like tiny pins pricking my throat and my eyes. It surprised me, so I bent back toward my plate, and we were quiet for a moment. Oscar Thibodeau poured himself another half-glass and held out the bottle. "Are you sure I can't tempt you?"

I looked at him, and shook my head. "No. I sort of ruined myself for all things alcohol when I was sixteen. It's probably psychological."

"That sounds rather dramatic," he said, taking a sip.

"Oh, it *was* that. And it wasn't even my fault, really. I mean, I didn't mean to do it. I just believed the guy with the rum and Coke when he said it was just Coke."

"Oh, dear. I'm guessing that ended badly."

"You could say that. It was my birthday," I told him, remembering just exactly how badly it had ended, remembering too how I had broken something in Poppy that night. "It's funny," I said, "but I can still see my grandfather standing there when the elevator opened onto our foyer. Just standing there. He didn't say anything. Not to me, not to Jasmine's dad—that's who'd brought me home. He just stood there as I stumbled into the entryway, sick. I was so sick I threw up all over the floor and then faded away to the sound of Grandy shouting." I looked at Oscar. "My grandmother never shouts."

There was nothing but compassion on the old man's face, and somehow his kindness invited my disclosure. So, in the home of a dead grandmother I had never met, to an attorney I did not know, on an errand I could not have imagined for myself, I shared one of the most defining moments of my life. I told him how I'd woken up in a pool of vomit and that sometimes I could still feel it on my face—like a sticky scar reminding me of that brutal night.

"I don't know how long I lay there," I said. "I just know that waking up to the sheer awfulness of my situation was nothing next to the terrible, terrible look on my grandfather's face. I'd never seen him like that. He was so hurt. I didn't understand what I'd done." I pushed some eggs around on my plate, then put down my fork. "Of course, it all came back in a rush. The party. The Coke that wasn't just Coke."

I looked over at Oscar Thibodeau. "You know a drunk killed my dad," I said softly. "And ruined my mother. And completely devastated my family. So, when I came home that night, wasted, I brought it all back for them. I hurt them horribly." I lifted an eyebrow. "So, by way of atonement, I drink a lot of Pepsi. And water," I added, holding up my Pellegrino.

His expression filled with even more compassion. "Your reasoning makes perfect sense, my dear, but aren't you being just a bit hard on yourself? You were sixteen."

"I was. But to them, if anyone should have known better, it was me. I am, after all, the poster child for alcohol-related worst-case scenarios."

Oscar Thibodeau patted my hand. "You are indeed, my dear. And I'm so, so sorry for that." He gazed at me for a moment. "For what it's worth," he said, "that drunk devastated this family as well."

"Really?"

"Oh, yes. And sometimes the worst consequence is running out of time to make amends."

"Do you think they would have done that?"

"I honestly don't know about Stephen—he was prideful to a fault. All I can tell you is he was crippled with regret after what happened to Claire, but I suppose that's what it took to get his attention. Rose was another story—she simply waited too long to defy him. But she was never the same after that accident."

I stared at him. "Tell me about them."

The old attorney cocked his head. "Oh, goodness, where to start…" he said, spreading jam on his toast.

"Just something. Tell me something."

He was quiet for a moment, studying me. Then he breathed deeply. "They were fascinating…in a rather dreadful way," he finally said. "I'd say they were the perfect…*complement* of disordered personalities, if you will. And in that sense, they were quite perfect for each other."

"How did they meet?"

"I'm not sure. But I do know they came from eerily similar backgrounds," he said. "Each of them had very driven and abusive fathers. Stephen's owned a manufacturing conglomerate, very successful but very ruthless. He taught Stephen how to spot weakness in competitors and exploit it—much to his peril. Rose's father was a tortured artist--mentally ill, but very acclaimed. I think she kept one or two of his paintings," Oscar said, glancing around the room. "They were both only children, both byproducts of vicious divorces." His eyes came back to me. "I suppose by the time they found each other, they both had something to prove and something to survive." He took a sip of wine. "People are highly complex, January; they're sometimes warped and fragile and yet amazingly resilient and resourceful at the same time. That was certainly true of your grandparents."

"Were they happy?"

"Oh, I don't think happiness was ever the reason or the goal between them. It was something far more strategic. An exaggerated *retribution,* if that makes sense."

"Did they love each other?"

"In their way. But I think they were really more about being owed and proving their own worth *through* each other. I don't think love was a conscious element between them until your mother came along."

This stung my eyes. "Did they love *her?*"

"Oh, yes. Very much. They just weren't very good at it. Rose was very proud of Claire, but she was also jealous of Claire's independence. That made her unpredictable, hard for Claire to trust. Stephen, on the other hand, equated love with discipline and success, measurable things. That's what he knew and understood. So, if Claire was compliant, obedient, all was well. But when your mother became her own person, someone he could no longer control, things went awry. He had no idea how to be in a relationship with someone, *anyone,* over whom he had no power." Oscar picked up his plate, frowned at mine, then carried them both to the sink. I followed him with the silverware and glasses. "Do you know anything about my mother and someone named Dennis Hyde? I think she was apparently supposed to marry him."

The old attorney looked up from his rinsing. He seemed pleased. "Denton. Denton Hyde. You found Claire's journals. Good."

"I did. Unfortunately, they are missing a few details."

He chuckled.

"It almost sounded like her parents disowned her for not marrying that guy. That can't possibly be true. Can it?"

He handed me a goblet to dry. "One would hope not," he sighed. "But sadly...."

"No way...."

"In truth," Oscar said, "it would have been a fine match—had they loved each other. That was the missing element. The Hydes were—are—a very influential and obscenely moneyed political dynasty. Denton is on the state legislature now; his father was a senator; his mother is an appellate judge. They're a very powerful family. Stephen saw that the union could have been utterly transformative to his interests. The Hydes were similarly enthusiastic but for their own self-serving reasons." Oscar handed me the other goblet. "And in the middle of all of this were two young people just trying to live their own lives."

"Did they like each other—my mom and this Denton guy?"

"Your mother had made it repeatedly known that she had no serious feelings for the young Mr. Hyde. They'd dated, mostly big events orchestrated by Stephen—in fact, I'm fairly certain it was your grandfather who introduced them. But your mother was attending Yale, competing and making a name for herself. Denton was, I believe, in law school at Stanford. They got together when they could, with both families pushing rather forcefully. And in truth, it didn't seem Denton was resisting much."

"Soooo, what was Grandpa's big plan to get them married?"

Oscar Thibodeau looked over at me with a grim expression. "It was actually quite heartbreaking. Stephen thought, presumably, that he could put Claire on the spot, *on his birthday, no less,* in front of all his essential society, and that she would not dare defy him. It was unprecedented and very short-sighted, but very Stephen."

I turned to Oscar, who was wiping down Rose's sink. "What happened?"

He lifted his brows. "Well, you have to understand that your mother had been raised to be obedient, to adhere to inviolate rules, one of which was to never embarrass her parents in any way. Stephen, I'm sure, was counting on her sticking with the program. Certainly, he never imagined that she would choose *that* night to rebel against him. It was his birthday, and he'd made a big fuss about *her* being his best gift—she'd just won a major competition, as I recall."

"He seemed really critical of her, from what I read in her journals."

Oscar chuckled. "Oh, always. He demanded perfection of everyone, but especially of Claire. Fortunately, that wasn't hard for her to achieve. Your mother was unusually gifted. For his birthday each year, they had this tradition. He always threw himself a grand soirée, and part of the festivities included Claire playing the masterpiece of Stephen's choice. It had been going on since she was a little girl; he loved to show her off for the who's who of his inner circle. That year she performed Liszt's "La Campanella." It was glorious. I remember that because it's a favorite of mine, and it was the last time she ever played here."

"Really?"

Oscar nodded. "That night was a true turning point in the life of this family. She performed flawlessly, of course, and Stephen was very pleased and naturally he was counting on her continued compliance. She took her bow, and I'm sure she thought she was home free. But then Stephen called Denton up. Made Claire stand there while Denton produced the little black box. He played his part beautifully, nervous but charming. And in front of God and everybody, he got down on that knee and asked that question, melted every heart in the room— just as Stephen had planned."

I shook my head, groaning. "My poor mom."

"Indeed. I just watched her, helplessly, because I knew she didn't have feelings for that boy, and I knew the terrible position Stephen had put her in. And when *she* grasped it...*whoa, Nelly.*"

"What? What happened?"

Oscar Thibodeau was leaning against the counter, his arms folded, and he was looking through me, seeing, if I were to guess, my mother that night. "January, it was as though every one of us spectators simply faded away—and the room was full."

"What do you mean?"

"I mean, it became a moment of absolute clarity for your mother. And right there in that tight little trio of just Claire, her father, and Denton Hyde—sixty witnesses be damned—your mother became Stephen's worst nightmare *and* his crowning achievement in the same instant."

"Tell me," I coaxed, impatient for details.

"Stephen was absolutely oblivious to her. He was just applauding and carrying on about *his future son-in-law...someday a senator...grandkids*—all that nonsense. And Claire simply said 'No.' It took her a minute, and she had to say it a couple of times before it registered, but she took control of the situation just as Stephen had always taught her a Winston should do."

"What do you mean?"

"I mean that Claire had spent her life to that point as both the beneficiary and target of her father's best strategies," Oscar said, nodding. "She'd witnessed first--and second--hand how he dealt with those who attempted to impose their will on him. So, as he rattled on and on about her future with Denton, she, like I said, quietly told him to *stop*. She said it softly at first, then louder. Then she said it again. Then she finally shouted it."

I grimaced. "That sounds...cringe-worthy."

"Oh, January...some moments stay with you a lifetime; that's one that never fades for me. The utter humiliation in Stephen's eyes, the resolve in Claire's voice, the crimson hue of Denton's face, and an audience of trapped onlookers afraid to breathe lest we be noticed."

"Where was Rose?"

"Sitting right next to me, glaring a hole through her daughter."

"Well, what was my mom supposed to do?" I snapped.

"That depends on whom you asked. The Winstons, naturally, expected Claire to go along with this spectacle. Any objections, umbrage, or refusal were to be handled privately, negotiated between themselves, socially managed by hired experts. In short, she was supposed to allow her father this moment, this victory. If you had asked Claire, well, she did what she'd always known she would one day have to do: claim her own autonomy."

I stared at him trying to absorb the enormity of what he was telling me. "This is unbelievable. Was Rose in on it? The scheme?" I asked.

"Rose was...*supportive* of a Winston-Hyde merger."

I shook my head in disgust. "No way! Did she know my mom didn't love Denton?"

Oscar frowned. "She knew. She used to say that Claire just needed to learn there were worse things than a loveless marriage."

I slumped, sickened. "Who *was* this woman?"

"She was...*complicated,* January. She was a woman who never really experienced...*love*. She wasn't born into it; she didn't marry into it. So, she had no real point of reference."

I swallowed, now deeply saddened. "Still, it must have killed her when Claire did what she did."

Oscar arched a brow and pointed a you-win-the-prize finger at me. "For Rose, the line between jealousy and admiration was infinitesimally thin, and that night I'm not sure she could have told you which side her feelings landed on. But she hid it all behind that glare."

I stared at him, my thoughts a tangle of conflict. "My grandmother says mother-daughter relationships are always complicated—I think she's just talking about mine, actually—but Rose and my mom sound like complicated on steroids."

Oscar nodded. "That's very true."

"Did they really disown Claire? That part isn't true, is it?"

"Well, it's decidedly more complex than that," Oscar said, thoughtfully. "Your mother did end up disinherited, but Stephen was certainly no victor. It was never his decision. In his mind, if Claire would have cooperated or apologized and atoned for her misdeed, all could have been forgiven, his pride and the relationship with the Hydes could have been preserved. But she went back to school, leaving Stephen to deal with the fallout. He led people to believe that Claire had defiantly walked away after humiliating everyone. He discussed this in all the right circles, which rendered him the sympathetic, roundly championed and betrayed father of a temperamental daughter."

My mouth dropped open. "He really *was* awful."

Oscar removed his glasses and rubbed the bridge of his nose. "It was scripted and performed to perfection, January. And it brilliantly left open the possibility of an epilogue that would further cast your grandfather in the glowing light of lavish forgiver should Claire come to her senses and return—which he fully expected."

"Genius."

"Indeed. But, of course, we know that *everything* changed while he was waiting for what never happened. Pride destroyed your grandfather's relationship with his daughter."

I stared at the old man. "My poor mom."

"In some ways," Oscar agreed. "But she found your dad, and ultimately Claire was truly happy. Stephen never was. He died a very bitter man."

I swallowed. "What a waste."

Oscar nodded, sadly. "Oh, my dear… you have no idea."

fifteen

Oscar Thibodeau left just after 9:30. I left soon after that with an armful of my mother's journals and the address of the Grove Crest Funeral Home in Philly. The attorney had said he'd meet me there on Friday and introduce me to my grandmother. I would also come back to Chestnut Hill that day and finish going through my mother's things. In the meantime, I had to figure out what to do about that glorious piano.

As I merged onto the I-95 toward Passaic, I felt restless and more than a little undone. I didn't feel like me. I felt like someone had knocked on my door and pointed a fire hose into my life, then opened the valve.

I spent the almost two-hour drive back to Duzy House lost in strange fantasies about the Winstons. Mostly Rose and Claire and me and the imaginary people we were all supposed to be—or should have been. When I'd first walked into that house, I'd seen us in my mind's eye, the three of us as extraordinarily ordinary women. Three generations of normalness sitting around just being a family: gossiping, laughing, teasing, catching up with each other's lives—basically, just belonging to one another in that unbreakable way people take for granted. In that fantasy I had a beautiful mother who knew all my secrets and kept them. So did she.

My mother *had* been beautiful. Once. And brave enough to stand up to her beast of a father in the midst of his chosen snobbery. She'd been strong—warrior strong. I'd only ever seen her broken. I'd only ever imagined her broken. I'd only ever given her that much consideration, and I suddenly felt very small for it. What was wrong with me?

And was I still making allowances for Rose? I'd heard everything Oscar had said about her. I had. What kind of mother would be okay with her only daughter marrying someone she didn't care about, didn't want to be with? Of course that was revolting. But had that bizarre grandmother really not known love? And had she really been watching me perform in secret? Why? What would she have said to me? And when did she plan to say it? I wished she were still alive just so she could explain herself to me.

***

It was very late when I pulled up to Duzy House, but the garage was open and the back of the van was empty, which meant Calvin was inside with the gurney. I was tempted to go straight upstairs. Instead, I scooped up Claire's journals, girded my tired loins, and went in to check out our newest delivery.

Calvin was filling out paperwork at the whiteboard when I walked in. He looked up at me and did a double take. "Where have you been?"

"Oh…I spent the day in Philly. Just got home. What have we got here?"

"Thirty-one-year-old female. Died giving birth to twins. I guess she bled out—I didn't know that still happened." He looked over the medical report. "Something called DIC." He shrugged. "Has some broken ribs from the CPR."

I grimaced. "Did the twins make it?"

"Not sure, but I want to say no."

I stepped closer to the cart and unzipped the bag. The woman looked younger than her stated age, with long red hair and a smattering of freckles across her nose and cheeks. I could tell she'd been beautiful in life. Now she was ghostly pale.

"Veronica Lawson," Calvin said, adding her name to the whiteboard. "Husband calls her Ronnie. He'll be here tomorrow afternoon."

I nodded. "Then I'll get her done first thing in the morning. Can you put her away?"

"Will do. You okay, Cookie?"

"I'm not sure. It's been a day."

When I got upstairs, it was dark, and I was glad because I wasn't in the mood to talk to anyone. I grabbed a bottle of water from the fridge, thinking I would just head to my room and read until I fell asleep. But when I turned around, Grandy was standing there. She was in her pajamas and robe and had taken out her contacts. In their place was a pair of thick, sturdy glasses she called her running-from-a-burning-building glasses, which she swore was the only time she would wear them in public. I liked them, actually.

"I thought I heard you come up," she said. "Are you okay?"

I looked at her, thought of lying. "Not really."

"Rough day?"

"A little overwhelming. Mostly interesting. And...sad."

"Anything I can do?" she said, belting her robe.

"I don't think so." The words came out cooler than I'd intended.

My grandmother narrowed her eyes at me, and for a long moment we just looked at each other. Then she said, "Can I make you something to eat?"

"No. I'm good," I said. "But thank you."

She nodded, stared, and sat down. "Is this still about the letter?"

"I don't know, Grandy. Maybe."

"I'm not sure what you need from me, January. I can't go back and undo the decision we made."

I looked at her. "I know. I just wish I'd known her..."

My grandmother's jaw hardened slightly. "I'm sorry, there is nothing I can do about that."

Her tone didn't sound sorry. "Right."

"Listen," she said. "If you're going to be mad at me, at least be mad with a little honesty. Own it, January. Let's get into it."

Sudden tears pricked my eyes. "I don't even know if it's you that I'm mad at."

"If not me, then who?"

"I don't know! Maybe it is you. I wanted to know her, Grandy."

"Well, I'm sorry you didn't get that opportunity," Grandy said coldly.

"You took that opportunity away from me!"

"No. Rose did that when she rejected your parents. Let's be clear."

"Grandy, my parents had nothing to do with that letter!"

She pointed her finger up at me. "I *know* you know that's not true. Your parents had everything to do with that letter. The Winstons disavowed their only daughter. They tore up their parent cards and, by extension, their rights to grandparent you. That's on them."

"Let's not talk about this!" I turned to walk away but spun around. "I should have been able to meet her. It wasn't fair!" I sounded seven, and started to shake with anger because of it. "I'm going to bed."

"Stop it, January! You know we don't deal in fairness around here."

"Of course I know that!" I shouted. "Look at my life! How can I not know that?"

"Excuse me?" Grandy slowly got to her feet, and her expression startled me. "What was that?"

"What?"

"I thought I heard you say, 'look at my life,' as though out of everyone in this family, you are the one who has suffered the most unfairness, the most loss. Is that what you're actually saying to me?"

I lifted my chin, but I was frankly alarmed by the tone in Grandy's voice. "I don't have a father," I said. "My mother is a shell of who she once was. Haven't I?"

Grandy glared at me, but her lip was quivering. "I don't know, let's take some inventory, shall we? Was it you who lost the love of your life? Did he die in a crushing accident, leaving you a widow—a disabled widow—at the ripe old age of twenty-four? No, that would be your mother. And speaking of her, did you lose your independence, the phenomenal talent you used to have, your career, your adorableness, your ability to speak, write, drive? No. That would also be your mother. Let's see, were your brothers, mom and dad, and best friend killed? Some shot in the head, some worked to death, some burned in a furnace? No. That would be Babka. Did you lose a brother who you idolized? No, that would be Tess, who had nightmares for three years after he died."

"Stop it Grandy…"

She leaned into me. "Did *your* precious son die horrifically? This amazing creature to whom you gave birth five weeks early, breech, who grew up to be a head taller than you, who teased you mercilessly and made you unbelievably proud and was supposed to bury you, instead of you burying him? No. That would be me!" Grandy was shouting now and weeping, and it was breaking my heart. "Poppy lost him, too, in case you hadn't noticed! Tanek was his hero, his best friend who fished, played baseball and soccer, and camped and repaired car engines with him. I can't tell you how much that man loved his son," she whispered. "What that loss did to him. So please…please enlighten me, January. What terrible unfairness, aside from the absence of parents you never knew, and the loss of a grandmother—who at any time in the past twenty-two years could have knocked on this door, but instead only wrote one lousy letter that we kept from you because we simply did not trust her. Tell me. Tell me all about your terribly unfair life."

I was trembling and with every word she'd shouted I felt smaller and more insignificant. I couldn't breathe. I couldn't do anything but stare unblinkingly at my grandmother as the tears ran down my face. There was nothing she had said that hadn't smacked of absolute, knife-slicing truth.

"I…I'm sorry…" I bawled through thick tears. "I'm sorry…."

"Diana. That's enough." Suddenly Poppy had appeared and it was as though the last two minutes caught up with Grandy. She blanched, collected herself and reached for me. "January…"

But I had to get out of there. I stumbled from the kitchen, down the back stairs, and out into the quiet night, Grandy shouting after me, Poppy shouting after her. I couldn't breathe. I wanted to scream, but I couldn't breathe, and I couldn't find my voice. So I wept at the sky as the echo of my grandmother's words buried me in shame all over again, my heartbeat pounding in my ears. What was wrong with me?

The moon was bright enough to see by, so I ran across the street to the park and headed to the Pinwheel Garden. Maybe the angel chatter would quell the terrible echoes in my head. As I approached, I slowed and used the light on my phone to guide my footsteps to the marble bench where I'd done so much soul-searching over the years. The chatter was lazy because there was no breeze, but I still found the sound irrationally soothing.

Maybe it was because my dad was here. In theory. I wished I could talk to him, but suddenly I wondered if he'd want to talk to me. After Grandy's huge declarations maybe I simply wasn't entitled to *feel* his absence. She was right; I didn't know him. He was just my father, the love of my mom's life…my mom who was broken but had once been unimaginably brave and beautiful and…good and smart and everything I aspired to be. And in my whole life I'd never missed her or needed her as much as I did right now. I doubled over in a sudden cataclysm of agonizing emotion. What right did I have to feel any of that when I had treated her the way I had always treated her?

This was hell. I was in hell.

"January?"

I didn't have time to be startled before Grandy had gathered me into her arms. She'd followed me, and I hadn't even realized it. I was sobbing and it was as though she had rescued me from drowning. She breathed "Shhh" into my ear and rocked me like I was a little girl.

"Janny...I didn't mean to be so harsh. I'm sorry, I'm so..."

"Grandy—" I croaked.

"Shhhh." She rubbed my back. "Shhhh."

I was so tired. *So* tired. "I don't know what's happening to me. Why am I like this? Everything you said—you...you weren't wrong."

"No, sweet girl. It was me...."

"No... no, Grandy, I know you lost a part of you when you lost my dad and I know I can't begin to understand that loss. I *wish* there was a sore place in *me* where my dad used to be. I wish there was a *bruise* that he left. I know that sounds weird, but I wish I had my own memories of him." I looked up at my grandmother. "I love you, Grandy. I envy your grief sometimes. But I never meant to hurt you."

A tear rolled down her face and glistened in the moonlight. "Oh, my darling girl." She kissed my forehead. "Sweetheart, I'm so sorry, too. About Rose. About the letter. We never meant to hurt you. Never."

"I know that. I do."

I leaned back against the bench, still holding her hand and let my heart calm. For a while we were quiet, watching the moon glint off the Mylar blooms.

Grandy sighed. "I so hate to fight with you."

"Ditto."

A warm breeze rustled the oak tree we were sitting under, and a few of the pinwheels responded lazily. "I really do love it here," I said still weeping. "Sometimes I imagine my dad talking to me."

"Me, too, Janny. I visit his grave, but honestly, I find more peace here."

I silently agreed. "Babi told me when she planted his pinwheel that I could come here whenever I needed to feel him. So…I like to imagine he knows me."

"I have no doubt he does, sweetheart. I'm so sorry that he missed out on being your dad. He would simply have adored you."

"I hope so."

"And you—you would have adored him back."

I gulped down a tiny sob. "I'm sorry you had to lose him. I don't know how you survived it, Grandy."

Her arm came around me. "I don't think we could have…except for you."

I sniffed.

"Poppy and I would have drowned in our tears if not for you, Janny. We still would, I'm sure because it never goes away—of course, it doesn't go away. We're around death all day, every day, but that's just death. Loss is something entirely different. It's a permanent *absence* that never goes away. But somehow your life just grows around it."

"I think that's what I miss…"

Grandy nodded. "Losing him was…was the hardest thing I've ever gone through. But God was so very kind to me, to us, in the midst of it."

"What does that mean?"

"Oh…Tan called. Just a couple of hours before. He'd called to tell me they were headed back to the hospital. He said, 'We think it's real this time, Mom.' They'd been there twice already that week. I hung up excited, and of course I couldn't go to bed. So, I took down the Christmas tree and tried not to burst—my first grandchild was on her way. Poppy was asleep on the couch, and I…I just took down the tree. And then about midnight, I think, maybe not quite, the elevator chimed, and I laughed because I thought it was your parents. I thought they'd been sent home again, and they'd seen our lights on and were coming to tell us." She swallowed. "But…it wasn't them."

"Oh, Grandy."

She sniffed in the dark. "By the time we got to the hospital, he was *gone*, and so terribly damaged. But in my heart, he wasn't really gone. He couldn't be. I'd been telling people for years that the soul part of us truly is immortal. I'd always meant it to be a comfort, but that night

I knew it was true—my own grief made it true. All of that personality, that kindness, that wisdom, all of my *Tanek*—that couldn't possibly just be *over*. He had to somehow *continue*. That was the only way I could accept what had happened."

"Do you still believe it?"

"Yes. Oh, yes. I need to believe like I need to breathe."

"Babka says the same thing."

Grandy kissed my temple. "Death and love...those two human experiences, intertwined, somehow open a path to godly understanding. It's really rather amazing."

I stared at the pinwheels and watched them distort through my tears. I felt bad for dredging all this pain up for my grandmother, but I didn't want her to stop talking.

"Poppy used to say that night was heartbreakingly dreadful with a side of joy," she said at length.

"Why would he say that?"

She leaned her head into mine. "We were with your father, trying to grasp what had happened, when a nurse came in. She said the doctor needed to talk to us, and my heart stopped because I just knew it was going to be more terrible news and I didn't know how I could possibly fit any more *terrible* in me. But we followed her down a hall to an empty room where she told us to wait." Grandy sighed. "I just knew that Claire had died and that we'd lost you in the process. It was absolute torture, Janny. But amazingly, that new *worry* had yanked us back from the shock of losing Tan."

She brought her free hand to her lips and was quiet for a moment. "I don't know how long we sat there," she finally said. "It probably wasn't long, but it *seemed* long, and then this doctor walked in holding an armful of pink." Grandy's voice broke when she said 'pink'. "She was so kind, January. I'll never forget. She said, 'Mrs. Duzinski, I have someone here I think you've been waiting to meet.' And then she put you in my arms and saved my life. I cried and I cried. I cried for my Tanek, and I cried for my Claire. And you. I cried because you were so beautiful. You had a bruise on your head, and your little eyes were very swollen, and they were worried about you because of your mother's trauma. But you were perfect, and I just...I just didn't understand how my heart could be so destroyed and at the same time ache with such unimaginable happiness." She brought my hand to her wet lips. "Dreadful with a side of joy," she rasped.

"Grandy…" I choked.

"That's what I remember most, Janny, about that night—that God was so kind to me inside such terrible." She blew out a breath. "And the dreadful, of course, is smaller now. It's the ache that never goes away—that's what dreadful does. But the joy…" she breathed. "The joy gets bigger every day."

"Oh, Grandy. Not on days like today."

"I don't know. Somehow, *especially* on days like today."

A tear that had been brimming spilled down my cheek. "I'm so sorry for everything, Grandy—it's been a very *emotional* day."

"It has indeed. But it's finished now." She kissed my head. "Sometimes love is harsh and it stings for a minute. But it's love; it can take it."

I nodded but couldn't speak over the knot in my throat.

She stood up and took my hand. "Let's go home, dear one. Let's go home and put this day away. I think it's rather worn out its welcome."

sixteen

I didn't sleep well. I kept dreaming that I was still fighting with Grandy and woke several times with a knot in my stomach. Finally, at 5:35, I gave up just as the sun was creeping into the sky. I'd maybe slept four hours.

I picked up Claire's journal and found where I'd left off. She'd driven home after her father's fateful birthday party in disbelief...

September 25, 1999 (11:00 am)
I still can't believe she slapped me...Denton had just left after the fiasco in the library. I was in the kitchen getting some food to take upstairs when Mom barreled in and barked at the caterers to get out. They scrambled, of course, and I wanted to go with them. Then she glared at me and said, low and mean: "How. Could. You?" I just ignored her and kept filling my plate. I had no intention of answering—there was no point. That was when my plate suddenly frisbeed into the wall, prime rib and salad flying everywhere. She hissed, "I asked you a question, Claire!" I couldn't believe it. I told her it was a stupid question, that she'd known I was never going to marry Denton. She told me to grow up and reminded me for the twentieth time that there were worse things than a loveless marriage. I

told her I'd have to take her word for it. That was probably a mistake.

And that's when she slapped me. I didn't even see it coming. I probably deserved it, but I was completely shocked. I think Mom was, too. She looked like she might cry, but she couldn't bring herself to say anything. She was going to, I think. I think she was going to apologize. But she didn't. Of course, she didn't. She just walked out of the kitchen. It was surreal.

It still is. She even turned off the lights and left me sniveling in the dark. It took me a minute to calm down and think straight. When the caterers came back in, I told them my mother was mentally ill and apologized for the mess. They both looked at me with such naked pity that I left and went to McDonald's where I got quite a few stares: alone, all dressed up, handprint on my cheek. I ate in my car and sat there for a long time. But when I got home, I'd decided to come back to school.

Everyone was gone, and I was packing when Dad slid a note under my door. It said simply "Come to our room. Now." I took my time and finished gathering my things. They were in bed reading, and when I walked in, Dad glared at me for a long time, waiting, I'm sure, for my apology, which he didn't get. He finally got up and snarled his disappointment in me. I ignored him, which made him furious. Then he started in on me like I was two. Could I even comprehend the gravity of what I'd done? How I'd ruined everything. He got into my face, said I'd humiliated this family and disgraced an esteemed political ally—apparently Denton's grandfather is a bigwig of some kind. That's when he shoved his finger at me and told me he'd done his best to explain my *cold feet*, but that I was going to do whatever it took to make things right with the Hydes! I've actually never seen him that desperate. When I told him no, he was livid, yelling, pacing, ramming his hands through his hair. He scared me—I thought he was going to have a stroke. I asked him what *he'd* done that made what *I'd* done so terrible, and I will never be able to unsee the look on his face. He tried to hide whatever his real motives were behind my supposed best interests. He barked that he refused to be sorry for wanting what was right for me—for *me!* and that there was absolutely nothing wrong with that boy and that I was going to repair the mess I'd made!

When I told him no again, that it was his mess and I was going back to Yale, Mom spoke up, said I wasn't leaving. I ignored her, too. She'd slapped me and I had no intention of talking to her. But when I tried to leave, Dad grabbed my arm and told me if I left not to bother coming back.

I must have laughed because he leaned into me with such rage that it shocked me. He said I wasn't going anywhere! He practically spat it. I've never been afraid of him, not like that, but he was acting insane. I pulled out of his grasp and started to walk out, and he yelled that if I *dared* to leave rather than do as he said, I was not welcome back in *his* home. *His home.*

Mom suddenly got nervous, and at some point, she started to cry—which never happens. It was unreal. For a minute I just stood there, dumbfounded. I didn't know what was happening. But I knew I couldn't stay. I couldn't. So I left...

I blew out a breath, not realizing I'd been holding it. My mother's words painted such a vivid picture I could almost see it. I could see my grandfather's growing rage, his irrational demands of my mom. It was almost like I'd witnessed a beating.

As I was lying there, heart pounding, feeling irate and exhausted, two women showed up in my mind: Stephen Winston's daughter and my mother. His daughter was brilliant, funny, obedient, savvy, strong, and privileged. She'd performed all over the world, won numerous awards, graduated with honors from Yale, and still he'd rejected her for choosing to live her own life. My mother, through no fault of her own, was grossly disabled, made strange noises, and walked with a halting gait. She slapped her knees when she got excited and blinked her yesses and nos because she couldn't speak. I too had pushed her away for my own irrational reasons and now I suddenly wondered who was the more despicable—my horrible grandfather or me.

It was almost unbearable to consider myself in the same category as Stephen Winston. But here I was, barely eclipsed by his shadow.

My poor mom.

And Rose. She was perhaps the biggest mystery of all.

I turned the page to find tucked in the fold two paper butterflies, which surprised me. Their placement there seemed to have some specific purpose, so I read on.

My mother absolutely infuriates me. She slapped me, which makes her even more ludicrous than usual. I shouldn't have mocked her over her loveless marriage, but she shouldn't have slapped me. She is an absurd woman! I love her, but I hate her sometimes too, and I pity her, and I need her. I don't understand her, and I do understand her, sometimes perfectly. And because she is weird and wounding, and always has been, and because I'm a smart girl, I have to remind myself what is true and abiding and a little bit sad: Mom loves me the best she can. But loving me, loving anyone, doesn't come naturally to her. I don't know if she was born that way or if her father or mine simply quashed the goodness—most of the goodness—out of her. I just know that what little remains is mine. I grabbed these butterflies from my wall to help me remember that. They're faded now but just as meaningful as the day Mom pinned them there. They are a forever testament of that strange, rarely seen, hard-scrabbled love she has for me. When I was 8 or 9 and sick, and recovering from surgery on my appendix, Mom never left my bedside. As she watched over me, she cut out dozens of these paper butterflies—all colors—and pinned them on the wall above my bed, arranged in a big multicolored swarm. I've never taken them down and she's never asked me to. Dad thinks they're cheap and gaudy, but they represent something deep and unsaid and real between her and me. At random times a butterfly has said what we couldn't or wouldn't utter. A journal with a big sequined butterfly on the cover she left on my bed—never saying a word. A mug with a neon butterfly I found at a flea market and left on her nightstand, a calendar that showed up in the mail at school, a watercolor I left on her desk. A card, stationery. Our little secret—a winged "I love you" to or from a woman rather incapable of saying it or hearing it...

I thought of the mural of butterflies I'd seen at the care center in Claire's room, maybe three feet wide, arranged in a wave, the swarm doubtless a replica of the faded one above the bed in Chestnut Hill. The art a secret nod heavy with meaning. *Complicated.* But why now? Why after all this time?

I fell back asleep imagining my grandmother showing up at Potomac Manor, just walking in one day with dozens of butterflies to pin on her daughter's wall. Dozens and dozens of unsaid *I love yous...*

*****

I got a late start on the morning thanks to my fitful wanderings through dreams and journals and arguments with Grandy, but by just past ten, I was downstairs and fully in death mode. As I skimmed Veronica Lawson's notes, I gulped a Mountain Dew, steeled for the sugar and caffeine rush. The woman had died at Holy Christus Medical Center at 16:10 yesterday. She'd been pregnant with twins but presented at the ER with heavy bleeding that could not be controlled despite delivering the eighteen-week-old fetuses. The DIC Calvin had mentioned was spelled out in parentheses: Disseminated Intravascular Coagulation. I didn't know what that was, but it had caused her to bleed to death, which explained my deceased's extreme pallor.

After all my verifications of identity and permissions were double-checked, I opened my music streaming app, scrolled to Norah Jones, hit Shuffle, and got to work, distracting myself from my own upheaval to focus on the death in front of me.

After I thoroughly washed Veronica and shampooed her hair, I set the young woman's features. I inserted eye caps and loosely sutured her jaw shut and arranged her mouth in the faintest of smiles—one aimed to bring a portion of comfort to her bereaved. That was my number-one job: make it as easy as possible for her loved ones to say goodbye. This was going to be a tall order considering they hadn't just lost her, but her babies as well.

When I had her expression fixed, I filled my tank with chemicals and gloved up, then made an incision in her common carotid. As the infusion was pumping in and what little blood she had left was flowing out, I dried her hair and talked to her about the terrible time she'd had, imagining the pain and horror that surely no one had seen coming. I voiced my sad and very close-to-home amazement at how the world could so drastically alter over the course of a only few short hours. "I so hope you just slipped away, Ronnie, and did not have to suffer. And I'm sorry about your babies, your poor husband, your parents. I've come to understand there is nothing harder than burying a child who was supposed to bury you—"

Behind me, Poppy cleared his throat, startling me. "You remind me of your dad," he said.

"I didn't hear you come in," I said, wondering how long he'd been eavesdropping. "Veronica and I were just chatting about bad days."

Poppy walked over and took in Ronnie Lawson. "Pretty girl," he said.

"I'm flying a little blind, but she's making it easy."

He picked up her hand, pressed her thumbnail to assess the color and nodded approvingly. "Your father used to talk to them, too," he said. "He was very tender, like you are. He'd reassure them, talk to them like they were just gently dying instead of already gone."

"I do talk to them sometimes."

Poppy winked at me. "I know you do." He checked the color of Veronica's feet and again seemed pleased. "One Christmas," he said, absently. "Well, Claire was pregnant with you, so it was…it was that December, just before Christmas. We got a young boy in here who'd skied into a tree. He was maybe seventeen, and he was a mess, as you can imagine. His face was absolutely ruined. I remember your mom and Diana had been shopping and they'd brought home dinner. But Tan wouldn't come up. He'd met with the family, and it was very traumatic, very hard on everyone, including your dad. It was the holiday, the kid was just a kid…" Poppy sighed, remembering. "Tan was exhausted; it had been a long day. But he stayed up all night reconstructing that boy's face, and I know he talked to him the whole time. But by that morning, those parents had their beautiful son to say goodbye to." Poppy looked at me, his eyes filled with emotion. "He was very good, your dad. And you're a lot like him."

"I love to hear that," I said over the knot in my throat. "Thanks, Poppy."

"Thank *you,* my girl, for the memory." My grandfather sat down on the rolling stool and looked at me. "You and Grandy okay?"

"I think so. We just had a *moment.*"

He nodded. "That's what she said."

I chuckled.

"January," my grandfather said soberly. "I hope you know we've always done what we *thought* was best for you."

"Of course I know that. I'm sorry I made such a big deal of that letter."

"I think I get it."

"It was a glimpse into a possibility…I don't know." I shrugged.

"I understand," he said.

"I am sorry, Poppy. I'm sorry that all my *crap* has had to fall on just you and Grandy."

"All what crap?"

"Me—raising me, dealing with me. You were kind of done with all that by the time I came along. And Mom. Sometimes I can't believe you did that. It seems to me that the Winstons…they shouldn't have gotten off so *free.* They should have stepped up. I went a little nuts over that letter, but really, it got me thinking that I should know them in all their absurdity because *they* should have been involved—with me, with Mom from the beginning. Finding out they—well, Rose—

wanted to know me after the fact…it's just such a waste. For me. For them. For Claire. For you."

"Well, I guess that's one way—"

"I just can't believe they dumped everything on you and Grandy. How could you have let them get away with that? It wasn't right."

"Whoa, whoa," he said, holding up his hand. "What are you talking about? Nobody dumped anything on us, January. It's true the Winstons didn't want the burden of caring for your mother, but they took responsibility. Long before Claire was ever released from rehab, even before she'd come out of her coma, they had arranged for her to be placed at Potomac Manor…*if she lived.* And you…" Poppy paused, took me in. "They…they had adoption papers drawn up before you ever left the hospital."

"What?" The word gushed out of me along with my breath.

"January, Claire was their daughter. They made arrangements for a private adoption—or their team of lawyers did. But none of that mattered to us. We would never have given you up. We were frankly shocked that we didn't have to fight them for you. We were prepared to go to court if we had to, but it never came to that."

Still open-mouthed, I stared at him over the sheet-draped Veronica Lawson. "They never wanted me?"

"They *didn't want* Tanek's child more than they *did want* Claire's. Does that make sense? It had nothing to do with you. You have to know that. Besides, Claire would never have wanted them to have you. Not for one moment. So, for once, Stephen Winston—and I have no doubt it was Stephen—and his hatred of Tan worked in our favor." Poppy smiled, sort of.

Of course, this all rang true to me. But it still stung.

"Months later," Poppy hurried on, "when the rehab finally released Claire, we brought her home, too."

I resurfaced at his words. "Why did you do that? I mean, she must have been so much work. Why did you take that on, Poppy? She wasn't even your daughter."

"She was your mother," he declared matter-of-factly. "She needed you. And, though she's not our *daughter* daughter, she *is* our daughter." He shook his finger at me. "I'll tell you a little story. The night before your parents got married, we had a traditional Polish wedding feast—your Babi insisted. It was very nice. We all blubbered.

And afterwards, after the dinner and the blessing and the toast, I took your mom for a walk. Claire didn't want to go, and she scolded me for leaving everyone else to clean up. But that was my plan: to get out of the dishes." My grandfather danced his eyebrows. "We walked across the street to the park where I asked her if she was really going to marry my Tan. And you know what she said, January?"

"What?"

"She said, 'I have to. It's too late to get the deposit back.'" Poppy laughed.

I did, too.

"I asked her if she was sure she wouldn't come to her senses. She said, 'Nope.' Then we got serious, because there was a reason I had stolen her away."

"What was it?"

My grandfather was quiet for a beat, staring at nothing. "We had paid her parents a visit—the first and last—and I wanted her to know."

I stopped what I was doing—which was spreading emollient on Veronica's lips—and looked up. "You'd never met them?"

Poppy shook his head.

"Were they awful?" I asked.

"Yes. To be fair, I think we may have caught them in the middle of an argument. But they were polite—cold, but polite. I'm pretty sure they thought we were missionaries. And after we told them who we were, I think they wished we *were* missionaries." Poppy chuckled. "Claire's first concern was if she needed to apologize for them. "

"I can understand that."

"I told her I never wanted her to feel like she had to explain or apologize or defend anything. Not to us. But between you and me, Janny, that Stephen Winston was just the most preposterous man I'd ever met. I mean, he was a pompous ass: arrogant, insulting, pathetic, but mostly just absolutely preposterous. He told me that my son had cost Claire her inheritance and that if she was going to settle for a *Polish undertaker*, she was no daughter of his."

"What?"

"It's a long story, but that man was out of his mind. It was inconceivable to me that Claire was his daughter." Poppy looked hard at me. "January, we could not have handpicked a finer woman for our son, and I told her that. Then I told her that if she'd let us, we'd be her family. There would be no such thing as 'in-law.' She would be our daughter, my mother's granddaughter, Tess's sister. Always. And I meant it. I still do."

Tears stung my eyes. "Poppy…"

"You know, Janny, my father used to say time was too brief and unpredictable to be wasted in turmoil. Very wise counsel from a man who had survived what he'd survived. I didn't always grasp that, but I do now. I believe there's grief. Of course, there is—we see it every day. But there's a much worse grief that's born of regret. I suspect the Winstons grew to regret, very much, what had happened between them and their daughter."

"According to Mr. Thibodeau, Rose did," I agreed. "I don't know about Stephen."

"Pride is an expert liar, January. Sometimes it takes a lifetime to realize you've been duped by it. But you learn."

I glanced at him, unmoved. "I'm not going to feel sorry for him, Poppy."

He wagged his finger at me again. "You sound like Grandy."

"Like minds…" I said, wheeling Veronica into the fridge.

"Thank goodness your mother was kinder—and more forgiving. On the way back from the park, I asked Claire for her forgiveness in advance."

"For what?" I said as I shut the door and adjusted the temperature.

"The countless mistakes I was destined to make because…you know, I'm me. The toes I knew I would step on, the bad jokes, the times I'd show up uninvited to dinner—and yes, I did that a few times—and of course the severe spoiling of her future children."

"You said *that?*"

"I did. Claire laughed. But then she had a favor to ask of me regarding these *future children,*" Poppy said with a sad smile.

"What was it?"

"She asked if I'd be willing to do double duty since their kiddos would probably only have one grandfather…And she'd probably only have one father."

I sat down on the stool next to him. "What did you tell her?"

"I promised to do my best."

I eyed him for a moment. "That's why you brought her home."

"That's why we brought her home, Janny. She's ours, and you're ours, and she needed to be near you. Moms need their babies—no matter what shape that mom is in."

I stared at him. I'd been walking around in a bubble my whole life with such little awareness of...*anything*. "I think you're pretty much a rock star, Poppy," I said softly.

"Oh, yes, just call me Mick Jagger." He winked. "I believe we're about the same age."

I laughed. "But it was hard, right? It had to be."

"It was, I won't lie. Those early years were exhausting. I don't think your grandmother slept for two years, maybe three." He shook his head. "I was down here all the time doing her job *and* mine. Tess was in school. We had *some* help—physical therapists, occupational therapists—who came to the house a couple of times a week. But it still seems we were always taking Claire to appointments. And you...it had been a long time since we'd had a baby in this house. Let's just say you and Claire were a full-time job for Grandy. I, of course, was my usual supportive self from, you know, the land of the dead three floors down."

I rolled my eyes. "Of course you were. And you didn't resent the Winstons? Even a little?"

"Have you met me? I resented the hell out of them. But what good was resentment? We'd made our decision; we weren't going to unmake it, even if sometimes things were hard—even very hard." He leaned over. "But I did occasionally fantasize about sending those horrid people truckloads of dirty diapers—yours and Claire's."

A laugh coughed out of me.

"If I could have just sent them the poop...the mountains and mountains of poop...I think I would have felt fine about the whole arrangement." He lifted a brow. "Other than that, almost everything else was worth it—especially when you both finally got toilet-trained."

I suddenly got a visual of my poor grandmother. "I had no idea."

He shrugged. "Why would you?"

"Poppy, be honest. Was the fire kind of a blessing? You know, with Claire moving to Potomac Manor. I mean that's when you changed your mind, right?"

"Well, after the fire, we didn't have much choice. Claire was in the hospital for quite a while, and then we took the Winstons up on their offer of Potomac Manor. But that was just because Margaret could barely accommodate *us*, let alone take care of Claire while she recovered. You remember we stayed with Aunt Margaret for nearly five months."

I always forgot that Claire didn't go straight to the care center—she first spent time in the hospital for her burns. "So, Potomac Manor was supposed to be temporary?" I asked.

"Well, yes. But, if I'm being *honest,* it did turn out to be a kind of blessing."

"Because of me."

"Because of *circumstances,* January. Yes, you had a rough time because of everything—it was very traumatic. But Potomac Manor was the perfect solution. Claire's been happy there. She's been well taken care of, much better than what we were doing. It was a blessing borne of a tragedy. A *tragedy,* Janny."

I didn't say anything. I'd been told this many times: The fire had just been a terrible tragedy. That Claire was hurt saving my life—hurt on top of being so terribly damaged already—was not my fault. That my four-year-old self had so grossly misread what happened that night was a justified reaction. That my long-held avoidance of the mother who adored me was part of the trauma. I'm old enough to know that none of this was ever my fault, but sometimes I wondered if I would ever be old enough to believe it.

Poppy stood up. "Stop thinking what you're thinking and let's get back to work." He planted a kiss on my forehead.

"Thank you, Poppy," I whispered.

"For what?"

"For stepping up. For being my one and only grandfather."

He sighed dramatically and pounded his chest. "Well, it's a big job, *Serce,* but somebody has to do it."

seventeen

It was just after three when Grandy called down to say I had a visitor. I wasn't dressed for visitors, but I'd grabbed my gray pencil skirt and black blouse for my meeting with Derek Lawson. And since I was finished embalming for the time being, I changed and ran upstairs. My visitor turned out to be Tyson Pierce, which surprised me. He was sitting on the sofa nearest the piano when I stepped off the elevator, and for a moment I just sort of drank him in. He was wearing light gray pants and a navy sport coat, white shirt, no tie. He looked good. He was on his cell—listening, not talking—and for a moment didn't notice me. And then he did. And I have to say the *look* he gave me made me smile.

"Hey, you," I said walking toward him. "What's going on?"

He stood, still taking me in. Still with the look. "I was just thinking about you—hope that doesn't freak you out. I knew you had a big day yesterday. And you mentioned how Krause's white chocolate pretzels were your favorites, and I just happened to be in Patterson this morning, so…" He grinned, turned back to the sofa, and picked up a familiar red box and handed it to me.

I looked at it then back at him, eyes wide. "Tyson, are you kidding—thank you!"

He smiled. "You're welcome. And this is from my mom." He handed me an ivory envelope the size of a large greeting card.

"What's this?"

"You made quite an impression on her. She wanted to say thank you."

"For what?"

"For taking such good care of Ash…and me."

"Oh, that is so kind. Can you sit for a minute?"

He checked his watch. "I wish I could. I actually didn't expect you to be here—I thought you'd still be in Pennsylvania—so I'm on my way to court."

"Oh."

"But, believe me, I would if I could." He grinned.

I smiled. "Well, at least let me walk you out."

"That'd be great." As we made our way through the foyer and out into the heat, he asked, "How did it go yesterday?"

"A little intense, but it was…very enlightening."

"Good enlightening?"

"Humbling enlightening. But good, too," I said. "Thanks for asking. And thank you for lunch. And for listening to me. That was a lot to unload, and I didn't realize how badly I needed to talk. You were a stellar audience."

"Oh, I could have done that all day," he said, sweetly. "So…you're okay?"

"I'm different, I think, than I was yesterday. But yeah, I'm okay."

"Well, if there's anything I can do…"

We'd reached his car, and I looked up at him, shielding my eyes from the sun. "Actually, maybe there is," I said, recalling something he'd mentioned. "Did you tell me your brother owns a moving company?"

"My uncle. Why?"

"It seems I need a grand piano moved. Does he do those?"

"Oh, yeah. Whenever you see someone hoisting a piano up to a New York City penthouse—that's my uncle. And china cabinets and big statues, all the stuff rich people can't live without."

"Really?" I laughed. "Would he go to Chestnut Hill?"

"Pennsylvania? He would if I asked him."

"Are you serious? That would be great," I said, rather amazed. "I'll figure out the details and call you later?"

"That works."

"Thank you," I said. "For everything. Just so you know, I'm having chocolate pretzels for lunch. Late lunch."

He smiled. "Excellent."

Just then, a dirty black jeep pulled into the parking lot. I watched as a man stepped from the driver's side, then proceeded to help his passenger out. They both looked to be in their thirties, the passenger slightly intoxicated. I instinctively knew it was Derek Lawson.

I turned back to Tyson. "I have to go." I reached for his hand and squeezed, but when I tried to let go, he wouldn't let me.

"January," he said. "Do you think sometime soon we could, I don't know, go do something?"

I smiled. "Like a real date?"

"Yeah."

"I'd like that."

Now he squeezed, then let go. "I'll call you."

My phone rang as he drove away, leaving me no choice but to shift gears. It was Grandy letting me know Mr. Lawson and his brother were in her office and they'd like to see Veronica. I told her to give me ten minutes, then I hurried in, grabbed the pretzels and card I'd left on the piano, and took the elevator back downstairs.

I moved Veronica Lawson into our tiny receiving room and was just finger combing the woman's red hair over one shoulder when Poppy showed the men in. Derek Lawson was a wreck of a man whose pain radiated off of him like heat. He was tall and the tiniest bit overweight, not particularly attractive, and at the moment, he looked unwashed. He smelled of alcohol. As he approached his wife, even held up by his brother, his knees nearly buckled. My heart broke for him. In less than twenty-four hours, this man had lost everything: his wife as well as two daughters who were supposed to have been born healthy and howling at Christmas time. I could have cried for him. I wanted to. Instead, I introduced myself.

"Mr. Lawson, I'm January Duzinski. I am so sorry to meet you under these circumstances."

He nodded.

"I'll be taking care of your wife," I said. "I wonder if you could...if you could tell me a little about her. Sometimes that helps me...I'd like to capture her as authentically as possible."

"Oh...yeah. Okay. I'll try," he coughed. "What...what do you want to know?"

"Anything you'd like to tell me, sir."

He looked down at the woman. "She never wore her hair like that," he said. "But I loved it down. I love her hair," he sniffed.

I swallowed. "How would you like me to style it?"

"Up. Here's a picture." He handed me a photo that looked as though he'd been clutching it for hours. In it her hair was piled loosely back, messy, stray tendrils at her neck.

I took the photo from his trembling hand. "I'll make sure you get this back, sir."

The other man handed me a paper bag. "Here's the dress."

"She liked black," Derek said. "And she almost never wore shoes. Does she have to wear shoes?"

"No. Not at all. Her feet won't show, but you'll know that she won't be wearing shoes. I did notice some black polish on her toenails. I'll paint them again."

He looked at me, nodded again. "Thanks. Can you do her fingers, too?"

"Absolutely."

He then reached in his pocket and pulled out a sandwich bag filled with rings and leather cords. "Ronnie made jewelry…Can you…" his voice faltered as he handed me the bag.

"I will."

He looked at his wife again. "Can I kiss her?"

"Of course you can. She's very cold, just so you're aware."

Grandy rescued me right after that with some questions she had for Mr. Lawson about the service. Upon parting, the man hugged me as though I held far more significance to him than I actually did. His brother, who barely said a word but did a lot of throat-clearing, shook my hand with tears in his eyes. It was a good meet. A hard meet, but good.

I'd been instructed that Ronnie Lawson was to be enhanced with as little makeup as possible, which meant a bit of lip gloss and mascara only. She'd be dressed in the simple black tank dress I'd been given and would be wearing her own leather and beaded creations around her wrists and long thin neck. It was an easy transformation. I piled her hair loosely on the top of her head, and after I'd painted her nails, I slid the five rings Derek had given me onto her slender fingers. Then I glued her hands together. Per her husband's wishes, she was barefoot.

Start to finish, Veronica Lawson took me just over an hour to complete.

***

I spent the rest of the day making arrangements for my mother's piano. It looked like it was going to cost me a good chunk to have the concert grand moved a hundred miles, and that was with Tyson calling in his family discount. But of course, it was really nothing to owning a Steinway, so I wasn't complaining.

The real challenge had been finding a home for my new bequest— I had no idea what to do with the nine-foot-long behemoth. After several dead ends, I called the Steinway Piano Gallery over in Paramus. Thankfully, they had storage space available but wondered if I might be interested in making a little money instead. Naturally I was intrigued. The manager told me a request had come in yesterday to rent a grand piano for the staging of a home over in Alpine. He didn't have the immediate inventory, but he'd told the realtor he'd keep his eyes open. Now he gave me his number.

After a short conversation, I managed to rent Claire's beloved Steinway to Piedmont Properties for almost as much as it was going to cost me to move it. The best part was that they would pay for its transport to the Piano Gallery who would house it for me until I decided what to do. It was a win-win, and I'd solved the dilemma of storage. For the time being, anyway.

With Veronica Lawson casketed and a deceased set up in each of our chapels ready for viewings tonight—one of which was our rower, who looked amazingly unscathed—we were caught up for the moment. Tess had gone home, and the whiteboard was cleared, but I'd heard the garage door a few minutes ago, so Calvin had undoubtedly been called out on a collection. I had some time, so I sat down at the desk and opened the card Tyson had given me. It was an ink drawing of a stick girl holding out a bouquet of stick flowers. She was looking down, and a tear had fallen from her eye into a puddle that she was standing in. Written inside the card, it said:

Dear Miss Duzinski, January—

I cannot tell you what your tender care of my beloved Ashley has meant to me. I was not prepared to lose her; perhaps no one is ever prepared for such a loss. But your gentleness with her, your attention to detail, somehow softened my pain and touched me more than I can express. Many thanks as well for your patience with my son, who was a bit overwhelmed when called upon to take care of things his father and I were unable to attend to. You were truly a godsend. Your kindness made all the difference at this difficult time for our family and will never be forgotten.

With much, much gratitude,
Nicole Pierce

I swallowed over a sudden swelling in my throat. How sweet was that? No wonder Tyson Pierce was such a nice guy. I read the card again, remembered how kind Nicole Pierce had been in her wounded grief, how appreciative. We got cards like this every once in a while—even today, I carried one around in my wallet that had belonged to my dad. Poppy had given it to me the day I graduated from mortuary school. Notes like these tended to make up for the rough days and reminded us—me, especially—that there was more to death than *death*. My dad used to say that, according to Poppy.

A knock on the door brought me back, and I looked over to see my grandmother walk in. "Hey."

"Hello, dear one. All caught up?"

"For the moment," I said.

"Well, I'm headed up to get ready for those viewings, and I wanted you to know there's some chef's salad in the fridge, if you're interested."

"Thanks. What time is it?"

"Just about 6:30. You okay?"

"Yes," I said, handing her the card from Tyson's mom.

She smiled as she read it. "Your Babka got one as well. They are a lovely family." She handed the card back. "Tyson looked nice today."

"Yes, he did," I agreed.

When my grandmother figured out that's all she was going to get from me, she shook her head and moved on. "Sweetheart, I did have a favor, an errand I'd like you to run."

"Okay."

"Poppy and I have been trying to figure out when we can get over to Potomac Manor, but we've been tied up every night. And we've got these two viewings tonight, and a full day tomorrow. Anyway, how would you feel about driving over there and telling Claire what's happened?"

It took me a second to process what she was asking me. "She doesn't know about Rose?"

"No. Mr. Thibodeau offered to tell her, but I thought it should come from one of us, and it needs to be face-to-face. We just haven't had the time. Janny, will you please do it? I don't think we should wait any longer."

"Oh. I…I can do that," I said hoping my reluctance wasn't too obvious.

"I think it will mean a lot coming from you."

"Do you really think she'll know Rose?" I asked even as a swarm of paper butterflies materialized in my mind bringing with it a probable answer.

"Oh, I don't think there's any reason to believe she wouldn't have some recollection of her mother—but then again…. They told us after the accident that over time her poor little brain could heal… To what extent, they didn't know. So, we don't know. But either way she needs to be told about Rose."

I nodded. "Okay."

Grandy kissed the top of my head. "You'll do fine, sweetheart."

eighteen

Because all I'd eaten all day was the entire package of white chocolate pretzels Tyson had brought me, I decided the chef's salad in the fridge was probably a good idea. I filled a plate, grabbed a yogurt and a bottle of water and headed to my room.

My bedroom was a disaster, the clutter only adding to my feelings of angst and unrest. What I *should* do tonight, what I really *should* do, was go find another apartment. I could totally expand my radius from Duzy House, maybe lower my standards, maybe up my budget—that would open up more possibilities, and I could get myself out of this mess. I sighed. Or…I could just be patient for a little bit longer and hope that someone would die or get arrested, and a spot would open up on one of the four perfect waiting lists I was already on.

I sat down on the bed and attacked my salad—I was starving. I'd leave in a half-hour, I told myself. Claire's journal was face down, keeping my place where I'd left off this morning. I picked it up as I bit into a tomato.

September 26, 1999, (10:10 pm)
   There is no way this is even the same day! I've been talking to a total stranger for the past three hours! Except he felt so *not* like a stranger that I think I could have let loose all my circus-freak parts and it would not have scared him. Amazingly, none of my bizarreness even

came up, which I have to say was rather lovely after having lived it for the past two days.

I can't quite believe he called, and I can't believe he asked me out. How did that happen? Well, I guess I did proffer my phone number—to him and the world—so there's that. Was that just yesterday? I guess it was.

It was just after Monica and I had finished lunch in Midtown where the waiter couldn't stop flirting with Mon and didn't charge us for dessert. He'd made us late, so we had less than two hours to get to Bloomingdales, find the perfect dresses for Dad's party, get back to my car, and out of the city. We were hoofing it up 5th Avenue when we ran into that parade. I'd wanted to backtrack, but Mon said we had to stop and watch for a minute—she's a newbie in the city and thought she might have to comment intelligently on it to someone, somewhere. She's hilarious. It was the Pulaski Parade, and it was actually cool—named for a Polish general who fought for American independence—that's what the banner said, and it was kind of awesome to be right there in the middle of it. And that's when I saw him: not Pulaski, but someone much more alive and better looking.

He was maybe twenty yards away and looking right at me, which surprised me. He was staring like he knew me, but I'm pretty sure I'd remember if we'd met. He was my kind of good-looking with longish dark hair pushed off his forehead with his sunglasses. Tall. Great smile. The dangerous kind that pulls you in without trying. And he just stood there smiling his dangerous, easy smile, and it made me laugh. But I didn't know him.

He waved, so I waved, and if I'd been standing next to him, I'd have introduced myself, and I know we would have had a conversation—probably a long one. He mouthed something I, of course, could not understand, so I laughed. He did, too. It was fun. And because the distance between us had grown, and I was feeling a little reckless, I did something slightly insane. Mon had a legal pad in her backpack, so I borrowed it and wrote my phone number, one big digit per page, and held it high above my head. He was confused at first, but then he scrambled to write it in his palm. I still can't quite believe I did that, because there is nothing in my extraordinarily proper upbringing that would ever have allowed for that. But there was just something about the way he was looking at me.

Monica said he was probably an axe murderer—this from the girl who had just done something similar to the purveyor of free desserts. And it was only after I'd lost sight of him that it hit me that he actually might be an axe murderer—or worse, that 59 actual axe murders might now be in possession of my phone number. But the parade broke up and he disappeared, and Mon and I sprinted to Bloomie's to power-shop before we left the city for Dad's party where I was ultimately expunged from my family. I hate to admit it, but with everything that's happened, I didn't even remember being on 5th Avenue until he called.

At first there was nothing but air, and I almost hung up. But then a voice I didn't recognize asked if I was Claire Winston. There was more silence, so I asked who he was, and he kind of stammered that we'd sort of met yesterday in Manhattan, to which I said he clearly had the wrong number. That's when he reminded me that I'd flashed him—and half of NY—my phone number. I kind of choked as it all rushed back, and I didn't know what to do because he sounded nice, but I had never flashed my name, and the whole thing suddenly felt creepy.

But it actually wasn't creepy at all. Turns out he recognized me from the Dabrowski competition Friday night where he'd had second row seats. How cool is that? And even cooler, he had been there with his grandmother—not a date. Apparently, she's Polish and she loves Chopin, so my parade stalker had surprised her with tickets. I think that's adorable! He must have told me I was incredible ten times. Sorry, but that never gets old.

He apologized for freaking me out at the parade, but he said when he saw me, he thought it couldn't be me. But, if it wasn't me, I looked a lot like me and somewhere in there, he said he couldn't quite believe he was actually talking to me, like I was some kind of celebrity or something. He was cute. And nice. And nervous, so he was ticking all the boxes.

I liked him even before he asked me out. But I had to make him work for it. I had to tease him, telling him that most guys I met at Polish parades were of fairly dubious character. He laughed. He has a great laugh. His name is Tanek. Tanek Duzinski. I gotta say, I love that name.

I dropped the journal and almost dropped my bottle of water. This…*this* was how my parents had met? At a parade? A parade where my dad had stared, and my mom had flashed him her phone number? I couldn't believe it. I'd never even wondered how they met, and here it was innocently playing out in front of me on the pages of my mother's journal. My parents' first conversation. I could hear it, and I couldn't process the emotion swimming through me.

Before yesterday, I had never been at all interested in Claire's life—or simply had been unable to imagine her having a life in the first place. And now, here I sat, hanging on every word she'd written.

This guy is utterly fascinating. He's Polish. Half Polish. He told me all about his family. His Busha (Grandmother) is the Chopin aficionado, and the way Tanek talks about her, it's clear they are very close. She has one son, Tanek's father, Stasio—another very cool name—who married a nice American girl. He has one sister, and they all work their family mortuary in Wallington, New Jersey. Tanek graduated two years ago with a degree in mortuary science but even without it, he said he would have joined the family business. He said he liked death that much—that's a line you live your whole life never imagining you'll hear. I told him I'd never known a mortician and he said he'd never known a virtuoso, so we were even. He's adorable.

He asked about my family, of course, and I told him I'm an only, gave him a superficial rundown of Rose and Steve, and quickly circled back to him. I couldn't help it; I was fascinated by this peek at something that seemed so genuine, so easy. I also didn't think him knowing I was a brand-new orphan would add to my allure.

He was insanely easy to talk to about everything—school, friends, food, sports, travel. When my battery finally gave out, I hung up having had my belief in God and fate and kismet reaffirmed. Tanek. Tanek Duzinski. His name felt good on my tongue, and his voice felt good everywhere. He asked if he could call me tomorrow, and I said of course. Now I can't wait to wake up in the morning.

Well, hello my 14 y/o self, long time no see.

"14 y/o self"…I loved that.

It's been a long day—pivotal, I think. And I survived it. I have a strange life, no doubt about it, but I think it must be no accident that my strange life—or the orchestrator of it—tossed a beautiful Polish boy into my path at this exact moment. Especially one who wants to drive the hour-and-a-half from New Jersey just so he can take me for sushi. I love that a guy with a nice smile, who loves his grandmother who loves Chopin, would show up with her to see me win a competition, then spot me in a crowd and somehow dazzle me into flashing him my phone number so he could call me on the worst day of my life, making me forget for a while that it was the worst day of my life, but somehow remind me that I had survived it. Big, fat run-on sentence there, but I don't care! I might just have to go out with the cute undertaker with the *dangerous smile from Wallington, New Jersey, and see where it leads.*

Oh. My. Heart! I checked my watch and couldn't believe it. 7:40! All I wanted to do was keep reading! But I had someplace to be.

***

As I made the 20-minute trek to Potomac Manor I thought of the woman I was discovering compared with the one I had always been content to accept just as she seemed. One was a damaged woman with such limited depth as to be uninteresting—and I cringed admitting it. The other was fast becoming a fascination to me.

I'd never heard my mother speak, yet somehow over the last two days, I'd heard her voice, clear and distinct in the words she'd written. She'd been witty and brave and intriguing. Claire Winston had been raised in a bubble to be a proper girl who would never flash her phone number to a strange man, and yet, she had done just that. And that one act of rebellious street flirting had led directly to me. I liked that girl. I'd never imagined someone like her was who my mom could have been.

And suddenly I felt desperately sorry that neither one of us had access to her now. I certainly had no tools to excavate her, and Claire had no ability to share her with me, even if she could remember the details. It all seemed so unbelievably futile. And sad.

As I pulled into the parking lot at Potomac Manor, I was a knot of frustration. If there was any good news to be had, I hoped it might be that Claire wouldn't clearly remember Rose either, and my job here tonight would be just a brief conversation about the death of someone she used to know.

On an easel in the foyer was a poster welcoming guests to 'An Evening with the Baxter Brothers.' Taped to it was a photograph of two teenage boys. Both were wearing tuxedos, one had braces, one had dreadlocks. Each held a violin. I followed the soft strains of Bartok to the gathering room where it looked like the recital was winding down.

The Manor did this kind of thing often, had local talent come in for an evening of entertainment. I'd played here several times. Sometimes full ensembles performed, with a harp and flutes, strings and guitars—high school kids frequently, but the Master of Fine Arts program at Bloomfield had contributed a lot of talent over the years as well. Nights like this were usually quite a production. Families were always welcome, and the residents were expected to dress up a bit. From the looks of things, tonight had been another success. Bless Harry Golding, who had always been very big on promoting culture at Potomac Manor.

I sat down in an empty side chair. The sofas had been pushed to the center of the room and arranged in a semicircle around where the boys were performing. Chairs were set up behind the sofas and behind them, the dessert table. It was a modest crowd, and the music was lovely. I spotted Claire near the front on the opposite side of the room. She was sitting alone on a loveseat. The side of her facing me was her bad side—her most injured side—and as I sat watching her, I tried to imagine the girl my father had stared at on Fifth Avenue. I wanted to see within that profile a shadow of what he had seen and been so drawn to. But the reality was too distorted, the lovely young tease too crushed beneath it. I was staring at Claire, thinking all this, when she suddenly turned toward me as if she sensed I was there. Many feet and quite a few people separated us, as we were at opposite ends of the room, so she looked past me. But she came back to me several times, like she recognized me, but not in this context. I waved, but it didn't seem to register.

Finally, Harry Golding stood and thanked the young violinists for sharing their remarkable talent. They took their bows, and the residents applauded and started to disperse. As Harry walked the boys out, I made my way over to Claire. When I got close enough for her to recognize me, elation filled her expression.

"Hey, Mom." I saw the joy turn to slight confusion, which shamed me. I imagined her thinking: *This can't be January! Here? By herself? No one dragging her kicking and screaming to see her mother?*

With decided effort, Claire got to her feet and steadied herself. Then, up came her skinny arms to lock me in fierce hug, the purity of her affection so generous it made me weep for my task. She was very bony, all planes and sharp edges. It was like embracing a small tree.

"C'mon, Claire," I said, pulling away from her. "Let's sit for a minute."

She blinked, then narrowed her eye around a question.

I cleared my throat, scrambling for safe footing. "Did…did you enjoy the recital? They sounded good, I thought."

She blinked her yes, then kept her eye on me as we sat, her stare a laser of inquisition. I didn't blame her. My being there at 8:30 at night had to be alarming. I blew out a breath.

"Mom, I know it's weird that I'm here. I came…I came because Grandy asked me to—she would have come…" I cleared my throat and avoided Claire's eye. Then I turned away completely, realizing I didn't know how to do this. When I felt my mother's little hand take mine, it should have helped, but it didn't. I turned back to find her looking intently at me—knowing if she could speak, she would ask me what on earth was bothering me. I breathed deeply and pushed out the words. "Mom, I don't think you'll—well you might, I don't know… But… Well, Mom, I'm so sorry, but… Rose died. Rose… your mother."

Completely blank stare.

And met with that completely blank stare, somehow relief washed through me. Claire didn't remember her. She didn't know who I was talking about! I sighed as my heart calmed and then I babbled on. "It happened the other day. I guess, because, well, Rose, she was... She had a brain bleed…some kind of brain aneurism. Her attorney came by… Mom, what's—are you *crying*?"

She didn't blink, but the saddest tear had filled my mother's eye. I swallowed my surprise and wasn't sure what to do. "Mom, do you know who I'm talking about?" Claire looked at me—through me—and blinked one time as the tear spilled down her scarred cheek.

"Mom. It's been so long, I didn't think…" I shook my head, no idea how to finish my thought. "Mom…I'm so sorry."

After an interminable moment, Claire let go of my hand and got herself shakily to her feet. I stood, too, unsure of what she was doing. She steadied herself by taking my elbow, and then we walked slowly out of the gathering room and down the hall. I had never felt so awful in my life. We walked in silence to the room where the big picture of me was taped to the door, and I followed her inside. The first thing I saw was the butterfly mural above her bed, identical to the one I'd seen in her bedroom in Chestnut Hill. Claire looked at me looking at it. "Rose?" I said.

One blink. Another tear. And as she stared at the butterflies, the tear became a steady stream.

"Mom, has Rose been to see you? Has she been coming here?"

One blink. And a tiny moan at the back of her throat.

"I don't understand." I was throbbing with anxiety. I didn't know what to do, not for her, or for me, and I hated feeling this useless, this much at a loss. She must have sensed this because she reached up and patted my cheek. It wasn't smooth, it wasn't gentle—Claire couldn't really do that—but it was something comforting a mother would do, even one hurting like she was.

"Mom, I'm—"

There was a knock on her door, then an aide looked in. "Oh, I'm sorry," she said. "I was just going to help Miss Claire get ready for bed, but if you'd like—"

"No, no. I was just leaving," I practically barked. "Come in. *Please.*" I turned to Claire, feeling *exposed* in my obvious relief at being rescued. "I have to go, Mom," I said.

She stared at me, her nose running.

"I'll see you soon," I told her, then I backed past the aide standing in the doorway and made my way out of the room. I must have looked insane! What was I doing? I only made it to the foyer before I knew I couldn't leave. I couldn't leave her like this. I didn't know what to do, I just knew there had to be something better than dumping this hurt on her and running away. Claire knew Rose. She *knew* her mother. Did she remember everything? Or had Rose just shown up one day last week and told Claire who she was after all this time? What had happened? Whatever had happened, for however long it had been happening, Claire obviously cared about her mother. I thought I would burst with this realization. I paced for a minute as I chewed my thumbnail, then I sat down and tried to just breathe. Then I got up and paced again. When I thought I had calmed down sufficiently, I walked back to Room 13, where the young aide was just coming out. She smiled at me. "Oh, I just put your mom to bed, but she's not asleep yet."

"Thank you." I stepped into the dim lamp-lit room and found my mother lying on her side, facing the wall. I took a shaky breath and walked to the bed and sat down. Claire rolled over, again surprised to find *me* there. She'd been crying, which made me cry.

"I'm so sorry, Mom," I rasped, tears clogging my throat. "I could have done that better. I didn't mean to hurt you. I really *never* do. I just didn't realize—I'm sorry."

Her little hand found mine, forgiving me, which I did not deserve.

In this soft light, with her short hair, her tininess swallowed up by the queen-sized bed, Claire looked like a little girl, and I suddenly felt uncharacteristically protective of her. I swallowed with effort. "Rose's funeral is Monday, Mom. Do you want to come with me?"

Her good eye widened just slightly. Then she gave me one wet blink and a nod.

nineteen

I hate self-examination—that clawing feeling of disequilibrium brought on by not being able to hide from myself. I'd hurt her, again—I'd hurt Claire with my eternal clumsiness the way I always managed to do. What was wrong with me? She was my mother. It was true that other people's pain made me squeamish, but I was usually braced for it, prepared with acceptable reactions. Tonight, I had not considered that pain would enter the equation at all. How could I have gotten it so wrong?

When my phone rang, it took a moment for it to register, I was so lost in self-recrimination. By the time it did, Tyson had hung up and I'd missed his call, which was just as well, I supposed. Tyson Pierce suddenly seemed a few too many rungs ahead of me on the ladder of normal. I was so busy wallowing that I didn't even listen to his message.

Instead, I called Jaz. If anyone could talk me off this ledge it was her. She'd done it before. Many times.

She answered on the first ring. "Hey! I was just thinking about you."

"You were not," I said shakily.

"I was, too. I came in the bathroom to text you. I'm studying the most boring garbage with the most boring group of boring people at the most boring house you can possibly imagine. Save me, January!"

"I can't, I called so you can save me."

"What's going on? You have that tone. Has something happened?"

"Oh, Jaz..."

For the next twenty minutes, my best friend just listened and best-friended. Jasmine Holloway said all the right things, telling me she had all night, though I knew she didn't. I told her what had happened with Claire, and she agreed that it hadn't gone well but said at least it had ended softly. No platitudes from Jasmine. Ever.

I told her about my mother's journals and everything Oscar had said about my grandfather trying to manipulate Claire's engagement. I told her how my mother, *my mother*, had stood up to her parents and walked away. I told her about how she'd met my dad at a parade and flashed her phone number at him and that he'd called her, and they'd talked for hours and fallen in love. And Jaz, with all the wisdom of whom I needed her to be, said, "Is that killing you? Reading about this awesome woman you'd probably give anything to know…knowing it's, you know, Clairy?"

She'd nailed it. Of course she had.

"Jan…"

"It's doing something to me," I pushed out. "That's for sure."

"I'm sorry your life is so twisted," she said in the nicest way possible.

"Me, too. Thanks Jaz. Thanks for letting me vent. I think I'll live now."

"You will. Undoubtedly. And you'll rock doing it," she said. "You always do."

I laughed anemically. "I so miss you."

"Backatcha. Especially tonight. Did I mention I'm drowning in boring? Even the pizza is boring, January."

***

It was after ten when I got home. The van was gone, which meant Calvin was out on a pick-up, but the parking lot was empty, so the viewings had wrapped up. I went straight upstairs, hoping not to run into anyone. But I found Babi sitting at the kitchen table, reading a magazine and waiting for the kettle to sing. She looked up at me and smiled her funny smile.

"Kochanie, I have not to see you for so long time. How is my love?"

I stooped to kiss her downy head. "I'm good," I fibbed.

"You were to see our Claire?"

I nodded.

"Sit with me, my Janny. Tell for me how was your talk."

I sat and shook my head. "I blew it. I made her cry."

Babka's hand found mine, gave a squeeze. "Is sad news when the *matka* is die."

"I didn't know." I shrugged. "I didn't know she would be sad. I didn't realize she...would *care* after everything that's happened. Or even remember...How could I have gotten that so wrong?"

My great-grandmother patted my hand again. "Oh, Kochanie. Is hard to know what is Claire remembering."

"It was awful, Babi. Apparently, there's more in that broken little brain than I ever imagined. I so hope there are happy things floating around in there, too." I sighed. "I'm reading her journals, you know. Oscar Thibodeau gave them to me—and I was thinking on the way home tonight that it would be awesome if she could remember Dad, meeting Dad, talking with him. I just read that, actually. That would be such a happy memory for her. They met at a parade."

"This I know!" Babi waved her finger at me enthusiastically. "A Polish parade."

"Yep. In New York."

"Yes, yes. But is not the first time he see her."

I smiled.

"I was with my Tanek when we saw Claire play the Chopin. Never I did heard 'Valse Brillante' played so much the beautiful. She won the contest this night, but this is not where they meet. Was later when he see her at Pulaski Parade. Pulaski brought their paths to cross," Babi informed me. "Your father wrote to me a letter. He was mad for her from first moment he see her."

"My dad wrote you a letter? About my mom?"

"Yes, yes. I will find for you, Kochanie." She smiled. "Claire told me once that my Tanek saved for her life that day. She was to marry another, I think."

I nodded, mutely. "See, that would be something glorious to remember—Dad saving her."

The kettle whistled, and I was jolted from my wanderings. I retrieved it and poured the boiling water into Babi's mug. As her tea steeped, I cut her a lemon.

"Thank you, my Janny. You are good to old womans."

"Just you," I said, smiling. Then I kissed her head again. "I'm going to bed, Babi. Find that letter."

My room assaulted me. Again. It looked like the home of a hoarder, with a small footpath from the bed to the bathroom to the closet. And I'd be adding more boxes when I brought home the things from Claire's room. I groaned. I really had to find my own place.

I took a long shower, and as the water pelted my skin, I tried to let go of the evening. But it wasn't just the evening I was grappling with— it was everything. I didn't feel like me. This was my body, but somehow it felt like a completely different person had moved into it: the daughter of a real mother and the granddaughter of troubled grandparents, people who'd only been ideas to me before yesterday. And apparently, I'd come close to not even being *me* at all, according to the "arrangements made for my adoption before I even left the hospital." I felt like Gwyneth Paltrow in that old movie *Sliding Doors*. Except for a few well-timed decisions, I could have been another person entirely.

But I couldn't imagine who I'd have been if I wasn't the daughter of a man who had spoken to the dead like I did. Who would I have been if I hadn't been raised playing my mother's piano? Living here with a Holocaust survivor and grandparents who'd been willing to raise a child from the ground up when they'd long finished with all that years before? Who would I have been if not for all of them?

I dried my hair and pulled a tee shirt on over some loose shorts. I was exhausted and didn't want to think about it. But on my pillow, I found something that kept me up a little longer. It was a letter addressed to Rahela Duzinski, and it had a thirty-two-cent stamp on it. In the place where the return address should have been, it simply said Tanek.

I sat down on the edge of my bed and rubbed the yellowed envelope. My father had written this. I pulled out a single sheet of paper covered with his impeccable handwriting.

Dearest Busha,

Remember when I was little, and Athena Burgess had written me a love note and I wanted to die? Remember how you settled me down and told me about the magic that would come with the one God had already chosen for me? You said not to fear, that Athena was not my Serce. You probably had no idea how those words saved me, and the next ones, which were: When you meet her, Tanek, you will know. From the masses she will emerge with a smile that will reach deep inside you to light your soul. And you will know. I laughed then, I know I did, because I was 10, and I'd been saved from the fate of Athena Burgess. And to tell you the truth, Busha, not until today did I remember any of this. But I remember it now. And everything you said is true. I've seen her. Surrounded by the masses of nothing too impressive, her smile found me. Me. And it was like a blessing and a miracle.

Do you remember the beautiful girl who won the Chopin competition last week? It was her, Busha. It was her! She was at the Pulaski Day Parade in the city. With at least a hundred people separating us, we somehow kept finding each other, flirting with our eyes. She is absolutely gorgeous! I called her, Busha! And would you believe Claire Winston sounds as nice as she looks? She's smart and funny and a little bit wounded, somehow. She graduates next year from Yale, and she said she was in New York today, apparently just to meet me. We talked for three hours, and there is something about her that makes me want to know everything about her. It can't be an accident! I have to believe that God and Pulaski himself made it possible for me to find her. Oh, I sound like a girl, but I don't care. I found her, Busha! I found her—and I had to tell you.

Now be my little secret keeper, and we'll talk soon.

Love, Tanek

I smiled through my tears and read the note again. My father's enthusiasm bounced off the page, and it made me laugh that he'd shared it with Babi. He was smitten. I glanced over at the little photo of my parents staring back at me from the nightstand. *That* happiness started with *these* words. I slipped beneath the covers and propped myself against an extra pillow. I was tired but suddenly hungry for more of my mom's story, *their* story. I picked up her journal and flipped to the page where I'd left off—right after that long first conversation with my dad.

October 8, 1999

It's been a busy week. Class. Tutoring. Study. Practice. One upcoming performance. Getting to know one yummy Tanek Duzinski. It is amazing to me the things we talk about. He actually walked me through an entire embalming. Fascinating. We're shooting for a football game sometime soon. And sushi, of course.

Orphan update: No word from Mom and Dad. They have not called me. And they do not answer when I call them, which I have done more than I'm proud of. I honestly don't know what I'd say if they actually picked up. I think I just want to check the temperature. That's me in denial—no answer tells me exactly what the temperature is. I just didn't realize, I guess, that there would be an 'absolutely no contact' clause in my "Unwelcome Home." But it's sinking in. And this morning something felt different, something I didn't anticipate. The hurt is scabbing over with something much less tender. Today I'm just mad. Not paralyzingly so, but the kind that leaves the people you cared about vastly diminished by what they've done. Dad especially. He's always been difficult, a hard man who has forever straddled the fine line between being feared and revered. But as my dad, he'd always landed on the revered side. Until a week ago when he didn't. He probably has no idea what he's lost in me. My respect is no great forfeiture, I'm sure. I'm just a daughter, after all—'a decent consolation if he was never to be graced with sons'—he said that to Oscar once. I overheard it. So, maybe Dad and I had not far to fall to be this altered. But I am worried about Mom. I wrote her another letter today. We'll see if she answers.

October 12, 1999

Been thinking of something extreme. It's crossed my mind before, several times, and it's something I am seriously considering now, but I have to be sure of my motives. Considering what's happened with Dad, it's easy to think I'm just reacting, but I don't think I am since this is not the first time I've considered it. The Denton thing has simply clarified my decision—I think. I have a meeting with our attorney next week to discuss it. I don't think he will be happy—Oscar is a worrier. But looking my future in the eye and seeing what it could look like if I don't take control of it motivates me more every day. And this feels right. If my father has taught me anything, he's taught me self-reliance—accidentally, I'm sure. His aim has always been for me to depend upon him. The glaring lesson that has become all too clear, however, is this: some prison bars are made of gold.

October 22, 1999

I usually hate, hate, hate first dates, but that was before Tanek Duzinski made the trek to Connecticut so we could watch my Yale Bulldogs lose to Columbia, which they did in spectacular fashion. It's after midnight and he just left, and for some reason I just really want to stay awake until he gets home around 2, so I'm documenting.

Kick-off was at 5, and he was right on time at 4, but he showed up at the wrong condo, banging on the wrong door across the way. I quietly opened my door and watched him, and oh, my, I was a little surprised by the true extent of his gorgeousness. I'd forgotten how tall he is, how broad, how his hair kind of hangs past his collar. He looked pretty fantastic in his blue turtleneck and snug jeans, leather bomber and mirrored sunglasses. I just wanted to look at him for about an hour. But when he caught me staring, I grinned and told him it looked like he'd been stood up by my neighbor, Bevan Pruitt. And he looked so cute and sheepish and embarrassed. He thought I'd said Unit B, not D.

We had a few minutes, so he came in and had to give me a hard time about my tiny place. He told me I was lucky I was small. He's funny. He asked if I have a roommate and I told him I couldn't find one willing to bunk with my piano, but that I have a dog. This lie just slid out, and I was rather surprised by it. Of course, I don't have a dog, but apparently my superego was on red alert, reminding me I was alone with a strange man. A man who'd spent three weeks calling me and who now had driven all the way from New Jersey to take me to a football game. Since I couldn't really back the dog story up, I asked to see his wallet—another surprise that just fell out of me. I told him I knew it was a weird request, but that I'd heard that everything you need to know about a man could be found in his wallet. He was a good sport and let me have it, which earned him lots of extra points—like he needed extra points! Please, this guy is almost perfect!

His driver's license said Stasio Tanek Duzinski, 6'3 ½," 184 lbs. Brown eyes. Utterly gorgeous. It didn't say that part, but it should have. He had business cards from funeral supply places and casket manufacturers, and one from Mercedes who makes hearses—who knew? His business card had his name superimposed over the image of a very cool building and the name DUZINSKI FUNERALS. It had a great pic of Tanek in a white shirt and black blazer; his dark hair combed back, a kind, no-nonsense expression on his face. *Nice,* I said. (*Really nice,* I didn't say.) When I asked to keep one, he handed me two and told me I never knew when I might need his services. He was too cute.

When I spotted the ticket stubs from the Chopin competition where he'd seen me the first time, he shook his head and said they were his grandmother's. That made me laugh. I found a picture of his Busha, and she was so tiny next to him, she could have fit in his pocket. There were several pictures of his family—one with his dad on a fishing trip, one of him together with his mom and his sister—and they were all laughing. I don't know what it was, but I was fascinated by them all. There was one of a little boy with the Busha that he told me was him on his first day of school. It was adorable. And cursed, he said. Evidently if he didn't carry it always in his back pocket, his grandmother could not protect him. I thought that was too sweet. He pretended he couldn't remember what the curse was—sudden death, incurable rash? He's hilarious. I was putting everything back in his wallet when I found a note tucked between some cash, and I kind of looked for permission to keep snooping. He played along and I dug it out, pretending to wonder what it was: fan mail from a satisfied customer? He seemed ok, so I read it. It was the most gut-wrenching note from the parents of a little girl who had been murdered. They praised Tanek for his tender care of their daughter. I was so unexpectedly touched by their words that I almost cried. When I finally looked up at Tanek, everything had changed. This is a man who honestly fascinates me.

He said the words keep him grounded, help him remember there is more to death, than...death. We stared at each other for a long minute, and when I handed him his wallet, our fingers kind of touched and neither one of us pulled away. Not our eyes or our fingers. It was a weighty moment. *Good* weighty. He finally put his wallet in his pocket and broke the spell by asking for mine. Of course, I told him he was insane.

He shook his finger at me. It was cute. My oh-so-sorry Bulldogs lost excruciatingly in what we agreed was an awful game. And wouldn't you know, Timper's Sushi Garden was closed for renovation, so we walked by the much-ballyhooed Skull and Bones Society because Tanek was curious. But no creepy or world-hanging-in-the-balance vibe seemed to be going on there, so we decided to come back here and have blueberry pancakes. We ate damp because Tanek burned the bacon, which set off the smoke detector, which then triggered the ceiling sprinklers in the kitchen. Thank goodness the pancakes were warming in the oven because everything else was ruined. But somehow it didn't matter. At one point, Tanek choked on a laugh and actually told me it was completely obvious that I was falling in love with him. And I almost couldn't cough up my "No Way!" because I was laughing so hard. He called me a beautiful little liar—*a beautiful little liar*. I'll never tell him, but I kind of liked that! Tanek Duzinski is pretty brazen. Cute—severely cute—but pretty damned brazen. And I have to say, as first dates go, it was just about perfect.

I was laughing through my tears—laughing out loud. Reading this felt like I'd been right there with them on their first date. My parents' first date. I could see them, I could hear them, and they had never, *ever*, been so alive to me. My parents navigating the awkward first of many firsts. But the way my mother had written it, it didn't seem awkward at all—the wrong condo, the ceiling sprinklers, the wallet, their fingers touching and neither of them wanting to be the one to move away first…

And the note…I swallowed over a thick mass of sudden emotion. The note in my father's wallet, the note my mother had found and read and wept over, the note that had *kept my father grounded*. That note now belonged to me. My grandfather had given it to me. But now it had history. My mother had read it. My father had shared it with her. Somehow knowing all that bound me to my parents in a way I had never felt before.

After that first date, apparently my mom and dad had started meeting halfway between New Jersey and New Haven on Sunday nights—to squeeze in some face time and fall in love. And evidently, they'd both pretty much lived for that precious time together and made it last as long as possible. I thought of my lunch with Tyson and the way the time had just slipped away so naturally, and I thought I understood a bit of what they had gone through.

Reading between the lines, it seemed my dad had been falling fast and hard for my mom, and Claire had been falling too, but she had also been keeping Dad a little in the dark about her life.

I could understand that.

twenty

I was already awake when my alarm went off at 7:20 the next morning. I was in fact battling with myself on whether to stay in bed another hour and read more of the Claire and Tanek story—which I desperately wanted to do—or get up and face whatever Calvin had left for me downstairs. My work ethic won out, and it was a good thing since he'd left me two: Doreen Kim, a fifty-six-year-old female who'd suffered a seizure and drowned in her bathtub; and sixty-year-old Patrick Magellan, who'd died of a heart attack. The man was morbidly obese and would be more work than the hundred-thirty-pound Mrs. Kim. I'd start on her, then Tess and I would tackle our cardiac victim together later when my aunt decided to grace us with her presence.

By nine, I was pretty much right on track. I had just gotten Mrs. Kim washed and the chemicals were flowing when my phone pinged. I pulled off my gloves and dug my cell out of my scrub pocket. It was a text from Jaz:

> Just checking on you, Jans. Did you make it through the night.

> I'm good. Another successful talking off the ledge. Thx, my little life coach.

> That will be new shoes or lunch sometime soon—price of my services has gone up.

LOL. Deal. I vote shoes!

You so get me! Gotta run. Stay cool til after 10, when I get off.

No promises. Thx, Jaz

I so missed that girl. If I didn't have someone who knew what I was going through first-hand, at least I had someone who acted like she did and didn't judge me, and that was almost as good.

As I was about to stow my cell, I noticed the tiny phone icon in the corner of the screen was lit up, indicating I had a message. I suddenly remembered that Tyson had called last night, and I'd been too self-absorbed to call him back. I opened my voicemail and listened.

Hey, January—Just getting back to you about my uncle and your piano. He's got a truck available tomorrow afternoon, or he said he can help you next week. Just let me know what works so I can get back to him. This is Tyson, by the way. And it was great to see you today. I'd like to do more of that— seeing you. Talk to you soon.

He really was such a nice guy, I thought, remembering the way he'd surprised me with the white chocolate pretzels yesterday. That he'd even picked up that I'd liked them pushed him way ahead of most of the guys I'd been out with. That he'd "just happened to be in Patterson, near Krause's" had to be the sweetest lie I'd heard in a decade. And now, a delicate Steinway transport at his family discount tomorrow afternoon? Wait…tomorrow afternoon? That was *today.*

I pressed redial. On the second ring, I heard him say, "Hello, this is Tyson Pierce."

"Hey. Hey, Tyson, it's January."

"Oh, hey! I was hoping I'd hear from you. My uncle just called to see if we're on for today."

"I'm so sorry I didn't get back to you last night. I went to see my mom and it got late—anyway, I got your message. Today would be great, if he can still do it. Do you know what time?"

"Perfect. I'll let him know and find out. Then I'll text you his ETA."

"And he's really okay, you know, trekking to PA?"

"He is. Can you text me the address?"

"I will as soon as I hang up. I really appreciate this, Tyson."

"No problem. Happy to help. Is there anything else you need? I mean, what else can I do to help you?"

"Nothing! Believe me, this is fabulous. I so owe you!"

He laughed. "No, you don't. Text me that address, and I'll let you know when he'll be there."

"Thank you, Tyson!"

I texted him Rose's address on Moon Hollow Court, and within a few moments, he'd texted back that a truck would be there by 1:30. It was just after 9. In order to meet that truck in Chestnut Hill, I'd need to leave by 11:15 at the latest. I could finish Mrs. Kim, but Tess and Poppy would be on their own with Mr. Magellan. Calvin should be in and out, and he could lend some muscle if needed.

But best laid plans…

Seems Mrs. Kim had an ex-husband and children and a new husband and stepchildren plus a sister and a niece, which made for enough contention on all sides that virtually no decisions could be made. Thankfully, my job had been easy—no one disputed embalming. But the discussion of what to bury her in—and if, in fact, to bury her or cremate her, how to style her hair, arguments over the shade of nail polish, jewelry versus unadorned hands, should she wear her watch, wedding ring, etc.—became ludicrous in its vehemence. Grandy was exhausted, and I hated to leave her. But I did, with a naked, unfinished Doreen Kim awaiting final verdicts in my fridge because she had trusted her loved ones to be adults rather than make her own wishes known.

***

I was late due to an accident on the New Jersey turnpike. But thankfully, when I got to Moon Hollow Estates, there was no massive moving truck waiting at the curb. I breathed a little sigh of relief and got out of my car, grabbed the bundle of boxes from my trunk, and headed inside. Everything was as I had left it. Same emptiness. Same ghosts. Same untenable history. Same silence. I said hello to the portrait of my mother, the one softness in the cavernous entry, and walked up the stairs.

At Claire's door, I set down the boxes, fully intending to start filling them. But instead, I decided to explore a bit. Oscar Thibodeau had shown up the other night before I'd had a chance, so now I took advantage. It was so peaceful up here: soft and inviting, big windows filling the space with afternoon light, everything enhanced with creamy, soft colors. Next to my mom's room was an open area, a family room that looked like a hotel lobby with its overstuffed furniture, big pillows, and the flat-screen TV on the wall.

There was a guest bath attached to this family room, and just past that big room was an alcove that led to a set of double doors. I instinctively knew this was my grandmother's bedroom. I pushed the doors open and stepped inside. This room, too, was filled with sunlight, albeit less bright because the shutters were half-closed, but it was lovely, completely undisturbed and immaculate, as though no one had ever lived in it. It would have been less eerie if something, *anything*, had been out of place.

I stepped farther inside. It was pretty and monochromatic, the bedding the same ivory shade as the carpet, large cherry-wood furniture all around. Everything was high-end but a bit boring, like an elderly person had inhabited it—although that was an unfair stereotype on my part, since Babi's room was drenched in color and photographs and Polish pottery. Not so in here. The only actual color in this room was found in the paintings on the wall. I walked over to study them. There were two. One was of a little girl no more than three or four with a garland of tiny flowers in her light brown hair. She was dressed in a very frilly sea-foam-colored dress, asleep in a large leather wingback. Her head was leaning in the palm of one hand, like she'd gotten tired posing and the artist had just gone with it. It was so innocent, so vulnerable, that it made me ache. It had to be my mother. Next to it was a portrait of a beautiful woman with long, golden hair. She was looking down, clearly in love with the baby girl she was holding. Rose? Rose cradling my mom? Who else could it have been?

These two paintings were on the wall directly across from the bed, which meant they were the first and last things Rose would have seen each day. It didn't exactly jibe with the impression I'd been fed of her. There were no photographs of my grandfather, no evidence of him anywhere in here. There was a framed picture of my mother and Rose on the dresser—it looked like high school graduation—and an empty crystal vase. But aside from that one photo, the space was almost clinical in its perfection, seemingly washed clean of any personal touch. I stood there for a long moment, taking in the paintings again, the perfect draping of the bedspread, the folded throw on the footboard, the fresh vacuum tracks in the carpet.

The nightstands were massive, tall, curved wood polished to a high gleam. Three drawers. I walked over to the side where the throw lay and slid open the top drawer. I don't even know why. I suppose I was looking for proof of inhabitance, proof that someone actually lived— *had* lived—in this room. I found it: a planner, a Bible, and a small bottle of Excedrin PM. The planner was large, overstuffed, and had the initials RW monogrammed in the corner. I lifted it from the drawer and brazenly thumbed through it. It was a daily calendar, the pages filled with past and future appointments, events, and obligations.

There was a section for phone numbers and addresses, and there were sticky notes on top of notes. Tickets and bills and letters protruded, and the whole thing seemed about to burst its binding. Grandy had one that looked eerily similar—she called it her Life. As I flipped through the planner, it was clear that Rose's days had been very busy. Even the day she'd died, she'd had a hair appointment, a lunch with K.B., a meeting at the library, a fitting, and it looked like she had planned to attend a winetasting that night. I sat down on the bed, and on a whim, I flipped back to March. I swallowed hard when I saw it—my name penciled in on the 22nd at 8:00, the Spring Review. She'd saved the program and written in the margin, "January was exquisite—so like her mother, I ache." I blinked back a sudden tear. I was both disturbed and flattered, but mostly just sad. Farther back, I found evidence that she had attended a Christmas program in December where I'd performed and a competition I'd won back in October. "Rose was very impressed," Oscar had said. Had I seen her? Had I walked right past her and not even known it? I was lost in this thought when a letter protruding from the back of the planner caught my eye.

I probably would not have cared except I saw a tiny, sketched butterfly where the return address belonged. The envelope was old, the paper soft and tattered. I hesitated, feeling like a snoop and suddenly aware that what I was doing was probably wrong, like none of this was my business. And yet…there was no one here to object. There never would be again. And I was curious.

The letter was dated December 19, 2000, the paper fragile in the folds from its many readings:

Dear Mom,

It's me. I'm just checking in to wish you happy holidays, hoping you actually get this letter because I have important news. I wanted to tell you in person and even drove home last week, but your new housekeeper said you were in Savannah with the weaver's guild—I'm glad you're weaving again. Anyway, I hope you are well. I worry about you. I'd love to see you.

Mom, Tanek and I are having a baby. A baby, Mom. I'm going to be a mother, and you are going to be a grandmother. She's due five days after Christmas, less than two weeks away. I think that would be the perfect time for us to start over, don't you? Can't we please just close the door on everything else?

Mom, I'm pregnant, and I'm overwhelmed by the love I have for the baby girl swimming inside me. And her father. I'm ridiculously happy, Mom, and I so want you back in my life. I've missed you terribly. Dad will hold me forever in contempt, but not you. You and I have not destroyed each other beyond what can be forgiven. I know we haven't.

I need you, Mom. And you need me. I am the one person who knows what you've been through—and what it's cost you. Please take this one step back into my life. Tanek is such a good man. I promise that you'll regret not knowing him. But more than this, you'll regret not knowing our daughter. She is a miracle in the making—destined to be stunning, talented, strong-willed, bold, and brilliant. I adore her already and you will, too.

Let's start over, Mom. Please. New year. New life. New start. You don't want to miss this. Come be part of our family.

I love you.

Claire

My hands dropped to my lap, heavy with futility and wasted time. Twelve days. Twelve days after this letter had been written, everything went terribly and irrevocably wrong. I read it again and devoured my mother's descriptions: "… the love I have for the baby girl swimming inside me…And her father…I'm ridiculously happy, Mom…ridiculously happy. Ridiculously happy." My outrageous grandmother had gambled with time and lost. No wonder she was tormented. Torment was all she'd had left.

Such a waste. Rose's life all alone in this perfect house, sleeping in this perfect room, all ugliness dusted and vacuumed away, superior *everything* drawing the eye away from the brutal heartache printed on this faded, precious, almost twenty-three-year-old sheet of paper.

What a life. What a tragic life.

I replaced the planner in the nightstand but put the letter in my pocket. I straightened the bed where I'd sat to remove all trace that I'd been there, and then I walked out. I shut the door on my grandmother's sterile room with a heaviness in my chest and left the empty to the empty, making my way back through the big family room to my mother's room. I could not imagine my grandmother's life—living alone in all this luxurious sadness. It made me ache.

I picked up the boxes and pushed open the door to Claire's room where the contrast overwhelmed and the sadness for my grandmother deepened. This room was the exact opposite of Rose's. It felt so very lived in, so loved. It was not hard for me to imagine that my grandmother had found sanctuary here—a lovely place of memories. I looked around, drinking it all in again. But as my mother's room breathed its peace to me, the door chimes sounded.

I hurried down the stairs to the entry and peered thru the sidelight where I saw a large mover's truck in the drive, "Pierce and Sons Property Transport" emblazoned on the side in huge Cooper Black font. I opened the door. "Hi," I said to the tall middle-aged man sporting a baseball cap with the same logo.

"You January?" he asked.

"I am. Are you Tyson's uncle?"

"Yeah, this is my Uncle Nick," said Tyson, making his way up the walk with another man—a kid, really. "And this is my cousin Brandt."

I swallowed, unable to hide my honest surprise. "Hi...I didn't know you were..."

He shrugged, offering me a grin as he took in my jeans and peasant top. "It was a slow afternoon, so I took it off. I'm helping out." He made his way to the porch and held my eyes until his uncle cleared his throat.

"So, how 'bout you show me this piano, Miss January?" Nick Pierce chuckled.

"Right. It's in here."

I held the door open for them, then they followed me down the hall. "Nice place," Nick said.

"Right?" I agreed.

"Whose house is this again?" Tyson asked under his breath.

"My mom grew up here," I told him. "I never knew my grandparents; now they're both dead, and I've been gifted with my mom's piano."

"Nice."

We reached the double doors, and I stepped aside to let the movers pass. Tyson's uncle took in the enormous room, his gaze landing on the piano. He walked over, circled it, considered its dimensions. "What do you think?" he asked his son. "Probably back the way we came?"

Brandt Pierce had walked over to the French doors that led to the backyard. He stepped out and, after a moment, stepped back in. "Yeah. I think the access is better through the front."

The older Pierce nodded. "I'll grab the trolley and some more tarps. You start wrapping the legs."

"What do you want me to do?" Tyson asked.

"Help Brandt," his uncle said, then looked at me. "This shouldn't take too long, Miss January, and we'll be out of your hair. Did you decide where we're taking it?"

I handed him the address the realtor had given me, along with his payment that I'd been carrying in my back pocket.

"Alpine," he said. "From swanky to swanky."

"It's for a house staging. They said someone should be there all day."

Nick Pierce checked his watch. "We're a bit behind—there was a wreck on the turnpike—but we should make it by 4:30." Then he nodded and walked out of the room. I felt decidedly useless all of a sudden, with everyone else on task, so I said to no one in particular, "I'll be upstairs if you need anything."

Tyson looked up at me from the floor where he was wrapping the music shelf his cousin had just handed him. He seemed to want to say something, but he just lifted his eyebrows with a little grin.

As I passed through the entry and glanced at the portrait of my mother, I had the thought that she would probably like Tyson Pierce very much. Then I headed back upstairs and got to work.

Oscar had told me to take whatever I wanted, which felt strange. Picking through Claire's belongings made me feel a bit like a scavenger, even though I knew that my motives were purer than that. The items that most interested me had little value—the notebooks, the scrapbooks, the pictures taped to her mirror. Her music.

I started to gather those things onto her bed. Pieces of my mother's life would now be pieces of mine. I carefully lifted the painting from the wall, enchanted all over again by the little girl's bare feet dangling from the piano bench. Yes. This would hang in my daughter's bedroom—if I ever had a daughter. I leaned it next to the desk.

Attached to my mother's huge bathroom was a closet the size of a small bedroom. A rack the width of the room held nothing but dresses, many zipped in plastic. These were custom designs, formals, dresses that were surely what Claire had worn when she performed. They were gorgeous, some dated, naturally, but many were timeless. When I recognized the red gown from the portrait downstairs, I couldn't help myself. I slipped it off the hanger and held it up to me. Claire was shorter than I was, so the dress hit me above my ankles, but I knew if

I put it on, I would love it. I couldn't imagine I would ever wear it, but I carried it to the bed.

On the dresser, there was a long box made of inlaid wood. Inside were dozens of necklaces, rings, and bracelets—nothing too bold, which was more my style, but all of it was lovely. In a velvet pouch, I found a black ribbon with a single ruby hanging from it and a pair of matching earrings. My mother had worn these when she'd posed for the painting in the entry. I dropped the jewels back in the pouch and carried the wooden box to the bed. I also added the photograph of my laughing mom with her laughing mom to the pile.

It was a big pile; I had no idea where I'd put all of this when I got it home, but I'd figure it out. Sooner or later, I'd have a place of my own.

I filled a box with the rest of her journals, fingering each book, nearly getting lost once more in the story of her life. One day soon, I would start at the beginning of these diaries, and if it took me a year, I would read every page. I packed her sheet music and composition books. She had devoted an entire folder to my own personal foe, "Fantaisie Impromptu," and I was heartened to see detailed notes in faded red ink written in the same places I had always struggled. How could it be that Claire, *Claire,* and I could have this glorious piece of *tortured* music in common? Unbelievable.

I went through her desk drawers for other significant memorabilia. And it was all significant. I pulled the pictures from her mirror and added them to the box, then carefully wrapped an art deco lamp from her desk in newspaper.

On the window seat, I picked up an afghan that was puddled next to the book I'd seen there yesterday. It felt like cashmere and smelled faintly of patchouli, and I wondered whose scent it was, Rose's or Mom's. The book was open and lay face down, the dust jacket faded, and I couldn't fathom how long it had been lying there. *A Confederacy of Dunces.* Could this really have been the last book my mother was reading before she left that night? I doubted it. So was it Rose who'd been reading it? I couldn't quite see that, either. I picked up the novel. Whoever it was had gotten to chapter nine and was a bit of a ponderer, judging by the scribblings in the margins. I flipped to the front of the book and found a short note on the title page written in very precise script.

Claire,

Between these covers lies another installment of our must-read Pulitzers. This one is hilarious, and you so need to laugh, my friend. Trust me, it's destined to be a favorite. Interesting sad fact: The author killed himself 10 years before this story was published because no one wanted to publish it. There could be more to it than that, but either way, JKT lost faith in himself, which is very tragic and a great lesson to humanity: Never give up—true success could be just around the corner, give or take 10 years.

Enjoy Ignatius and praise JK Toole.

Love Monica

The note made me smile, wonder about JK Toole, and want to read this book. I fanned the pages, imagining my mother and her best friend discussing old literature and suicidal authors. As I did, a photo fell out from between the pages. It was a picture of two little girls, a postcard, I thought initially. But looking closer, I could see it was an actual photograph. The girls were maybe six or seven, both were in ballet togs, both were grinning. One was missing her two front teeth and the other had a black eye. I turned it over to find it covered with titles and what I assumed to be the year they had been read—*The Color Purple*—'91, *Angle of Repose*—'92, A *Confederacy of Dunces*—'93, *Executioner's Song*—'96, *The Optimist's Daughter*—'94, *The Reivers*—'94, *Ironweed*—'95. There were more, and if I had to guess, they were all Pulitzers. I looked closer at the picture, and this time it stung my eyes—one of these little girls had to be my mom, the same little girl who'd been scolded for not performing Liszt well enough, for walking on a rug and being ridiculous for liking science…and then, of course, for marrying the wrong man. The photo blurred beneath the sudden tears that had filled my eyes. *My poor mom!*

"January?"

I looked up, startled and embarrassed by my emotion.

"I didn't mean to scare you. I just wanted to let you know we're done," Tyson said. "We got it loaded."

"Oh," I sniffed, composing myself, and ran a hand under my eye. "That's...that's great. That was fast."

"You okay?"

"Yeah, of course," I answered a bit too ardently. "I'm fine." I blew out a breath. "I have a check for your uncle."

"You gave it to him. Downstairs."

"I did? Oh, that's right. Does he need anything else? I think I gave him the address."

Tyson walked over to me. "You did. He's all set. I just..." He shrugged. "I just came up to say goodbye. Are you sure you're okay?"

I nodded away his concern. "Absolutely." I waved the picture of the ballerinas in his direction. "Just lots of ghosts here," I sniffed. "But it's all good. You don't know how much I appreciate this." He was wearing a snug black tee shirt, and I reached over and patted his chest. "I need to buy you lunch or something. And your uncle. And your cousin."

Tyson smiled. "No, you don't—not them, anyway. I'm just glad it worked out." Then on cue, a horn blared from the driveway. Tyson glanced at the window, then back at me. "I'd better go."

I offered an exaggerated smile. "I'll let the realtor know you're on your way. Thanks again." I sniffed and nodded.

The horn blared again, and Tyson sighed, seeming to want to stay. But instead, he gave me a reluctant good-bye and walked out.

I listened to his footfalls on the stairs, the sound of the front door open, took a settling breath and pulled out my phone. When the girl from Piedmont Properties answered, I coughed away my leftover emotion and informed her that my new piano would be arriving at the address in Alpine by 4:30. Then I asked if I could come by and check on it later tonight.

The nasally woman said they would be setting up for the open house and someone would be there until at least nine. I was welcome to drop by.

"Thank you," I said, watching from the window as the massive Pierce and Sons moving truck pulled out of the neighborhood. It felt so odd to stand in my mother's old bedroom, watching a truck drive away with a Steinway that now belonged to me, and a guy I thought I could grow feelings for but shouldn't because he'd come along at the exact same time as the piano, which had introduced serious upheaval into my otherwise rather mundane existence. I rubbed my forehead with the side of my wrist.

I was still holding the picture of the little ballerinas. I took another look at them and turned the photo over to the inventory of Pulitzers. Per the crude tally, *A Confederacy of Dunces* had been read in 1993. Finding it now on the window seat meant...what? Had Rose come in here to be near my mother's things, to read her books, listen to her music? Breathe her scent from a blanket Claire had slept with? Feel badly that her only daughter had a daughter that she'd never gotten to know? Why did I care? Why was that depressing thought the one that suddenly overwhelmed me? I pulled the letter my mother had written to Rose from my pocket, and through my emotion, I read it again. Had she even considered answering? Had my grandmother even for a moment thought of *a granddaughter* with any trace of lovely excitement? Had she cared at all? My hurt made me so angry that my breath shuddered out of me, and of course, there were tears; I was so sick of myself that I wanted to scream. And then I *did* scream because I had not heard Tyson walk back up the stairs, and when I turned to find him standing in the doorway again, it scared me. I involuntarily dropped the letter and the picture as I jumped.

"I—I'm sorry," he said, looking apologetic and truly unsure of himself. "I didn't mean to scare you—again—but I was worried about you and...I couldn't leave you. Not like this."

I stared at him, feeling completely exposed and weakened by it and irritated that I *was* weakened. " *What are you doing?* "

He took a tentative step into the room, but stopped, shaking his head. "I'll leave if you want me to, but it didn't seem right. I...you don't seem okay."

"I'm fine," I whimpered.

"Okay. But you don't seem fine. You seem pretty *unfine.* "

I pushed out a breath to regroup and ran a hand through my hair. "I'm...you're sweet. I'm a little unfine, but I'm okay." I picked up the things I'd dropped, then lifted my chin and did my best to not look so pathetic.

He stared at me. "Look, I know you're going through something," he said. "And I was just worried."

"I am. Going through something. But it has nothing to do with you."

Tyson raked his hair back with both hands but stayed where he was, looking at me from the doorway. He seemed very torn, uncertain. "I don't know what to do here, January," he finally said. "You're like this exotic bird who's crashed into a plate-glass window, and it's knocked the wind out of you. I can see you're a mess, and I just...I want to help you, but I don't know if you want help. Maybe you just need a friend, I don't know—I just want to get to know you. I don't care that all this—whatever all *this* is—is happening in your life. But I'm afraid if I make a wrong move or get too close or say too much, I'll scare you away and I don't want to do that."

I shook my head and tried to smile. "It's more complicated than that, Tyson. This is my life—this didn't just *happen* to me—it *is* me. Some of the details are new, but this is my life." I waved my arm. "This was my mother's bedroom, and I never knew it because I never knew her—or who she was before—and I never knew her because I never wanted to." I lifted a brow in a bit of a challenge, then held out the letter I was holding. "She wrote this to my grandmother about me— my *grandmother*—who never wanted to know me because her daughter married the wrong guy. And I'm no better. I never wanted to know her either." I didn't mean to sound glib but knew that I did. I shook my head. "Tyson, my life is one big guilt trip, which you somehow—at first glance—thought seemed interesting. It's not. Believe me, it really isn't."

His brows came together, and for a moment he seemed to be weighing his thoughts.

"January, do you think you're the only one who's ever lived with guilt? You don't own that mountain. I have a condo there."

I stared at him.

"I know I don't have the whole picture," he said. "But I think I've figured out the gist: The most horrible thing that could possibly happen happened the night you were born, and you think that's somehow your fault. But not really, because you're smart enough to know better, but that really doesn't change the way you feel—"

"Please be quiet," I said. "You don't know me, Tyson."

He looked at me. "Really? Which part do I have wrong?"

"You don't know me!"

"I don't know you," he said evenly. "But what I do know is that you have this thing going on with your mom. And now here you are, pushing the world away so you can do penance on the guilt hill because you don't love her enough or you don't know *how* to love her enough or you don't want to love her enough, or you're mad because she's her and you never loved her enough. Am I getting close?"

Every word stung. "You can't talk to me this way!" I croaked. "You don't know me!"

"And it doesn't look like you're going to give me the chance. But I know this story, January. I've lived this story. I had a sister I didn't know how to love enough. I know guilt. I know the mind games it plays. And you're right; it's not one bit interesting. But it can sure eat away all the interesting parts of you."

I felt slapped by his words. I couldn't move. I just shut my mouth and felt my heart start to pound and my face start to tingle as Tyson Pierce stared at me for a long, deafening moment. Then he walked away. He just turned and walked away. I heard him walk down the stairs, and I heard the front door open and close. And still, I couldn't move.

twenty-one

He wasn't wrong. But how could he have spoken to me that way? How dare Tyson Pierce speak such awful truth to me? That man had seen me—seen *into* me—and I *hated* that I had been seen. How did I let that happen?

I slumped onto the window seat and fell into my own lap, pummeled and humiliated replaying his terrible words: "...you don't love her enough...you're mad because she's her...you never loved her enough...never loved her enough...never enough..." It was unbearable.

I don't know how long I sat folded in on myself, but I was eventually saved from the wretchedness when my phone rang. I didn't answer it, but when it stopped ringing, I listened to Grandy's message. The sound of her voice like a life-preserver, even if all she wanted was some lost paperwork.

I dragged myself upright and took some deep breaths, wiped my nose, and rubbed my scratchy eyes. Then I splashed my face with cold water in my mother's palatial bathroom. I looked like hell, and I was making myself sick obsessing about how unhinged Tyson Pierce must have thought I was. I tried to hate him a little for making me feel so bad. But how could I do that when he'd admitted something just as rough about himself?

It was a moot point anyway; I was never going to see him again, which was probably better for all egos concerned. Especially mine.

This is what I told myself as I got on with gathering my mother's books—some of them, anyway. I knew I couldn't take them all, but I suddenly very much wanted the ones listed on the back of the photo I'd found. It was a good distraction. An excellent distraction that kept my hands busy and my mind focused.

I'd been at my task a few minutes when the chimes rang. I had no intention of answering the door since I was such a mess and not in the mood to talk to anyone. But the chimes sounded again and then again, and I realized my car in the driveway made it clear that I was there, so I reluctantly made my way downstairs, swiping the lingering evidence of my bad day off my face as I went. It was probably Oscar.

But it wasn't.

When I opened Rose's massive door, I was surprised to find—leaning against the frame on an outstretched arm, looking both sheepish as well as commanding—Tyson Pierce. He didn't smile. In fact, he looked decidedly nervous. "Hi, January."

"Hi."

"This is awkward…" he said.

I didn't say anything.

He drew a dramatic breath. "Funny story…My phone is in my uncle's truck…and it seems I'm two hours from where I live."

I lifted a brow. "That's not good."

"No."

"What have you been doing all this time?"

He rubbed his forehead. "I've been sitting on this porch trying to get the courage to knock on this door and beg for a ride home."

I arched a brow. "That took some courage, huh?"

"You have no idea…"

We stared at each other for a long, moment. Then I opened the door wider with a weary smile and he walked into the foyer, where we stood, again awkwardly sizing each other up.

"You've been crying," he finally said.

I nodded. "I'm kind of a mess."

"I'm so sorry," he said kindly. "I didn't mean to make things worse for you."

I shrugged. "You weren't wrong. The truth is just hard to hear sometimes."

"Do you hate me?" he said.

"I tried for a minute," I told him. "But… maybe a little."

Small smile.

Eyeing him, I said, "What about you? Did you come to your senses about me?"

He slowly shook his head. "I told you, January, I like you. The *something big* going on in your life right now doesn't scare me. I think it scares you, though, so I just don't know if you—and I understand if you don't…I just don't know how to do this. Tell me what to do so I don't mess this up." He took in a deep breath, let it out. "Tell me what to do."

I swallowed and didn't move. Neither of us moved. For a long moment we just looked at each other as we stood on this…this *edge.* Then I took the two steps that separated us, shedding what was left, if anything, of pretense—I was too drained, too tired to hide. I looked up at him. "Do you think for now I could just…do this for a minute?" I said, resting my head against his warm neck.

"Absolutely," he said softly, his arms coming around me. "Absolutely."

It felt strangely safe to be standing here so close to this man when less than twenty minutes ago, I'd been completely horrified that he'd *seen* me. But apparently, there was something intensely sanctifying about my worst shame being understood, and I sank into it, almost weeping with relief as he gently stroked my back.

I don't know how long we stood there—long enough, I suppose, that it felt all right to ask him to tell me his worst guilt story. I asked this while still nestling into his chest, and Tyson didn't hesitate, but I could swear I felt his heart speed up. "They all feel like the worst," he said softly. "Now that Ash is dead."

"Tell me anyway…please."

He took a breath and ran a hand down the back of my hair. "One time I blamed her when an antique teapot got broken," he said a bit shakily. "It was my grandmother's grandmother's—so my great-great-grandmother. My friend broke it, but I told Mom that Ash bumped into the hutch and knocked it over…"

"How old were you?"

"Twelve."

"Did anyone ever find out the truth?"

"I finally told them, when I couldn't stand it another minute."

I lifted my head from Tyson's chest and met his eyes. There was a story there that I wanted to know. I took his hand and tugged him to the stairs. "I want to hear this."

He sat down by my side, our thighs touching, and looked over at me. "I blamed Ash for the teapot so my friend wouldn't get in trouble. So, basically, I sacrificed my disabled sister to stay in good standing with the guys I hung out with. It was my first true moral dilemma. I knew it was a lie, they knew it was a lie. And Ash knew it was a lie. My friends didn't care because they were twelve, you know, and in their words, Ash was *retarded*, so what was the big deal? Ash..." His gaze slid away from mine. "I betrayed her, and she knew it, but she got so snotty at being blamed that she *seemed* guilty. My grandma was sad because the teapot was an heirloom, but she didn't want to be mad at Ash, because Ash was Ash. But Ash was being a butt because she was hurt." Tyson shook his head. "It was such a mess. And I just floated under the radar, feeling awful and hoping it would all just go away. But the whole thing made me sick. Literally. The guilt was making me throw up. I couldn't eat. And at school, trying to pretend with my friends that everything was cool when everything wasn't—I was going crazy. I thought I was going crazy."

"What did you do?"

"Well, it came down to running away, killing myself, or telling my dad."

"Tyson—"

"And I was too scared to run away and too chicken to kill myself. So, one day I got up early and hid in the car so I'd be there when Dad left for work. And when he got on the freeway and couldn't pull over and strangle me, I popped up from the back seat and told him I had something to tell him."

I stifled a laugh. "Oh, my gosh!"

"Yep. Nearly gave the old man a heart attack *and* almost caused a commuter pileup."

"So, what happened?"

Tyson shook his head, and I watched his eyes mist at the memory. "I told him what I'd done, and he listened. Didn't say much until we got to his office."

"Was he mad?"

"Oh, yeah. It was brutal." Tyson looked over at me. "But after he was done yelling, he said, 'I always knew you were a good kid, Ty. And I still know it, because only good kids feel this much guilt.'"

"Ooohh…" I crooned. "That's really nice."

Tyson sighed. "Yep. Very much my dad's style. Utterly destroy, then utterly save."

I smiled. "So, you were forgiven."

"Oh, I had to earn it—and lose a few friends along the way. My dad helped me fix the teapot with this gold stuff—it's a Japanese thing. They believe that when you fix broken things, you make them more valuable for the effort, or something like that. So that's what I did— had to work Saturdays for my dad to earn the money for the gold clay. Then I told my mom and Grandma what really happened. I told Ash I was sorry I'd lied about her and bought her a bunch of candy. And I told Eric Philpot he was a jerk and I didn't want to be his friend anymore. And ultimately, I stopped throwing up."

I chuckled. "Did she forgive you? Ashley?"

He nodded. "She did. She always did. You'd be surprised at the healing power of candy." He almost—but not quite—laughed.

I bit my lip, thinking about my mom and how she was the same way. "It must be a trait of the people we're not good at loving," I sniffed. "They just keep forgiving us."

Tyson nodded, then nudged me a little with his shoulder, and we were quiet for a long moment.

I looked over at him. "Thank you," I finally said.

"For what? Showing you what a jerk I could be?"

"Something like that."

"Not my finest moment. But…"

I studied him, studying me. We were so close I could feel his warm breath on my face. I so appreciated his *nakedness*, and his seeming acceptance of mine—lesions, warts, cried-off make-up, and all. It was a bit intoxicating.

I'm not sure who leaned in first. I think it might have been me. I do know that as first kisses go, it was just about perfect: soft, tender, tentative, and then not tentative at all. It was like something exploded between us then, something that, if I'm honest, might have been simmering since the moment we met. It was a deliciously intense kiss that eventually morphed into something soft again, deeper and slower, and we lingered in it for a long time.

Long enough that for a few moments on my dead grandmother's stairs, everything just fell away. All the old and new, the sad and wrong and broken pieces of my strange life just fell away.

twenty-two

Had I meant to do that? Was that what I wanted? Kissing changed everything. Lips on lips, tongues tonguing, senses on fire, emotions emoting. Mine, anyway. I've done a little of it in my two decades, but this kiss felt like an official *Let me unlock the door and grant you entrance into my bedraggled life.* Had I really just done that?

Tyson looked at me looking at him. It was a great kiss, no denying that. I got brave and spoke first. "You're right," I said. "I'm a bit of a train wreck at the moment. Obviously. Are you sure you want to be here? *Here?*"

His face was inches from mine. "Do I *look* like I want to be anywhere else?"

I tried for a smile, but it just made my eyes sting.

"January," he said softly. "I don't care that your life is your life right now. If you're okay with me in it, I want to be here. Your call."

I believed him. I *wanted* to believe him. If he saw me as a weird, exotic bird lying in a twisted heap and was still somehow drawn to me, how could I not be okay with that? "I *will* get through all this," I whispered.

"I don't doubt it for a minute."

"How 'bout we take it a day at a time?" I said.

"I'm good with that."

I nodded. "I think I am, too."

***

As pre-payment for his ride home, Tyson helped me load boxes for the rest of the afternoon. Totally his idea, he was an insistent negotiator, which made me laugh…and feel normal again. In fact, it seemed Tyson had a knack for diffusing my discomfort, and I appreciated it more than I let on. After our emotional fall through the ice, loading books and music into boxes and talking nonstop while we did it was like being able to breathe again. It was lovely.

Tyson asked a lot of questions about Claire, and I was generous with details, to the extent that I knew them. The story I'd started at lunch a few days ago, I brought up to date with what else I'd learned, namely, how her dad had tried to marry her off to a guy she didn't love, and how refusing to do it had pretty much ended their relationship. I told him how Claire had met my dad, and how her parents had hated him because he was Polish.

"That's so cold," he said. "That's…were they clinically insane?"

"Apparently," I said, stacking books.

"Cool about your parents, though."

"Yes. Very," I agreed.

"Guess how my parents met?"

I looked up at him and lifted a brow.

"My mom ran over my dad's briefcase."

"What?"

"True story," Tyson grinned. "It was my dad's first day at his first real job, right out of college. He set his briefcase down to get something out of the back seat of his car, Mom pulled in the parking place next to his and—splat."

I laughed.

"The best part: the only thing in that sucker was a ham sandwich and a thermos of milk that exploded on impact."

I laughed harder, and it felt delicious.

"You have no idea how we've tortured my dad with that—big, empty, self-important briefcase with nothing in it but a ham sandwich and milk. My mom felt so sorry for him she asked him out. That's love."

"That is so sweet!" I smiled, thinking of Tyson's mother, the note she'd written me, and how kind she had been when I'd met her the day of Ashley's funeral. "I like your mom," I told Tyson.

"She likes you, too." He grinned.

The afternoon slipped by comfortably, with no more awkwardness thanks to Tyson's skill at calming my waters. He listened and shared, was interested as well as interesting. He was remarkably easy to be with, which was a gift.

When we got hungry, we ate water crackers with imported cheese, olives, and tiny corn we found in Rose's pantry and chased it all down with fancy French lemon sorbet we found in her freezer. I took him on the grand tour of the house and introduced him to the grandparents and, of course, to the beautiful girl my mother had been. He was understandably awestruck.

The last thing we did was go through Claire's closet, where Tyson helped me pick out something funeral-worthy for her to wear to Rose's upcoming service. My mother only owned one dress and that was a blue flowery number Grandy had made her wear to Tess's wedding two years ago. Fortunately, her twenty-five-year-old wardrobe was built on classics—undoubtedly thanks to Rose. We found a black short-sleeve dress that I was sure would still fit her and a white sweater. Timeless. Perfect for a funeral.

Tyson didn't believe Claire really had just one dress, but it was true—she had skirts, the kind that were easy to step into and pull up, but no dresses. My mother simply had no need or desire for frills. Truth be told, she would be utterly content if nothing she wore ever had to be zipped, buttoned, or accessorized at all. Claire abhorred fuss of any kind—a far cry from the girl she'd been, considering the dozens of formals in plastic hanging in her dressing-room-sized closet. And she didn't like much help. My mother was as independent as she could successfully manage to be—slip-on shoes, no laces, short hair she could push around with her hands, no makeup because she couldn't do that by herself. Although for an occasion such as her mother's funeral, she might let Grandy fix her up.

***

It was almost nine when Tyson and I pulled up to what looked like a hotel in the suburb of Alpine. I checked the address to be sure, then noticed the Piedmont Property logo on the car in the driveway. "This is it," I said, cutting the engine.

The neighborhood looked a little like Moon Hollow Court in Chestnut Hill, but less spread out and not gated. This massive Tudor was the crown jewel of the cul-de-sac with its impeccable grounds, spotlights illuminating the shrubs, a tiled walk rimmed with ornate pots overflowing with petunias and daylilies. I looked over at Tyson. "Not bad," he said.

We walked up the steps and knocked, but the door was open, and no one seemed to be around. "Hello," I shouted as we walked in. "Hello!"

A woman hurried into the room, flustered. "We're not showing the property until tomorrow, but—"

"No, no, I just came by—I'm January Duzinski. I came to check on my Steinway."

"I beg your pardon?"

Tyson cleared his throat. "We're here to make sure it was delivered safely and intact this afternoon. The Steinway concert grand? My company should have been here by 4:30."

Suddenly the light dawned in the woman's eyes. "The *piano*, yes," she said with relief. "I didn't know what you were talking about, but yes, it's here." She started walking, so we followed. "It's stunning, by the way."

She led us to the round turret room, rimmed in floor-length windows. The centerpiece, naturally, was Claire's Steinway, which glistened under an ornate chandelier.

"Wow," Tyson breathed.

"That looks amazing," I said over him. "May I?" I asked, not waiting for permission. I pressed a key, and the note pierced the room. I couldn't help myself; I sat down and played the first thing that came to mind, which was Debussy's, "Arabesque." I played it slowly, savored my mastery of the harmonic favorite—especially on this impeccable instrument. The room embraced the melody and sang it back with its perfect acoustics. The sound drenched me in loveliness and threatened to carry me away. But after a few moments, I caught myself when I glanced up to see the twin expressions of wonder on my small audience. I lifted my hands self-consciously and stood up. "Well, it looks like it made it one piece," I said, pulling down the fallboard. "And she sounds fine. Thank you so much for letting us drop by."

The woman's hand was on her collar bone. "Thank *you*. We'll take good care of it."

As we walked out, Tyson tugged on my hand until I looked over at him, then he said, "Who *are* you?"

It made me smile.

I dropped Tyson off at his office, which was where he'd left his car, and of course, our good-bye threatened to be awkward because second kisses don't really know their place yet. Somehow, they can seem more fraught with familiarity or expectation—but are they really? Or was I just overthinking? Apparently, I was, because Tyson simply leaned over and softly touched my lips with his in a perfectly unassuming way. He then backed up a few inches and asked me if I was all right. I knew instinctively that he wasn't asking about the kiss—or us or what had happened between us. He seemed truly to want to know how I was.

I looked at him for a long moment. "I honestly don't know how to answer that," I finally said. "But I can say that being with you today helped. So, thank you."

He smiled. "Anything I can do for you tomorrow…or the next day, or the day after that?"

I chuckled and leaned my forehead into his chin. "Tempting, but probably not. I'm headed back to Chestnut Hill tomorrow to actually meet my grandmother." I gazed back up at him and lifted a brow. "That should be interesting," I said, suddenly feeling exhausted because I had agreed to make the two-hour trek yet again to meet Oscar Thibodeau at the funeral home.

"What is that? Like three times this week?" Tyson said.

I nodded. "I wasn't totally planning on *today*." I smiled. "But having that piano taken care of is a huge relief. So, again, thank you, Tyson. For *everything*."

"I'm glad I could help." He sighed. "Well, I'd better…"

"Yeah…"

He looked at me.

I looked at him.

Then I tugged on his collar, and he kissed me one more time.

***

It wasn't terribly late when I pulled into Duzy House, which probably explained the still half-filled parking lot. It had been Teagan Lowe's viewing tonight, and the family had warned Poppy that it would be a large gathering—they hadn't embellished the turnout, apparently. I imagined lots of highschool kids. The van was in the garage, which was a good omen, so I headed downstairs to check the whiteboard. If there were things to be done, I wanted to do them before I went to bed since I was headed back to Pennsylvania in the morning.

But the death gods were smiling on me for the moment: we were caught up. No new deliveries since our two this morning, and Mrs. Kim's family must have reached a consensus, because she was dressed, and her hair was styled. No nail polish, but she was wearing her watch.

Mr. Magellan was embalmed. He'd been shaved, his hair gelled into a businessman's respectability. Tess was good. He wasn't dressed—that was going to require some help, maybe the pulleys—but there was an enormous navy-blue suit hanging on the door at the ready. Tucked into the breast pocket was a picture of our deceased, along with a pair of Oakley sunglasses. He'd been a happy man if the picture was any indication—his smile was all teeth. The sunnies were evidently his signature, to be worn for his viewing. He'd look very sharp, I thought. "I wish I could have known you, Mr. Magellan," I said as I shut the fridge door.

Upstairs, since it was quiet, I grabbed a sleeve of Ritz crackers and a bottle of water and headed to my room. I was tired, but not the kind that sleep cures, not necessarily a *tired* tired, just full-of-new-things tired. I thought of Tyson and smiled. I thought of how easy he'd been to be with, to laugh with, despite everything. I thought of the briefcase with just a ham sandwich in it that had led to a lifetime together—that had led to Tyson. I thought of my mom holding her phone number high above her head and my dad writing it in his palm and then calling her on the worst day of her life to start something that had led to me.

Mom's journal was under my pillow exactly where I'd left it this morning. My parents had been going out for a little while, and my dad was falling in love. It seemed obvious from her entries that she felt the same about him. But she was holding back—she hadn't told him about her *orphan status* yet. I got into my pajamas and slid into bed. Then I opened the book.

November 14, 1999

Tanek Duzinski is getting very hard to resist. Even for a rational, goal-oriented, single-minded girl like me—preoccupation with family drama and orphan status notwithstanding. He's persistent but not annoying and patient but not needy, and thankfully he's as busy as I am. So, we're getting to know each other the only way we can: slowly through late-night phone calls and email, and for the last 3 Sundays, dinner at the Compton Grille in Stamford—halfway between us. It's kind of a miracle that we can manage even that.

Tanek does almost all of the embalming and trauma reconstruction for his mortuary, and 18-hour stints are not uncommon. He's a slave to the Reaper—his words. My dual degrees, performing schedule, tutoring, and Cliburn prep are keeping me crazy. Oh, and of course, I'm looking for a job, since Dad cancelled my Mastercard. I knew that was coming. This marks my 6th week in exile. (Side note: still haven't heard from Mom—6 letters mailed, none answered.) I applied at the Foundry Music Company since I spend so much time there already.

Anyway, because of logistics and time and the sheer need to look at each other, T and I sort of live for Sunday nights. And because of that, I've completely put off broaching the meat of my life. It's all so unseemly that I've just ignored it. I don't know what I was thinking. Yes, I do. I was thinking I was never going to have feelings strong enough for this man that would require me to expose my lineage to him.

And then when I did, it turned into a fight—kind of a fight. Tanek doesn't really fight, which is annoying because I like a little heat in a heated discussion. Anyway, tonight was the night—I couldn't put it off any longer. I told him I needed to tell him about my family. I wasn't smiling, but he was, and it bothered me because I needed him to be serious. I told him we couldn't get any closer without him knowing the screwed-up mess I came from, and I didn't want him to like me under false pretenses. I'm not sure why, but that made him laugh, which annoyed me.

I'd been thinking about this conversation a lot and I wanted to get it right, but he thought I was joking around. He finally got serious and asked me what I was talking about, and as I was trying to figure out where to start, he asked me to tell him the worst thing he should know about me. I'm so full of myself, I drew a complete blank, which was embarrassing. He laughed, and it made me mad all over again. But when I couldn't come up with anything about me, he wanted to know the worst thing about my dad. I almost started to cry, which finally got his attention.

I didn't have a clue where to begin, but once I started spewing, I didn't stop until I'd told him the whole ugly story of Dad's party, Denton, the proposal, my refusal, and being disowned for it, though I told him I'm still hoping that wasn't entirely real. Tanek's smirk was replaced with something worse: pity.

I got angry all over again, but I didn't know at whom exactly—T for feeling sorry for me, which I hate, Dad for putting me in a position to be felt sorry for, or myself for exposing my sorry life in the first place. I got stupidly weepy. But I was on a roll. I whimpered my way through telling him about all the letters I'd written since that awful night and that I hadn't gotten one in return. And that next week was Thanksgiving, and I wasn't going home and...blah blah blah.

Pathetic! At that point I told him I needed a moment. And I went out and sat in my car and hated everything about myself and the last ten minutes but especially Dad for making me have to explain it all in the first place. T came out and asked me if we were fighting, and I said I thought we should be. And he said he wasn't really good at fighting, but he'd give it a try if I wanted to—and that made me smile and then it made me cry.

I told him this was my bloodline and that I'd understand if he never called me again. He didn't bat an eye. So, almost like I was trying to push him away, I vomited up even grittier details about how Dad doesn't hesitate to hurt people he can't bring into compliance—wife and daughter included. And quite possibly boyfriends of said daughter.

T said he wasn't afraid of my dad. He said it all macho, and I know I rolled my eyes because he has no idea. But he got very in my face, and told me again that he wasn't afraid, but if I was afraid because Daddy wouldn't be pleased about me liking T...that was different. He said that was my deal. It was humiliating because he was right.

I am afraid of Dad. But only because he could hurt T.

Tanek switched gears to Mom, but by then I was done talking. I think I just apologized for being bad company and told him I wanted to leave. The truth was my family drama had left me feeling very sorry for myself and ashamed of them. And it's Thanksgiving, and I'm dangling outside of everything I've ever known, and I don't like it.

I think T must have figured out that's what I was feeling, because when it was time to go, he told me he wanted me to come to his house for Thanksgiving. How pitiful is that? Not the invitation, which was lovely, but the fact that I needed an invitation—that was just sad! I told him no. Absolutely not. He said yes, absolutely yes. He said, "Please come, my family thinks I've made you up." That made me laugh. I had to argue. But every time I opened my mouth, he kissed it, so he was pretty persuasive. He even issued me a challenge: He told me if I came, I would be in love with him by the time I left—in fact, he dared me not to be. I told him he should give up the dead and sell used cars. Then I kissed him quickly and drove away before he could see me start to cry again. I'm so sick of myself!

Thanksgiving in Wallington, New Jersey, with Tanek and his family...as lovely as that sounds, I don't think it's going to happen.

twenty-three

I fell asleep before I found out what Claire actually did that Thanksgiving. And though I wanted nothing more than to sit in bed and read once I woke up, my day had other plans for me. It started with company breakfast, which I actually forgot about, but because I was fully awake and dressed when I walked into the kitchen, I looked like I'd remembered.

"Good, Janny. You remembered," my grandfather announced. "I thought with everything you had going on yesterday, you might have forgotten."

I swallowed, thought of Tyson and the way my life had taken such an unexpected side trip yesterday. What did Poppy know? "What?" I stuttered.

"The piano. You did get that taken care of, right? What did you think I was talking about?" my grandfather said, his eyes narrowing.

"Nothing. Yes—all taken care of. And of course, I remembered *company breakfast*—it's on my calendar in big red letters," I fibbed, pouring myself some juice and avoiding Poppy's confused stare.

Once a month, Poppy holds what he calls The Company Breakfast. He makes pancakes and eggs and invites Calvin. Tess is supposed to be there, and she is about half the time—I waved to her across the table. Sometimes our accountant Mr. Dennison comes to tell us we're doing a bang-up death business or, if it's been a lean month, to advertise more. Babi's always there—I sat down next to her now and kissed her cheek—and Grandy, of course. Poppy usually talks about things that have gone well that month, what we can do to improve, if we're acquiring a new piece of equipment, that kind of thing. Sometimes casket people come to present their latest and greatest, sometimes chemical people come to do the same. But there were no salesmen today. Just my apron-wearing, spatula-wielding Poppy, who opened with how much he appreciated us and wanting to know if we had any concerns.

It was the opening Grandy had been waiting for. "Stas," she said, "I've placed an ad for a part-time funeral director. Don't be mad."

Poppy groaned.

"Good! We have to be thinking about this," Tess chimed in. "I *will* be taking some time off with the baby, and when I come back, I'm probably…I'm thinking twenty hours a week will be plenty."

My grandfather's mouth fell open.

"It's time, Poppy. You know it's time," I offered supportively.

Thankfully, Calvin's phone rang and broke the spell of Poppy's harsh reality.

After a short conversation, our number one—read, *only*—assistant grinned and said, "Cheer up, Stas, Sisters of Mercy has a DOA with our name on it. It's gonna be a good day." With that, Calvin grabbed a pancake from the stack, scooped a spoonful of scrambled eggs on top, folded it like a taco, and walked out.

And with that, we reverted to an ordinary family breakfast, sans Zander, of course. Poppy was brooding, but that was to be expected because money had entered the discussion. In an attempt to distract him, I said, "I'm available for the next hour or so, then I'm headed back to Chestnut Hill to meet with Mr. Thibodeau."

Grandy smiled at me from across the table. "You look very nice, sweetheart. Are you meeting him at the mortuary?"

"I am. He wants to introduce me to Rose."

"He is nice man, this Mr. Oscar," Babi said.

"He is," I agreed. "I like him very much. He was a big fan of Claire's."

"I knew I liked that guy," my grandfather said, settling down and pouring syrup.

"How goes the journal reading?" Grandy asked.

"Good, I just wish I had more time." I set down my fork. "Last night I read about an argument Claire had with Dad over Thanksgiving. He wanted her to come be with you all, but she thought it was too pathetic—she'd just told him about her parents, and I think she thought he felt sorry for her. But that's as far as I got. Did she come to Thanksgiving? Do you remember?"

My grandmother laughed. Poppy gave me a look, then gave Grandy the same look. When he came back to me, he said, "Have we lost our minds here? Of course we remember! Not likely to forget the first time you meet your future daughter-in-law."

Babka spoke to Poppy. "Remember how she play the Chopin for me? This will never I forgot. So wary beautiful."

"And she was soooo nice," Tess said. "Easy. She helped me do the dishes, and we just talked and talked and talked. Like we'd known each other forever."

Grandy winked at me from across the table. "Yes, my sweet, as you can see, we have very *vague* memories of that Thanksgiving."

I chuckled. "So, she came here, right?"

"Yes," Poppy said. "Tan had given her directions, but he wasn't sure she'd actually show up. But I'd been watching for her, and sure enough, I found her wandering around downstairs by the chapels. When she realized she wasn't lost, I showed her around."

"You didn't show her the Final Resting Retail room, did you?" I teased.

"I absolutely did. I *think* I did," Poppy said. "And I'm sure she loved it."

Grandy rolled her eyes. "We're lucky she stayed to dinner."

"She was a pretty little thing," Poppy mused. "Very put together. I remember being inordinately impressed with *my son*." He laughed. "He'd done well for a Duzinzki." He looked over at Grandy and lost his grin. "Course, I'd done the best of all! I showed her around. She liked the pianos, I do remember that, and I told her I'd heard she could play, and she said she played a little. She was quick."

Grandy chuckled.

"Was where is she played for me the Chopin," Babi put in. "Downstairs, I heared her playing."

"I don't remember that," Poppy said. "I just remember I took her downstairs, and she gagged when the formaldehyde hit her, but she was a trooper. I thought Tan's eyes were going to fall out of his head when he saw her. He had it bad for that girl."

"Understatement," Tess said. "Huge understatement."

Poppy started to laugh. "I caught them smooching in the workroom where Tan hadn't put his deceased away. Course I had to give him grief about romancing his girlfriend in the company of a corpse."

"Oh, jeez!" I noised, appalled. "Did she freak out?"

"No!" Poppy laughed. "She agreed with me that it was unseemly to be carrying on in front of the dead. I told you, she was quick."

I shook my head, loving this. To imagine my mother—funny, quick-witted, pretty and put together—fed my soul. "So, you liked her?" I clarified, looking at my grandparents.

"She laughed at my jokes," Poppy shrugged. "What wasn't to like?"

Babi wagged a finger at my grandfather. "You lucky you not scare her away with your wary bad not funny talk."

"Mama, I'm hurt."

"We liked her a lot," Tess said.

Grandy was nodding but seemed lost in a thought. "Margaret and Leon were there for dinner that day, and Mar told me later that she predicted Claire was the *one*." She smiled. "They were cute together. And yes, she was very easy to like."

Tess stood up with her plate. "I'm serious about the dishes. Everyone scattered, the way everyone does, and she just started clearing. I'll never forget that."

"She seemed reluctant to leave," Poppy said. "Remember that, Di?"

"I don't remember that," Grandy said. "I just remember hoping she'd come back."

"No, Mom. Dad's right. It took her a long time to go, and when she did, Tan was all mopey. But then she came back a few minutes later. Don't you remember? I don't know what happened, but it was something good because later that night, Tan told me he was going to marry that girl."

"Really?" I said.

"I did not know that," Grandy said.

Babi leaned over to me conspiratorially, "He knew when he write to me the letter, he was marry Claire."

Poppy's phone rang then, and Grandy sighed. Tess drained her juice at the sink and grumbled something about the heartburn she was going to have as a result.

Babi patted my knee. "Was wary lovely Thanksgiving when Tanek brought our Claire home. Thank you to remind old womans of such long time ago rememberings."

I leaned into her. "Thank you for remembering the rememberings."

***

Three hours later, I'd replayed the entire conversation a dozen times in my mind. I'd imagined my family spending that first Thanksgiving together so much and so intently that it almost seemed like I had been there. I loved knowing that Claire had made such an indelible impression on everyone. I loved knowing that they'd loved her from the beginning. And my meanderings did not stop there, of course. They kept meandering in and out of the odd place I found *myself:* reluctantly rummaging through my mother's life at the same time a very nice guy decided this—*this*—was the time he wanted to get to know *me*. So naturally, I had no choice but to dissect what had happened with Tyson Pierce yesterday. I was so lost in these thoughts that I missed the turnoff and Google Maps annoyingly and repeatedly had to nag me to make a U-turn.

I obeyed and ultimately pulled into the parking lot of the Grove Crest Funeral Chapel at 11:45. I took a moment to clear my thoughts before I got out of the car, then made my way to the entrance, checking my reflection in the glass door—white sleeveless dress, hair pulled back in a knot, rather tired eyes—thanks to lots of late-night reading and seemingly endless roundtrips from Jersey to Pennsylvania.

A funeral was in progress, so I was duly respectful as I approached the somber dark-suited usher whose job it was to inspire reverence. He silently indicated the placard that said Cleve Moriarty, under which an arrow pointed down the hall. I shook my head and whispered. "Is there someone I can speak to about viewing Rose Winston?"

"Are we expecting you?" he asked, softly.

"No, I don't think so. I'm not sure. Her attorney may have contacted you on my behalf. I'm her granddaughter, and I've come from out of town."

His face bent in apprehension. "Have a seat, dear, and I'll see what I can do."

I knew unscheduled viewings could be disruptive, and I could empathize with what I was asking today, but then again maybe Oscar had taken care of it. "Take your time," I said. "I'm not in a hurry."

He turned down the hall while I sat and watched the latecomers to the Moriarty funeral. One of Poppy's many jobs at Duzy House was to check on people who were waiting, as I was waiting now. He used the time to offer a bottle of water, a tissue, or the opportunity to talk. He'd taught me early that grief is highly individual. Some people need space, some need a shoulder, and some need a confessional. Since this wasn't exactly grief for me, I wasn't sure where I fit into the equation.

As I was sitting there lost in my own head, Oscar Thibodeau sat down next to me and smiled. "Good morning," he whispered, then checked his watch. "It is still morning."

"Good morning," I whispered back, rather surprised by how happy I was to see him. "I'm glad you made it. I didn't want to do this without you."

"Well, Rose would have insisted on a formal introduction, so I'm pleased to oblige." He patted my hand. "You look tired, my dear."

"Not getting much sleep these days, I'm afraid."

"Well, your life has been significantly disrupted."

"Yes."

"Have you had a chance to read any more of your mother's diaries?"

"That's part of the reason I'm tired. They're hard to put down."

Nodding, he smiled. "I can imagine." Oscar considered me. "After Stephen died, Rose allowed me to read a few. Your mother was very good at pulling one in with her words."

"She was," I agreed. I turned to fully face the man. "Oscar, when you came to see me in Wallington last week, why didn't you lead with the journals? Why not just bring them to me?"

"I could have. I thought of it," the attorney admitted. "But discovery is everything—as is ambiance, you know. I wanted you to get a sense of your mother's world, how she'd grown up."

"It worked," I said. "There is something to say for being in a place so full of her, so full of evidence that she lived…it's brought something very tangible to her story."

He lifted a brow. "You never knew Rose," Oscar said, "or the Claire whom I was so fond of. You were robbed of that opportunity, January. I'm pleased you could have this strange bit of experience with both of them."

I nodded and smiled.

The attorney again looked very lawyerly, grey suit pressed and pleated, red tie against a crisp white shirt, bald head buffed to a high sheen. He glanced around. "It's nice here," he said. "The Groves prepared Stephen. There was no funeral, as I told you. But shortly thereafter, Rose made her own arrangements with them."

"Some people do that," I said. "And it's nice when all the decisions are made beforehand. Makes my job easier, for sure."

"I can imagine it would. So, your family, were they always…funeral people?"

I lifted a shoulder. "No, it kind of just happened. Poppy was a little kid when his family moved into our building. The ground floor had always been a mortuary, and when Poppy was about twelve, the owner spilled a body on the curb. Poppy helped him get it inside…and the rest is history. He calls it divine manipulation, but he loves it."

Oscar smiled. "And you? You've always wanted to follow in your grandfather's footsteps? What about music?"

"I love music. I got a scholarship to Seton Hall, but…" I shrugged. "When I looked into those two futures—death won." I chuckled. "When all was said and done, I think it was really my dad's footsteps I wanted to follow. He'd grown up with it like I had, and doing what he did makes me feel connected to him somehow. He loved it, and I think I love it because of him—it started out that way, I guess. But now I just love it because I love it. Poppy says it's a calling." I looked at the attorney, debating, then leaned down and picked up my purse. "I read in my mom's journal that on their first date, she asked to see my dad's wallet."

Oscar grinned. "That sounds just like your mother. But to be fair, it was Rose who always said a man's whole life could be found in his billfold. A woman keeps hers in her handbag."

"That's probably true," I said, rifling. When I found the note that I'd kept in my own wallet for the past two years, I handed it to Oscar. "My grandfather found this the night of the accident—the night I was born. It had apparently been in my dad's wallet to remind him maybe of why he did what he did—like a talisman. Poppy gave it to me when I graduated from mortuary school."

Oscar opened the note slowly, and since I knew the words by heart, I heard them in my head as he scanned them.

Dear Mr. Duzinski—Tanek.— We would be remiss indeed if we did not take this opportunity to thank you for your kindness at this most devastating time. You were so very gentle with our broken hearts and our broken spirits. When we could not transcend our grief to make a single decision, you were there to gently guide us. To lose a child in such a horrific manner is hell on earth, and we will forever mourn her. But in the midst of our paralysis, you made our final goodbye to her as soft and lovely as possible. Mr. Duzinski, there are angels on earth who masquerade as ordinary human beings—you are such a man.

With deepest gratitude, the Portmans, parents of Lila, age 6

Oscar seemed genuinely moved by the words. When he looked over at me, there was honest emotion in his ancient eyes.

"That little girl was murdered," I told him. "I think Poppy wanted me to understand what my father understood: We do sacred work. Now that letter is my talisman."

Oscar scanned the note again, then met my eyes. "Well, I guess that tells you everything you need to know about your father, doesn't it?"

"It tells me a lot," I said. "And I think it told my mom a lot, as well."

He handed the note back. "You are a fascinating young woman, January."

I grimaced. "No. I'm not."

"Yes. You can't help but be. You are the best of both of your parents, and you never even knew them. I think that's rather extraordinary."

"I wish that were true, Mr. Thibodeau. But if I've learned anything over these last few days, it's that I have not been a good daughter. That's not extraordinary—it's shameful."

The old man studied me for another long moment, then placed his hand on mine. He seemed about to say something when the soft approach of footsteps kept him from speaking. The usher stopped in front of us and asked that we follow him. He appeared to recognize Oscar and nodded. "This way, please."

We followed in silence to a small visitation parlor. It was simply appointed with two sofas and seating around the room. An open casket of rich mahogany was in the corner. "I'll leave you with your grandmother," he said to me. Then he walked out and shut the door.

I moved closer to the casket, not expecting to feel anything, and I didn't. Not really. Rose was the grandmother I'd never known but had heard enough about to dislike with impunity. Until now. Now I knew she had probably memorized every word in my mother's diaries, had secretly been watching me perform, had sat reading in her daughter's window seat. I needed a face to go with that woman.

Rose Winston was laid out in a Batesville casket of superior quality on a cushion of ivory satin. She was wearing a navy-blue dress with a pale pink scarf at her neck, and she held a strand of pearls in her carefully positioned hands. Her pretty face was minimally lined thanks to devoted skin care when she was alive and skillful postmortem enhancement. Her hair was silver, cut in a bob, and cemented in place. All in all, I thought my grandmother was a lovely woman, expertly preserved to reflect her high station. I couldn't have done a better job myself.

Next to me Oscar, chuckled. "She hated her 78-year-old neck with a passion. Trust her to cover it up."

"I guess that's why she's not wearing the pearls?"

"Probably," he mused, seeming a little preoccupied. He caught himself and, clearing his throat, he told me, "Your mother brought them back from Tokyo, where she'd been for a piano competition. I think she might have been seventeen, maybe sixteen. Japan is known for Akoya pearls, and Rose loved pearls. These were especially meaningful to her, a just-because gift from her daughter. She prized them."

This surprised and confused me, and I'm sure it showed on my face. "I don't understand. If she loved my mom so much, why was she so..."

Oscar seemed to sadden at my question. "Rose was an enigma, January. A complicated woman. But don't take everything you've heard—or read—at face value."

"I just don't understand how they could have made her leave. Who disowns their daughter for not marrying the right guy, and then never speaks to her again?"

"I know it sounds irrational, and as I've said, I don't think it was the intent. But you have to understand that in the time period that was meant to teach her some sort of lesson, Claire fell in love and got married. Six months. Six months was not so long that Rose and Stephen could not have assumed that she would come to her senses and return, their penitent daughter. Plenty of time for any damage to be repaired. But of course, that didn't happen. And in the meantime, Stephen's hold on your grandmother only tightened."

"Why didn't she just leave him?"

"Oh, January. It's very complicated for a woman living with someone as powerful as Stephen. He would have ruined her. He couldn't lose his daughter *and* his wife. And after what Claire had done to humiliate him, if Rose had chosen her over him, he would have destroyed Rose. She knew that, and it made her a prisoner." Oscar looked hard at me. "She never would have left him. But as insurance, Stephen threatened to ruin the Duzinskis if Rose got any ideas."

I felt my breath catch. "What are you talking about?"

"My dear, your grandfather made his money by crushing people like Stasio Duzinski."

I stared, open-mouthed, unable to process what he was saying.

"There's a park across the street from your home, correct?"

"Yes."

"After your parents got together, Stephen had me look into acquiring that park for him."

"Why?"

Oscar nodded, taking my elbow. "Let's sit for a moment, January," he said, leading me away from Rose's coffin.

As we sat down on the sofa, I narrowed my eyes at the attorney. "Why would my grandfather be interested in our park? You can't buy a park, can you?"

"You can if the price is right and the city is willing. But if plan A wasn't possible, plan B was the dry cleaners at the top of your street."

"I don't understand what you're saying."

"January, Stephen was actively looking for space where he could build a mortuary."

"What? Why?"

"So he could directly compete with your grandparents. It would have been state-of-the-art. He would have cut prices to the bone—which he could have afforded to do—until he put your family out of business. Make no mistake—Stephen would have destroyed them. Their livelihood certainly, their standing in the community, perhaps their professional reputation—he wasn't beneath slander when it would benefit him. And a byproduct could very well have been the destruction of your parent's marriage."

I looked at him in disbelief.

"He never did it, obviously, but as I said, he used the threat of it as leverage to keep Rose in line. And Rose stayed in line." There was sadness and soft rebuke in Oscar Thibodeau's eyes as he let that statement sink in. Then he sighed. "So, before you judge your grandmother too harshly, January," he finally said, "know that she fell on her sword to protect her daughter's happiness."

"And Claire never knew?" I said, sounding small.

The attorney simply looked at me with deep sadness. "Rose was flawed," Oscar said with a catch in his voice. "Very flawed. But never assume she didn't love her daughter."

I thought about this. "What about after, after everything was ruined? Why didn't Rose leave then?"

"I don't know. Guilt. Shared shame. After the accident, Stephen became very *unstable*. What happened to his daughter broke him, January. Your grandmother…" Oscar glanced at the coffin. "Rose took care of him. She took care of *everything* because I think she saw herself as complicit in the tragedy, damaged by it beyond repair. With Stephen, she was shielded somewhat because he shared the same shame, if that makes sense. It was a communal burden, a shared torture that rather bound them to each other. And because they had each other, it was possible to survive what had happened. Like I said, she would never have left him. Never."

I stared at the old gentleman, who was doing nothing to hide his sudden emotion. "You... you loved her," I said.

He looked at me for a long moment and did not deny it. Then he shrugged. "I did," he said. "Someone had to. But there was nothing untoward between us. I was contentedly married until my wife died in 2015. And after Stephen died last year, it was clear Rose wanted only a friend."

"So...she didn't love you back?"

"Not to my knowledge," he said regrettably.

"I'm so sorry," I said, suddenly finding life unbearably unfair.

"As am I, Miss January. As am I. But all things considered, it was probably for the best. Since Stephen died, I've watched your grandmother finally stand firmly upon her own two feet. And she needed to. As always, I have performed my role as advisor and friend, but she stepped into a life she was reinventing. She took control of the business entities, began the tentative reconnection with your mother, and was preparing to do the same with you. I believe that Rose was on her way to becoming the woman she had always dreamt of being— even at seventy-eight. It was actually quite glorious to behold."

I gazed again at the coffin containing the remains of the dream Oscar spoke of—the unencumbered, enigmatic Rose Winston. I sighed. "I honestly wish I'd met her."

"I do, too, my dear."

"Do you know how long she had been seeing my mother?"

"This last Christmas was when she finally mustered the courage to pay her first visit to Claire."

Christmas. Just seven months ago. I looked at Oscar. "I can't imagine what that would have been like."

"I can tell you. I was there."

I stared at him. "Did Claire know her?"

Oscar nodded. "Almost instantly. It was very tender. Rose was terrified of—I'm not sure what. I guess of what Claire's reaction would be to her. But we knocked on the door, and when Claire answered, the two of them stared at one another for a long moment. I think Rose said something like 'My darling girl' or 'Hello, my darling,' and Claire just started to weep."

A tingle spread up my spine. "No way. After all that time? After all that had happened? She *knew* her?"

"There was a very long embrace and many tears," Oscar said. "Rose made repeated apologies, and Claire made a lot of noise that to me sounded like absolute forgiveness. I didn't stay long after that; it seemed an intrusion. My job was actually just to get Rosy through the door. But I can tell you that when I picked her up later, she was a different woman. Buoyant."

"Amazing," was all I could manage.

"Are you all right, my dear?"

"I don't know, Mr. Thibodeau. Sometimes I wonder if I'm ever going to be all right again. I went to see my mom the other night. I went to tell her that Rose had died. And she...she cried. It was awful. It was heartbreaking. She'd just barely reconnected with her, only to lose her a few short months later. That's heartbreaking."

The old attorney patted my hand. "Well, at least Claire has you, Miss January."

His words made me want to crawl into a hole.

Thankfully, Oscar's phone buzzed from inside his breast pocket. He retrieved it and, after studying the screen for a moment, excused himself, which left me alone with my strange grandmother. I walked back over to the coffin and gazed down at the woman who had so upended my life over the last few days. Lying there so serenely, she didn't look capable of all the uproar she had caused—in my life, in Claire's, in Oscar's. She also gave no hint of what she'd survived. I imagined her hiding out in my mother's girlhood bedroom, reading the same journals I was reading now. Was there really nothing else she could have done?

"January," Oscar said, sidling up next to me. "I have to run back to the office to sign some papers. I shouldn't be long. Do you have time for some lunch?"

I looked over at him, preoccupied. "Oscar, why didn't Rose return Mom's calls or answer her letters? Her journals say she wrote all the time and Rose never wrote back."

"Rose never got those letters, January—Stephen made sure of that."

I stared at the old man. "What are you talking about?"

"Now that's a story you should hear. Do you have time for lunch?"

"I'll make time."

"Good. Meet me at The Simon Café. We'll dine alfresco. It's on Germantown Avenue, just up the street about a mile, on the left. I shouldn't be more than half an hour."

twenty-four

I found the restaurant with no problem and parked in the shade. With twenty minutes to spare before I expected Oscar, I decided to wait for him in the car. I thought of lowering the seat and resting my eyes—it was a pleasant enough afternoon—but I was afraid I'd fall asleep. Then I remembered why I was so tired and reached for what I'd thought to toss in the back seat: Claire's journal. If I'd had the time this morning, I would have read the rest of what had happened on that Thanksgiving so long ago.

My curiosity had been so ignited after breakfast that I'd almost, *almost,* opted to read rather than help dress the enormous Mr. Magellan. Instead, I'd done my duty by Tess. We'd gotten him dressed and casketed, but at just shy of 400 pounds, the task had required all of us *and* the pulleys. But he looked amazing in his custom suit, white shirt and silver tie, wet-look hair, and sunglasses. I'd left Calvin and Poppy maneuvering the double-wide coffin into the elevator and grabbed the journal on my way out the door, thinking I would catch up on my reading when I stopped for lunch on the way back from meeting Rose Winston. But this worked, too.

I skimmed Mom's entry for Thanksgiving 1999, and her version mostly mirrored the story my family had told me over pancakes. Her impressions of Poppy were hilarious. She'd written:

T's dad asked how we'd met, but before I could answer he said he'd heard that I had spotted Tanek in a crowd and chased him down 5th Avenue, tackled him, and tattooed my phone number in his palm. I gave him a look and told him that was exactly how it happened, and he cracked up. He told me I was quick and that he liked me. I didn't tell him, but I liked Stasio Duzinski almost immediately.

She wrote about playing Chopin for Babi, and that her accent was thick, but she had no trouble understanding her.

Rahela Duzinski said the sweetest thing, I had to write it down. She said:
"There is wary much goodness in you. Is why God has blessed you to play such magnificent, to stir old woman's soul."
I told her she was going to make me cry. She smiled and squeezed her eyes shut. It was adorable.
Stasio had mentioned that she rather liked Chopin, so I asked what her favorite was and she said the Etudes—"These I love," she said.
I fingered a few notes, but it wasn't right, so I asked her to hum her favorite, and when she did, I recognized it immediately. I moved over, and she sat her tiny self down. Then we were off, Tanek's little g-mother and me, on a journey of the heart by way of E sharp. When I finished the Etude Mrs. Duzinski looked up at me with wet eyes and I thought I would cry when she said, "Such beautiful." I told her my music prof believes that Chopin, played well, evokes lovely pain that leaves you wanting to hurt more. She got that. She said, "Always this music makes me to weep." I love the way she talks. I love her.

It seemed Babka and Claire had bonded from the first moment. In fact, the way my mom described her first impressions of my family made me weep for its familiarity. This was my life.

In my 22 Thanksgivings, I've never spent one I enjoyed more than the one I had with Tanek's family—and that's sad, actually. Conversation came so easily. Laughter came easier. There was absolutely no undercurrent of unkindness. There was teasing, a lot of it, but these people had a genuine regard for each other that I found intoxicating. They also seemed to like me. A lot.

We talked and laughed for two solid hours, and by the time dessert was served, they were all telling me funny funeral stories. My favorite was the woman whose husband had wanted a solid mahogany casket, but she didn't want to pay for it, so she opted for cremation. If possible, she wanted hubby piggy-backed with another planned burn—for half price, of course. Stasio was appalled and very dramatic in his retelling. She then wanted to rent the dream casket on an hourly basis. And so, an empty Batesville (apparently a very pricey coffin) was wheeled into the chapel for everyone to weep over during the thirty-minute service. It was then solemnly loaded into the hearse by the pallbearers, who, if they wondered why the casket was so light, said nothing. Afterward, it was whisked off under the widow's subterfuge of a private burial at a secret location, when in truth it merely circled the block and came to rest in the garage with no mourner the wiser. The Batesville was buffed and back on display with twelve minutes to spare—which the woman expected to be refunded for, of course.

I laughed until my sides hurt and didn't want to leave, especially when Stasio wrapped me in a bear hug and told me he had a hundred more stories to tell me, so I'd better come back. Even more especially when Diana cupped my chin and begged me not to let his silly stories keep me away. I laughed and promised. T's aunt whispered in my ear that in her opinion, her nephew had never looked better than he did next to me. I almost cried. I wanted to hug Rahela, but she had fallen asleep, so I made T promise to tell her that I loved playing Chopin for her.

At my car, T slipped his arms around me and pulled me close and said he wished I didn't have to leave. I wished the same thing, but I had a performance the next night and lots of practicing to do. We stared at each other for a long time, and I knew he was hoping I'd say something, which I didn't. So he kissed me deep and a bit rough and told me I'd better go before *he* said something I'd regret—I knew he was talking about his over-confident prediction that I would be in love with him by the end of today. And he was right. If he'd told me he loved me, it would have been awkward. It was anyway, because when I pulled onto the street and he waved his somber little wave, it kind of broke my heart.

I drove away with an ache in my chest that only got worse the farther I got out of town. It had been such a wonderful day. The perfect day to have fallen in love with Tanek. But had I? The atmosphere, his home, was so filled with it, love, that it had to be that I'd just fallen under the spell of his family, right? Right? I mean, I was feeling something, but it was them. Right? I was just about to the freeway when I asked myself that question out loud. Tanek's family had been so soft on the open wounds of my life that I probably had fallen in love with them today. But not Tanek. Not today. No, I didn't fall in love with him today.

I started to shake with such bald realization that it actually scared me. I'd been so busy worrying about all the reasons this couldn't possibly be happening that I'd failed to notice that it already had. I turned my car around, and when I was facing the right direction, I called T; fifteen minutes later he was waiting for me where we'd said goodbye. He looked upset. When I got out of the car, he asked if I was okay, which was a good question since I was holding back tears. He asked me what was wrong, and I was amazed—I still am—at how sure I was when I told him I'd come back to tell him I hadn't fallen in love with him today. He looked a little stricken and asked if I came back to break his heart, which broke my heart a little. I slipped my arms around his waist and looked up at him through a wet blur and told him I'd come back to tell him he was right all along. I fell in love with him over the pancakes, just like he'd said. His beautiful face bent from confusion to relief to awe.

He couldn't believe it. And I almost didn't either. But I do. I love him.

I didn't expect to, and I guess I've been worried that maybe I shouldn't because of all the garbage going on with me, or that maybe I just couldn't trust it right now, or that maybe he shouldn't trust it right now. But somehow it happened anyway, and it's real, and I do. I just plain love that guy, and that's what I told him. It wasn't exactly movie-caliber romantic, but the way he looked at me, I could tell he knew what I was trying to say. He did much better than I did, and I wish I could remember his exact words because they were so beautiful and whispery.

He said he fell for me the minute he saw me at the Lincoln Center. And when he spotted me on 5th Ave, he fell some more. And when I waved my number at him, he knew his life was about to change. And he said he just keeps falling more in love with me every time we're together. At some point I just reached up and kissed him. I kissed him like he was mine and I was his, and he kissed me the same way. When we finally emerged from that kiss, all that was left of Tanek and me was an undeniable Us.

Undeniable Us. Oh. My. Gosh. My mother was a poet. And I suddenly loved that I had a front-row seat to my parents' *discovery* of their love for each other. What was written on these pages was incredible to me. I ran the back of my hand under my leaking nose and turned the page.

> Of course, the fact remains that I am going through something, so I had to spend the hundred miles and the hour and thirty-five minutes it took me to get home examining the fine print of my life. As I did, it seemed suddenly very important that Tanek meet my parents. Sooner rather than later. There was no point moving forward until we got past that. And I so wanted to get past that because I was making space in my life for this incredible man—if I'm honest, I'd probably been doing it since the day we met. How long have I craved the sound of his voice? How long have thoughts of him been nearly omnipresent in my day-to-day? When did his interest in me become so utterly addicting? It started with the pancakes, just like he said. And it could all come crashing down when he met my parents. So, he had to meet them. He had to see who made me, even if it proved to be a deal-breaker. Better to find out now before I couldn't unlove him.

I read that last line again. If I didn't know how the story ended, I would have been worried. I can only imagine what that would have been like, after all that had happened; it wouldn't surprise me at all to learn that Stephen was a jerk. But did she do it? Did Mom take my dad home to meet her parents?

November 29, 1999
> Flowers from T with a note that said he loves me more than he did yesterday. We talked for two hours. That man! I broached the issue of T meeting the parents. He said he'd love to meet them. He has no idea...

December 2, 1999—

It was a big day—lunch with Oscar in New York between his business meetings for Dad. It has taken some time, but he finally came through with the contract, and I have no regrets. I am free—or I will be. I just wish it hadn't had to come about this way. But the timing appears perfect, given what's happening in my life. Even OT agrees. I've long stopped calling home because Mom has not once picked up, and she doesn't return my calls, but today I made an exception and left a rather lengthy voice message letting them know that I was bringing Tanek home to meet them next weekend. I guess we'll see. I also sent a letter informing them of the same. I still write every week, and my letters still go unanswered, but at least there's a paper trail, and—

A soft knock on the hood of my car jolted me from my reading. When I looked up, Oscar Thibodeau was making his way around the side of the car.

"January, my apologies," he said through the open window. "That took longer than I intended."

He'd startled me, but I quickly recovered. "No problem. I stayed busy reading," I indicated Claire's journal before stowing it in my bag, then I got out of the car.

"Anything interesting?"

"Always," I said as we made our way across the parking lot. "I wish I could just lock myself in a hotel for a month and read them all, start to finish."

Oscar chuckled.

"Did you ever meet my dad?" I asked.

"I did. Once. I met him the day your mother disinherited herself."

I stopped. "What? Disinherited herself from what?"

Oscar smiled as he held open the door to the restaurant. "Everything her father owned."

I swallowed. "But I thought…I thought *they* disowned *her.*"

twenty-five

The hostess showed us to a table on the patio, and Oscar smiled his approval as he removed his suit jacket and hung it over the chair. She handed us our menus and told us that our server would be right with us.

I looked around, took in the elegant grounds—complete with koi pond—and sighed appreciatively. "This place is very cool."

"I'm glad you think so," Oscar said. "It's a favorite of mine. And the menu is world-class."

"Good. I'm starving."

"Well, it is two o'clock. Again, my apologies for the late hour."

I waved his words away as our waitress approached. We ordered and she poured ice water into our glasses. She offered Oscar the wine menu, but he declined and requested a pitcher of water. I asked for a Coke.

When she walked away, I leaned over. "So...my mother disinherited herself? How did I not know this?"

He shook his head. "I suspect that because of the dynamic between the two families, there is probably much you don't know."

"So, tell me. What did Claire do?"

"A little background, January," Oscar said, once the waitress had brought my Coke and his carafe. "Though I was first and foremost Stephen's business attorney, I was also the attorney of record for the Winston family. And I was a friend, which was a fine line to walk, but it put me in the position of seeing this household from all angles."

"I bet that was *interesting.*"

"Your mother—I can't describe the strength of her character. I can't do it justice." He seemed to search for words. "She...how can I explain this? She gleaned much of her savvy from her father, but she used it with more humanity. She was kinder. Easier going. She rejected the very entitlement that Stephen demanded, if that makes sense."

"Not really," I admitted.

"Well, it was like this: Your mother grew up with very high standards—very high expectations. She was loved, but she was also strategically groomed to become something she had virtually no interest in becoming. As Stephen Winston's only heir, she stood to inherit his empire. And to that end, much preparation and grooming—molding—was required to ensure this eventual transfer of power. But your mother—much to her parents' displeasure—was never very interested in the privilege that went along with being a Winston. I don't know if she consciously rejected it or just didn't absorb it, but either way she wasn't all that impressed with being a Winston. Claire was very much her own person. She recognized no class distinction, enjoyed all types of people, had friends from all walks of life, and was very self-determined. All this caused her parents a lot of...*heartburn*. They had a very narrow view of who she should be."

"I got that impression from her journals."

Oscar nodded. "I think Claire knew the day would come when she would have to lay claim to her own life. That day just happened to coincide with the Denton Hyde episode, though it would have come regardless. But I don't think Stephen ever imagined his daughter would actually reject his wealth."

"That really happened?"

"Oh, yes. And it was rather earthshattering."

"Tell me. Tell me everything."

"Well, she'd been thinking about it for some time. We'd discussed it before Stephen's birthday celebration, but afterwards, she became very committed. She wanted me to draw up a document of intent to emancipate from her inheritance. I tried very hard, like the good attorney I am, to talk her out of it—it was a lot of money, not to mention a lifetime of security—but she had made up her mind. She was extremely bright and essentially said that if I didn't do as she asked, she would obtain legal representation elsewhere, and I trusted that she would do exactly that. I also understood what motivated her, so I did as she requested."

"And her parents never knew?"

"Not until she brought your father home to meet them. It certainly wasn't my place to tell them, so although I was walking a fine line as Stephen's lead counsel, I said nothing." He sighed. "I think part of me was holding out that Claire might change her mind, but of course, that didn't happen. I got a call from her a few months after the Denton incident. She was coming home to introduce your father to her parents, and she wanted me to be there. I was naturally surprised; the occasion didn't seem to warrant my presence. But then she told me she planned to inform Rose and Stephen of the petition we'd drawn up, and she wanted me there in case there were legal questions."

"Were you nervous?"

"Like a condemned man facing a lethal injection."

I laughed.

"And to add another element of angst to my predicament, I remember distinctly that I had just hung up from speaking with your mother when your grandfather called demanding my attendance at the same meeting."

"Why?"

"He told me to come prepared to defend the terms of his will because Claire was bringing someone home and he wanted to make it crystal clear to her what was at stake if she did not toe the Winston line."

"So, wait a minute, he was going to threaten to disinherit her? Because of my dad?"

"Exactly. Your grandfather was a man who rarely lost—and he wasn't about to lose his daughter to anyone. And there was no engagement announcement. Claire hadn't brought your father home to do anything but introduce him. But Stephen was making it abundantly clear that Tanek—or anyone who had not garnered his pre-approval—was not welcome. He was sending a clear message, a warning."

The waitress arrived at our table with our salads and a bread basket. As she refilled our drinks, Oscar buttered a roll, and I picked up my fork. She informed us that our entrees would be out in a few minutes, and I thanked her.

We'd missed the lunch crowd, and our table in the far corner of the shaded patio offered superb privacy. I looked around, still preoccupied with thoughts of my beast of a grandfather.

Oscar seemed to follow my gaze. "This is one of my favorite places for lunch. Your grandmother was quite fond of it as well." He winked as he stabbed a forkful of salad.

Poor Oscar. I buttered a roll, took a bite, then sat back. "Soooo. That day…the big meeting. That was the first time you met my dad?" I asked.

"It was." The old man nodded. "And I have to say, my initial impression of him was not particularly favorable."

"Why not?" I said, surprised.

"Two things, really," he said. "No one was ever going to be good enough for your mother, as far as I was concerned, so he entered the scene at a disadvantage. Secondly, I assumed he'd be out of his depth, and I was concerned for him. Stephen didn't give men like your father the time of day," Oscar said. "But I needn't have worried."

I took a sip of my Coke and sat back. "Tell me what happened," I said, folding my arms. "And don't leave anything out."

He dabbed his mouth. "When I arrived that day, your parents were just getting out of their car, and your father looked completely awe-struck—hence my impression. He'd had no idea of the wealth your mother came from. And as I recall, Claire looked quite anxious about the whole thing as well."

"Because of my dad?"

"Him, and her task, I'm sure. You have to remember your mother had not seen or spoken to her parents in weeks, so the whole ordeal was destined to be awkward. And I do recall that Rose just looked at your poor father like he was a stray dog Claire had dragged home." Oscar grimaced with disgust. "She showed us into your grandfather's den, where he was sitting, glimmering like new money, the way he did. I do remember that he stared at Tanek over the top of his glasses with utter disdain, much like Rose had. But Tanek was very gracious. In fact, he seemed almost amused by Stephen's antics, which is what made the whole encounter so memorable for me. He was not impressed with your grandfather at all."

I chuckled and felt uncanny relief—I'd been somehow worried about my dad.

"Stephen was on the sofa, and Tanek and Claire were opposite him—calculated seating I'd seen many times, designed to intimidate. But, again, as I recall, your dad never broke a sweat." Oscar smiled.

I smiled, too. "Go Dad."

"Exactly, and it frustrated Stephen, to say the least. He dearly hated to fail at terrorizing."

I laughed, gratified.

"Moreover, he hated not being in control. I remember the tone was set when he thanked *me* for being there. I remember this distinctly because Claire piped up that *she'd* been the one to invite me, and I had to acknowledge this, which surprised your grandfather. Stephen Winston did *not* like surprises. He started glaring at me then and didn't stop." Oscar sighed. "If a man could die by glares, January, I'd have died a thousand deaths."

"What did he say?"

"Nothing that I can remember." He just glared—over small talk, I'm sure—which was his way of warning me that my sedition was unappreciated.

"Oh, charming."

"At some point, he picked a fight with your mother, telling her he didn't appreciate her giving them such little notice that she was dropping by with a *friend.* And Claire said something to the effect of: 'Well, Dad, much has happened in my life, and this man is a big part of it, so I thought introductions were in order.'" Oscar looked at me. "To be honest, I thought they were there to announce their engagement. But that wasn't it, like I said. That would have concerned me, made me question her motives, given what she'd done with her inheritance." He ran a hand over his shiny head. "But I had to admit, January, they looked very much like they belonged to each other—your parents."

"That makes me happy."

"Yes. They made a very handsome couple. Of course, Stephen was simply annoyed by the whole thing. He went on and on about Claire being childish and hell-bent on making a *point* and was it really necessary to use this poor boy to get back at him—that kind of thing. Very rude, and very awkward for your dad."

"You're kidding! What did Mom do?"

"I can't remember exactly, but I think she probably apologized to Tanek for her father's behavior. And I remember how your dad, who, again seemed completely unaffected by Stephen's boorishness, said something like, 'Your dad is just as charming as you said he'd be.'" Oscar laughed. "That's when I stopped worrying about him. I'm an old man, and I can't remember most days if I've changed my underwear, but I'll never forget that!"

I laughed, too. "Really? My dad actually said that?"

"He did—something like that. And Stephen was just livid. It was quite...*extraordinary*."

I stared at him, envisioning the icy scene. "What about Rose? Did she say anything?"

"Not that I recall. But then Rose didn't typically engage. Her style was more suited for pointed, well-timed remarks—few and far between. And if you want to know the truth, I think she rather enjoyed watching Stephen lose his footing. Don't get me wrong, she wasn't happy about Claire's conduct—or Tanek's—but seeing Stephen compromised was always a treat." He winked.

After a moment, Oscar stroked his chin. "But when powerful men think they're losing ground, they resort to insults, and this was very true of your grandfather. So, around this time he asked your dad what he did for a living. And when Tanek told him he was a mortician, Stephen jeered."

I felt myself stiffen with familiar disdain for this man I had never known. "What did he say?"

"Oh, I'm sure he was rude, and then I'm sure he got mean—that was his style. I know he said something to the effect of, 'You're an *undertaker*? Well, isn't that *impressive*!'" Oscar leaned closer to me. "But your dad's response was absolute perfection. It was a speech for the century, and I wish I could remember everything he said—I wrote some of it down, since I always kept notes of my meetings with Stephen. Had I known we were going to be discussing this, I would have read over them. However, as I recall, with every word your dad spoke, Stephen shrunk by degree."

I leaned in.

"Tanek said that without his services, when Stephen died, he would bloat and start to stink to high heaven. His bowels could explode, which would be a huge mess and very unpleasant for everyone. He'd liquefy and putrefy and mortify—he used the best words, I wish I could remember—but he painted a profoundly gruesome picture of human decay, and he smiled as he did it. Then he said something like, 'So, thank you, sir. I, too, think what I do is pretty impressive, and I'm very proud of it.' I don't think I'll ever forget the look on your grandfather's face."

For some reason, I was crying. Happy, proud, triumphant tears. Some mine, some, by proxy, for a man who had looked his enemy in the eye and smiled. "My dad said all that?" I croaked.

"He did—and it was a thing of beauty. Round one to the mortician," Oscar crowed. "And Stephen wasn't one bit happy about it. But as I live and breathe, my dear, when I glanced over at Rose, she was smiling at the floor."

These people, I thought, ashamed and fascinated at the same time. I was so lost in this reprisal that I was surprised when my salmon Florentine had been placed before me. I looked up just as the waitress asked if I needed anything else. All I could do was shake my head.

"Enjoy," she said. Then she walked away.

I looked over at Oscar. "The more I hear about my grandfather, the more grateful I am that I never met him."

"It was entirely—*entirely*—his loss, my dear."

I acknowledged the compliment with a wave of my fork.

Oscar Thibodeau had ordered a steak, which he attacked with gusto, and for a moment we ate in companionable silence, me lost in the image of my dad giving as good as he got.

"So how did Claire tell her parents about the inheritance?"

"Oh, she tried to broach it a few times, but Stephen was too focused on knocking your father down. At one point, I recall very clearly him saying, 'Tanek Duzinski is an interesting name.' And your father thanked him. And you know what your grandfather said?"

"What?"

"'Oh, son, it wasn't a compliment.' He actually said that, January, and, of course, Claire was horrified. I think that's when she said they were leaving, but Stephen told her to stop using this *Polack* in an attempt to humiliate him! He actually called your father a Polack."

"He did not!" I nearly choked.

"He did. And your dad…" Oscar grinned. "Your dad looked him right in the eye and said, cool as a cucumber, 'Gosh, I don't think I've been called a Polack since junior high. And that was by a twelve-year-old girl.'" Oscar laughed out loud. "Something like that. And again, Stephen lost his mind and started shouting, gesturing...I tried to intervene, but Stephen reminded me, in no uncertain terms, for whom I worked."

"What did you do?"

"I told him that day I worked for his daughter, and by extension Mr. Duzinski. Then I did a little glaring of my own."

"Well look at your bad-ass self," I laughed. "He could have fired you."

"I wish he had," Oscar sighed. "I've wished it many times. But, as they say, I know where the bodies are buried, and Stephen would never have risked that." He winked at me.

"Do I even want to know what you're talking about?"

"Probably not."

"Hmmm," I said, stuffing delicious salmon into my mouth. "What happened after that?"

"It got uglier. It was around that time, I think, that your father thought they should leave, that Claire had been abused enough. And that enraged Stephen—no one *ever* walked away from him. He got all puffed up and asked your dad if he thought he was a match for him—kind of challenged Tanek. But your dad never took the bait, which again infuriated Stephen. He just said he loved Claire and if they had a future, he'd spend it protecting her from Stephen's nonsense." Oscar pointed his fork my way. "I remember he used the word nonsense, because nothing could have diminished a man of Stephen's self-importance more. And believe me, it hit its mark."

"Wow," I breathed.

"He was something, your dad," Oscar said. "And he wasn't one bit afraid of Stephen, which essentially crippled your grandfather. So, what could Stephen do but get in his face? And he did. He told Tanek that if he was any kind of a man, he'd let Claire live the life she was intended to live. That they both knew she was worthy of much more than the likes of a *Polish undertaker*. And Tanek, graciously, *disarmingly*, agreed with him, but said ultimately it was Claire's life. Her decision."

This burned my eyes. "And Rose never said anything?"

"I think somewhere in there she made some noise about how the mortician—the *Polish* mortician is what she meant—would never be accepted in their world." Oscar rolled his eyes. "They really did not know their daughter at all, January. Claire could not have cared less about her parents' world—obviously."

"Obviously."

"Then Stephen played what he thought was his ace in the hole. He asked your dad what he thought she was worth."

"Who?" I said.

"Your mother. He asked him what he thought your mother was worth. Naturally, Claire was mortified, and I remember Stephen was so incredibly arrogant. And when Tanek couldn't answer—he had no idea—Stephen told him Claire was worth millions."

I coughed. "Mi—Millions? Was that true?"

"Yes. And your poor dad was absolutely shell-shocked. Stephen launched into a litany about how Claire was their only child, that their net worth was her net worth, and that he had every right to expect that she not marry *down*. And that surely an *undertaker* could understand that."

"Oh, Oscar—" I gasped.

"It was pretty awful. Even for Stephen."

"That—that makes me sick," I said.

Oscar shook his head with antipathy. "Oh, he wasn't done. Stephen then explained that if Claire chose him, she would forfeit everything earmarked for her, and said he'd invited *me* there so I could answer any questions. But he assured them both that he was well within his legal parameters to place these conditions on Claire's inheritance."

"My poor dad. What a position to put him in."

"Exactly. And you can probably imagine he was astonished—but not about Claire's prospective wealth. No. He couldn't believe Stephen would actually do that to his own daughter, and he told him so. And Stephen, ever so smugly, turned it on him. Said it was entirely in Tanek's hands. I'm sure your father felt completely manipulated."

"What happened?"

"Claire finally did what she'd come to do. She told Tanek that her parents were wealthy but that she wasn't, she didn't want their money or their life, so he was there to understand that none of anything they were standing in belonged to her. Essentially, she was letting him know that if he was interested in her for her money, there was no money—which he obviously wasn't because he'd never known about it. Then turning to her father, she told Stephen she had petitioned to disinherit herself from him and gave him the letter of emancipation." Oscar shook his head, again revisiting that memory. "It was more eloquent than that, but you get the gist."

"My gosh! What did he say?"

"Stephen could not fathom that his daughter would relinquish her birthright. He thought she'd done it for your father. He kept saying, 'For him? For him? You'd give up your inheritance for *him*?' And Claire just looked at him with such sadness and said, 'I would, Dad. But I didn't. This was all because of you. I made this decision long before I met Tanek.' She told him that I'd drafted the petition before she and your dad had even gone out on their first date. You should have seen Stephen's face, January. He was...*floored*," Oscar said, softly. "I can count on one hand the times I've actually felt badly for that man, but that was one of them."

"Oh, my gosh."

"And your father..." Oscar shook his head, recalling. "You could say that he was the victor in all this, but I'm not sure he thought so. He'd just witnessed a proud, arrogant man lose his last hold on his only daughter. I remember Tanek kissed your mom on the cheek, told her he'd be in the car and to take as long as she needed. And then he left."

"Did he say anything to Stephen?"

"I think he would have. I think he started to, in fact. But Stephen wouldn't look at him. If he had, I'm sure Tanek would have said something respectful. Instead, it seemed to me that he'd chosen to honor Stephen's pain and leave without a last word. It was really quite kind, I thought," Oscar said refilling his water glass.

"Wow...that was my dad?"

"That was your dad. I only met him the one time, but as you can tell, he made quite a lasting impression."

"Thank you," I said softly. "I don't have any of my own stories about him. Now I do. So, thank you, Oscar."

"My pleasure, Miss January."

I ran a hand under my nose and took a drink. "So how did it end?"

"Still more heartbreakingly, I'm afraid. Claire was leaving, but she turned back, and with great emotion, she asked her mother why, when she'd written every week since the night she'd left, Rose had never written back."

"The letters…" I breathed.

"The letters. And the news of them shocked Rose," Oscar said. "She knew absolutely nothing about any letters, January. And when Claire realized it, when Rose realized, you could have heard a pin drop. Claire turned to her father with such fury. So did Rose. Not one word passed between them, but he knew he'd been found out. He didn't deny or admit intercepting the correspondence. He just simply lifted his chin in a bit of sad, pathetic triumph."

"Good Lord!"

"It was a long, fraught moment. But Rose finally got up and walked over to Stephen and spat, with utter disdain, 'How *dare* you?' She was absolutely seething. Of course, he said nothing, but he looked very small. She then turned to your mother and told her if she had any desire to communicate with her in the future, to do so through her attorney. She gave me a look that made me complicit."

"That sounds a little cold."

"I suppose it could have been perceived as such. But it was actually a quiet reclamation of control. Rose had openly utilized what little power she had, flaunted it, in fact, in front of Stephen. And then, in a very uncharacteristic show of stilted affection, Rose gave Claire's arm a little pat, then she walked out of the room."

"That was it?"

"That was huge, January. In less than a minute, Rose took one small step away from Stephen and toward Claire over a mine-infested battlefield. For her, it was huge and very brave."

I thought of my lavishly caged and reigned-over grandmother, her pathetic privilege, and I could suddenly see exactly what Oscar was saying. "What did Mom say to her?"

"I can't remember if she said anything. All I can still see is the way she looked at Stephen. Hurt—profoundly wounded—and disgusted. And for all his bluster, Stephen absolutely withered under the intensity." Oscar stared at me and shook his head. "That man was such a fool. He looked so empty standing there, dispossessed of the only power he really cared about." Oscar sighed. "And I remember Claire

234 - Ka Hancock

was just about out the door when he asked if she was actually thinking of marrying that *Polack*."

"What?"

Oscar nodded. "And you know what she said? She said they hadn't even talked about it, and after what Tanek had just witnessed, there was no way they ever would, which was a shame because she couldn't have imagined anything better than spending her life 'making music and babies with that amazing man.' Isn't that just lovely, January?"

A little sob burst out of me. "She said that?" I rasped.

Oscar nodded. "Music and babies...with your dad. But she told Stephen they had both lost that day. She'd lost Tanek—she thought she had—and Stephen had lost her, for good. Then she walked out." Oscar shook his head. "I don't think Claire ever spoke to her father again," he said. "Your mother was a force, my dear. An absolute force."

I chewed my lip because I could not speak.

The old man reached over and patted my hand.

"And Rose?" I said at length.

Our waitress was back, and this time I was a bit annoyed at her timing.

"Can I get you some dessert?"

"None for me, thank you," I said.

"Cheesecake with extra strawberries. No cream," Oscar said.

"You got it," the girl said, gathering our dishes. When she walked away, I drained my Coke and let a piece of ice slip into my mouth. As it melted, I thought of everything the attorney had shared with me.

"Are you okay, my dear?"

"I don't know," I said. "I just can't believe those people were my grandparents. What about Rose?" I asked again. "Did she ever get the letters?"

"I don't know what became of them," Oscar said. "But about a month later, after the holidays, I got a package in the mail. It was Claire's journal."

"She sent you her journal? Why?"

"She wanted me to give it to Rose—she'd sent it to me, as Rose told her to—so that Stephen wouldn't have the opportunity to intercept it. I think she desperately wanted her mother to see inside her life. Apparently, it was everything she'd written to her about in the letters." Oscar shrugged. "I think Claire wanted it back, her diary, but Rose never returned it." He looked at me, smiling sadly. "Paints a lovely picture of your parents falling in love, don't you think?"

"It does. So, you've read it?"

"With permission."

"What about my grandfather? Did he ever read it?"

"I don't know about that. I'd be surprised if Rose ever allowed it."

"He was a monster, wasn't he?"

"Many thought so," Oscar said. "He was damaged, so he damaged back. He decided when he was just a boy that he would someday steal his father's company out from under him—it was the driving force in an adolescence filled with intense abuse and degradation. If there is a reason or blame to be had for Stephen's choices, some of it really must be placed at the feet of his father."

I pushed out a breath. "Did he do it? Did he steal his father's company?"

"He did. He ruined his father—using all the tools his father taught him. He lured the best employees away with promises and opportunities which left his father's organization without leadership. That then exposed crippling vulnerabilities to the nervous stockholders which could not unload their investments fast enough. Then Stephen set up a successful competitor when his father's company went belly up."

I sighed into my hand. "I really am glad I didn't know him. But it's weird—I do appreciate knowing some of his story, and Rose's. And my mom's—*especially* my mom's. *Thank you*, again, Oscar."

"You're welcome, January. And now it's part of *your* story—your unique and imperfect and tragic, but wholly fascinating, story."

I looked at the old man. "I had no idea who my mom was, Oscar," I said softly. "Now I want to know everything about her."

He smiled sadly.

"That is why I'm here, isn't it? You wanted me to know her."

"I did, my dear," he admitted. "But I'm only on the errand of your grandmother. Rose knew that she was the keeper of much of her daughter's history—the bad, the difficult, as well as the splendid—and there was much splendid because *Claire* was splendid." He arched a craggy brow. "And I have no doubt, Miss January, that Rose very much would have liked the opportunity to share her every fond memory with you. But it didn't happen, so I'm doing my best for her. Because she was my dear friend, and she would have wanted me to."

"She was very lucky to have you, Oscar," I said, marveling at his devotion and the probable depths of his unrequited love for my strange grandmother.

He winked at me as the waitress set between us an enormous piece of cheesecake piled high with fresh strawberries. She had included two forks.

"Will there be anything else?" she asked, as Oscar handed her his credit card.

"No. I think you covered it nicely."

As she walked away, the lovely old man turned to me and said, "Now, you must help me eat this in honor of Rosy. It was her favorite dessert."

twenty-six

It was late afternoon when Oscar drove away from the Simon Café. We'd talked for almost two hours, and he'd left me awash in new understanding. Between the things he'd told me, the things I'd read, and the things I'd been raised knowing, my mother was taking shape in a way she never had before. I was beginning to see the woman she had been. I'd known Claire was educated and talented. But I had no idea she'd been *privileged*—at least, not in an actual *eligible-to-inherit-millions* kind of way. Nor in a *never-wanted-it* kind of way. I'd had no idea about that. Or that she'd been mistreated. Manipulated. Threatened. I knew her parents hadn't approved of my dad in a spectacular way, but the rest…I'd never known how unflinching she'd been to stand up to all that.

The woman Oscar had described, the woman I had read about, knew herself, and knew the liability of being who she was. What was it she'd said in her journal? My dad had to meet her parents, he had to see what she'd come from even if it proved to be a deal-breaker—before she wouldn't be able to unlove him. I'd never known anyone like her…

Suddenly, into this reverie screeched Grandy's indelible words: "Did you lose the love of your life? Did he die in a crushing accident, leaving you a disabled widow at the age of twenty-four? No, that would be your mother." Those biting words echoed out of nowhere, stinging even worse than when she'd shouted them the first time.

I shuddered. My mother, *my* mother, my broken little mother, over the last few days, had *become* someone I desperately wished I'd known—wanted to know. A heartbreaking image of her filled my mind. It was the last time I'd seen Claire: curled up on her bed, sad, weeping, and alone—so very alone.

I started the engine and pulled out of the parking lot.

***

The normal ninety-minute drive from Chestnut Hill to Wallington took well over two hours thanks to commuter traffic, and I nearly talked myself out of stopping at Potomac Manor when I saw the standstill on I-95. But I hung in there even as the pit in my stomach pulsed. I took the Glen Ridge exit, asked Google where the nearest florist was, then followed the directions only to find *The Rosebud* closed. I called two more flower shops and got the same result. So, I hit the Costco in Clifton where I picked up a vase and two dozen white roses. I arranged them in the restroom and felt infinitely better for having done so. Now I had an actual reason to see Claire—and flowers to hide behind.

When I got to Potomac Manor, Harry Golding was sitting at the reception desk with his sleeves rolled up. He looked a tiny bit out of place. As PM's owner and proprietor, he wasn't typically seen doing manual labor. He smiled warmly. "Well, hello, January. What a lovely sight *you* are." He looked more than the usual surprised to see me.

"Harry," I smiled back. "Adding to your job description these days?"

He chuckled, preoccupied. "Just momentarily. How strange that you're here. I was just thinking of calling your grandmother."

"Why?" I said, setting my flowers on the counter. Indicating them, I explained, "Not sure you heard, but Mom's mother died."

"Yes. I know. And our Claire is having an awfully tough time of it. Hence my concern."

"What?" I said, alarmed. "What's happening?"

Harry sighed. "I just think she'll be very happy to see you. She hasn't really engaged much today. In fact, I don't think she's left her room at all, which is not like her. I know an aide took her dinner in because she didn't come to the dining room this evening."

"Oh…" Suddenly I cowered, not sure there was anything *I* could do. I wasn't even absolutely sure why I was here. Not really. I'd had the plan to drop by, bring flowers, but other than that…. Now Claire *needed* me?

"January?"

I refocused again on Harry, whom, in truth, I'd been staring at all along, just not seeing. "Yes?"

"She's in her room. Maybe you can get her to eat something."

I picked up my flowers. "I'll try," I said feeling unequal to this task. But then I stopped, put the flowers back on the counter and held up a finger. "I'll be right back," I said.

It was probably a mistake, but if Claire was this affected by the loss of her mother, it might help. Outside I popped the trunk of my car, which was crammed with the boxes Tyson and I had packed yesterday. I dug through a couple of them before I found what I was looking for, and when I did, I put it in my purse. I was just about to shut my trunk when the dress I'd found for her caught my eye. It, along with the white sweater, were still on the hanger inside a dry-cleaner's bag Tyson had taken from another outfit in Claire's closet. I pulled it out now—another good excuse to be here, and something to talk about. I draped the dress over my arm, shut the trunk and walked back into the building, where Harry had been joined by Zuli Morrison. He and the receptionist were discussing the expected arrival of a new resident, so I picked up my flowers and did not disturb them.

At Mom's door, I steeled myself before I knocked, as I always did. But this time was a little different. This time I knew what I was walking into. I cracked the door a couple of inches. "Mom? It's me."

The room was a bit dim with early evening shade, and Claire was just sitting. No music. No TV. No light.

"Mom?"

I walked in, and she smiled at me—a smile slightly less joy-filled than usual.

"I…I brought you some flowers," I said, placing the vase on the small table separating two chairs near her bed.

Her eye widened in surprise, and she tried to stand, but I kissed her cheek and told her not to get up. Then I pushed the vacant chair a bit closer to her and turned on the lamp. "I felt bad about Rose," I began. "About how I told you about her. I'm so sorry, I just didn't…anyway, I love white roses, so I brought you some."

She breached the small space I'd created between us and pulled my hand to her lips, tugging me toward her in the process. There was a tear in her eye, and it made my eyes sting.

"Oh, Mom…" I said, at a loss.

Claire took in the plastic-wrapped dress puddled in my lap. I'd forgotten about it, and now I was happy to have something else to say. "Oh, I picked this out for you to wear to the funeral." I held up the dress and the sweater. "I think it will be perfect."

If she recognized it, she gave no indication, but again, her good eye welled up when she heard the word *funeral*.

I cleared my throat and didn't know what else to say, so I stood and hung the dress on the back of the closet door. Then it was awkward and brittle, my mother as far removed as possible from the fascinating woman of strength and self-assurance I had been hearing about. She was looking at me now with such naked aching that it hurt my heart. I had wanted to come, but now that I was here I felt completely useless.

I was about to tell her that I'd just stopped by to check on her and couldn't really stay, when I noticed the dinner tray on the ottoman and remembered what Harry had said. The plate had a plastic dome over it to keep it warm. I walked over and removed it. Pork chop, broccoli, rice pilaf. There was a soda beaded with sweat, an éclair, and a bowl of applesauce. All untouched. It was just past 6:30. Dinner had been served an hour ago. "Mom, you have to eat."

She covered her face with her hands, and I heard her whimper.

I didn't know what to do. "Do you—should I cut it for you?"

She moved her hands and blinked twice for no.

"How 'bout the applesauce? You like applesauce."

Two blinks.

I sat back down and looked at her, a little amazed at how helpless I felt. When I couldn't think of anything else to do, I reached over and popped the top on her soda and placed it in her hand. "At least drink this," I said. "It's totally bad for you, but it tastes good."

That got the tiniest smile. And a sip.

"Good girl," I said, feeling inordinately victorious.

After a few more sips, she set it down and again reached for my hand. It was nice but awkward, the way one-way conversations are. "I'd better go, Mom. I've been gone all day, and I'm sure the bodies are stacking up."

One blink and another tiny smile.

When I reached for my purse, I could see what I'd placed there.

"Oh…" I looked at my mother, whom I had a history of hurting unintentionally. Would I do it again by giving this to her? "Mom…" I hesitated. "I was thinking that if…if I lost you, if something happened to you, I think it would help me if I had a picture of you. I don't know if that's how you feel, but I…I took a chance…." I handed her the photograph I'd found on the dresser in her room. Of course, I had no idea the occasion, but the laughter you could almost hear, the mussed hair and the soiled clothes had all comprised a memory she'd made with Rose. And it had clearly meant something to my mother at one time. Amazingly, her reaction now seemed to indicate it still did.

One hand floated to her chest and the other trembled as she took the photo from me. The sound at the bottom of my mother's throat was both cry and laugh. She clearly remembered her mother, which by now was not a surprise, but she also seemed to remember the circumstances of this photo. Oh, how I wish she could tell me about that day. Claire brought the picture close, studied it, stroked it with a shaky finger, seemed to get lost in it. And suddenly it didn't matter that I didn't have the details. She did. In fact, she was so lost in the memory that I started to feel like an intruder. After a moment, I quietly stood, kissed her head, and walked out. I don't think she even noticed.

No one was at the reception desk when I left, so there was no one to tell that I hadn't gotten Claire to eat anything. But twenty minutes later, when I returned with Mom's favorite Quarter-Pounder with Cheese, no pickles, and large fries, Zuli was at her station and nodded her approval. When I walked back into Mom's room, she was still staring at the picture, but she looked up at me with a tear running down her face. I'm not sure she realized I'd left. I held up the McDonald's bag and her eye widened.

"Okay," I said. "No excuses. Now you *have* to eat."

One blink, still the tear, but now a smile.

twenty-seven

Saturday left me little time for reflection. I'd wanted to check in with Tyson, to fill him in about my lunch with Oscar, my visit with Claire, and to see if things felt cool between us...or awkward. But unfortunately, I never really got the chance. His mother was back in the hospital, this time with an infection, and it sounded serious. When I'd called, Tyson had been edgy with me—or just edgy in general, but I took it personally, which I shouldn't have. Nicole Pierce was at Sisters of Charity Med Center being prepped for surgery—of course he was edgy. I thought of sending flowers, but when Calvin said he was on his way over there to pick up a body, I had him stop in East Rutherford for Krispy Kremes and leave them with Tyson's family. The gesture seemed to hit its mark. I got a lengthy text a while later that was rife with unnecessary (but appreciated) appreciation.

I texted Tyson a quick "Good luck" and told him I was thinking about him and his mom. That was all I had time for, because by then I was knee-deep in a very sad burn case. Ethan Bale was a Mormon bishop who had been on a campout with a group of scouts when his trailer caught fire. He'd gone in after five boys. They'd survived; he had not. The Medical Examiner's office had just released his remains, but the accident had happened the night before last at the Panther Lake Campground.

Poppy, Tess and I stood over the man, his arms and chest and lower face badly scorched, parts even blackened—one hand appeared encased in a glove of hardened soot.

"We can't fix this," Tess said.

"No," Poppy said, shaking his head.

"Do we embalm?" I asked.

He chewed on the question for a few beats. "Topically," he finally decided. "I think that's our only option. Wash him down thoroughly—use a gallon of Neutroline if you need to. We have to get rid of the smell before we let the wife see him."

"Poppy…"

He sighed. "She's a nurse, so that helps—she's seen gruesome things. She's also insisting that she be the one to dress him."

"Noooo, Poppy," I groaned. "Please, no."

"I think it will be all right. It's just the consult tonight; I've asked her not to come alone, and she said she'll bring her brother. I'm actually more concerned about him."

I gazed down at our deceased. "Are you sure? Why are we doing this?"

"They're Mormons; their dead are dressed in ceremonial clothing, and we respect whatever they require of us." He eyed me with emphasis. "I met the wife. I have a feeling it will be okay—this is very, *very* important to her—and with your help, Janny, I think it will be okay. They'll be here around five, so you have all afternoon. Do your best. You'll be fine."

"No, I won't…" I whined.

But if anything takes you out of your own woes, it's meeting the new widow of a man who kissed her goodbye two days ago, piled his two sons and three of their friends into the family SUV, and headed to the lake, only to die saving those kids after a propane tank exploded too close to the gas line that fed their trailer. Or something like that. The petite blond woman explained it to me with such detached poise that I was too fascinated by her to fully grasp what she was saying. Belinda Bale said each boy had a slightly different version of what had happened, except for the part where her husband had run in after them. He apparently threw two of them out the door while two others followed him out on their knees. What got him in trouble was going back for the boy he hadn't known was already out and cowering under a picnic table. Mr. Bale was still inside when the camper exploded.

The woman told me all this as her brother somberly held her hand.

"Of course, there will be no viewing," she said. "*No one* is to see him."

"Of course."

"But I would like to help dress him, when you get to that point."

I nodded. "Probably tomorrow evening."

"And my children will each have a note for him, which I would like you to place in his hand before the funeral, if that's okay."

"Absolutely."

"Thank you," she said, her voice trembling.

I was simultaneously saddened and intrigued by her. "I'm so sorry, Mrs. Bale."

"Me, too."

Her brother put his arm around her, and she leaned into him. "Let's go, Mitch," she rasped.

It was a few hours later when I finished wrapping Mr. Bale's limbs in plastic sheeting. He'd been topically embalmed and was lying on an absorbent bed of foam, air drying. After he was dressed and his wife had said her final goodbye, the man would be wrapped securely in another layer of sheeting—as was our protocol with the badly burned. Then the coffin would be permanently closed.

"You have a very nice wife, Mr. Bale...Bishop Bale," I said softly. "I'm so sorry you had to leave her this way. But...saving all those kids...that probably got you to the head of the heaven line. So, well done, sir."

"Oh...this smell...this smell I know..." Babi moaned, suddenly at my side. "Is hurts my heart."

"I didn't hear you come in," I said, turning to my little Babka. "You need to make more noise."

"You need more better ears."

"Are you okay?"

With her hand over her nose and tears misting her eyes, she said, "I make especial pinwheel for this fine man. I heared the news on the TV what he did do."

"That would be nice," I said eyeing her as I wheeled him into the fridge. "I know you don't usually do this, but can you make four?"

Babi looked at me.

"He had four kids—two that he saved."

"I can do for this. Now come up and eat the something."

"Are you sure you're okay?"

"Bad rememberings is this smell. Let's go up, Kochanie."

***

It was a wickedly busy weekend, and I was bone tired when I finally crawled into bed on Sunday night. Besides finishing up with Ethan Bale, I had done an embalming, and dressed and made up a middle-aged woman who'd been brought in Friday while I was in Chestnut Hill with Oscar. And just when I'd thought we were caught up, we'd gotten a trauma that had taken Tess and me deep into the night to put back together. So, I'd been busy. But despite this, I kept hoping I would hear from Tyson. I never did. Around six—before we dove into our trauma case—I had texted, "Thinking of you. How is your mom?" But I never heard anything back, and I didn't feel like I could reach out again without being a nuisance. Now it was far too late. But I was a little bugged. And I was a little bugged that I was bugged.

To distract myself I got out of bed and retrieved Claire's journal from my bag. I wasn't bothered so much that I hadn't heard from him—not true, I *was* bothered—but it was more not knowing what had happened. What kind of infection compels surgery and a family camped out in the waiting room? I just truly hoped everything was okay. I liked Nicole Pierce. And I liked that she liked me. I checked my phone again for a possible text from Tyson. Nothing. Since yesterday.

After a moment of staring at the ceiling and imagining too hard, I opened Mom's journal with a sigh. I'd left off on December 2, 1999—Mom had been in New York and met with Oscar about her plan to emancipate from her inheritance. The contract was in place, and she'd reached out to her parents to let them know she was bringing Dad home to meet them the next weekend.

> Oscar has agreed to be there to answer any legal questions. He's a gem and I worry that I have put him in an awkward position with Dad. But he has assured me that he is as much my attorney as he is his, so I shouldn't stress. Easy words. I'm just grateful it's done and off my plate. It paved the way for a fabulous time in New York.

It was just going to be me and Monica, the tree-lighting at Rockefeller, some Christmas shopping, and a little Broadway for Mom's birthday. But as luck would have it, things turned out even better: At the last minute, Tan was able to break away and come to the city, and Mom's new honey, Jonathon, was just waiting to be included. The four of us swam through the humanity to see the tree, then gorged on Italian food. Then we went dancing, which was so not me, but was still the most fun I've had in ages.

It killed me to have to say goodbye to Tanek, but he had to get back—he had two in the fridge and one he'd left with a hose in his thigh. (I didn't ask.) Before he left, he gave me a note from his mother and invited me to come back to Wallington for Christmas. I just smiled because, honestly, who knows what's going to happen after T meets Mom and Dad next week?

This was the fabulous little card from Diana Duzinski. Taping it here so it never gets lost. I love that woman!

Dear Claire,

I just wanted to thank you for spending Thanksgiving with us. You were such a lovely addition to our holiday, and of course my son simply glows with affection for you. As does our Rahe— she was very sad when she woke to find you had gone. Needless to say, dear girl, you have many fans here in NJ. I won't presume to understand the difficulties going on in your family right now, but I am sorry that you're experiencing them. Please know that you're always welcome in our home and we would love to see you again any time. Christmas, perhaps?

Best wishes,
Diana

December 9, 1999

My father died today. He's still breathing, but today was the end of us, and I'm mourning, I truly am. I'm mourning the death of him and me, and I'm mourning the awful meeting, and I'm mad that I'm mourning. I've never been so mad. It oozed out of me—and it keeps oozing out of me, this rage. I don't know what I expected when I planned to reject my inheritance, but suffice it to say, it was a thousand times worse. And I really, really don't know what I was thinking to combine that task with the intro of T to my parents. I just know it was important that Tanek understand what they were about, and what I was walking away from. But it turned out so ugly. So very, very ugly.

I'm so sure that Dad's horribleness has cost me my relationship with Tanek that I've lashed out at him, seemingly to make sure. I'm insane, I've gone completely insane! But I just couldn't take T's goodness. I couldn't take his understanding. And it irritated me beyond reason. I don't even know why. We argued, and I pushed him away—why? Because he was trying to help me wrap my head around what had happened—that my dad had schemed to trap me with his money? Tanek was too...*calm* about it. Too rational. I couldn't take it, and I made him leave, and now he's called five times and I haven't picked up once. Who am I? What am I doing? I can't find myself! I can't land on the way I'm supposed to feel. I can't even describe it. It feels like a death. Again. How many times can a man betray his daughter?

Dad beat T up mercilessly. And me, too, so of course I question T's motives for still loving me? I'm an idiot! I'm deranged! And I hate, Hate, HATE my father for doing this to me, to Tanek—especially to Tanek. I hate him for injecting his poison into us, into beautiful us.

I can't believe the words that actually came out his mouth, the names he called Tanek, the way he spoke to him, how he belittled him. I've never been so ashamed to be Stephen Winston's daughter. And I can't believe how my Tanek just took it. How can I ever face him again?

It's over. Dad and I—we are truly severed. And Tanek and I, we're over, too, before we ever even left the gate. And I'm truly sick—because I really can't imagine a better life than being with him. But that will never happen now.

In the back of my heart, I was worried that I would be scared when it came right down to telling Dad what I'd done. And I was...a little. But it wasn't as frightening as it was lifesaving. So why am I so, so angry, so heartsick? I've been set free from an underwater bear-trap—that's what it feels like! I made it to the surface, panting and damaged, with casualties all around me. But I'm breathing, dammit...I'm breathing! And now I don't know how to feel—sad, mortified, furious, disgusted...scared.

I'm a liar because fear has floated to the top of my cesspool of emotion. Actually, I'm terrified. I'm terrified that I will never see Tanek again. His last message broke me, as if I wasn't broken already. He actually said he didn't deserve to be treated like this (and he doesn't!)—he'd done nothing but love me. And if that wasn't enough then he wished me well, but said it was probably for the best I figure things out on my own. I thought that was a good idea for about 10 hellish minutes then I called him. But his phone just rang and rang. This is such a mess! Please call. Please call just one more time and love me at my most unlovable. I'm so sorry! I warned you! I did. I tried to warn you.

My poor mom. If Oscar hadn't told me what went down, I wouldn't have such a clear picture of what she'd gone through. This was painful. This was agonizing.

December 11, 1999

I guess somewhere in the fine print of the best friend's handbook, it apparently says you must call out truth—even when it devastates. T never called again. Not for two days! And I was whining to Monica about it—which I pride myself on seldom doing, whining—when she rather meanly laid the whole thing at my feet. She asked what I expected when I'd pushed the nicest guy in the world down the stairs after my father had already pushed him down the stairs. Said I was rather horrible, that maybe I didn't deserve him. I was stunned and hurt and even more so when it sank in that she might be right. I hung up on her—which was seemingly the extent of my maturity at that moment. But when she called back, she called me on it—again. She said she loved me, and she knew that I knew she was right. Then she said, "You're welcome!" and hung up on *me*.

I mulled and wallowed until the truth she'd so eloquently revealed set in. Then I drove to Wallington in a panic. All I could say when I saw him was: "I'm sorry—completely, utterly, absolutely, consumed by 'sorry.'" T probably had a dozen things he should have said to me, had every right to say to me, but all he did was open his arms and let me weep. I hate being fragile. I hate it. It's never served me well. But there I was, the textbook definition of breakable in my sweats and unwashed hair, unmade-up face, red-swollen eyes—amputated from a father and having placed what felt like my lifeline at risk, trembling inside that lifeline's embrace. I said what I went to say about a dozen times—I'm sorry—and he let me say it, ad nauseum. I took that as a win. I'd yanked him from his work in the middle of the afternoon, and I knew he had to get back, so I asked him just one question: Had I lost him?

T started to cry a little and said, "No." Actually, he said, "Hell, no! Then he hugged me so hard I almost couldn't breathe.

It scares me how much I love this man. And just like Monica said, I soooo, so don't deserve him.

Oh. My…I pulled the journal to my chest like it was child that needed comforting. I could feel what they'd felt in that moment. Both of them. It was raw and tender and painful and overwhelming. I fell asleep weeping.

twenty-eight

I was already awake when my alarm went off the next morning. It had been a short night, and I woke with the same words I'd fallen asleep with—my mom's "Have I lost you?" and my dad's "Hell no!" as he'd crushed the breath out of her. That scene was now forever carved in my gray matter.

The whole journal entry was so heartrending. The pain and confusion she'd felt was palpable. I loved that she'd described what had happened as the death of her father. It was weird, though, and sad, that Rose had not been mentioned at all aside from being a possible casualty. In the terrible aftermath of that pivotal meeting, my mom knew she could never have reached out to her strange mother. I thought that was beyond tragic.

I sighed. In a couple of hours, I would pick up Claire and take her to the funeral of that strange mother, a woman with whom she'd had the most bizarre relationship. Bizarre, yet weirdly tender, and one Claire apparently mourned, which continued to astound me. Rose was such an enigma. Yes, there was much to dislike. But there was also much to pity, and probably reasons for all of it.

I still wished I had met her.

Poppy loves to say, "Ice has no choice but to melt." Could Rose have melted if I'd gotten the chance to know her? Of course, thoughts like these were complete treason to my father and, by extension, my grandparents. No wonder I wasn't sleeping.

I rolled over and stretched, checked the clock. I had time. I picked up Mom's journal to where I'd fallen asleep—the lovely make-up scene. Four days later…

December 15, 1999
    After the big showdown, I thought I might hear from Mom, but that would be a no. She makes me so tired…

I chuckled at the thought that Rose had probably disrupted Mom's sleep, too. For years.

    …But I'm settling into my new skin, nonetheless. I've balanced my checkbook, had my tires rotated, and put the utilities in my name, all things Dad had always taken care of. But most importantly, Tanek and I have been able to dissect and process what happened last week, and we're back on track—my words. He says we were never off. I love that about him! He's asked me again about spending Christmas with his family, and it looks like I will, but it still feels a bit pathetic—orphaned girl saved from lonely holidays by big-hearted boyfriend. Sigh.

December 20, 1999
    So far December has been a blur. Study, finals, holiday concerts, parties I've been hired to play, and my YSM recital is coming up in two days. That's a big deal and very stressful because I'm performing my original composition for my department. It can't come fast enough! I live for Sunday nights when I meet T for dinner, and can I just say, it's getting harder and harder to say goodbye to him. It's almost as if we've drawn closer thanks to what Dad did. I'm not prone to infatuation, so I have no choice but to trust this thing that seems to be growing between us.
    I heard from Monica, who heard from her dad that my dad is on a world apology tour where I'm concerned. Apparently, he's telling people that I'm too embarrassed

to show my face in Chestnut Hill society this season after what I did to Denton back in September. He's saying that he's tried to reason with me, but it's hopeless, I'm hopeless. That seems par for him, and exactly how he *would* explain my absence at his company bash.

December 21, 1999 (1:48 am)

It's late (or early, I guess), and I'm in NY again, this time for a Christmas performance. Mom's gone to bed, but I can't sleep...I woke up in a funk this morning, and the day followed suit. I was so preoccupied that I may have bombed my music history final. I'd reserved a piano studio for practice, but for two hours I played like a robot. It's because it's the 20th—or it was until a few hours ago, and I can't remember a time when I've been excluded from the festivities of that night—20th of December every year. Even the year I was recovering from my tonsillectomy, Dad still made me play for his big night. But not this year, and I'm heartbroken—not because of Dad, but because that party *is* Christmas.

All evening I imagined the ballroom at the Four Seasons in Philly filled to capacity. I have such great memories of that standing black-tie soirée—the room, the tree, the grand piano, the tables, the candles, the dancing. To not be part of it this year has hurt me more than I expected. Earlier today I actually considered just showing up and taking my seat per usual at the piano like nothing was amiss. But of course, everything is amiss.

So instead, knowing my parents would be gone, I decided to drive home. It was silly, really. I was headed to New York, and I would be doubling my travel time with that detour. But somehow it didn't matter.

I hate to admit it, but I cried a little when I got there. I so love the neighborhood all Christmased up—I always have. I sat in the driveway for a long time. I think

I was actually afraid to get out because I half expected the locks to have been changed. But my key still worked, and I stepped into the evergreen memories of my childhood and the crisp pine scent that always takes me there. I love that smell.

The house was, of course, simply and tastefully decked, and I just breathed it in. The silver angels on the entry table, the soft white lights casting the foyer in that great shadowy twinkle. Enormous, long-needled swags, glowing with a pearlescent shimmer. It was lovely, so lovely. All of it. I'd missed my house—I'd missed the happy times.

The tree was in the library, of course, and it, too, was simple and softly lit. I just stood in the quiet, and it felt so very strange to be there—strange and full of memories, mostly just the good ones. I'd grown up in that room, lost myself in the books that filled those shelves: *Memoirs of Hadrian*, *The Sheltering Sky*, Dorothy Parker, Edith Wharton's *House of Mirth*. I'd lost myself there in Bach and Schubert and Chopin as well, even some Nirvana.

Maybe I'd just lost myself, period.

I'd loved all the trappings of the season—the whole month of celebration. And the presents. Of course, I figured out early they were kind of a stand-in for actual affection, but the bigger the gift, the bigger the statement of such, so that was nice. The Barbie Dream House I'd wanted once with just two occupants vs. the custom-made castle that I actually received. It was as tall as I was and came with ten Barbies to attend a specially commissioned Barbie that looked just like me. It was way over the top, but I remember Dad was beyond excited to give it to me, and that was the real gift. One year, I got a miniature car. Literally. Gas pedal, power steering, windows that rolled down. That year, Dad laid an asphalt track around the lower garden for me to drive on, which doubled as a walking path for Mom. That turned out to be especially nice because she and I spent a lot of time together on that path.

The gifts weren't always so appreciated. Like the year I got a new school uniform and was told that after the holiday break I would be starting at Christman Academy. Amputated from my friends and budding social life in one clean slice, and under the guise of a lavish gift I was not allowed to be ungrateful for. So, no, not my best Christmas—even if I ended up loving Christman. Three years ago was good, though. A linen envelope that had held the notarized document printed in gold. It said that since I'd earned a full ride to Yale, I'd need a place to live. The gift was a deed to an off-campus condo. I now owned real estate in New Haven—which was a true blessing considering my current situation...

The tree was pretty, but it was barren underneath except for a couple of emergency gifts for those brave souls who would show up with an unexpected offering. They were pre-tagged with "Warmest Wishes—The Winstons." I added my small package to the sad pile—A hand-painted silk scarf, the color of burnt lavender. Mom loved scarves, and this one would look fabulous with her hair. I'd wrapped it in utility paper and holly berries, which would make it hard to miss.

I didn't expect there to be anything for me, but I looked anyway. The small red box wasn't under the tree, it was in the boughs, hidden, but not well, with a tag on which my name had been written in Mom's handwriting. I opened it and started to weep. The delicate butterfly was fashioned from Swarovski crystal—small enough to fit in the palm of my hand, big enough to break my heart. Our secret language—my mother's and mine. This is how I knew she still loved me.

There was a tiny parchment printed in calligraphy and signed by the artist: "The butterfly is the very evolution of beauty: exquisite, graceful, intelligent, fiercely independent, ferociously admired. Free." Free, was underlined. Oh, Mom.

It all felt so stupidly futile, so wrong, so broken. I almost left then, but it felt too undone to just walk out, so I sat there a while longer and watched the tree and the ghosts of my life. My heart was pretty scabbed over where Dad was concerned, but Mom...I ached for her and me—the her and me that we should have been.

Upstairs in my room, I did the only thing I could think of: I took down two of the faded butterflies from the swarm above my bed. Their absence didn't make a dent. Then I placed them on my mother's pillow. At least she would know I had thought of her, too.

I was almost to New York when Tanek called. I tried to keep things light, but he knew. Small talk is not really our thing, and it didn't take him long to get around to asking what he was dying to know—he's so transparent. He told me his Busha's Polish Christmas Eve was a pretty big deal at his house, and he wanted to make sure I was going to be there. What could I say? I—

My phone rang, yanking me back to my own world. It was Oscar, but at 7:45 it seemed a bit early for him to be calling.

"Good morning," I said with a bit of trepidation.

He chuckled. "Good, I didn't wake you. I *didn't* wake you, did I?"

"No. But what's going on?"

"I was just wondering if you could arrange to get here a few minutes early today. I need to speak with you."

"Should I be worried?"

"No, but it's important."

"Then I'll be there," I said, getting out of bed. "11:15 is about as early as I can promise. Will that work?"

"I'll see you then, January."

Before I jumped in the shower, I texted Tyson, but when I got out, he had not texted back. I didn't know what to think, but I decided there was nothing else I could do. I'd hear from him when I heard from him…or I wouldn't. Then I said a tiny prayer that his mom was okay.

I dressed in a fitted dark-gray three-quarter-sleeve dress and red heels, took time with my makeup, and borrowed some diamond studs from Grandy. She said I looked pretty.

We were shuffling responsibilities this morning. Tess would fill in for Grandy, Grandy would fill in for me getting Claire ready and bringing her to the funeral so I could meet with Oscar. Calvin would run interference while Poppy filled in for Tess with an embalming before he left. Tess and Calvin would then handle a funeral that was scheduled at Duzy House so that Poppy could get to Rose's service in Chestnut Hill by noon. My fingers were crossed that nobody died near Wallington until this afternoon. Fat chance.

I was quite proud of myself as I took the elevator down at 9:30 with all my ducks in a row—as Poppy would say. I had my needed hour and 45 minutes to get to Chestnut Hill. I'd be missing most of the commuter traffic, so I'd even have time to stop for a Coke before I got on the freeway. But then as I walked through our lobby, I saw Tyson coming through the glass doors. He stopped when he saw me, took me in and smiled. He looked beaten up and exhausted.

"Hey," I said, surprised.

"Hey."

I walked over to him. "I've been so worried," I said. "What's happening?"

He shook his head.

"Tyson, is your mom…"

"Yeah," he breathed. "Yeah. She's okay. Took a little trip to hell, but she's okay now."

"What happened?"

He blew out a breath. "She…I don't even know for sure. She got so sick, so suddenly. They took her into surgery—then about six hours later they took her back into surgery." He blew out a breath. "She's stable now. They think they'll move her out of ICU tonight."

"Why didn't you call me?" *Did I sound annoyed? Don't sound annoyed!*

He groaned. "Someone stole my phone. That's a whole other nightmare. But I couldn't even call you on another phone because your number is in my stolen phone, and I don't know it." He pulled me into his arms. "Kill me now. I'm so sorry. I'm just glad I didn't miss you. I know this is a big day and I just...I wanted you to know that I know it's a big day, and I'll be thinking about you."

"What? Are you kidding me?"

"No." He squeezed me a little, then let go. "How did it go, anyway? You know, *meeting* your grandma? I think that's what you were doing when you went back yesterday—to the mortuary."

"It was," I said, still processing that he was here for *me*. "And I'll tell you all about it. Soon. But go home now. Get some sleep. We'll talk about me later."

He smiled wearily, nodded, took me in again. "You look *really* nice."

"You're sweet."

"I'll call you later," he promised, then caught himself. "I guess I mean I'll be in touch...*somehow*. What's your number?"

I laughed and grabbed a business card from the entry table. "My number's the same except it ends with a 5."

"Got it," he said tiredly pocketing the card. Then he leaned over and kissed me the way people do who've been kissing each other their whole lives: quick and a bit mindless, but fraught with belonging. I liked it. We looked at each other for a few beats. He didn't say anything and neither did I. Then he *really* kissed me, and I walked him to his car.

twenty-nine

It was a few minutes later than I'd promised when I pulled into the Grove Crest parking lot next to Oscar Thibodeau. But all things considered, I wasn't sorry. He smiled forgivingly and got out of his car. I checked my face in the rearview mirror and got out of mine.

Rose's attorney, and my new friend, looked very crisp in his black three-piece and respectful gray tie. Silver cufflinks caught the sunlight but were not ostentatious, and he smelled nice. "Thank you for coming early-*ish*, January."

I offered a wry smile as we walked. "As I recall, you didn't really give me a choice."

"That's true," he said, holding the door.

The same greeter I'd met when I was here before welcomed us this morning with the same somber bearing, same thin smile. Oscar asked him if we could meet privately for a moment, and the man led us to a small office across from the receiving room where my grandmother reposed peacefully. Rose was in the corner amid a garden of floral monstrosities—a gaudy contest, it would seem, of one-upmanship among her peers.

Oscar looked annoyed at the display but said nothing. Once we were seated, he didn't waste any time. He checked his watch and opened his briefcase. "I'm sorry if this seems so cloak and dagger, January, but I ran across this in Stephen's safe, and I really wanted it in your hands before the legatees meet this afternoon to begin the process of disassembling the estate."

I looked at him. He looked at me. Then Oscar Thibodeau handed me a large envelope. From it I pulled a photograph of a young, very lovely—if dated—sophisticated family. Stephen Winston looked every cent his net worth, impeccable in a tuxedo and bow tie; Rose was in royal blue and pearls, her blond hair long and flowing down one shoulder—a '70s vibe, for sure, but classically comported. Neither were looking at the camera, but were both fixated on the sleeping, baby girl nestled between them, twin looks of adoration infusing their expressions. My mother, only weeks old, was angelic in her long blush-pink, sleeveless gown, a delicate bracelet around her chubby wrist. They looked royal, my mother and her parents. Regal and somehow insulated as if nothing would have ever been allowed to intrude upon their little circle of privilege.

I looked over at Oscar, now slightly blurred with my tears. "Why would the legatees care about this picture?"

He handed me a box emblazoned with the Cartier logo. "It's not the picture they would care about, my dear."

Inside the fancy box was another, this one velvet, and inside that one lay the miniature bracelet my infant mother was wearing in the photo. I lifted it from its soft enclosure. It was a circle of tiny diamonds, exquisitely crafted, perfectly adorable, and absolutely stunning.

"Stephen had it custom made—of course," Oscar said. "Here's the certificate. He paid $21,000, forty-plus years ago. I had it loosely appraised yesterday for more than triple that."

I fingered the stones then looked at him. "Wow."

"I'd like you to have it, January."

I swallowed. "What?"

"Again, this bracelet falls into that ambiguous category of once belonging to your mother. But I knew Stephen. I know how his mind worked, and I think this *heirloom* was actually meant for you. And if your father had been that much-ballyhooed senator-to-be—and not the amazing Polish mortician your mother chose—you would have received it. I'm almost certain Stephen imagined side-by-side portraits—" Oscar tapped the photo. "He and his daughter, his daughter and hers, the bracelet the unifying factor."

Again, I gazed down at the sparkling sadness I was holding in my hands, eternally unworthy of it in my grandfather's eyes because I had the wrong father. "I don't think I want it," I said. "It's lovely, and it belonged to my mother, but—"

"Yes, you do," Oscar interrupted. "Your mother would want you to have it. Maybe especially because your grandfather didn't."

"I don't know…"

"I do. At any rate, my dear, it's nearly inconsequential compared to the rest of the estate, but the legatees would definitely make a case for it." He flipped his hand. "It's the down payment on a house, for heaven's sake…or a lovely bequest for a daughter of your own someday. And it's a good story. You have to admit, it's a good story. You could also consider it a legacy from both Rose and Claire."

"I don't know what to say, Oscar." I leaned over and kissed his cheek. A Steinway and now diamonds. Lovely *things*, no question, but the true prize was this man who'd so generously taken me under his wing. "Thank you," I said. "I know I'll come up with something better *eventually*, but for now: *Thank you*. So much."

"You're very welcome, January. I also went over early this morning and had the portrait of your mother taken down. At the moment it's in the kitchen, tagged as unavailable—for the legatees. But I'll have it moved to my office first thing, if you decide you want it."

"I definitely want it. Thank you, Oscar."

"Good." Oscar Thibodeau smiled, cocked his head. "I've very much enjoyed getting to know you, Miss January. I truly hope today isn't the end of our acquaintance."

"Me, too, Oscar. Me too."

***

It was about 11:45 when Oscar and I finished up, and people were gathering in earnest for Rose's service. Evidently, my grandmother had organized things herself as a sort of wake. People did that—made their own arrangements—for a variety of reasons, one of which might be to entice an audience, which seemed would have been important to Rose. But if my grandmother had feared no one would attend her final send-off, she need not have worried. It looked to be the social event of the week. Air kisses and firm handshakes, gentlemanly backslaps and aggrieved countenances were all on solemn and tasteful display amid high fashion and cloying perfumery.

In the room where Rose was reposing, I looked around and didn't see my family—or anywhere to sit—so I decided to pay my last respects. My grandmother had been freshened, her hair re-puffed, her lips re-moistened. She looked nice. As I gazed down at her, I thought of all that had transpired over the last few days. I'd never met Rose, but I'd had enough of a glimpse of her to mar the perspective ingrained in me, and I was grateful for that. To know now that Stephen Winston had had the power to destroy my grandparents—their livelihood, their business, quite possibly my parents' marriage—and that Rose had sacrificed herself to prevent it was remarkable to me. How could I feel animosity for this tragic woman? I reached out and ran a finger over the strand of pearls she was holding—the inexpensive but priceless gift from my mom. It seemed few realized that at the end of the day, Rose Winston truly did have a mother's heart.

As I stood there, rather lost in these thoughts, two women walked up to the casket. I stepped aside to give them a bit of space.

"Rosy, Rosy, Rosy..." the taller of the two said softly.

"She looks pretty good," the older one remarked. "Don't you think?"

"Rose was always beautiful. On the outside."

"True enough, Monica," said the older lady, who was now glancing around. "Do you think there's any chance she'll be here?"

"Of course not, Mom. Claire wouldn't even know Rose. And you know she's bedridden."

The older woman sighed. "Oh, I know, I just thought..." She sighed. "The whole thing is just so sad. Oh, look, there's Barb. I'll see you inside, sweetheart."

My heart was rather thumping as I stole a glance at the woman standing next to me: mid-forties, gorgeous, with shoulder-length reddish hair and very cool glasses, but she was still a shadow of the girl I'd seen in so many of Claire's photos. Her mother had walked away, but this woman seemed in no hurry to follow her as she continued to gaze down at my grandmother.

"She'll be here," I said, softly.

The tall woman looked over at me. "I'm sorry. Were you speaking to me?"

I nodded. "My mother. She'll be here."

Confusion.

"You're Monica, right?"

Her brows knit together. "Do I know you?"

"I'm January. Claire Duzinski is my mom. Is that who you were talking about?"

For a moment, my mother's friend stared at me, her jaw slackening as she did. Then her hand came to her throat. "You're...you're January?" she breathed.

I nodded. "I'm Claire's daughter."

"Oh, my...are you serious?" Both hands came to her lips. "You can't be my Clairy's... Oh, my goodness..." she whispered. "But of course you are. You look just like her." For a long moment the woman took me in. Then she held out her arms. "Come here...come here, you darling girl."

I walked into Monica's embrace, and it almost felt like walking into my mother's arms, what my mother would have felt like had she been whole. She held me for a long, hard, trembling minute—and I her—and when we let go, we were both a bit teary. I didn't know what to do or what to say. I had not expected this. "I can't believe you're here? Do you still live in Chestnut Hill?" I stammered.

"No. No. I've been in Virginia for years. I teach at William and Mary. I just happened to be here for a few days helping my mother when we heard about Rose." She shook her head and bit her lip as she stared at me. "And I certainly *never* expected to meet you," she finally said.

"I know. It's...it's surreal. Wait, I have something..." I reached into my bag under the box Oscar had given me and found it protruding from my wallet. I pulled the photo of the ballerinas out and handed it to my mother's best friend. "Is that you, by chance? Is that you and my mom?"

Monica took it from me and studied it open-mouthed. "Oh, where did you get this?"

"It was in a book."

"I can't believe we were ever that little. My mother took this. We crashed and burned in ballet class—Claire's teeth met my eye during a dress rehearsal of *The Nutcracker*. This was taken that next night." She tapped a place near her left eyebrow. "I still have the scar." She chuckled, then her eyes misted. "Where did you say you found this?" she asked, still staring at the picture as she moved to a nearby chair.

I followed her. "In one of her books," I said, taking the seat next to her. I turned the photo over, revealing the timeline of Pulitzers read.

As Monica studied it, the mist turned to actual tears. "We decided to read Pulitzers so we could pad our college applications. We read *everything* back then. But she *ate* books. I swear, Claire could read three books a week. On top of her studies and practice and performing schedule. And she remembered all the weird things, the details, obscure quotes, things nobody else ever noticed." Monica looked at me, pained. "She was brilliant. Absolutely brilliant. I...I am so sorry about what happened to her."

I felt this woman's ache as real and piercing as my own, but I did not know what to say to her. I just nodded.

She reined in her emotions, clearing her throat. "You look amazing, January. Where are you living?"

I shrugged. "I'm with my grandparents—in New Jersey. Still. I'm trying to move, but it keeps not happening. Soon, though, I think. I'm on a few lists."

"I'm sure they'll miss you terribly when you leave."

"Do you know them? My Duzinski grandparents?"

"I met them years ago. I spent a night in their home. Loveliest people on the planet. All terrible things considered, January, you are so lucky to have scored such a wonderful family."

I looked at her and swallowed over my swelling throat. "So...you knew my dad?"

She smiled sadly. "I did, sweetheart. Loved, loved, loved your dad. He made your mom so happy. He told me once that God, Chopin, and a dead Polish general had conspired to help him find her." She chuckled. "They met at a Polish parade. I was there."

I smiled through sudden tears. "I just read about that in her journal!"

"Oh, honey, the stories I could tell you..."

I was suddenly hungry—starving—for what she knew and was about to tell her that when a sort of hush fell over the room. It was startling. Something had altered, transmuted into a reverence that reached beyond the existing reverence. I watched as Monica's hand again floated to her mouth and some of the color drained from her face.

Then I followed her gaze—and most everyone else's—to find standing in the doorway, flanked by my grandparents, my little broken bird of a mother. She was wearing the black jumper and it seemed to fit her perfectly. She also had on black hose, which I had never in my life seen her wear. She looked like a little girl. I got up and walked across the room. I could see that she had let Grandy put a little makeup on her, and her hair was combed over the most prominent scar on her forehead. She looked nice and completely overwhelmed. When I got close, she let go of Poppy and Grandy and reached for me. I held her for a long moment, and she clung to me like I was the mother and she, the child. "It's okay, Mom. It's okay," I said. Then I took her hand and walked her over to Rose's casket.

The receiving room was full of wealthy, fragrant people who parted to give us a wide berth. They became invisible to me, and I'm honestly not sure Claire even saw them. Not then. No, as we slowly approached the coffin, everything and everyone seemed to fade away until it was just me and my mother and Rose. And as we stood there, I heard what no one else did, a tiny wail at the back of my mother's throat, a kind of smothered, heartbroken keening. I put my arm around her, and she leaned into me. She was trembling. I thought of the butterflies on her wall at Potomac Manor and Oscar's story of Rose knocking on Mom's door just this last December.

After all that time—a lifetime, my lifetime—after all that damage, all that hurt, Rose just walked in and said…what? What had she said to my mother? And what had she said since? I swallowed over the lump in my throat as more futile tears stung my eyes. What did it matter now? It didn't. We were what we were: three generations of Winston pain and convoluted love standing in this small circle of *too late, goodbye,* and *grief.* What did it matter?

But then my mother reached out and shakily, so shakily, touched Rose's face, and I felt something undeniable transcend it all. I felt Claire's infinite capacity to forgive her flawed mother. It pulsed through her like a current. That's the only way I can describe it. It was a tenderness that flowed from her to Rose and back through her to me. It bound us to one another, daughter to mother to daughter. I felt it, a connection so real that it took my breath away. I choked on a little sob, and this time Claire patted my back, comforting me, and I was again her child. For a moment we stood there, arms entwined, gazing down at Rose, both of us thinking our own thoughts. Then Claire once more reached in, and this time ran her bent finger down the strand of pearls dripping from Rose's hands.

"Do you remember those, Mom?" I asked softly.

She looked over at me, puzzled.

"They're from you," I sniffed. "Oscar said she prized them above everything else. You brought them back from a piano competition. Japan, I think he said. Because she loved pearls. You were just a girl. Do you remember?"

Dawning filled her good eye, and she blinked her yes over a slow flow of new emotion. She remembered. Claire looked back at Rose and openly wept, and I would have given anything to know her thoughts. And then, I think I did.

My mother stood on tiptoes, leaned into the casket, and gently— gently for Claire—kissed her mother's marble cheek.

thirty

Rose's service was short and, if not exactly sweet, then interesting, and clearly penned by my grandmother. Most of it, anyway. The only speaker was Oscar, who eulogized her beautifully, as she'd no doubt known he would. He did it with the practiced dispassion of her attorney and not someone who had genuine feelings for her, although I thought some of that leaked through a time or two. He extolled her life of charitable service, citing the many committees she'd served on, the monies she'd raised, the relief efforts she'd taken part in, the extreme generosity that had frequently chagrinned her husband—that got a laugh. It was an impressive accounting of misery put to good use, and I admired Rose for her artful sublimation. Oscar also skillfully broached what he coined the heartache of Rose's life: what had happened to my mother. But I could tell he was uncomfortable doing it. Poppy, sitting next to me, stiffened the tiniest bit, and I imagined his brow—one brow—raised in ready challenge. I saw Grandy pat his knee—a settling gesture. I'm sure they were both poised for outrage. *The heartache of Rose's life? Really? So heartbroken she could have nothing to do with her daughter? Right.* But they didn't know what I had learned. They didn't know what Stephen might have done had Rose not bent to his will.

At the podium Oscar cleared his throat, and for a long, awkward moment, he referred to his notes. Then he placed them in his breast pocket and looked at my mother.

"As many of you know, tragedy struck the Winston family several years ago when their daughter, Claire, was in a devastating car accident that claimed the life of her husband—Tanek Duzinski. He was the love of Claire's life." Oscar said, and I heard a tiny moan come from the depths of my mother, who was sitting on the other side of me. "Claire nearly died as well from her injuries, many of which she has yet to fully recover from." He nodded, his warm eyes on my mother. "The Winstons were estranged from their daughter when this tragedy occurred. And this, *this* was the heartache of Rose's life." Oscar sighed, clearly off script.

"Today, Rose very much wanted the Duzinski family acknowledged for their unwavering devotion to her daughter and the superb raising of her only granddaughter, January, who was born that painful night." For a moment, he eyed my family, and there was honest regard in his expression. "I've had the opportunity over these past few days to acquaint myself with January," he said. "And I think I can say with authority that in not knowing her, Rose missed out on a great deal of loveliness." Oscar then smiled at me and I wanted to cry. Claire did.

I had no idea what Rose actually intended for Oscar to say, if anything, regarding my Duzinskis, but I doubted very much that it would have been this generous of heart. In fact, I thought it was much more likely that my grandmother had penned a quite different description of the heartache of her life, one that would have elicited more genuine sympathy for herself and cast her in a less rejecting, less prideful light. But I would never know. No one would, and again, I would love Oscar Thibodeau forever for saying what he did. But in fairness to Rose, I had to give her high praise for having earned this man's friendship in the first place. All in all, it was a lovely service for a grandmother who had grown exponentially more and more intriguing to me.

In true Rose fashion, she'd tasked Oscar with arranging a luncheon following her interment at Laurel Hill. She'd left a list of acceptable restaurants, and the winner was the one able to accommodate ninety-plus guests with little advance notice. The Priory on Germantown Avenue won the day. Poppy, of course, was eager to get home, so he left from the cemetery. But Grandy, Babi, and I stayed with Claire, and I have to say, we were treated like celebrities. It was a little weird for me, and I know it overwhelmed my mother. Throughout the luncheon, a steady stream of Rose's friends took the opportunity to get a good look at us under the guise of kindly offering condolences. It was understandable, I guess. They hadn't seen Claire since I didn't even know when—probably my grandfather's party when he'd tried to marry her off, certainly not since the accident—and they'd never seen me. We were a curiosity, destined to become a story to analyze, a history to retell. But for now, we were Rose's daughter and granddaughter, and there were kindnesses to be imparted, sympathies to be extended, assessments to be made of the damage to my mother. Of course, all this took some time, and it was exhausting for Claire.

Thank goodness for Oscar. He was very solicitous, introduced us to the people clamoring to engage us, reminded Claire of how she would have known them—though if she actually did was anyone's guess—hurried them along so we could breathe, and was kind enough to keep us all in bottled water.

And I kept him in water, too. Oscar was an old man, and by midafternoon he looked done. When the flow of well-wishers finally started to thin, I made him sit. Grandy took that as permission to sit herself, and when she did, she linked her arm through his. "I have to say, Mr. Thibodeau, this has been a lovely send-off, and the tribute was superb. I think Rose would have been very pleased."

"Well, maybe this no," Babi piped. "You make Rose to sound like woman she only wish she would to be."

Oscar wagged a finger at my ancient Babka with a gleam in his eye, then looked over at my mother. "What do you think, beautiful? How'd I do?"

Claire blinked one time with a small smile.

"That's all the matters," he said.

"Clairy?" came a tentative voice.

I followed my mother's gaze to the woman who had walked up on her blind side. When Claire turned to see Monica it took only a couple of beats before absolute glee erupted from deep within her. Then she was up and clinging to her friend in a sort of dance that made it clear that nothing had been lost to her. And again, I could not contain my own tears.

With everything else going on, apparently the luncheon was the first real opportunity Monica had had to approach my mother, and now it was a complete weep fest for everyone—even Oscar, who had known these women as little girls. The moment was so beautiful that I took out my phone and snapped a picture. I captioned it "My mom and her best friend" and sent it to Tyson, the tiniest bit surprised that I wanted to share it with him. I sent it just before I remembered his phone had been nicked.

When they parted, Claire was beaming her lopsided smile, but Monica looked decidedly shaken. She wiped away tears that seemed to have overtaken her. "I...I'm so sorry, sweetie," she coughed. "But I have to go. I have to get Mom home, and then I have a plane to catch. I'm in Virginia now, I just...I just couldn't leave without saying hello." She extricated her hand from Claire's grip. "I have to go," she said, again. And then she walked away. Quickly. I watched her hurry toward the exit alone, saw her mother at a table chatting with a group of ladies as she ate a slice of cheesecake. I glanced back at my bewildered little mother and my Babi, who looked just as confused as she put her arm around Claire. Then I excused myself to follow my mother's friend out of the restaurant.

Outside, I watched the woman fumble for her keys, drop them, pick them up, and press the fob. I called her name before she could get into her car. "Monica? Hey, Monica?"

She turned, visibly shaken. "Oh, Lord. January..."

I looked at her. "You...you forgot your mom."

She coughed, trying to camouflage her emotion, but gave up. "I'm sorry. I'm so sorry."

"For what?" I asked. "What's happening?"

She looked at me. "I...I haven't seen her for...since..." She bit her lips and looked away. "I haven't seen your mom for years. I wasn't prepared for..."

"What?" I pressed.

She pushed a tear off her cheek. "She *knew* me. She actually *knew* me."

"So it would seem."

"I had no idea. I—January, I thought...I don't know what I thought. I never...I didn't know she would be like *that*. Rose and Stephen made it sound so hopeless. For years they said she was..."

"What? What did they say?"

"They said she would never recover—that she *had* never recovered. Or maybe that's just what I heard."

"I don't understand."

"I lost touch with her after the accident. Not at first. At first, I saw her every day. But when she didn't…" the woman shook her head. "I had to go back to work. I was in school. Lord, listen to me make excuses!"

I watched her squirm and had no response.

"The last time I saw Claire, you were just a baby, and she was still in terrible shape." Monica looked at me through eyes pleading to be understood. "I lost contact with her, but Rose said she…" Tears spilled from her eyes. "How could Claire *possibly* have known me?"

"What did Rose tell you?"

Monica shook her head, truly stricken, then dropped her gaze, embarrassed. "I'm sorry," she said again. "When Rose said she would never get better, I just never imagined that she would be *functional* ever again. I moved. I got married, and I just…got on with my life and…" Monica looked up at me, slumped. "She doesn't speak?"

"She blinks. But that's all she can do."

"But she knew me?"

"Apparently," I said, honestly just as surprised as Monica.

"I don't understand," the woman sniffed, genuinely pained.

"It's…she got hurt on both sides—her *brain* was damaged on both sides, but mostly the left, where speech happens. That was ruined. She comprehends things, which they say is sort of amazing—that's why she remembers you, I guess. But she only communicates with her eyes."

My mother's friend seemed truly disturbed by this.

"She's had lots of tests," I offered unnecessarily.

"January, you have to believe me. I had no idea. I'm sorry. I'm so, sorry. I should have stayed in touch with her. I should have stayed her friend. Then I would have known."

I had no idea what to say to this flailing around pathetically, guilt-ridden getting-on-with-my-own-life spiel. Probably because it was like looking in a mirror.

"I'm sorry," she said for the umpteenth time.

"I am, too," I said. Then I turned and walked back into the restaurant.

thirty-one

By the time the last mourner walked out of the restaurant, it had already been a pretty long day. Babi was totally wilted, and Poppy had called Grandy twice, begging her to be home by 6:30 for double viewings we had scheduled at Duzy House. So, at just past four, my grandmother pecked my cheek and hugged Claire, then she scooped Babka into the backseat so she could nap on the way home, and they left. Oscar had long since been called back to his office to deal with some missing documents, so that left me to wrap things up and get Claire back to Potomac Manor.

We were the last to leave, and the hostess loaded us up with leftover cheesecake and appetizers. She helped us carry everything out to the car and was very sweet with my mother. For a moment I wondered if I was supposed to pay her, but she must have noticed me wondering because she said that Oscar had taken care of everything and that it had been their pleasure to serve our family. And if I wouldn't mind, could I leave a nice Facebook review? I said sure.

Because of the hour, I was rather dreading the commuter traffic, so I asked Mom if she'd like to drive around her old stomping grounds before we went home. She looked at me as though I'd offered her a bucket of money. Big blink. It made me laugh a little. So, as I pulled out of the parking lot, instead of heading to the freeway, I turned up Germantown Avenue, not sure where I was going. It didn't seem to matter. Claire was glued to the sights—shops, museums, eateries, bookstores. I had to assume she'd been in most of them. A couple of times her head turned so far back, watching something, that I ached to know what memory had been sparked.

When I turned into Moon Hollow Estates, I really didn't have a plan. In fact, I wasn't even sure we should stop since Oscar had said that the legatees were meeting today to begin the work of dismantling Rose's estate. But they must have been meeting elsewhere, because there were no cars at my mother's childhood address, no activity at all. I pulled up to the curb so she could take in the house in its impressive entirety. "Do you remember this place, Mom?"

Claire looked at me and somberly blinked one time.

I cleared my throat, the tiniest bit unsure I was doing the right thing. "Um, Oscar gave me the code. Do you want to go in?"

It took a long time for her to answer me. She seemed to be considering it, studying the massive home where she'd grown up, imagining *something*. She finally turned to me with a bit of uncertainty and blinked. One time.

I nodded. "Okay."

I walked to her side to help her out, and Claire took my hand. But she didn't move.

"Mom?"

She stared at me.

"We don't have to do this. Should we just go home?" I made a move to let go of her hand, but she gripped it tighter. Two blinks.

She stepped out of the car.

"You're sure?"

One blink. And a death grip on my hand.

She didn't let go. Not as we walked to the porch. Not when we walked into the entry. And not as we stood there for a very long moment in the world she'd once inhabited.

I let her decide where she wanted to go. And at length we walked up the stairs, slowly, a step at a time. At the top, she took a right to her bedroom and pushed open the door without the least hesitation. She stood at the threshold and seemed to marvel as she took it in.

Tyson and I had left the space as clean as I'd found it. And though I'd taken her journals and several of her books, pieces of music, quite a few pictures, and her jewelry box, the room itself was not lacking. Claire walked in and looked around. Her gaze stopped at the faded butterfly mural over her bed, and I watched her eye fill. Mine did, too.

"This was special, wasn't it Mom?"

One blink, and the tear fell.

"Should we take one?"

Claire looked at me.

I walked to the wall and removed a green butterfly. "This one?"

Her eye widened and she reached out her hand, then she held the paper butterfly like it was a living thing.

"Can I have one?" I asked as I unpinned a blue one. When I turned back to Claire, she looked like she had a story to tell me, and I so wished she could have shared the memory of her mother sitting at her bedside, cutting out butterflies. For a fleeting moment, I thought of telling her that I already knew, but that somehow felt like trespassing on something sacred, something that was Claire's and her mother's alone—something to which I had no right.

The moment passed and Mom carefully, awkwardly placed the butterfly in the pocket of her dress.

She then walked over to the window seat and picked up the throw that I thought smelled of patchouli and held it to her face. It was so intimate, so deliberate that it took me aback. She breathed deeply of its scent, then leaned her cheek into its softness. I would have killed to know the significance. She then turned to me with another tear bubbling in her good eye and held out the blanket for me to smell. I did—I pretended to be surprised at the fragrance. I pretended because suddenly I did not want my mother to know I had been there. That I'd been pilfering, reading her journals, helping myself to her belongings, that I already knew what the blanket smelled like.

"Was this your blanket, Mom?" I asked.

Two blinks.

"No? Was it your mom's?"

One blink.

I swallowed. So. Rose had hung out in here, in her daughter's window seat, reading her daughter's novels. Wow. "You should take it, Mom," I said. "I think she'd like that."

My mother smiled through that tear and clutched the scented afghan to her chest.

We walked through the rest of the second floor, Claire taking her time as we went: the big family room, her parents' bedroom, where she drank in the paintings on the wall, a large room at the end of the hall that was set up as a gym. That got kind of a giggle out of her. There was a cluttered workroom filled with huge spools of thread and several looms that looked like an abandoned hobby, but Mom stood in the doorway for a long time, recalling *something.* What I wouldn't have given to be a fly on the wall of her stifled mind.

Downstairs she seemed to remember her father's den because we stopped briefly at the open door. But she barely glanced inside, showing no inclination to enter or linger. I remembered Oscar's account of the woeful meeting with my dad and assumed it had been in that room, but it could be that my mother simply had no interest in recollections of her father whatsoever.

We made our way through the halls to the double doors of the library. This was where she discovered her beloved Steinway was missing, and her reaction nearly did me in. She was visibly shaken to find it gone. Her hand came to her chest, a moan erupted. She looked around in disbelief as if it must have been moved to another corner of the room. Her questioning eye came to rest on me as though I had the answer, which of course I did. "It's okay, Mom. Oscar didn't want your piano to be sold as part of the estate. So, it's been moved." I nodded, taking her hand. "It's okay."

I know I should have said something more, but again I was too ashamed for her to know that I'd been there and was complicit. So, I played dumb and felt awful as all my old familiar guilt started churning inside me. I was hurting her. Again. And today of all days. Why had I brought her here?

I couldn't think of anything to do, so I hugged her, told her again that it would be okay. I tried to distract her: draw her attention to photographs, point out her trophies, the art, the creepy coat of arms behind glass. But my mother distracted herself. As I rattled on about her awards, she let go of me and made her way to the fireplace and the portrait of her and her parents—the one I thought screamed of ownership and unhappiness. I watched her stare up at it for a very long moment, but with little emotion. It seemed to calm her, focus her, but not in a warm way.

It took her quite a while, but she finally looked over at me.

"Have you seen enough?"

She blinked.

We walked back toward the foyer, and when we reached the hall to the kitchen, I tugged her toward it. "Should we see if Rose had anything to drink? A snack for the road?"

Mom blinked, so we walked into my grandmother's industrial-feeling galley, equipped with two refrigerators, two double ovens, and a ten-foot prep space. I let go of Mom's hand and went straight to the nearest fridge, where I found a case of Pellegrino (*no!*) and a case of Diet Coke. I grabbed two Cokes and thought to at least offer Claire the sparkling water. But when I turned to ask her, I found her attention captured elsewhere.

Propped next to the bar was the beautiful portrait Oscar had taken off the wall in the entry. A small tag stuck to the corner marked it as unavailable, just as the attorney had promised. Now my mother had walked over to that lovely painting of the girl she used to be and was gazing at it with such awe that it made me weak. When I heard the sob at the bottom of her throat, it broke my heart. I set down the Cokes and put my arm around her. I felt responsible somehow for her pain. I'd brought her here, exposed her to sad things, stolen her piano, was going to steal this painting.

I tried to tug her away, but she wouldn't budge. So, there we stood, Claire gazing at herself as the girl she had once been, me gazing at the woman she now was.

The side of Claire facing me was her blind side—her most damaged side. In my whole life I could not remember seeing her this clearly, or maybe I had just never looked at her this closely. I could plainly see the scarred evidence of what had happened to her, and now I couldn't look away. This side of her damaged-beyond-repair face did not move, at least not much. She had an artificial eye that kind of did its own thing, but since it had always been there, I'd never really taken much notice of it. However, this close I could see it was slightly larger than her real one, and that the lid drooped a little. Her mouth on this side also drooped. I knew her smile was lopsided, but this close I could see the scar that made it that way. There was another thick scar on her forehead that started somewhere in her hair and ran down through her eyebrow and across her cheek until it disappeared under her ear. All along it, the skin was puckered, and beneath it, if there was a cheekbone, it was very flat, which made this side of her face appear a bit caved-in.

I stood there, following that scar with my eye, and as I did, the accident that had caused it bloomed in my mind: my parents' little car spinning in the snow, the unstoppable pickup landing on top of them, the roof giving way, glass and steel buckling—crushing my father to death and damaging my mother for life. It made me lightheaded.

Claire was still staring at the portrait of the girl she used to be, and I followed her gaze. This, *this* was who my mother was meant to be— the grown-up version of this lovely girl brimming with *possibility*. Instead...I turned to find Claire now studying me intently. The story in her eye was one of such pain that I started to weep. I could see it. I could see inside my mother's life. In her eye, I could suddenly see the depths of what she had lost.

I shuddered. "I'm so sorry you didn't get to be *that* girl, all grown up."

My mother cocked her head, and a tear filled the eye that told all her secrets. She cupped my face and I leaned into her touch. Suddenly years of cruel indifference filled me and pushed past me and flowed out of me, disgrace filling its wake.

"I'm sorry for so many things, Mom."

thirty-two

That moment in Rose's kitchen had been a turning point, a connection so liberating that it almost felt like a rebirth. Claire's tangled emotions, her memories with no voice colliding with my artless shame was a bridge to understanding. It was surreal and overwhelming and bonding all at once.

My mother had been an incredible young woman, and today she was even more so for all she had lived through. How was I just comprehending this?

On the way home, she'd fallen asleep holding my hand, and I couldn't stop looking over at her. And now a day later, I was still thinking about her.

It was making it hard to concentrate.

I was just wrapping up my second embalming of the day (or trying to)—a seventeen-year-old who'd died of meningitis. Sloan Tipton was a beautiful boy—tall and athletic, with thick hair, clear skin, and straight teeth. A kid in his prime who'd been no match for the vicious little microbe that had stolen his life. He'd been sick with the flu, his mom had thought, when he went to bed. He'd died in his sleep. For most of the afternoon, Poppy had been running interference between Sloan's divorced and devastated parents, who blamed each other for this tragedy. They could barely be civil enough to coordinate a service. As hard as my job had been preserving the boy—infection risks require extra precautions—Poppy's had been worse. And at least Sloan had been a very attentive, if not active, participant in our conversation about my mother.

I'd also spent the morning babying the corpse of an emaciated woman just shy of her hundredth birthday with skin so papery it split apart in places as I prepared her—that was always hard. So, it had been a busy day. My saving grace was that I had a date, *a real date*, with Tyson in a few hours. We both agreed we'd earned it: his mom was out of ICU and doing much better, and I'd gotten Rose Winston buried—not to mention the breakthrough I'd had with Claire. Plus, he'd found his phone, as evidenced by the funny voicemail he'd left me last night:

Hey, it's Ty—calling from MY phone. Long story, but it was found. Intact. Hey, I just wanted you to know I'm still thinking about you. I'm sure it's been a long day, and I hope it's about over and you can just chill. I play basketball on Monday nights with some college buddies, and I wasn't going to go tonight, but they moved my mom to a regular room, and she booted us all out, so I am. It usually goes late, so I'll call you tomorrow. I really want to see you, ba—oh! I almost called you babe. He laughed. Self-consciously. *Sorry. Or not. Probably too soon to call you babe, right? Not sure. It felt kind of natural. I should probably erase this and start over since I don't know if we're there yet.* He fumbled and there was beeping and then: *Hello...hello? January? Obviously, I don't know what I'm doing. But if you get any portion of this message, I thought maybe we could, you know, go do something. I'll call you tomorrow—from MY phone. Oh, this is Ty, by the way, if none of the first part of this message came through. And if it didn't, it's because I almost called you babe and I thought it was too soon, but now I'm thinking I hope that's cool with you. Talk to you tomorrow.*

He was adorable. And it was cool with me if he called me babe. Wasn't it? Or it would be by tonight. Tonight, he was taking me into the city for dinner and something called Dueling Pianos.

Almost three-and-a-half hours later, I had just finished mopping when Poppy knocked and poked his head in. He looked frazzled. "The Tipton boy. How does he look?"

"Good," I said. "He's finished."

He stepped in. "The dad wants to see him," he grumbled, heading to the fridge.

"Want some help?" I asked.

My grandfather rolled the boy into my workspace, then pulled the curtain to hide the embalming equipment from view. Our tiny receiving room was already being used by Calvin, and Mr. Tipton apparently was not to be put off. Poppy looked irritated. "No, this is fine, Janny. You need to go upstairs, anyway. You have a visitor."

"Is it Tyson?" I said. "He's way too early."

"It's Monica Fairchild."

"Who"

"Monica Fairchild. She's a friend of Claire's. She said you met her at the funeral."

"I stopped. "I didn't know her last name. What does she want, Poppy?"

"I don't know, January. Go find out," he snapped, clearly not inclined to elucidate.

In the hall bathroom, I stripped off my gown and gloves and smoothed my sleeveless navy tee over the white jeans I was wearing underneath. I headed upstairs with a little pit in my stomach. *She'd said she had a plane to catch.*

Monica Fairchild was sitting on a sofa near the piano, and she stood when I stepped off the elevator. She was wearing a teal linen shirtdress, belted, with the sleeves rolled up, and sunglasses pushed back in her great hair. She looked nervous as I approached, and that somehow put me more at ease.

"Hello, January," she smiled.

"Hi," I said. "This is a surprise. I thought you went back to Virginia."

She sighed. "About that...I took a chance. I should have called."

I waved a hand, dismissing her words. "No, it's fine. You caught me at a good time."

She looked around. "Is there somewhere we can talk?"

I hadn't seen Grandy, so I wasn't sure if the coffin room was in use, but I led Monica in that direction anyway. We walked in silence, and at the door I knocked and peeked in. The room was empty, but it was in retail mode. "We can talk in here. If you're okay with a few coffins...." I pushed open the door.

Monica smiled. "I've seen it before. I think it was the first thing your grandfather showed me when I met him." She looked around. "Still a bit unsettling though."

She walked to the sofa and sat down, and I pressed the button on the wall, closing the curtains over the alcoves. Monica watched. "Well, that's impressive. He didn't show me that part."

I chuckled. "It's been years in the making, and believe me, it adds quite the dramatic flair to his spiel." I sat down across from her. "I remember you said you spent a night here years ago, and I wanted to know about that, but we got *interrupted*."

My mother's friend smiled. "I came for your parents' wedding," she said.

"That was here?"

"It was at an inn not far from here, a charming little place. It was lovely."

I only knew of one inn, and it was oddly reminiscent of one portrayed in *Gilmore Girls*. "It wasn't the Copperfield?" I said, sitting down across from her.

Monica nodded. "I think it was. That sounds right."

"Wow. I never knew that. Why didn't I know that?"

"Well, you weren't exactly there, my dear."

The wheels were spinning now. "Were Rose...I guess Rose and Stephen..."

"They didn't come, no," she said. "They didn't take part in the wedding at all. Well, there was the wedding dress, but they didn't attend. Your grandparents, your Duzinski grandparents, arranged everything. Your mom wanted to elope, but Diana wouldn't hear of it."

"I didn't know that either," I muttered. It was awkward then for a few beats, and I cleared my throat. "Monica, I thought you had to get back. What are you doing here?"

She took a moment to answer me, smoothing the dress at her lap. "I couldn't leave. And I'm here for a purely selfish reason, I'm afraid. I have felt awful since I saw you—and your mother—it's been eating me alive. And I thought...I thought maybe if I could explain, which is ridiculous, I think, but..." she shrugged. "I am just so sorry."

"You don't owe *me* an apology."

"I think I might, but this isn't really an apology. It's more of an admission, I guess. I'm just sad to my very core that I let this happen, that I let all this time go by and let my friendship with your mom die. I didn't even realize what that friendship still meant to me until I saw her." Monica bit her lip. "Until she wouldn't let go of me. I told you, I was simply not prepared for the way Claire was, and I'm ashamed of how I reacted." She met my eyes and looked truly distressed. "Did I hurt her, January?" she said. "Is she...is Clairy even aware enough...you know, to *be* hurt? Is that a dumb question?"

I was careful with my answer. "I think you might have *confused* her," I said, softening the truth the best I could. "And yes, she is aware enough to be hurt. And no, that's not a dumb question. My mom can be hard to read if you don't know her."

Monica's face crumpled slightly. "Good Lord, what you must think of me."

I shook my head. "I'm the last person who should judge you, even though I did for a minute the other day. I'm sorry about that."

Monica looked at me, her eyes begging for an explanation. I didn't give her one. "I don't think your friendship is dead," was all I said.

She smiled sadly, pushed her hair back. "I'm just so surprised at myself—and not in a good way. Claire was my dearest friend, and I didn't know how to stay close to her—after the accident, I mean. So, I didn't. I went through the motions for a while. I sent cards. I think I sent flowers once, on her birthday." She blew out a breath. "But seeing her the other day shocked me. Not just how she looked, but the way she hugged me, like I hadn't abandoned her twenty years ago, like we were still best friends and nothing had changed. I couldn't believe that. I told you, I had no idea she had recovered to that degree. I had no idea she was functional at all. I thought—I was under the impression that she was being taken care of twenty-four hours a day, was entirely bedridden, and fed through a tube." Monica sighed and looked down at her hands.

"Well, she has lived at Potomac Manor for many years—it's very upscale assisted living. But she's not bedridden. Obviously. Why would you think that?"

"Because that's what Claire's parents told everyone. At least in the beginning. And I guess it was true for a long time—I know she was in a coma for years."

I stared at her. "She was in a coma for six months."

Monica's eyes widened. "No. It was years."

I shook my head. "Just six months. She was in a rehab hospital for a long time. But then she came home. She came here. She lived with us until I was four. Then…"

Tears swelled in Monica's eyes, and her hand rose to her lips. "I should have stayed in touch," she croaked. "I should have visited her. Then I would have known." My mother's friend pulled a tissue from the box Grandy kept on the coffee table, and for a minute we were quiet.

"You need to go see her," I finally said. "You need to tell her what you just told me. My mom blinks up a storm and she giggles and she cries and she hugs and she smiles on one side. And somehow, with just those limited means, she manages to communicate almost perfectly. I promise she'll understand, and she'll forgive you, and you will know it within five minutes."

Monica looked at me, and agony filled her face. "I couldn't," she whispered. "Twenty years of rejection—that's too much to be forgiven for."

"You'd think…" I said softly.

She narrowed her eyes around a question as she wiped her nose.

"A couple of years after my mom came home, there was a fire. It was a long time ago; I was just a little kid. She couldn't get me out, so she got on top of me." I looked away from Monica's probing eyes. "I didn't know what was happening and thought she was trying to hurt me, not protect me. It took me a long time to understand what had really happened, and in the meantime, I just…" I shook my head. "I pushed her away. Far away. I hurt my mother terribly."

"Oh, January."

"I was horrible to her," I said, meeting Monica's eyes again. "She caught on fire trying to save my life…and I blamed her for trying to hurt me. And when I finally figured it out, I couldn't stand to be around her because of my own unbearable guilt at getting it so wrong. So I kept rejecting her, which just kept hurting her. It seemed there was no way for me *not* to hurt her. So, it might not be *exactly* the same, but I understand how you feel. I do."

Monica stared at me. "But I watched you with her. You were so lovely, so tender. She clearly adores you."

"I know she does," I sniffed. "And I saw her with you. She clearly adores you, too."

We were quiet for a moment, and my thoughts again filled with the terrible scars on Claire's back. I'd seen them again last night when I helped her get ready for bed, and she'd known, like she always knew, my stinging, futile remorse. I hadn't shied away as I usually did, but I *had* gotten emotional. That's when she'd put both her bent hands on my face and pulled me to her. When she'd kissed my forehead, I'd wept with shame.

Now it was my turn to reach for a tissue. "Do you have any children, Monica?" I finally said to break the silence.

"Two sons," she smiled. "Jake and Topher. They're fishing in Alaska. My husband's father took all the testosterone in the family— five men, eight boys—camping in Denali National Park."

"Wow."

"So, I came to spend some time with Mom. Needless to say, it's been quite a trip."

I lifted a brow.

She blew out a breath, then reached into her purse and pulled out a large envelope. "When I got home yesterday, I was desperate to find my copy of that picture you showed me. After what happened at the restaurant, I was kind of possessed, I think. So, I tore through my mom's attic—she never throws anything away, she just relocates it."

"That sounds like Poppy. Did you find it?" I chuckled.

"I did. I found a few things, actually. And while I was stumbling around up there in my childhood, I realized I'm probably one of the few links you have to who your mom was before she was your mom. I brought you some pictures. I hope that's okay."

"Are you kidding?" I said, stunned.

She wiped her nose again and walked around the coffee table to sit next to me, pulling a handful of photographs from the large manila envelope. Monica Fairchild then spent the next half-hour describing the occasion captured in each image: A school play when they were eight—Mom was a tulip and Monica was a weed. A church concert where they sang a duet. A Halloween bash with friends where they'd all dressed up as the cast of Ghostbusters. There were class pictures and prom pictures and random shots with friends. There was one of my mother and Monica with a group of kids at a Habitat for Humanity project, mom adorable in overalls.

"Oh, and this one was taken at the Mutter Museum," Monica said. "Have you ever heard of it? It's famous in Philly, and Claire got a summer job there—for about five minutes until Stephen made her quit. There is a tumor from John Wilkes Booth in that museum."

"Ewww. Why did she have to quit?"

"Who knows?" Monica said. "I think Stephen blamed it for interfering with her piano practice, but I think he just couldn't stand a daughter of his working for minimum wage."

"Oh, right. I can totally believe that."

From the envelope, she next pulled a large drawing, and sighed before handing it to me with a sad smile. "I thought you'd like this. When we were, I don't know, eleven, maybe ten, Claire was sleeping over one night and we decided to invent our future husbands. That's what she came up with."

It was a sketch of a tall man with dark hair, drawn and detailed with colored pencils. To anyone else the figure surely would have seemed nondescript—a child's rendition of a lanky, long-legged boy. But it was my father, and he blurred beneath my tears. He was wearing jeans and a blue shirt. His big hands were on his hips, and he was smiling. His hair was long and dark and hung over one eye. I looked over at Monica, rather shocked. "That's...*amazing.*"

"I know. Now read what she wrote," she said, pointing to another sheet of paper stapled to the drawing. On it was a list.

My future husband will:

Be gorgeous,

Be kind,

Be funny,

Be smart,

Be happy,

Be gentle,

And will not be afraid of my dad.

Again, I looked over at Monica, who was now also blurred by my tears. "She found him."

"She did indeed."

"Oh...I can't—thank you," I rasped, feeling myself tremble.

She hugged me sideways. "We were funny little girls," she whispered at length. "Clairy used to tell people we were sisters, and I

286 - Ka Hancock

loved that." Monica swallowed over sudden emotion. "She was my best friend, January. And I was her sanity."

I instinctively knew what this meant. "Thank you," I said, again. "Given my grandparents, that was probably a huge job."

Monica nodded, looking wistful, and then teasingly submitted, "I want you to know that I take credit for you, dear girl—you might not be here if not for me."

"What does that mean?"

"She almost let your dad walk away."

I gaped at her. "What?"

"Your mom was stubborn, and it didn't help that her dad did a number on her. I guess there was a time when he tried to bribe her away from marrying Tanek—or at least he let your dad know what she was worth—money-wise, because that's all Stephen cared about—and that if he married her, she would lose everything."

"Oh, I know about this. Oscar told me."

"Then you know it wasn't true. But because Stephen was Stephen, and he was, well, *hideous*, Claire momentarily convinced herself that she was too tainted by association, was too unworthy of your dad. She lost her way for a minute and almost let him slip through her fingers. I had to slap her around a little—figuratively speaking." She half-grinned. Then she sighed.

I recalled reading about Mom's trek to New Jersey to apologize to my dad.

"It was just fear," Monica said, softly. "Sometimes when you're raised with a warped version of love, you have a hard time recognizing the real thing. Which your dad was."

"Well, thank you for *intervening*."

"Wasn't really me—not *all* me. A lesser girl would have been ruined by the Winstons—I have no doubt. But not your mom. They were hard on her, but probably much to their dismay, what they demanded of Claire ended up being everything she needed to survive them: insane talent, poise, confidence, intellect. She just had a little trouble trusting anyone but herself. Thankfully your dad fixed that." Monica nodded. "Your dad fixed that beautifully."

I tried to swallow over the sudden knot in my throat. I thought of my mom's description of driving to Wallington to see if she had lost my dad—and his resounding *Hell no!* in response. "I've always heard he was a good guy," I whispered.

"He was, sweetie." Monica got very quiet then as she pulled another photo from the envelope. She looked at it for a long moment before she handed it to me. It was a picture of my mother in her wedding dress. Claire was also sporting a baseball cap, which she had on backwards, and she was crying. I thought she was absolutely beautiful, and I looked to Monica for an explanation, but again, I couldn't really speak.

"That's a funny story. Funny sad, actually," she said. "Your parents' wedding came together very quickly, and of course Claire let her parents know, but she never heard a word from them. Not a word. But a couple of weeks before the big day, Rose came to my work. She had this big box and told me she knew I'd be seeing Claire, and she wanted me to give it to her. I think I argued that she should take it herself, but you really couldn't argue with Rose." Monica rolled her eyes. "Anyway, that's what was in the box." She pointed at the picture.

"The wedding dress?"

"That very dress." She nodded. "We had a friend we ran with in school who wanted to be a fashion designer. She borrowed a ton of money and created a collection; her name is Shine Lacroix."

"No way! I have a Lacroix jacket! It's a second, but still."

"Yep. She's famous now, but at the time she wasn't a name brand; she was just a cute little round girl with a big dream. We all went to her debut and took our moms. At that fashion show, Claire fell in love with *that* dress. Fast forward two years and some change, Rose moved heaven and earth to get that dress for Claire. Your mom was cleaning the toilet when I showed up with it—hence the baseball cap. I think there are rubber gloves somewhere in that picture." Monica looked more closely. "Anyway, she must have called her mom a dozen times while I was there, but Rose never picked up."

"Why? That's so sad," I said.

"It was your grandfather, I'm sure. He was a piece of work."

"I know, I've heard. But the dress is *beautiful*," I said. "It must have meant so much to my mom that Rose would do that."

"It's why she was crying," Monica said, thoughtfully.

I smiled through my tears. "My christening dress was made from the train. Some of it."

"Really? And you didn't even know you were blessed in a Lacroix!"

We laughed.

Monica then handed me the last picture. It was a shot of my parents in the kitchen upstairs. They were seated at the table with Poppy, Grandy, Tess, and Babka, who were all leaning in on either side. Candles provided the only light, aside from the camera flash. My parents were beaming. Everyone was holding a glass, and my parents' free hands were bound with a white cloth. "What's happening here?" I asked. "Looks like a happy occasion."

"That was the night before their wedding. I wasn't sure I should have been here—it was such an intimate family gathering—but Claire insisted, and it honestly took about a minute and a half, and I was completely comfortable. It was incredible. You have a wonderful family."

"I do."

"I remember the table was set with candles and this beautiful china and stemware. Your mom and dad were across from me, and I was next to your Aunt Tess—that's her name, right? She told me I was in for a treat, but I had no idea. Your little grandmother, what did you call her?"

"Babka."

Monica nodded. "She said she had a gift for Tanek and Claire. 'It was tradition,' she said. And when everyone was ready, she brought this little tray over and set it down in front of them. There was a tiny loaf of bread, a little pile of salt, and two glasses of wine—I think. Oh, and that white scarf." Monica tapped the picture.

I studied the photo. I'd never seen anything like it.

"Your grandfather—he was pretty emotional—he picked up the white scarf and asked Tanek and Claire to hold hands. Then he tied it around their wrists. He held their hands over the bread and said —I wish I could remember exactly, it was so beautiful—he said in Polish tradition, their bound hands meant hope that they would never be hungry. The salt was a reminder that life would be hard sometimes, and they must always help each other through it. And the wine was a symbol that they would never know thirst and that they'd have a life of happiness with good friends. It was something like that. I remember he kissed the top of your dad's head, and Tanek cried." Monica put a hand to her heart. "It was so sweet, January. Then he kissed Claire and she cried." Monica then got further swept up in the remembering, and it took her a few beats to compose herself. "Then your grandfather toasted them," she sniffed. "And I remember this part; he said, 'To the happiness and abundance that abounds at this table.'" Monica again tapped her heart and lost her voice. "It was just the loveliest night."

I watched tears run freely down her face as she studied the little photo. "They were so happy, January. Your parents were so very happy. I could not imagine them, either one of them, capable of any more joy." She looked over at me then. "But they proved me wrong when they found out about you."

I swallowed. "Really?"

"Oh, yes. They were completely in love with you from the moment they knew you were coming. I know you were robbed of the life you were supposed to have, January—you and my Clairy. But before that happened, sweet girl, there was unimaginable love. And joy."

I wrapped my arms around her neck, fighting a sob of my own. "Thank you, Monica. Thank you for all this. I'm so glad you came."

"Me, too, sweetheart."

"Go see my mom."

"I just might." Monica said into my hair.

thirty-three

When Monica and I emerged from the coffin room, Duzy House was decidedly in afterhours mode. There was no viewing scheduled, so no one was roaming around, and it suddenly hit me that we had been holed up for quite a while. As Monica checked her phone, I glanced at my watch and was shocked to see that it was after seven. Tyson was supposed to have picked me up at 6:15.

"Oh, my goodness," Monica said, stealing my thoughts. "Look how late it is. I had no idea."

"Me neither," I said. I heard voices then, lighthearted, spiked with soft laughter, and when we rounded the corner into the main foyer, there was Tyson chatting it up with my grandfather. If he hadn't looked so relaxed, I would have been worried.

When Poppy spotted us, he stood, mid-laugh, and walked over with arms outstretched to swallow Monica in a hug. "I was hoping I'd get to see you before you left," he said. "I was in the middle of something sticky when you got here earlier and very preoccupied. How are you?"

They spoke for just a moment as I apologized to Tyson with my eyes. He just grinned. When Poppy released Monica, she turned to me. "Thank you again, you sweet thing." She glanced at Tyson then back at me. "I can see I've probably messed up your evening."

I just smiled. "I'm glad you came," I said, meaning it.

She then handed me her business card. "I want to stay in touch with you, January. Call me anytime. Or email. That's all my contact information."

"I will. And I'm January@DuzinskiFunerals. Easy." I hugged her then and whispered in her ear, "Let me know how it goes with my mom."

She smiled without committing and walked out.

Then it was just me and Tyson. And Poppy. My grandfather slipped his hand into mine and squeezed. "How did it go, Janny? You okay?"

"I'm good. We had a nice talk."

"So did we." He grinned over at Tyson, and I followed his gaze. Tyson had stood up, and he looked great. He was wearing jeans and a fitted gray Henley with the sleeves pushed up. His thick hair was combed back, and he'd moved close enough that I could smell his cologne.

"I'm so sorry," I said to him. "I had no idea what time it was. I don't know why"—I turned to my grandfather—"*someone* didn't let me know you were here." I turned back to him. "I didn't know she was coming."

"No worries," Tyson smiled.

"I offered," Poppy announced cavalierly. "But Ty here said he wanted the dirt on you, and since you stood him up, the least I could do was accommodate."

Tyson laughed.

Poppy grinned. "Well, Grandy has lasagna upstairs if you're interested. I'm going up." He reached past me and shook Tyson's hand. "Good to see you again, son. Remember what I said."

Tyson nodded, and I grimaced. "Oh, that sounds bad."

Poppy winked at me and walked away.

"Do I need to apologize for him?" I said.

Tyson laughed again.

I looked at my watch. "It's 7:15. Have I ruined everything? What should we do?"

He smiled. "Hit Dueling Pianos the next time they're at the Green Room. They're there all the time. It's not a big deal."

"Really?"

Tyson reached for my hand and tugged me toward him, planting a quick kiss on my lips. "Really."

I leaned in, and he kissed me slower. "You're awfully understanding," I said as we parted.

"I am, aren't I?" He grinned as he led me back to the couch. "Why don't we just sit here, and you can catch your breath. Then we'll make a new plan," he said, slipping his arm around me.

I leaned against him, surprised at how chill he seemed. "You're not in the mood for lasagna, are you?" I ventured.

"I am, actually," he said. "But at a very cool bistro over in Ridgefield."

I looked over at him and grinned.

And then neither of us moved. I took a deep breath and let it out slow, settling in. This felt surprisingly good. Easy. I leaned my head on Tyson's shoulder and laced my fingers in his. I was in no hurry to move.

"How is your mom doing?" I asked. "Did she come home?"

"Tomorrow. She's much better. Weak, but infection-free. My dad's taking the week off to take care of her. They're going to drive each other nuts," he laughed.

"I think that's sweet."

"Yeah. Put a scare in my dad, that's for sure." Tyson was quiet for a moment, presumably thinking about this near miss in his family.

"Soooo…" I sighed to pull him back. "Do I want to know what you and my grandfather talked about?"

"Just you."

"Of course. I'm sorry."

Tyson chuckled, then I felt his lips at my temple. "He sort of adores you, you know."

"Well, that's his job. He's my grandfather."

"He told me you're a lot like your dad."

"Poppy loves to talk about my dad."

"He loves to talk about *you*," Tyson said, tugging me closer.

"What can I say? I'm just *that* fascinating."

"Don't I know it! Funeral school grad with honors. Youngest embalmer in New Jersey. Turned down a full ride in music—well, you told me that. *Aaand* you were the New Year's baby. When were you going to tell me that little noteworthy piece of your history?"

I laughed. "Clearly, never."

"A year's worth of diapers, January? That's the stuff of legend."

"And formula," I clucked. "And a preschool scholarship and free dental until I was five—all for being born on New Year's."

He laughed. "So, I guess that explains your cool name?"

"Actually...that was because my dad won. If I had been born in December—I was due the 30th—my mom would have won, and I would have been named Elizabeth after her grandmother. If I made it to January, the deal was Dad got to name me January Ann. So my grandparents named me...for him."

Then it was awkward.

Tyson groaned, turning toward me. "And I'm an idiot! I've been teasing you about the night...your parents... I don't know what I was thinking."

"You're not an idiot," I said. "I was still the New Year's baby."

"I just...I know you've had a rough week, and I wanted to give you a break from everything, and then I go and...*talk*."

"Tyson, shhhh. Stop. Besides, there's been some amazing in my rough week, so, you know... not all bad."

Tyson Pierce stared at me, then narrowed his eyes. "You don't like that, do you? Pity—not that that's what I was doing."

"Does anyone? Like pity?"

He studied me for a few more beats and I let him. Then he pushed out a breath. "Rewind. Tell me something amazing, January."

"Okay...something amazing. Oh." I picked up the folder Monica had left and pulled out my mother's drawing.

"What's this?"

"Apparently, my mother always had a pretty good idea of what she was looking for in a husband. She drew that when she was a little kid, and it looks just like my dad."

"No way," he said, studying the sketch. "He really looked like this?"

"You wouldn't believe." I stood up and reached for Tyson's hand, and we walked across the hall to my grandfather's office. Poppy's space was soft and leathery like an old slipper, the walls wood-paneled, the art by Grandy, the photographs mostly of our family. I picked up an eight-by-ten of him and my dad that had sat on his desk for forever.

Tyson, who was standing behind me, looked at it over my shoulder. "This is my dad," I told him.

The picture had been taken on my parents' wedding day, and my father was standing next to Poppy. Their smiles were the kind of happy reserved for once-in-a-lifetime occasions. They were both in tuxedos, and my very handsome dad with his too-long hair was towering over my shorter, grayer, goateed grandfather. The contrast was striking, but the love between them was identical.

"Wow," Tyson said, softly. "She nailed it. How old was she?"

"Right? I don't know, ten, maybe."

"Is this her? Is this your mom?" Tyson said, picking up another picture on Poppy's desk, this one of a bride.

"No, that's my Aunt Tess," I said. "She's my dad's sister. She's the other embalmer here." I turned Tyson toward the wall and pointed to a large portrait of my parents. "That's my mom."

The photo had been taken at Tomahawk Lake, so my dad wasn't wearing a shirt and his great hair was wet. Claire was wearing a tank top and shorts, and her long hair was kind of blowing to the side. They were both laughing and looked incredibly healthy and happy, like they belonged on a magazine cover.

"These are your parents?"

I nodded. "Yep. Poppy had it blown up. He says what makes that pic frame-worthy is that I'm in it. See my dad's big hand on my mom's little belly bump? That's me," I said. "Family picture."

Tyson looked at me, then back at the photo. When he again found my eyes, the soberness in his expression was so intense I had to look away.

"Is it *pity* if I'm just sorry?" he ventured.

"I don't know. I don't think so, because I'm sorry, too."

He took my hand. "You got a raw deal, January. You and your mom. And your grandparents."

"We did."

He looked at me. "And I'm officially at a loss."

I smiled through a threat of tears, because in his eyes I found such genuineness that it caught me off guard. It was so candid and so refreshing that I leaned up and kissed his cheek.

"What was that for?"

"Just because."

"So we're okay?"

"Of course we're okay."

"Good. Because I don't want to do anything to ruin what might be happening here."

I looked up at him. "Me neither. I get a little weird sometimes about my story. It's just that there's a fine line between being sorry about what happened to me and feeling sorry *for* me. That might not make sense to you, but believe me, I can tell the difference."

He nodded. "How am I doing?"

"So far, so good, I think," I said softly.

"Just tell me if I cross any lines." Then his mouth was on my mouth, and all thoughts of pity and lines and strange life stories vanished at the taste of his kiss. It felt so nice to be held by him. Safe, even, like something truly honest was blossoming between us.

"Soooo," I finally said in his ear. "What did my grandfather mean when he told you to remember what he said?"

"He told me I had one job tonight."

"Was it this?" I teased.

He chuckled, his lips against my neck.

"What was it? Seriously."

"To make sure you laughed."

"What? What does that even mean?"

"I guess it means he thinks you're a serious girl surrounded by serious things, and you need to cut loose a little."

"Oh, really?"

"Really," he said, stepping back to look at me. "So, I'm thinking since you blew our plans tonight—sorry, but you did—we should go for lasagna in Ridgefield, then I know this crappy little dive bar in Paramus where a half-decent band is playing tonight."

I grimaced, owned it. "What kind of band?"

"Stone-cold country."

"Oh, I don't know," I protested. "I do *country* on a limited basis only."

"Well, if you hate it, I promise next time we'll find a Beethoven bar."

I laughed out loud. Mission accomplished.

***

Tyson was right about almost everything. Angelino's in Ridgefield did have world-class pasta, and the Eagle's Nest in Paramus *was* a dive—actually, dive was too generous a descriptor. But he was wrong about the band. The AP Project was a surprise—three guys, one on drums, one on bass, one vocalist on lead guitar. Tight jeans and cowboyed up, the lead singer knew his stuff, and I was impressed. I tried to tell Tyson that, but I couldn't be heard over the noise; the crowd in the small space was intense.

When the band wrapped up their first set, Tyson kissed my cheek. "I'll be right back. See if you can find a table, and I'll grab us some drinks."

"Coke for me," I winked.

"You got it."

I looked around and saw no place to sit, so I inched my way toward the pub tables lining the walls, ready to pounce should someone vacate, which wasn't likely.

"January?"

"Yes?" I didn't recognize the liberally made-up woman with the shocking cleavage who'd walked up to me, but she seemed to know who I was.

"This is so crazy, doll," she said. "I just left you a message. Well, an hour ago."

"What?" I suddenly realized I did not have my phone. "You left *me* a message?"

"That townhome you lost a few weeks ago...another one just came available in the same complex. The guy wants out of his lease—job transfer, I think. You were the first person I thought of. Single, non-smoker, no pets, right?"

"Right. Right. Oh, my gosh! I didn't realize who you were. You look so *different*— Sa...Sabrina, right?" I guessed at the name of the pushing-fifty-year-old property manager.

She grinned. "I'm partying. I'd *better* look different."

"You're talking about the one in Hasbrouck Heights, right? Off Prudential."

"That's right. Urban Pikewood. It's not the furnished one, but if you want it, come by tomorrow and lock it in."

"I will! Thank you! *Thank* you! That's awesome! And you look great, by the way!"

She laughed. "See you tomorrow."

I looked around, feeling suddenly giddy. I'd been packed up and living out of bags for a month. I'd already said the hard things to Grandy and Poppy, and Babi had known my intentions for the past year. I'd mapped out my radius and nailed down only places within a five-minute commute from Duzy House. Hasbrouck Heights had been my first choice, and now I'd scored a lease on a townhome—furnished would have been better, but I didn't care. I was moving. *Yes!* I wanted to share my great news with Tyson, but I couldn't see him anywhere.

The band had come back, and Mr. Tight Jeans was re-welcoming the crowd to thunderous applause. He calmed the room and said, "I have a message for my brother's date, Miss January Duzz…Duzing—what's her name, dude? Duzinski. Okay. January, if you're wondering where Tyson is, my bro is gonna sit in on this set. He owes me twenty bucks, and this is how I'm collecting." With that, he bellowed, "Hit it, boys!"

My mouth dropped open. Tyson was on stage going to town on a rhythm guitar. And he was having a blast doing it. I moved onto the packed dance floor as close to the stage as I could get. And when Tyson finally saw me, he grinned, big and toothy, jutted his chin at his brother, then at me. I got an arched brow and an approving nod from Mr. Tight Jeans, which apparently constituted our official introduction. And then I was dancing, as much as wall-to-wall bodies would accommodate. And I don't know if it was the twang and sexy lyrics, or my great new address, or the people soup I was swimming in all by myself, or the fact that the guy I liked had a secret passion and was showing off for me—I just knew I was having a great time. And I was laughing.

thirty-four

It was well past midnight, and we were driving back to Duzy House, but I was still feeling energized. So was Tyson. In fact, he was a talking machine, clearly pumped by his performance. It seemed the gig for the AP Project—AP was short for Aaron Pierce—came about last-minute. "They knew I had plans with you," he explained. "And we've played a man short before, so it wasn't a big deal. But when you and I ended up, you know, not going into the city…" He'd grinned at me. "It was kind of a win-win, right?

"Absolutely! In fact, the way I see it, we're even now. You didn't know I was a celebrity infant, and I didn't know you were a quiet numbers guy with a secret life. And groupies."

He laughed. "The groupies are all Aaron's. By day my brother designs commercial buildings in his sweats, by night he pours himself into those man leggings and jams for free drinks and phone numbers."

I grinned. "Well, I'm sure he gets plenty of both."

"Yeah. His girlfriend isn't too happy about that."

"Price of fame, I guess."

"We're just having fun." Tyson squeezed my hand, and we were quiet until he pulled up to Duzy House.

"I had a great time," I said, smiling. "And I'll tell Poppy you kept your promise."

He cut the engine and leaned over to kiss me. It was the kind of kiss that could have lasted all night. "I had fun, too. In case you didn't notice."

He walked me to the entrance and gave me another long kiss. "I'd better go," he groaned, looking like that was the last thing he wanted to do at the moment. I knew just how he felt.

Once inside, I flipped on the light and took a deep breath. Then I took another one. I'd had a fabulous time with a fabulous guy, and it had been a while since I'd felt this good. That had to be a good omen for a first date.

I spotted my phone on the sofa where I'd left it and almost dreaded checking it. If we'd had deliveries and anyone had tried to reach me, we were probably behind. I picked it up and headed downstairs to check the whiteboard. In the elevator I listened to the only message I'd received. It was from Sabrina Hastings, the manager of Urban Pikewood, and it made me excited all over again. My own place! *Finally.* And the death gods were shining on my life because had been no deliveries while I'd been gone, and we were caught up at the moment. Someone had even sanitized the equipment. I must be dreaming.

It was quiet upstairs, so I tried not to make any noise as I grabbed a yogurt and headed to my room. When I turned on the lamp, the mess I'd left assaulted me again. I'd been living like this for too long, but right now I felt rather bittersweet about it. I was beyond excited to have my own place, but at the same time, this room was my mooring—my tether.

My gaze fell on the portrait of my beautiful mother at her piano. After that pivotal moment in Rose's kitchen, I hadn't been able to leave it. I'd wrapped it in sheets I'd stolen from Rose's linen closet and laid it across my back seat. At nearly four feet long and three feet wide, bundled, I was lucky it had fit. Again, not wanting Claire to know I'd been there, pilfering, I'd simply told her I was taking it. She had giggled as a tear fell—seemingly in full support of my supposed naughtiness. I had so loved being conspiratorial with her.

By happenstance, I'd leaned the portrait in the same corner where Claire's rocking chair had been when I was a little girl. It seemed fitting to find my mother's eyes gazing upon me now as they had then. I'd unwrapped the portrait to show Grandy and Babi, and they had reacted with much the same awe as I felt seeing it again now. I moved closer.

I never imagined how strong, how willful, how determined my mother had to have been to be her own person. Now I found that woman completely fascinating. I wished she was here now so she could tell me, as only a mother could, that I'd be okay on my own. I knew I would, of course. I knew it in theory. But I imagined that a mother could say it so it would penetrate, truly penetrate, the supposed adulthood that came with being twenty-two down to the child who might be a little unsure. I suddenly wondered if part of us always stayed a little bit of a child in our mother's eyes, and therefore always entitled to that kind of unconditional reassurance. It was a lovely thought—and as I looked at Claire's beautiful portrait, knowing what I now knew about her, I could almost hear her whispering, "You are your own mooring, January, and you will be just fine. You are my daughter, after all."

The thought was jolting and very real. And as it settled on me, in me, I knew—*I knew*—it was something she would have said to me and I loved her for it.

I thought of my dad then, too—my supposed-to-be-here father. He'd carry this painting into my new home—assuming he'd let me have it—and hang it lovingly on my wall. Then he'd probably attach a dead bolt to my front door, just like Poppy had on all his doors, and call me at night to make sure I was safe—the way I knew Poppy was going to do. The apple wouldn't have fallen far from the tree.

***

It was nearly nine when my phone rang and woke me up. I sat up in a panic, wondering where I was supposed to be. Nine o'clock! In the morning? I missed the call scrambling for my phone, but it was Tyson, and I stretched like a cat in the sun as I listened to his message.

"Hey, babe—yeah, I'm calling you babe now. If you have a problem with that, you're going to have to stop keeping me awake all night." He laughed. *"I just wanted to tell you I had a great time last night. I want to do it again. And again. And again. I was actually hoping we could get together tonight, but my boss just called, and I guess I'm headed to Boston. Want to go to Boston?"* He laughed again. *"One of our clients is being audited, and I think it's going to be bad. For him, not me. I*

should be back tomorrow night, maybe Friday. But feel free to distract me anytime—that means call me...or, you know, show up. Have a great day. Later. Babe.

I listened to the message again and smiled. I should get up, but no one was pounding on my door which meant I had a little time. I felt around under my bed for Mom's journal, planning to read just a few pages then I'd head over to Urban Pikewood with my deposit. I found the book and pulled it up by the edge of the cover. As I did, a note came fluttering out from between the pages. It was simply addressed *Mom*. I unfolded it.

Mom,

Because you never got my letters, and because so much more has happened since that fateful meeting with Dad, I'm having Oscar hand-deliver my journal to you. I know that's probably odd, but I want you to know what's gone on in my life since Dad's birthday, and I don't have time to re-write the last four months, so I'm offering this unconventional solution to bring you up to date. Everything I wrote to you in the letters is contained on these pages, as well as what's happened since our meeting—namely: I'm getting married. Naturally, the letters were much more filtered, so please don't be shocked by the details here. Feel free to skim.

You may not know this, Mom, but I keep journals because I've always felt rather swallowed up in everything 'You and Dad.' When I was little, I used to think I was crazy because I would remember things so differently than the two of you did—so much so that I would doubt my own experiences. I was very young when Grandma Winston gave me my first diary and I started writing down the truth as I saw it. Now I consider it proof of life for me. It has been my saving grace.

Read this journal, Mom, then I'd like it back. Since I'm getting married, maybe we could talk.

Claire

What? This was how Mom had told her parents she was marrying my dad? I guess that made sense. But then my heart sank because I'd read what was on these pages, and I rather ached for Rose reading these words. I got why Mom would allow it, but how hurt my grandmother must have been to read how her daughter pitied her, had seen her flaws so clearly, how angry she had been with her. But at least she'd *seen* her. Surely that had meant something to Rose. I read the note again, placed it back in the fold of the journal, then turned to where I'd left off: Christmas.

CHRISTMAS EVE, ALMOST CHIRSTMAS, 1999
Catching up the last few days: I got through my obligations, bowed to a standing O at my final holiday perf in NY, aced my departmental for the board, and passed my music history exam with a 97%. Then did my Christmas shopping—seemingly with the rest of Connecticut—at the Post Mall on December 23rd. All in all, a very productive week, which left little room for distraction. I never saw or heard from the parents.

I listened to Christmas music the whole way to NJ, and by the time I got there, I was fully into the holiday spirit. Yes, I went to Wallington for the holidays.

I'd been warned that Christmas Eve was all Rahela. And apparently it was quite a coup to be allowed in her kitchen to help out, but I was invited. I'd never seen so much food. T warned me that Christmas Eve was for Polish food. Carp and dumplings and cold beet soup, and things I couldn't pronounce and to just do my best because Christmas Day was all ham and potatoes and pie and pie and more pie. I helped T's sweet Busha set the table with Polish crockery and candles, and we set an extra place setting and even put some hay beneath the tablecloth, as was their custom. When it was to her liking, Rahela took my hand, and we stood back to admire our handiwork.

"Is wary special night to have you to be here." I had to write that down, she said it so sweetly. She said,

"*Wigila*—Christmas Eve—is time I always miss my family."
I couldn't think of anything to say, so I squeezed her hand.
We were standing in this lovely candlelit kitchen, and she
looked up at me, and out of the blue told me her father
believed love was like a precious stone. He was a miner,
hence the analogy—she said he used to tell her we were
very lucky to find this preciousness and that when we did,
we must hold it tight, guard it, because life could take
that stone—that preciousness—at any time and leave us
with only memories. She told me tonight, "I have only
memories of my *ojciec* and *matka* (parents, I had to ask
T), my brothers, my dear Ilka." T's tiny little grandmother
then looked me right in the eye and said: "If life lets you to
hold preciousness, dear Claire—hold it tight without fear.
There is no time for fear."

No one has ever spoken to me that way. That directly,
that boldly. It felt like truth and wisdom washing over me.
I will never in all my life forget that moment. To say it
was a special Christmas Eve would be a massive
understatement.

From the first star—which is the official start to
the *Wigila,* to the toast, to the breaking of the *Oplatek* (a
Polish cookie, kind of), the traditions were lovely. T's dad
broke the first piece of the *Oplatek* and thanked his wife
for being wonderful, then she broke off a piece and thanked
him for being a good provider, then it went around the
table, and each of us broke off a piece and thanked someone
for something. When it got to me, I was embarrassingly
emotional, but I thanked them all for embracing me
because I had truly never felt anything like being in the
heart of this family. Tanek was next and he was emotional,
too. He thanked me for filling his life with beautiful things
and I again remembered what his grandmother had told
me. I love this man. I truly do!

After that we opened gifts. That's Polish tradition. So, after Stasio and Diana had exchanged gifts with their children, Tanek's mother unwrapped the Kolinsky paintbrushes I'd anguished over giving her. I was so relieved when she liked them. And when Rahela hobbled over with a gift for me, she kissed my cheek as I gave her mine. We opened them at the same time. She gave me *The Yellow Fairy Book* by Andrew Lang and told me she had read these stories to her Tanek and Tessa, and now I would read them to my "childrens." I loved it! And my gift to her seemed to hit the mark, too, because she cradled the videotape like a lover, and it made me laugh. The 1945 movie *A Song to Remember* was just out on VHS. It starred Cornel Wilde as Frédéric Chopin—and by some miracle they'd had one copy at the Sam Goody in New Haven. She said I "made an old womans to swoon."

T was miffed because he got her a heating pad that she wasn't all that jazzed about. It was hilarious.

T gave me a Patriots stadium blanket and some long-hair boots that I adore! I gave him a Patriots sweatshirt and impossible-to-get tickets to the first playoff game against the Steelers next weekend—thank you, Oscar Thibodeau. T whooped. Stasio was on his feet insisting that game was sold out. I told them I knew a guy who knew a guy, and that there was a ticket for him, too. Merry Christmas very much! The look on his face was priceless, and I could never in a million years imagine Dad reacting to a gift from me that way. It's been an extraordinary Christmas Eve, lovely in a way I did not dare expect.

Before I left for Wallington this afternoon, I called home. There was no answer. But something told me that if they'd been in town, Mom would have picked up. Wherever they are, I hope my parents are having a lovely holiday because I certainly am. Aside from the fact that I'm on the couch in the den that Diana has made up for me and Tanek is across the hall, I'm having an outstanding time. I can't quite imagine how Christmas Day can possibly top it.

CHRISTMAS NIGHT

It's Christmas night and I'm home and I'm completely beside myself with regret. I don't know what I've done. I don't know how it all went so wrong. Tanek woke me up early this morning—this beautiful morning—before anyone else was up and told me to get dressed because it had snowed, and we were going for a walk.

It was lovely. We were the only two people awake, it seemed, on this cold but absolutely beautiful morning—the sun so bright, the sky so icy blue it hurt my eyes. T asked me how I was, and I told him I was pretty fantastic, because I was. I was! It was him. Being with him was simply too, too lovely. Not sure how he did it, but this amazing man had managed to erase almost everything that had made me ache, and that's what I told him. So why...why am I home tonight? How could I have blown it so horribly?

There's a park across the street from T's and I swear it was the most magical place I'd ever seen—Christmas Day, and we were wading through a sea of white. And it was so, so quiet.

T told me his first kiss happened there. He'd done it on a dare, and it had been categorically life-changing. He had been 7. I laughed, and it was like my laugh was the only sound on earth.

He told me he'd run away once—all the way across the street to that park—because he was in trouble. He didn't remember what he'd done (probably talked back to his mom), but his punishment had been so extreme in his view that he'd put some underwear and a comb and some peanut butter in a plastic bag and dramatically announced his departure from his cold, cruel family. I laughed again, loving every detail. He said Stasio just held open the door and asked him if he needed any money. T lasted about an hour, which was when his beloved Busha rescued him with a Popsicle and a pinwheel. That didn't surprise me.

I told him I loved his memories, and he told me he was hoping to make a few more. Then he said, if he ever had kids, he hoped they got to be kids here. How lovely is that? We walked all the way across that park to a playground and it, too, was magical. Snow was glistening on the swings and puddled at the bottom of twin slides. Even the picnic tables were buried. All except one. One had been brushed clean and there was a blanket on the bench and a picnic basket sitting on top. I looked at T and wanted to cry—he'd made me breakfast! Honestly, I couldn't stop kissing him.

I told him that I was really liking this love thing going on between us. His eyes misted and he looked hard at me. Hard enough that it scared me a little. Then out of the blue he said it. He said, "Then marry me." I didn't think I'd heard him right, so I just stared at him.

But he said it again. "Marry me, Claire."

I don't think I breathed. I didn't think it was real. I didn't think it could be real. Then he leaned closer and said it for the third time: "Marry me. Please." He put his cold hands on my face and said, "I know we haven't known each other very long, but I don't care. I come from a long line of married people who love each other, and I want in on that. With you. I love you."

And I can't believe what that felt like. It should have felt amazing, and it did on the surface. But underneath, it felt completely undoable, wrong, impossible. Everything I wanted seemed too far out of reach for me—I wasn't capable of being a wife. The thought of it utterly paralyzed me, and I was stunned by the feelings washing over me, the doubt, the quick and terrible doubt. I actually heard myself say "I can't...I can't marry you. I could never do that to you."

I'll never forget the look on his face. It broke my heart. Of course, he desperately reminded me that I wasn't my parents. He said, if I was anything like them, he wouldn't have been one bit crazy about me, and he was completely, off-the-charts crazy about me. But by then I was running across the park, and now I'm home and I can't stop crying and I'm hating myself and I'm loathing the people who decided a sham of a marriage was a good arena to raise a daughter in.

I dropped the journal. The scene hurt my heart. For both my parents. My poor dad...

I knew how this story ended, obviously, but there were only a few more pages left in Mom's journal, and I had to know what happened. So, I turned the page—and my phone rang.

It was Sabrina Hastings from Urban Pikewood. If I wanted the townhouse, I'd better get over there with my deposit because she'd already turned away two other interested parties.

thirty-five

Sabrina Hastings was still the tiniest bit hungover when she finally answered the door, and it took her a minute to place me. "Single, no pets?" she squinted. "Just about gave up on you."

"That's me. I didn't lose it, did I?"

She arched a brow. "Only cuz I like ya. C'mon. He's moving out today. I'll walk you over. Slowly."

She was wearing shorts and an oversized tee shirt, and her hair was a bit tragic. I smiled conspiratorially. "Good party?"

She grinned and put on her sunglasses. "From what I remember."

The unit I'd looked at before was a two-story with a large kitchen/family room combo on the main floor and a big bedroom with a walk-in closet and *en suite* bathroom upstairs. There was also a little office that I didn't really need—but I wasn't complaining—and a tiny half-bath as you walked in. I was assuming the unit I'd be renting would be comparable, and it was.

There was a lot of activity going on at No. 20, but apparently the owner was not around. Sabrina informed a mover that we were there to look around, and he shrugged his non-objection.

Of course, I wanted to check it out, but what I really wanted was to see if there was room for a piano. There was, but it was nowhere near the space needed for Mom's concert grand. If it were the only thing in the room, it still wouldn't fit. I knew it wouldn't. And I knew I had to figure out something else soon. I took in the room, imagined myself living there. I was going to need some furniture.

"I'll take it," I said to Sabrina. And I Venmoed her my deposit.

When I got home, Grandy was in the kitchen organizing cases of supplies into what was staying up here and what was going into storage downstairs. She was out of uniform, wearing slim jeans and a kimono over a black tee, sunglasses pushed back in her hair.

"Hey," I said.

"Hey, to you," she said over her shoulder. "Where have you been?"

"I finally snagged an apartment," I said, grinning. "Actually, it's a townhouse. Two floors."

"Oh?" Grandy said, temporarily frozen in her task of removing toilet paper from a big box.

"Yeah. Can you believe it? Another one opened at Urban Pikewood—which, if you remember, was my first choice. I'm so excited!"

The look on my grandmother's face told me I'd blindsided her— if being packed and ready to leave five weeks ago only to have it fall through and anxiously waiting for this very thing to occur could be considered blindsiding. My grandmother smiled sadly and resumed her toilet paper shuffling. "I'm happy for you, sweetheart. This is my happy face."

I laughed. "I'll be here so often, you'll wonder if I actually left, Grandy."

"I'm going to hold you to that." She was still smiling, still sadly.

"Grandy…"

She looked at me for a long moment, then rolled her eyes. "I'm just being a grandma. I knew you were leaving, and I've been preparing for it, but…I'm sorry, that empty room will break my heart a little. That's just a fact."

On my way to the fridge, I pecked her on the cheek. "Will you still feed me?"

"I don't know. I might be too busy redecorating that room. Margaret thinks I should turn it into a studio and paint in there because the light is so good, and my eyes are getting so bad."

I laughed. "Oh, good idea. And I predict an easel with Margaret's name on it in there, as well."

Grandy narrowed her eyes comically and nodded. "She's a sly one, isn't she? That was probably her plan all along."

I chuckled. My grandmother and her sister had always painted together, and they had always been best friends. The studio idea made me happy. "I'm going to make a sandwich," I said. "Do you want one?"

"Sure, there should be some turkey in there. And Havarti."

"Coming right up," I said, pulling out bread and mayo.

Grandy continued dividing case goods into pantry and downstairs items. "How was your date last night?" she asked as she worked.

"Great!" I gushed, with more feeling than I intended. Then I laughed. "I really like him."

"Really? I can't tell," she mocked. "So, he's nice?"

"Very. And he's in a band. And he's pretty good."

"I love a renaissance man."

I laughed.

Grandy walked over to add another slice of cheese to her sandwich. "Your dad always wanted to be in a band. But he had a terrible voice."

Another laugh barked out of me. My grandy *never* said anything disparaging about my dad.

"It's true," she nodded. "I loved him, but fingernails on a chalkboard were preferable." She pulled a funny face—she was on a roll. "He was a good drummer, though," she added, then bit into her sandwich. "Milk?"

"Pepsi," I said.

I pulled out chips and a couple of apples and carried everything to the table while Grandy filled two glasses with milk. I gave her a look when she handed me one of them.

"That's for moving out on me." She winked.

Then we sat across from each other, cases of canned goods flanking us on either side. It was like visiting each other in jail.

"I hear Monica came by yesterday. I'm sorry I missed her," Grandy said.

"She did," I said, with my mouth full. Then I looked around the cluttered kitchen, remembering that I had left the envelope with the pictures she'd brought me on the counter somewhere. I spotted it on a barstool and walked over and grabbed it. When Grandy saw the drawing that Claire had done, she smiled through misty eyes. "Can you believe that? Looks just like Tan," she kept saying.

"I know!" Then I remembered. "Grandy? I was reading in Mom's journal last night… Did she turn dad down when he asked her to marry him?"

My grandmother looked up at me. "What?"

"I read that she…he asked her to marry him on Christmas Day. Did she really say no?"

Grandy focused on me for a moment, then gazed over my shoulder, capturing the memory. "I could have wrung her little neck." She nodded. "We'd had this amazing Christmas Eve, and then we got up Christmas Day and she was gone." She shook her head, staring at me—*through* me—and put down her apple. "Tanek was absolutely beside himself. When I got up that morning, he was in the den. I can't remember if he was crying, I think so. He said they had broken things off. He was a mess, an absolute mess. He wouldn't talk to anybody; he didn't want to discuss it. We were just stunned."

"Did you know he had proposed?"

"I knew it was coming. And to tell you the truth I was a little concerned—they'd known each other all of five minutes." She gave me a look. "But I didn't know he'd done it until after. Stas finally got it out of him. Your grandfather was ready to drive to Yale and drag Claire back here by the hair and sit them both down until they figured things out. But of course, Tanek…whoa, no way. There was *yelling.* Lots of yelling."

"Did you know he made her a picnic in the park? On Christmas Day?"

Grandy put a hand to her heart. "Isn't that the most romantic thing you've ever heard?"

"How could she have said no to him?"

Grandy sighed. Then reached over and patted my hand. "Your sweet mom. I wanted to pinch her head off at the time, but I remember your Babka scolded us for being so hard on her. She said it was fear. And it turned out that's what it was—that's all it was." Grandy tapped her lips with a forefinger. Then after a moment she pointed that finger at me. "Those parents of hers…" She groaned.

"But they got married, obviously. So, what happened?"

Grandy smiled, and in that smile, of course I knew everything turned out just fine.

"As I recall," she said. "It was a very long week. But a couple of days before New Year's, Claire called me—and I don't think I was very nice, but she was. She was very understanding with my disappointment. I guess she and Tan had made plans to attend a New Year's Eve party in the city—some black-tie thing, and she was renting him a tux. Anyway, she called to ask what size suit he wore. It was strange, and I remember I was abrupt with her—I still feel bad about that—so I got off the phone fast. And then on New Year's Eve, oh gosh, maybe 8 or 8:30, the chimes rang and there she was." Grandy looked at me and her eyes filled with tears as she shook her head. "January, your mother..." Again, the head shake. "I can't even describe how lovely she was. She was wearing this beautiful gown, the color of pearls, maybe a shade darker. It was kind of Grecian—high neck, but bare shoulders and arms—she had on kind of a matching stole. She looked like Audrey Hepburn—do you even know who that is? She was gorgeous. Her hair was pulled back, with long, dangling earrings. She was just stunning. And she looked very nervous."

I had leaned across the table to capture every word my grandmother was saying, every emotion. "Where was Dad?"

"He'd just come up. He'd been working all day, and I think he'd come up to eat something, maybe. I'm not sure about that. I think your grandfather and I had been watching a movie in the den, and Rahe wandered out when she heard the bell. Tess wasn't around. So, I showed Claire into the den, which as I recall was really awkward because of your Poppy—then I went to get Tan. But when I came back..." Grandy sighed. "I don't know how she does it, but your great-grandmother has a way. She was just sitting there holding Claire's hand, smiling her little cat-swallowed-the-canary smile."

"What does that mean?"

Grandy shook her head, remembering. "Rahe wasn't worried. It's like she knew the secret. Anyway... We all sat there for a minute, very awkwardly, waiting for Tanek. I'm sure there was small talk, I hope there was. But then Tanek walked in and got a look at this *vision* that was your mother and—oh my, he was...*gone*."

"Really?"

"Well, he didn't know it yet, but he was."

I smiled. "What happened?"

Grandy chuckled. "I think he asked us to leave so he and Claire could talk. But Stas wouldn't move—you know your grandfather—and then Claire said, no, she wanted us to stay."

"You're kidding!"

"No. Then, bless her heart, she stood up and walked over to your dad. She was crying—or trying not to. She was shaky. But she said…" Grandy cleared her throat, tried not get emotional. "She told Tanek she'd made a mistake. I remember that."

"What did that mean?" I said, leaning further in. "About marrying him?"

Grandy nodded. "She looked at each one of us and said she was sorry. She said she didn't expect us to understand, but her experience with love was very different from ours. She broke my heart and said because of that, she wasn't sure she was capable of loving Tanek the way he deserved to be loved. But then she looked at your Babi and said a wise woman told her what she might be feeling was actually fear."

I stared at my grandmother staring back at me. We were both on the verge of tears.

"Rahela…" Grandy whispered.

"Of course…"

"Then Claire said this—something like this: she looked at Tan and told him she wasn't sleeping, she wasn't eating, her every thought had been of him. She said she was filled with fear that she'd lost him, and bottomless hope that she hadn't, and pain—pain in her head, in her heart, pain everywhere—that she'd hurt him. She told him she only wanted him, just him, that she needed him more than she needed to breathe—things like that—and that she'd decided that agony like that must actually be love, and if it wasn't, then she really didn't know what love was." Grandy shook her head. "I can still see her, hear her trembly voice as she laid it all on the line."

"Oh, my gosh!" I sang.

Grandy nodded, bit her lip. "I know. Then your sweet mom got down on one knee—"

"No way!"

"Yep. Of course, we were all bawling."

"And Dad said yes?"

Grandy wiped her nose on her napkin. "Well, he would have, but your silly grandfather beat him to the punch."

"What?"

Grandy rolled her eyes. "That man. What are you going to do? Claire said her—you know—Tanek will you be my husband? And Tan was so busy emoting that Stas just blurted, 'Of course he will!' But then I think, I'm pretty, sure Tan just scooped her up and said the same thing: 'Of course I will!' It was very sweet. Very...*memorable*. They were both crying. Lot of kissing going on."

"Wow," I breathed. "I had no idea."

Grandy's brows did a little dance over her wet eyes. "It was very special. And if we weren't already in love with Claire, we fell in love with her that night. And we have loved her as our own ever since."

"And Dad? I guess he completely forgave her?"

Grandy smiled. "Well, clearly. But I'm not sure it was forgiveness that was required. Janny, there is something wholly sacred—and irresistible—about being the person another person trusts with their broken life. And I think that's what happened that night. Claire handed your father her pretty but broken life, and Tanek wrapped it up in his own. That's bigger than forgiveness. That's what love really is. That's belonging."

I blinked back tears.

She sniffed. "I've said it before, sweet girl, and I'll say it again: Your parents were very special. Your mom still is."

I thought of that moment in Rose's kitchen, my mother's comforting hand on my face. "Thank you, Grandy."

She leaned across the table and kissed my head, then proceeded to gather our lunch things.

"I mean it. *Thank you.* This wasn't the life you imagined for yourself, but thank you."

She looked down at me. "It wasn't. But sometimes life gives you what you didn't even realize you wanted more than anything—a *January.*" She sighed. "And then life pulls a fast one and lets her grow up and move out." She shook her head. "Life is cruel. Obviously."

thirty-six

After we cleaned up, I told Grandy all about my new place. Mostly I told her how empty it was. She laughed. "So, what do you need?"

"Just about everything. I have my bedroom. And the desk you gave me for Christmas. And I have a laundry basket."

"Oh, dear," she said, with mock empathy. "We'd better make a plan."

For the next hour, we made a list of essentials I'd need to set up my new home: light bulbs, towels, dishwashing soap, utensils, dishes, a toaster, a couch, and a hundred other things. It was a bit overwhelming.

Grandy leaned back when we'd filled both sides of a sheet of notebook paper. "Before you shop for a thing, see what's downstairs. You know your grandfather throws nothing away. *Nothing.* I know there's a table down there, probably a couple. And sofas—not great sofas, but I'm sure there's one you can live with. And some lamps. There are things in that room that belonged to your parents—things we just didn't have the heart to throw away. Take whatever you want, sweetheart. *Please.*"

I checked my phone. Since no one had texted me, I was assuming we'd had no new deliveries, so I kissed Grandy's cheek and headed downstairs to see what I could find.

For as long as I could remember, the second floor had been a dumping ground, home to all of our excess. The fire that had destroyed half our home when I was small had taken out two rooms down here as well. One had been full of chemicals, and apparently it was a miracle that we hadn't been blown to bits. The other room had held the coffin inventory. That room was directly under our living room, which was next to my room. Because Duzy House had originally been a small apartment building, there were zones of reinforcement, which is why the fire had been contained to the northeast section but traveled all three floors. Massive renovations had been needed to bring everything up to code, and though better designed than the original, the second floor was still the designated overflow. Jasmine and I used to play hide and seek down here when we were little. I always won because I wasn't afraid to hide in the caskets.

I pushed open the door to our big catchall room—the mother of all closets—and flipped the light switch. I was immediately overwhelmed because it was true: my grandfather had an aversion to throwing away perfectly good...*anything*. But it didn't take me long to see that as a blessing.

I found an almost new cream-colored sofa that used to be in the foyer downstairs. Its companion loveseat had been long ago discarded after a grief-stricken and seriously intoxicated widow had thrown up a gut full of red wine on it. Red wine. Poppy had incinerated that, of course, but held on to the sofa, which was good news for me. Not really my style, but with some funky throw pillows, I could make it work for now. There was a table I'd never seen before with very cool carved legs. The wood top was pretty beat up, distressed, but I didn't think purposely. I could make it look more on-purpose and it would be fine. And I found a mishmash of chairs to go with it.

There was a quilt I'd never seen before which I unfolded to spread over the sofa I was claiming. It was beautiful—handmade, with small diamond shaped pieces of fabric in every imaginable shade of blue sewn together in uneven stitches. It was old, and I wondered at its history. That was a maybe.

I'd been down there for a while and my stash had grown impressively when I heard my grandmother's voice.

"Janny, are you still down here?"

"Over here, Grandy."

"Oh, this room!" she grumbled. "I told you, your grandfather is a hoarder." She found me between an ancient credenza and a steel shelf packed with old electronics. I was looking at a weird little TV that had a built-in VHS player. I laughed. It had an antenna. "Why on earth would Poppy save this?"

"Oh, I forgot all about this," Grandy said, sidetracked by the quilt I'd found. She ran her hand over it. "This was your mother's."

"It was? Where did it come from? Do you know?"

"I think her grandmother made it, but I'm not sure." Grandy fingered the edge. "It was in your parent's bedroom when we packed up their house. I couldn't let it go," she said softly. "But I didn't know what to do with it." She shook her head. "I completely forgot it was down here. I wonder if Claire would recognize it…"

Grandy looked around. "Somewhere down here," she said, "there is a little footstool. You'll want that, sweetheart. It was a wedding gift from one of your mother's piano teachers."

"Really? What does it look like?"

She held her hand about a foot from the floor. "It's beautiful. It's maybe this high, with a top, I don't know, maybe the size of a cookie sheet but covered in needlepoint. You'll know it when you see it."

"Diana! We going, or what?" Poppy boomed from down the hall.

"Oops, forgot about him," she laughed. "We're taking Claire to dinner. Want to come?"

I considered it for just a second. "No, thanks. I think I'll stick with this. But tell Mom that I'll see her soon. Sometime this week."

Grandy smiled. "I will."

"Taking Babi?" I asked.

"She's with the girls." Grandy leaned down and kissed my head. "Find that footstool."

***

It took some digging and some time, but I finally found it. And Grandy was right, I knew it when I saw it, and I knew it was special. I lifted it onto the table I was taking with me and inspected it. It was old, or just made to look old, and the top was again a piece of art made of small stitches. The scene depicted was a girl in a billowy dress blowing a dandelion, but the flying seeds were musical notes. I'd never seen anything like it. There was a small hinge, so I could tell it opened and after I played with it for a minute, I was able to lift the cushioned top.

Inside was a hollowed-out space where I found a stack of sheet music that had to have been my mother's.

I sat down and combed through it, smiling when I found Ravel's "Gaspard de la Nuit," Beethoven's "Moonlight Sonata," Vivaldi's "Winter" from his *Four Seasons*. When I saw Chopin's "Fantaisie Impromptu," I felt a tingle crawl up my spine. There was a note written in red on the inside cover: *Baby Girl knows a masterpiece when she hears it—dances inside me when I play. Clearly recognizes perfection just like her mama!* There were two smiley faces under the note.

Dances inside me? I went a little limp as that registered. I'd heard this piece—and danced to it—inside my mother. Amazing. I added the footstool to my growing pile and looked around, unexpectedly reminded that somewhere down here was the plastic bin where I'd found the sketch of Claire's injuries all those years ago. But that bin had been full of all kinds of things that had belonged to my mom; now, though I'd avoided it since my gruesome discovery, suddenly I was curious to know what else it contained.

I found it on an old bookshelf. It had *Claire* written in thick black letters along with *Do Not Throw Away* underlined twice. I carried the bin to the sofa and lifted the lid.

There was my baby dress that Babka had made for me. I'd forgotten it was in there, and now I wished I'd been able to show it to Monica. It was over three feet long with itty-bitty sleeves and pearl buttons at the neck, made from Claire's designer wedding dress. Now that I knew the history of that dress, I realized I had been prayed over drenched in Rose's love for her daughter as well as Claire's love for me, and it made me feel a little weak. In Babi's room, there is a picture of Babka holding me that day. That dress nearly reached the floor.

The newspapers with the terrible headlines and indelible crash pictures were rolled up and bound with an elastic band, and inside that roll I knew were the sketches of my mother's head as well as a copy of my father's obituary. I set the bundle aside. Not now.

There was a small box that held a smaller velvet box and a note. Inside was a silver ball about the size of a large marble hanging on a very delicate silver chain. It wasn't a typical necklace; it was rather unique, a little funky. There was a card with a picture of four hands, a man and a woman each holding a little hand of the child between them. The note said:

To my beautiful and burgeoning Claire, because it's almost time. I want you to know that even though our daughter is not yet here, I adore her already simply because she is ours—because she is the gift we will give each other in a few short days. No child could have a finer mother, and no man could want for more than this for his daughter. Baby, you have made me the kind of happy other men only dream of. You have no idea how much I love you!

Tanek

I was shaking all over as I tried to figure out how to open the locket. It was a smooth ball with a seam barely visible through the middle. I found a tiny pin, and pressed. The seam widened and I pulled the ball apart, which unfolded into three little round frames. There was a picture of my father grinning and one of my mother doing the same thing. The third frame was empty because my father had died before he could take a picture of me. I read the note again, this time through thick tears. He'd loved me simply because I was theirs. I put the necklace in my pocket. Surely, I could find a picture of me to fill that tiny empty frame.

There were movie stubs and playbills from productions my parents had seen. I found the letter congratulating my mother on her invitation to compete in the Cliburn. I couldn't even imagine what that would have felt like.

There was a half-knitted pink sweater that would have fit a brand-new baby when it was finished, the needles still threaded through the yarn ready to be picked up. Grandy told me once that Babi had been teaching Claire to knit.

I found a heavy book wrapped in tissue paper. It was old and worn, the leather binding cracked. The gold title had been rubbed off in places, faded elsewhere, but you could still make out Jane Eyre. The pages were brittle and yellowed and smelled ancient, and there was a note inside:

Clairy,

Since we have lived and died through this book, not to mention holding all men up against the impossible standards of Mr. Rochester, I thought you deserved a first edition. Happiness was always waiting for you, my friend, and tomorrow you will marry your Rochester. You deserve it all! No looking back. Now go forth and conquer everything wonderful that is waiting for you.

Love Always, Mon

Monica. Of course.

Inside the book, I found a letter addressed to Monica. It was stamped but not sealed, and as I opened it, a photograph slid from between the pages. It was my very pregnant mother and her best friend. They were laughing uproariously. Monica was standing behind Claire, and mom's protruding belly was covered with ribbons and bows. I stared at the picture of her—and me—for a long time. Then I read her note:

Mon,

I cannot thank you enough for the baby shower. Best. Party. Ever! Clearly, my daughter is off to a great start, and it's all your fault! Thank you! Thank you!

Oh, Monica, I am so excited about this next chapter in my life. I feel like I already know her. She will be beautiful and brilliant and kind and witty and all the things I wish I was, this daughter of mine. I want to be a good mom just like yours. You know it was your mom who taught me absolutely everything about mothering. Thank you for sharing her with me all these years. I can't imagine my life if you hadn't come along to be my "sister." No matter where our lives take us, I will always love you. Enjoy New York for as long as you're there, but don't let it change you. You are perfect the way you are! I'll bring the baby up this spring, and we'll have lunch at Tavern on the Green. Now go forth and conquer grad school but stay by the phone. You'll be the first to know when Elizabeth Ann Duzinski arrives. Or January Ann if she's born even one second into the New Year. (That's the deal I made with Tanek.)

Love always, Claire

I swallowed. If I'd been born when I was due, I would be Elizabeth Duzinski…and my parents would never have been on the road that night. We'd be a family, I'd have a brother or two, maybe a sister…

I kissed the photo. I'd make myself a copy, then I'd send the letter and the original and the book to Monica.

I found the beautiful velvet box holding the crystal butterfly my mother had written about in her journal. It was as exquisite as she had described and gave deep meaning to the paper swarm on both of her walls. The lovely note Rose had written about being free was in the box as well. It was heartbreaking.

The biggest thing in the container was a video camera. It looked brand new and seemed a little out of context with everything else. It was obviously a gift because there was still wrapping paper stuck to the bottom of the box it had come in, and there was a Christmas card. It looked like the camera had been taken out and probably used, because it had been put back a little haphazardly, with the cords still attached. It surprised me to think of Claire as a would-be videographer; she seemed a bit delicate to be lugging around this monster. I fiddled with it, but there was no tape, so I opened the card.

It seemed the camera did not belong to my mother. She'd given it to my dad for Christmas.

Merry Christmas to my funny husband. As you requested, aka begged, cajoled, wheedled, and ultimately found for yourself since they don't make them anymore, a Sharp Slim Cam. Now your job is to do exactly as you've promised—to document the life and times of our little one, and all the little ones that will come after her. They will probably hate it, but you're right, we will always have the memories, not to mention the blackmail material.

Speaking of memories, Tan, I'm sitting here reliving one of my most pivotal—last Christmas when you walked me to the park and asked me if I had any plans for the rest of my life. I know I freaked out terribly, and it took a few days for me to get it right. But marrying you was by far the best decision I ever made. I love you with my whole soul. And here we are, standing on the cusp of another brand-new year with a brand-new baby girl on the way. She came fast and was not exactly planned just moments into our story, but like you, I have come to believe that maybe the universe knows something we don't. All I know is we've made a little person, and I am so excited to be her mom and watch you be her dad. And if I miss anything, I know you will have it recorded.

I love you, Claire

P.S. The other thing you ordered for yourself is in the big box. Happy viewing.

Like her journals, I could almost hear the sound of Claire's voice talking to my father through these words. It was haunting, however, her reference to the universe. It made me shudder, and I slumped against the back of the sofa and closed my eyes. It had been a little over a week since Oscar Thibodeau came to see me, but it could have been a year for all that had happened since. I was not the same person. It was as though I'd fallen through a trap door into a room full of things I couldn't *not* look at. The luxury of my own ignorance had been stripped away. Rose dying had introduced me to my mother whether I'd been ready for that or not, and the dominos had just kept falling until here I was, wanting to know more and more.

I read the card again. Happy viewing. *Happy viewing?* It couldn't be that easy, could it?

I walked over to the metal shelf and the odd little television with the built-in VCR. I stood on tiptoe and tried to see if there was a tape in it. The slot wouldn't open. The TV wasn't large—it was meant to sit on a counter—but it was heavy and a bit unwieldy. I tugged it to the edge of the shelf and nearly dropped it, but I managed to get it to the table, then pushed the table to the nearest outlet. My heart was pounding. *Tell me there's a tape. Tell me my dad recorded something on that Christmas. Anything.*

I plugged it in and turned it on. The screen filled with black and white static, and I could hear whirring. I found the play button and pushed it, but nothing happened, then I pressed eject and the screen went dark as the little machine spit out a VHS tape. My hand was shaking when I pushed it back in and pressed rewind. When it stopped, I hesitated. If there was nothing on this tape, I was going to cry.

I pushed Play.

For a moment, nothing happened. Nothing but darkness and some muffled noise. But then I heard a woman's voice say, "*It's not working. Don't you have to push 'record'?*" A man said, "*It is recording—oh wait, forgot to take off the lens cap.*" Then he apparently did just that, and the woman giggled. "*To our future child, your father is not at all technologically savvy, and your mother is even less so.*"

I swallowed, my mouth suddenly bone dry.

Then the picture became clear and that mother, *my* mother, came into focus. She was beautiful, with the same long hair she'd had in her wedding photos, same lovely face, same smile that came alive as the camera zoomed in, then out, then in again. "*Tanek, what are you doing?*"

On the tape, my father laughed, "*I'm trying to find you. Oh, there you are,*" he said. "*I'm just trying to—okay, move over to the right a few inches.*" My mother did. "*Okay, perfect.*" Then the screen went dark as my father walked in front of the camera and sat down next to my mom. He took a deep breath and smiled. "*Welcome to the world, Baby Girl—Take One.*"

My mother laughed, and my father put his arm around her and pulled her close. "*We are your parents,*" he said stiffly. Then nothing. My parents became distinctly camera-shy, and in that moment of awkward inanimation, they were *brilliant.* Young and beautiful.

My father said, "*Oh, brother!*" And my mother laughed again, and the screen went black.

"No!" I yelped. "That can't be all there is!"

I was just about to rewind the tape when another picture formed.

thirty-seven

I don't know how long I sat there, transported. I only know I rewound the tape so many times that I lost count. I was completely overcome, like my heart had cracked open—not in a broken way, but in a way that made room for feelings I had never known.

No one was home to share this with, and Tyson was in Boston, so I called Jasmine, desperate to tell someone what I'd found. I got her voicemail and wanted to scream. "Jaz, call me," I warbled, as calmly as I could manage.

I thought of Claire then and what this would mean to her. I thought of simply loading the little television into my car and driving over to Potomac Manor. But would seeing this devastate her? How could it not—the love of her life speaking from the dead? I didn't know what to do, because the thought of hurting my mother one more time twisted me inside out. But how could I possibly keep it from her?

My father had made this tape just hours before I was born, just hours before he'd died, and suddenly I imagined that night in a way I never had before. My parents driving through a blizzard on New Year's Eve, another man in position to cross their path—a man who'd been drinking. The timing had to have been absolutely precise for that tragedy to occur—down to the second. What I had always seen as completely random suddenly seemed highly exact. And if it had been that specific, then what did that make me? The making of me? The timing of me? The rather miraculous way my parents had found each other on a crowded street? The woman my mother had decided to refuse to be which had made her accessible to my dad?

My head was exploding with these thoughts. And who gets married just six months after laying eyes on each other? And who gets pregnant five minutes later? And who gets sent home from the hospital twice, then waits until the exact moment they did to leave in the middle of a snowstorm—not one labor pain sooner or later—only to be at that exact location at that precise moment to be in the path of that truck? An hour before which my father had made this tape. I started to tremble as my life came into clear and glaring focus.

I imagined the impact, imagined that last moment between two people who'd adored each other…and adored me. Had my father known what was happening to him? Had Claire? My mother had been so hurt, so terribly damaged. Why hadn't she died? She should have died—*she was supposed to have died*—everyone said so. Surely, she could have gone with the love of her life; surely, she'd wanted to.

My gaze fell on the stack of sheet music sitting in the open footstool, Chopin's masterpiece on the top. "Dances inside me," written in my mother's handwriting.

I'd danced inside her. *I'd danced inside her.* Had I moved? Had I made myself known in the midst of that carnage, reminded her of where they'd been headed and why? A breath shuddered out of me. Was it possible that my mother had had a choice that night?

I was shaking and my heart was a hammer, and I didn't know what to do. And then I did. I picked up the music—my mother's music—and went downstairs.

***

Some people cope with big, unwieldy feelings by running, or drinking, or hurting themselves. I play because I feel more in control of my chaos when the space between my head and my hands fills with someone else's timeless emotion and marries mine. Music tempers unmanageable feelings in me, suspends my confusion in exquisite noise, detaches me. Chopin, especially, makes more bearable my own ragged secrets, wraps them in a kind of beauty.

That was especially so of "Fantaisie Impromptu."

I'd always been intrigued by its mysterious journey to fame. But now that I knew my mother had loved it as much as I did, I felt a deeper connection, not only to her, but also to the troubled genius who had never wanted the piece published.

I had the notes down, but the expression challenged me. An old piano instructor—Mr. Blood—had once told me that memorized notes were nothing but clothing on an old woman; expression was what revealed her scars and secrets. It was the scars and secrets, the heartache, which brought a piece to life. This is what made Chopin's work so deeply personal to me.

And tonight, I understood. Scars and secrets.

With his first G sharp, I entered that disturbingly ethereal realm. That octave echoing for eight full counts in the cavernous foyer of our dim mortuary was like an ominous portent, and in fact, I had always thought of this piece in terms of a building storm. Frédéric was pure genius and surely only part human. The other part had to be the stuff of magic because I simply couldn't understand how that eerie bloom of melody thought up by a sickly prodigy could so thoroughly drill itself into the center of me. Haunt me and soothe me at the same time. Especially now. *Especially now.* But it could, and it did.

Babka says it's because Polish blood runs through my veins. Maybe. All I know is that I have loved this piece since I was a child. When I first heard it, I think I had a spiritual experience. And right there in a library in Clark, New Jersey, the Impromptu had become my secret obsession. I didn't practice it much when anyone was around, but when I was alone with just my big feelings, it was the perfect diversion.

And now I was so focused on keeping the semiquavers my right hand was playing in correct time with the triplets my other hand was playing, that I was not even aware that anyone had walked in until I felt the blast of warm summer air. I glanced up to find my grandparents flanking Claire, who had kind of a silly look on her face. At least that's how it struck me in the nanosecond that it took me to take her in without losing my place. I should have stopped, but I couldn't risk the loss of momentum. Playing this piece was like running a hundred-yard dash, then slowing down for a deep breath before taking off again. The secret was all in the timing. It shifted quickly and required laser focus that was now completely compromised by this intrusion.

I'd been doing so well—likely thanks to the rawness of my emotion—but now I started to falter. I lost the rhythm, then the notes. Then I lost my cool and just lifted my hands.

Grandy's palm was at her chest. "Oh, Janny. That is lovely. What is it?"

"Nothing. It's just something I've been playing around with," I said, watching Claire make her way jerkily toward me. I braced myself for a bone-crushing hug, but my mother just sat down next to me and made her noise, the tonal noise at the back of her throat that means if she had words, she would say something profound. She was trembling and urged me on with the jut of her chin. There was encouragement in my grandparents' eyes as well, though they stayed standing a few feet from the piano.

I hesitated, but only for a breath, then I started again with that lone G sharp, that siren note Chopin surely had intended to cause one to sit up and pay attention. And then the wind and rain. Soft, lightly played at first, but extremely fast like a downpour. Beside me, Claire was bouncing excitedly, and I was suddenly feeling the same energy. Once more I got lost in the music, opposite sides of my brain dictating notes and timing to their designated hand. I sounded good and it felt amazing, exhilarating, even...*frenzied*. But then, as sometimes happens, my fingers were running ahead of my brain, and I tripped over one little sharp. Back up, start the measure again. But it's hard to start over in the middle of a blitz and enter at the right speed, and I messed up again. I was frustrated because I knew this part, and yet it sounded so wrong. I went back to the beginning of the measure, but I missed the note again and started to cry—not just because of the music, but the box, the tape, my father's message, my mother, everything. Suddenly, Claire was tapping down my arm, and everything collided; the floodgates opened.

"Claire! What are you doing?!" I cried. And then I began again.

But I made the same mistake and grew even more exasperated. This time, my mother took hold of my hand with both of hers. Of course, I resisted because I didn't know what she was doing. But she hung on, firmly, until she had my full attention. When I finally looked over at her, we were nearly nose-to-nose. I dropped my other hand to my lap and let the sound evaporate until it was quiet. My mother made no noise, she just looked at me, into me, and I could not look away.

More tears came then, unchecked, and I did nothing to hide them. I tried to speak but the words wouldn't surface. This seemed to worry Claire somehow, because she reached up and helplessly patted my chest as though reminding me to breathe. The moment was so visceral and unexpected that I just closed my eyes and leaned over the keys.

"Janny, are you alright?" Grandy said softly, approaching the piano, Poppy at her side.

I took a breath and looked up into their concerned faces.

My mother, who had not let go of me, gently nudged my hand back onto the keyboard and sort of motioned slowly up and down, which I took to mean that she wanted me to start again but to go slow.

I looked at her, a question in my eyes.

She did it again.

I breathed in, then out, and nodded, surprised that I was nodding. With eyes locked on hers, I found that everything had slowed down— my breath, my frustration, my heart—as I suddenly realized what was happening; I was sitting at the piano next to my mother, a veritable virtuoso, and she was tutoring me. My damaged little non-verbal mother was tutoring me through Chopin. Could that be? She tapped my knee and urged me on. I took a settling breath as my left hand once again softly keyed Chopin's masterful introduction. When I started the right hand, my finger memory took over—I knew these notes. Again, my mother motioned me to slow down. And I did. And amazingly, at this pace, I captured each note in its fullness. But I was still too fast per Claire, who made the slow-down motion once again. So, I did. I slowed down and played "Fantaisie Impromptu" like I'd never played it before. Slowly and deliberately. And my heart ached to hear it at this gentle, stirring tempo. The fast parts were more thoughtful, each measure, their own miracle. The brilliant melody became a respite, an embrace almost, in the midst of the chaos that bookended its softness. It had always been my favorite part, and it never failed to lift me and hold me, the beating heart of this piece. I felt Claire go the tiniest bit limp next to me, as though she was overcome as well. For a moment we were completely suspended, she and I, in the beauty of this opus, as under her guidance, I took the time to be precise and unhurried. The result, to my ears, was heartbreakingly beautiful.

It ended perhaps exactly how Chopin intended—like gently rousing from a dream. I let the final notes resonate, and then I looked up to find my grandparents staring at me, open-mouthed. Next to me, Claire's eyes were closed, but a tear was dripping off her chin. She knew this piece. She remembered it. And she had taught me how to play it. I'd never experienced anything like it before. When she looked over at me, I saw what I always saw, but deeper, more undeniable. I wrapped my arms around her and felt her weep into my neck.

After a moment, I gently peeled out of her embrace and wiped both of our faces with my hands. Then I reached for the music sitting on the rack. I turned to the inside cover and showed my mother what she'd written. At first nothing seemed to register. But when I read it to her, a small moan happened at the back of her throat and her craggy little finger found the words: *Baby Girl knows a masterpiece when she hears it—dances inside me!*

"Mom, do you remember writing this?"

One blink, a smile, and new tears.

I looked at Grandy.

My grandparents had moved close and could see what I was talking about. Grandy's hand came to her mouth. Poppy's eyes were wet.

I looked at my mother. "Mom, do you remember the night I was born? The accident?"

One slow blink as her eye welled again.

"And you remember Dad…"

One blink, a tiny sob. No hesitation.

"Do you remember what you gave him for Christmas that year?"

A furrow appeared in her forehead.

I hugged her again, my heart pounding in my chest. Then I looked at my Grandy. "What are you doing here? I thought you went to dinner. What made you bring Claire home?"

"I wanted her to see the quilt you found before we took her back," Grandy said. "I'm pretty sure her grandmother made it. And…she wanted to see you."

I swallowed. "Will you take her upstairs? I'll be there in a minute. Poppy, can you help me carry some things up?"

"Of course."

I looked at Claire and smiled through my tears. "I have a surprise for you, Mom."

thirty-eight

When we got upstairs, Grandy was telling Claire and Babka about my new townhouse. I could hear them in the kitchen when we got off the elevator, Poppy lugging the television, me holding the bin with Claire's name on it. Poppy hadn't asked any questions, but he'd eyed me with curiosity on the way up. "If you really want a TV for your new place, Janny, I think we can do better than this one."

I smiled. "I don't think we can, Poppy. Let's take it in the den." I pulled the piano bench into the center of the room, and he set the television down on it while I went for an extension cord. When I was ready, I asked my grandfather to get the others. Again, the curiosity, but he didn't ask. He just walked out shouting down the hall. "Diana, your granddaughter is acting very suspiciously. She wants us all down here. You too, Mama."

My family filed in and sat down facing the piano bench. I sat down next to Claire and pulled her hand into my lap. She looked over at me with a question in her eye.

"What's going on, Janny?" my grandmother asked.

I looked at them. "I found this downstairs, and...well, you all just need to see it." I blew out a breath. There was nothing else to say, but for a second, I couldn't move. I simply didn't know what to expect, especially from my mother, and it rather paralyzed me. Finally, I let go of Claire's hand and walked the two steps to the TV and knelt down. "I do want to thank Poppy for never, *ever,* throwing anything away,"

I said, looking over my shoulder at him. "I mean it. I will love you forever for being a hoarder."

He gave me a confused look but said, "Happy to oblige."

"What is it?" Grandy said.

I pushed Play. "Just watch."

For a moment, just like downstairs, nothing happened. Nothing but darkness and some muffled noise. But then the same: *"It's not working. Don't you have to push Record?"*

Then my father's voice.

"Oh...my," Grandy choked. "Is that..."

Then the picture became stunning as beautiful Claire came into focus.

I heard another sharp intake of breath from my grandmother, but I could not look at her. I couldn't look at any of them.

"Oh, Stas...it's...it's *Tan*," my grandmother said in a thin whisper.

I heard a gasp from Babi and a sob disguised as a cough from Poppy, and I was feeling it all, just as I had downstairs.

"We are your parents," my dad said on the TV, and I smiled through tears that had again surfaced because again my parents had become camera-shy for long enough that I could take them in. *"Oh, brother!"* my father finally groaned, and the screen went black.

"Is that all there is?" Grandy asked, breathlessly.

"No," I said. "Just keep watching...."

After a few seconds my father, looking very tired, reappeared on the tiny screen. He was wearing different clothes than he had been a moment ago, a blue shirt and a loosened tie, as though he'd been at work—it was a different day. He cleared his throat. *"Let's try this again, and I'll try not to be so worried about my weirdness being immortalized."* He chuckled and pulled his chair closer to the camera. *"Okay,"* he rubbed his hands together. *"Take Two—actually, take twenty-two, at least. Hello, Baby Girl. Your mom gave me this video camera for Christmas, and we gave each other this cool little TV so we could watch movies while we rock you. You can probably tell that I have no idea what I'm doing. But I'm learning."* He smiled.

I finally had the courage to look over my shoulder at my mother, where I saw everything I needed to know. She was sitting ramrod straight on the edge of the sofa, a tear brimming in her good eye. Her lips were parted slightly, which allowed passage for the little moan that voiced her memory of the man she loved.

"I just want you to know how excited I am to meet you," my dad continued on the screen. *"You're just about the coolest thing that's ever happened to me. The very coolest was meeting your mom, but that led to you, so you get to be the coolest kid. Someday I'll tell you all about the miracle of your mom and me, of how we found each other and how much money I cost her."* He laughed, but then rubbed a tear from his eye. *"I think I loved her from my first glimpse, and that probably sounds ridiculous, so I'll tell you that I knew for sure when I spotted her on a sidewalk in New York."* For a beat or two, he looked very thoughtful, and I heard another moan from the sofa behind me.

"She is so excited to be your mom—and you are so lucky to have her. You will be incredible because of her. Me, I have no idea what I'm doing, so it's a good thing I had a great teacher. Your grandpa—you'll call him Jah-dek, maybe Pops—he thinks he's funnier than he actually is, but that guy is my hero. Don't tell him, though—he already has a big head." He laughed, and behind me Poppy did too, a little. *"I will tell you this, little one, the blood of the strongest women I know will flow through your veins, and because of that you are destined to be amazing. You won't be able to help it."* He smiled and was again thoughtful.

From the sofa, Claire made a noise that sounded like an audible ache. Behind me, I heard my grandmother sniff.

On the screen, my father's handsome face had zoomed in, and he was laughing. *"Obviously, I've got a lot to learn about my new toy and which buttons do what and which ones not to push."* He zoomed back out. *"I really just wanted to introduce myself and welcome you to the world and—let's be honest—play with my new camera, which I plan to use to capture everything about you. It's what parents do. Apparently. Somewhere my mom has a mountain of all things* Me, *and now I understand why, and I love her for it. Prepare to be utterly adored, my daughter. Your grandmother does nothing by halves."*

He was right about that. I imagined Grandy's heart exploding, but I didn't dare look.

My father was quiet for a second. *"Right now, I just want you here safe and sound, but you are being a little stubborn."* He nodded, and we stared through the TV at each other until, off camera, a door opened. *"There you are. What are you doing?"* It was my mother's voice.

"I think I finally figured this thing out; if the light is blinking, it's recording. Come say hi to our daughter."

On the screen, my lovely mom laughed and walked over to look into the camera. *"Really? Again? You'll never fit all of me in that little, tiny frame."*

"Rolling, Mama."

She turned to the side and ran her hands over the basketball under her shirt that was me. *"Can you even see all of me?"*

"Barely," my dad teased. *"Say something to her."*

She chuckled. *"Well, the doctor says you are big, fat, and gorgeous, and that you'll get here when you get here. I, for one, wish you'd hurry, missy."* On the tiny screen, Claire sat down next to my father and laid her head on his shoulder, clearly worn out. She *was* beautiful. She was wearing a red turtleneck, and her hair was in a ponytail. And this time I noticed that she was wearing the little round locket my dad had given her. Seeing it made me swallow my own sob.

"You okay?"

"I'm just pregnant."

"Phew." My dad grinned. *"I didn't want to say anything, but you are getting a little chunky in the belly region."*

She punched his arm playfully.

My father then looked into the camera. *"Baby G, this is your awesome mama. She plays a mean Beethoven and Brahms and Jerry Lee, and I so hope you inherit her talent and courage and her big heart and her beautiful laugh."*

My mother smiled as she absently rubbed her enormous middle.

"You're not okay, are you?"

"Not really. But I just can't stand the thought of being sent home one more time. Not in this weather. So, I'm going to be fine. Until I'm not."

"C'mon, Baby. I'll rub your back while we watch Dick Clark ring in '01." He then helped my mother out of the chair and kissed her forehead. She looked up at him and didn't really smile, but said *I love you* without saying it.

I paused the tape as my dad reached over to turn off the camera, freezing their beautiful images. Again, I could not believe it. My parents on the night I was born. I tried to swallow, but my throat had swollen shut. Again.

There was not a sound.

When I turned to look at my mother, I saw new a tear brimming in her eye. No one said anything; no one even breathed as she slowly got to her feet and made her way to the television. For a moment Claire just stared down at the man on the screen. Then with decided effort, she bent to her knees and brought her shaky hand to his face. The tear fell then, but she wasn't crying so much as she was in awe. And despite her irregular features, you'd have to be blind to not see the pure love—and the memory of pure love—in her expression as she stared at my father.

A chill drove down my spine as I realized that her knowledge of him was completely intact. Had it always been? Or had her memory of him been a gradual restoration? These thoughts humbled and amazed me...

Behind me, my grandparents' tears were flowing, and Babi's tenderness saturated her wrinkled face. They had all adored him, and he had adored them back.

After a moment, Claire started pushing buttons on the TV in an effort to make the video start again. She only managed to eject the tape. I moved closer and helped her, and once it was rewound, we watched it again to the same reaction in all of us. This time, as my mom took in their frozen images, I asked her if she remembered the locket she was wearing around her neck in the video. She touched her heart and blinked, once more astonishing me.

I retrieved the necklace from my pocket and when my mother saw it, a tiny gasp burst from her throat. I opened the little ball to reveal the frames and told her I would find a picture of me to fill the empty one. She studied the small images of herself and my father, her fingers pressed to her lips. I slipped the locket around her neck, and when I did, she clutched it in one hand. With the other she patted my face.

Grandy walked over to us and knelt down, sniffing back emotion. "Sweetheart, I am so sorry... I forgot all about that. It's just lovely."

For some reason, I suddenly wondered if my mother had been wearing the necklace that night, or if she'd taken it off before they went to the hospital. I asked Grandy, but she was busy hugging Claire and didn't seem to hear me.

"She was," Poppy said softly from the sofa. "I thought it was ruined. But it just needed to be cleaned up."

I swallowed.

Grandy wiped her tears. "I'm going to grab that quilt, sweetie," she said to Claire.

While she was gone, I showed my mother some of the other things from the box I'd found. She giggled at the picture of her pregnant self with Monica, then held the little photo to her chest.

"That's Monica. You remember her from the funeral," I said.

She smiled and blinked.

"She was at Potomac Manor today," Poppy said. "She was just leaving when we got there. The nurse said she had spent most of the afternoon."

"Really? How was it seeing her, Mom?"

Big smile. Big blink.

I couldn't believe how happy this made me. "That's awesome, Mom!"

Another blink.

I found the crystal butterfly in the velvet box and opened it for Claire. When she saw it, her good eye widened then watered. Again, the strange relationship my mom had had with her mother seemed to boil down to a tangled devotion, complicated, brutal, but still love.

Grandy walked back in then, holding the quilt from downstairs and, with Babi's help, draped it over the sofa. Claire had been studying the butterfly and did not notice until I redirected her attention. When she saw the quilt, it wasn't immediately apparent that she recognized it. She looked at it for a long moment, then walked over and stroked it. When she cocked her head, I heard a little moan.

Grandy lifted Mom's chin. "Look familiar? It was on your bed. Yours and Tan's."

My mother blinked. Slowly at first, then with more animation.

Babka slipped her hand in Claire's. "Was made from your Busha, your Grandmama. You remember this?"

Again, Mom blinked.

"I was wish I could know this woman," Babi said, and Claire leaned into her as though she wished the same thing.

***

It was a night of memories for my mom and revelations for me—simultaneously stunning and joyful and heartbreaking. And exhausting. When Poppy stood and yawned and said, "I'd better get you back home, Miss Claire," I volunteered to take her.

We folded the quilt that would now be on Claire's bed at Potomac Manor, and when I picked it up, she buried her face in it for a moment. She then wrapped her arms around my grandmother's waist and squeezed her with gratitude. She hugged them all, and then walked over and indicated the little television with a question on her face. I told her that I would have a copy of the videotape made for her. "I'll go tomorrow, Mom," I said. "I'll get it transferred to DVD." Maybe Tyson could help me, I thought. Mom had a television in her room at the care center; I wasn't sure about a DVD player, but I'd get her one if she didn't have one. Then it would be easy. With the press of a button on a remote, she could watch my dad anytime she wanted. I told her all this and she looked intently at me, as though eliciting a promise. I promised, and she patted my chin.

My Babi then wrapped her once more in an old woman's bear hug. "Sweet Kochanie," she crooned over and over. They had a bond, those two, that surpassed friendship and admiration, even devotion. My mother had been the heart of my Babi's beloved grandson. That made her almost royalty to all of them, but especially my Babka, who seemed to feel love a bit *purer* than the rest of us—unfiltered and uncomplicated.

In the elevator I was sad to be taking her home. Suddenly, it seemed not such a bad idea that Claire be able to stay over once in a while. Maybe she could fight Grandy for my room when I moved out, or they could clean out her old room that she used to have before the fire had changed everything.

Tears stung my eyes as our *history* crept back in. She caught me staring, and her crooked smile widened. It did me in with its generosity. When the elevator stopped in the lobby, my mother was slow to step out, but when she did, I followed her in silence to the exit and out into the warm evening to where I'd parked my car. I put the quilt in the back seat and opened the passenger door, but Claire just stood there and looked at me.

"Mom? You okay?"

She cocked her head and reached for me. I walked into her embrace and felt it tighten around me. It seemed a very heartfelt *I love you* that I suddenly felt wholly unworthy of. I started to tremble and she squeezed me tighter. I began to weep...and then sob.

My mother stepped back to look at me, her expression bent in a way I'd never seen before: part surprise, part pain, and part worry. She didn't know what was happening. I started to shake in earnest as years of remorse bubbled to the surface. "Mom," I choked out. "I am so sorry. You have no idea how sorry..."

Alarm filled Claire's good eye.

"For all of it, Mom," I pushed through my swelling throat. "For every time I hurt you. For every time I was mean and cruel, and so, so awful...." I shook my head. "I was... Mom... I got it so wrong for so long. Can you ever, *ever* forgive me?" I could no longer see her for my tears, but suddenly her hands were on my face and she was pulling me toward her. And then she was wiping away my tears, kissing me, and holding me. My mother held me until I stopped crying. Until I was strong enough to look into her beautiful little face. When I did, I saw nothing but love and forgiveness there and I can't even describe the feeling.

"Mom," I finally managed. "Do you think... Can we...can we maybe just start over, twenty-two years late?"

When she smiled her crooked smile and offered me a single, tear-filled blink, it felt like absolution.

"I...I love you, Mom." Had I ever even said those words to her? "I do, Mom. You probably never knew that, because I was always such a brat, but...I do. And I have no idea how to...how to thank you...how to make up for..."

My mother touched her heart, and I wondered how to even begin to atone for all I had put her through.

thirty-nine

As I pulled onto the highway, I looked over at Claire and smiled, "You know, I have your journals," I confessed.

Claire cocked her head in a question.

I nodded. "That attorney, Mr. Thibodeau—he said I could have them. I hope it's okay. I guess Rose's estate is being dismantled, remember, and he wanted me to have them before the lawyers descended. So…anyway, I've read some of them." I cleared my throat. "I read about how you met Dad."

Claire smiled, and it was big.

"Can I just say that I loved, loved, loved that you flashed him your phone number on Fifth Avenue. That you made the first move. Do you remember that? That was extremely cool."

She made a sound that might have been a giggle.

"I know Dad loved you the minute he saw you—he said that in the video—but what about you? Did it take you long to love him back?"

My mother didn't hesitate. She shook her head and blinked. Twice.

I already knew this because in her journal she'd admitted that she had fallen in love with him over the pancakes. I laughed, recalling how my dad had set off the sprinklers in her kitchen when he'd burned the bacon. I laughed, too, because I realized I was having a conversation, an actual conversation, with my nonverbal mom, and we were understanding each other. She had been my age when she'd met my dad and somehow, in this moment, that made us peers.

"I've met someone," I blurted, glancing over at her.

Claire's eye widened, and she slapped her hand against the seat for details.

I laughed. "He's nice. Very nice. He likes country music too much, which seems to be his biggest flaw," I said. "But he has a job, and a degree, and plans, and a nice family." I laughed again, and it felt good.

Claire reached over and tapped my chest with her finger in what I assumed was a question about my heart.

"I like him, Mom," I told her. "I think I like him a lot."

Claire nodded, her half smile urging me on.

"And this might sound strange, but I really like the me I am with him. I'm not hiding from him or trying to impress him, or anything—I'm just myself. And that's a little off-script for me, but it's nice."

My mother nodded with vigor, and I had the distinct impression that she knew exactly what I was talking about.

"I think he's real, too," I said. "He was in a real place when I met him, and when you start there, there's no going back—if that makes sense. His sister died, and we did her service, so he was a little…bruised at the time. We probably shouldn't have started anything under those circumstances, but we did. Especially with Rose dying…and everything." I shrugged. "But it's a little late now. He's kind of rocked my world. So, Tyson—his name is Tyson—has had a front-row seat as I've unraveled a bit. But I haven't scared him away yet."

Claire reached over and squeezed my arm.

"I want you to meet him," I said softly. "I want to know what you think."

Claire's mouth dropped open, and she stared at me like she'd been waiting my whole life to hear me say something like that. And I guess she had, since I'd never once introduced her to anyone I'd gone out with. In fact, the only person in my life outside of my family who knew my mom was Jasmine. "Would that be okay with you, Mom?"

A tear had filled her good eye, but her smile said yes.

"Good. I'll bring him sometime soon. I promise."

Her crooked smile broadened, and it was beautiful.

I smiled, too.

***

It was almost nine when we finally walked through the arch and into Potomac Manor. They were having a recital in the gathering room tonight, so Claire and I went in and caught the tail end. A copper samovar was still set up amid the almost empty platters of fruit, cheese, and teacakes, so I fixed Claire a plate and we found a seat near the piano where a young tuxedoed man was playing Pachelbel.

"Looks like you missed a nice evening, Mom," I said as we enjoyed a lovely execution of "Canon in D."

My mother tugged on my arm and when she got my attention, she shook her head with gusto. I smiled. "Oh, sorry. You're right—we had a much better night."

We were quiet then, my mom running out of steam. She even laid her head on my shoulder. I should have put her to bed then, but we didn't move.

As I sat there drenched in the ambience of this big rotunda-shaped room with its high ceiling, paneled walls and pockets of plush seating, a thought began to form. I let it germinate as my gaze roamed the impressive art and tall bookshelves, the huge stone fireplace with its massive wreath above the mantel. This room was amazing. Arranged in the round, there was space enough for a small ensemble to perform from the center; certainly, a string quartet would fit, as well as a small choir. With a single pianist, chairs were frequently set up in rows, like now, or in a semi-circle radiating from the center. At times, I had seen a small stage erected. Whatever the arrangement, the acoustics were perfect in here, thanks to Harry Golding's architectural vision.

I closed my eyes and let Pachelbel's brilliance drift over me. I adored everything about this music, which was stunning played on the glistening Kawai. But as I sat there, rather floating on the loveliness, I suddenly thought how truly exquisite the "Canon in D" would have sounded in this room played on my mother's Steinway.

forty

It was after eleven when I got home, and I went straight upstairs instead of checking the whiteboard. If we'd had deliveries, they could wait until morning. They'd have to; I'd lived an entire year today—that's what it felt like—and I was exhausted.

Everyone was in bed, and it was dark except for the lamp at the end of the hall. I quietly grabbed a water from the fridge and made my way to my bedroom. The clutter assailed me as it always did, and I'd almost forgotten that this day had started with me signing a lease on my new home. Had that really just been this morning? It didn't seem possible with all that had happened.

I wanted to tell Tyson about this day; I'd tried to call him twice on my way back from Potomac Manor, but he hadn't answered. It seemed both a bit weird and totally natural to want to share all this with him. But he must have been either asleep or still working, because he hadn't called me back.

I washed my face and brushed my teeth and fully planned to just fall into bed and sleep for a week. But instead, I walked into the den.

The little TV was still on the piano bench, the extension cord still feeding it power. As I rewound the tape, I wondered how many times my grandparents had watched it. When my father appeared on the tiny screen, I was once more in awe that he was speaking to me. By now, I knew every word, knew exactly when his expression was about to change, when the tone, the cadence in his voice would fluctuate. He was beautiful. My dad was beautiful. When the screen went dark, I felt a little like he had kissed me goodnight.

I had just gotten into bed when my phone rang just after midnight. It was Tyson

"Hey, you."

"I took a chance you'd still be awake," he said

"I'm awake," I told him, turning the lamp back on.

He chuckled. "I got your message, and I didn't want to wait until tomorrow to call you back. But I will, if that's what you need. I'll hang up right now and call you back in the morning. Your call."

I smiled. He was cute. "No. I want to hear about your day."

"My day was long and tedious," he said. "But guess where I've been for the last hour?"

"It's late. Where?"

"The Holocaust Memorial."

"What?"

"This job I'm doing is just up the street from Boston City Hall. You can see the memorial from the office where I've been working all day. It's really striking in the daytime, but all lit up at night, it's really *something*. We finally wrapped up about an hour ago, and I wandered over. Have you seen it?"

"No. I've never been to Boston."

"January, it's awesome. It's sobering, but so awesome. From a distance, these huge towers look like they're made of frosted glass. There are six of them, and the guy I was auditing told me they represent the six concentration camps. But it's not frosted glass. It's glass that's been etched with numbers—the numbers issued to the people who were murdered there."

I swallowed. "Tyson. Wow. I had no idea."

"Your grandmother," he said. "She was at one of those camps?"

"Birkenau."

"And her family? They were there, too?"

"Some of them. Her parents and oldest brother died before they ever got there. But the rest of them…"

I heard him swallow, and then he was quiet for a beat. "Auschwitz-Birkenau is one of the towers," he said. "It just really hit me as I walked through that sculpture that I had a connection, a kind of connection, to someone…to her people who died there. It made me so angry and so sad. I was kind of emotional. You would have been embarrassed."

"No. I wouldn't," I said. "I would have been right there with you. We would have been emotional together."

"That would have been nice," he said.

"It would have. I need to see it."

"I'll bring you here sometime. It's very sobering," Tyson said again. "Tell your grandma—great-grandma—tell her I thought of her tonight."

"I will. That will mean a lot to her," I said, genuinely touched by him. "You're very sweet, you know. Thank you, Tyson."

"For what?"

"For being real. I like that. I like it a lot."

"I...uh...I feel the same way about you." He laughed. "I told my mom we went out the other night and she's all, 'Don't screw this up, Ty. Don't blow this. She's a beautiful girl.'"

I felt heat in my face. "That's funny," I said. "Just tonight, I told my mom about you."

"Yeah? Wait, what?"

"I did. It's been quite a day, and I really want to tell you about it when you get home. It's been kind of life-altering."

"Are you okay?"

"I'm good. I'm really good. But I need another favor. I need to move my mom's piano again. Can you talk to your uncle?"

"Sure. Is it going back to Pennsylvania?"

"No. It's not going far at all," I told him.

"Okay. I'll talk to him tomorrow. I'll call him from the airport."

"Thanks."

"Hey, I get in around seven tomorrow night. Any chance I could see you?"

"I think there's an excellent chance," I said, smiling. "Who's picking you up?"

"Uber. It's just from Teterboro."

"I'll pick you up. Text me your flight number."

"Really? That would be great. We'll grab some dinner. Maybe we can find a Beethoven bar—I owe you after last night. Oh, speaking of which, have you heard Ed Sheeran's 'Perfect'?"

"Of course."

"Have you heard the arrangement with the opera guy?"

"There's an opera guy? What are you talking about?"

"You know the song, right?"

"Uh huh."

"YouTube Sheeran's 'Perfect' with Andrea Bocelli. He's the opera guy."

I laughed. "I know who Bocelli is."

"Of course, you do," Tyson teased me. "YouTube it. Sheeran's lyrics are stellar. Very cool arrangement."

"I'll find it," I said, smiling. "Night Tyson."

forty-one

The day after the day everything changed, I called Harry Golding at Potomac Manor with a proposal. Harry had known Mom for years, but he was not aware of her history until I offered up the details of her accomplishments over lunch the next week. His jowly chin dropped in genuine amazement when I mentioned she had been a Cliburn candidate. The toupeed and bespectacled man had only ever known that Mom came from wealth and had a seemingly bottomless living stipend thanks to her imperious father—information I had only recently become privy to myself.

Harry was just absorbing the news of my mother's former life when I barreled ahead with my proposition: A trade—her impeccable Steinway for the lovely, tuned-to-perfection, glossy, mahogany-stained, upright Kawai that now sat in the gathering room—which would fit beautifully in my new townhome. Harry's forkful of pasta hung suspended halfway between plate and mouth as he took a moment to process my words. "I beg your pardon?" he finally managed.

I nodded. "It's a concert grand, and it belonged—*belongs*—to my mother. It's spectacular," I'd told him. "And it was made for that space. Please say yes."

"A Steinway piano? An actual Steinway...at the Manor? Yes. Yes!" he'd cried. "Of course. That would be incredible, January! But it doesn't seem like a very fair exchange."

"Oh, believe me, it's a win-win-*win*," I insisted. "My mother gets her beloved grand and can enjoy it whenever it's played—which I hope will be often. I get the stellar Kawai, and Potomac Manor gets a bit more snob appeal." I danced my eyebrows.

I could almost see the wheels turning as the proprietor gleefully considered the advantage of boasting a showpiece of this magnitude. "Well, the space can certainly accommodate it," he mused. "You know, my mother, rest her soul, loved that massive room; she loved the majesty of it. At one point she actually thought of turning it into a theater-in-the-round for small productions. After she got sick and we created The Manor, we opted for the elegance and intimacy of the big parlor for gathering, but with much the same capability as the theater." He nodded. "You're right, a grand piano would only add to the grandeur of that space." He winked then and said he could only do me *this favor* on one condition: that I agree to perform a recital.

"Of course," I agreed.

"We'll make an event of it," he said. "A launch, if you will. Introduce the concert grand as your mother's. Introduce her past *achievements*. Perhaps we could even display some of those awards? Can you get hold of them?"

"That's a great idea!" I said, thinking of the box I had packed away filled with her trophies and ribbons. "And I think that would be lovely for Claire. Thank you, Harry."

He smiled absently, preoccupied with the possibilities.

I called Oscar Thibodeau on the way back to Duzy House that day, and when he answered, I was a little surprised by how much I'd missed him. He seemed sincerely pleased to hear from me as well. Especially when I told him what I'd decided to do with Mom's piano.

"Oh, January. Of course. Of course, it belongs there. What a lovely gesture."

"It's a surprise. She doesn't know about it, but I think she'll be pleased."

"Of course she will," Oscar enthused.

"I'm not sure how long it will take me to get it to them," I said. "The house it's sitting in hasn't sold yet, but apparently there is interest, so it might not be too long. But the real reason I'm calling is to see if, by chance, you could be there…for the party?"

"I wouldn't miss it, my dear."

"Fantastic!"

A few days later, I called Tyson's uncle, who was more than accommodating. He was even nicer than when I'd first met him—familiar somehow—leading me to believe something had happened to increase my worthiness in his regard, something like being a topic of conversation in the Pierce household. Nothing said *arrival* like positive domestic scrutiny.

I explained that I didn't know when, but as soon as the property in Alpine sold, I wanted to move the Steinway to Potomac Manor. Nick Pierce agreed to not only transport Mom's grand piano to the care center, but also to move the Kawai to my new address.

I'd started to move out, but it was slow going because Duzy House had been bombarded with death, which had waylaid my best intentions. I had yet to spend a night in my new place. However, the boxes and bags that had cluttered my bedroom for weeks had been relocated and now cluttered my new home. But at least my kitchen was unpacked—mostly unpacked—enough so that I was able to bake a pizza for Tyson and even serve it on a plate. There hadn't really been time to put anything else away, but almost everything had been moved to my new address.

Tyson had helped with the heavy lifting, including hauling furniture from the hoarder's paradise on the second floor. He had been astounded by Poppy's massive collection of...*everything*, and when he'd admired a gun case my grandfather had squirreled away down there, Poppy had insisted he take it. Tyson only went through the motions of arguing, which made Poppy laugh.

Since he'd returned from Boston, Tyson and I had seen each other as often as humanly possible, which turned out to be not often enough. Something frequently came up with his work or mine, but we did our best and we talked every day. He'd even brought me—all of us—dinner just last night, when my work had interfered with our plans. We'd had reservations to see Dueling Pianos—again—but then Poppy had gotten a call we'd all hoped we wouldn't.

The floodgates had opened just past nine when the coroner delivered a family of five that had died in a murder-suicide. The story had broken over the weekend, shocking our community and putting Duzy House on red alert: In the bereavement trade, any death—or deaths—that make the headlines are deaths to avoid, even though you know they could end up on your table(s). All of them. And that's what happened.

As pragmatic as we all pretend to be with death, that kind of awfulness—murder/suicide—evokes a pall that is hard to dispel. The kids were five, eight and ten and had been poisoned by their mother, who'd then shot her husband in the chest and herself in the head.

It was all hands on deck.

I let Tyson know that I'd need a raincheck—again—on Dueling Pianos, and he was a little cranky about it. I didn't go into too much detail, but I did tell him it looked like we'd be pulling an all-nighter, which was not an exaggeration. I also told him that he was welcome to take someone else since this was the third time I'd had to cancel. I said it, but I didn't mean it.

My aunt, who was now in the throes of twenty-four-hour-a-day morning sickness, had left hours ago. But she came back in when Poppy called and she brought Zander, who gowned up for gofer duty. Poppy jumped in for embalming, which would take place in assembly-line fashion with Tess doing the prep work between bouts of dry heaving. Calvin was given the job of cleaning up the man and packing his chest cavity—repacking, that is; the coroner had done a rudimentary job—then wrapping him into leak-proof condition. My assignment was to begin reconstructing the woman's head and face. Fortunately, half of her was unscathed so I had good comparison for my task.

Babka had placed herself on pinwheel duty. She'd wandered down after Poppy got the call—he had been upstairs when it came in, so she was aware of what had happened. That left Grandy to handle all the paperwork and meet with family members at this god-awful hour. They'd insisted on accompanying their loved ones and wanted things handled as quietly as public fascination would allow, hence the late-night consult. This was one reason the entire family had been brought to us at this far end of the day: containment of sensational information.

As often happens, family members had a story to tell Grandy, one of mental illness and addiction and violated restraining orders. There were different versions, but all mourned the precious kids caught in the crossfire. The news reports blamed the wife, but Grandy was not so quick to accept that judgment since to her it was unclear who exactly had been the worst addict or the most mentally ill. She told us later that the whole sad incident struck her as the perfect storm of compromised people. She'd formed this opinion during the consult, which had been marked by tattered emotion expertly reined in by a very tired, very compassionate member of the clergy. It had left Grandy overwhelmed. She'd kept it together for the family but had buckled a bit under the weight of it after they'd left.

This was how Tyson found my grandmother.

She wasn't expecting him. None of us were—it was well past midnight. But there he was with sandwiches, chips, and caffeine—both hot and cold. I don't know what they talked about for nearly an hour, but whatever it was touched my grandmother to her core. And when she brought down the sacks of food and now same-temperature drinks, she kissed my cheek and said, "That one's a keeper. He's waiting upstairs, but don't be too long. I'm talking about Tyson, by the way," she clarified with a tired grin.

I was surprised, but too tired to make much of it as I slipped off my messy apron and inspected my scrubs. Not too bad. The rest of me was a bit undone, but I'd been at it going on eighteen hours and there was no apology in me. When I stepped off the elevator, he was standing in the foyer with his hands in his pockets. He looked a bit uneasy, like he wasn't sure what to expect since we'd argued just hours before. I walked over and kissed him as though he was mine—had always been mine.

"I'm sorry," he murmured. "I was an ass earlier."

"But you brought us food." I smiled. "And you made my Grandy cry. That makes you pretty much a rock star, Tyson Pierce."

He laughed without laughing. "I honestly don't know how you do it."

I sighed. "Oh, it's almost never like *this*. Thankfully. This is hard, and it's bad. But everyone's here, so that helps. And you brought us food, and you brought me *you*." I slipped my hands into his, and he pulled me close, and for a moment I just breathed him in. "Thank you," I said, laying my head on his shoulder. "Keep this up, and you're going to push me right off the far edge of *like* into…*that other place entirely*," I said sleepily, with no regret. Then I lifted my head and kissed his chin.

His steady eyes were on mine, and he was not confused by what I'd almost just said. Neither was I. And though I had not known those words were going to come out of me, they'd formed so naturally and so honestly that I had no regrets.

"Good to know," Tyson said, finding my mouth again.

He *was* delicious, and I didn't want him to leave. "I'd better get back," I whispered reluctantly.

He walked me to the elevator and pulled me once more into his arms. "Just so you know," he said into my ear. "I think I might have already fallen off the far edge of *like* into that *other place entirely*." He kissed my neck and didn't see me smile. "Good to know," I said.

As the elevator doors closed, shutting away Tyson's beautiful face, my rational, educated, grown-up self knew it was too soon to feel this way about him. But I wasn't imagining it. I'd been out with enough guys who'd sparked absolutely nothing in me to know what was real and what wasn't. I thought of my father falling in love *almost instantly* with my mother as she'd played the music of angels. I thought of Claire having enough of an inkling of the same thing to do what she'd done on the most famous street in New York City. Could it really be that belonging to someone was that cosmic and that simple? And that you just had to be paying attention when they walked into your life?

***

It took us all night, but we finally got that little family put back together, their faces devoid of the pain that had ravaged them. As we stood together in our embalming theater, exhausted, bedraggled, emotionally burdened and in need of showers, my grandfather said something profound. First, he thanked us. Then he said, "Don't let this damage you. It's only death, and God will sort out the details. "

My grandmother walked over and wearily kissed his cheek. "Let's go to bed, old man. We have to be up an hour ago."

Calvin pulled a handkerchief from his pocket and wiped his nose. "I'll grab a nap and be back by ten with the collection from Sisters of Charity."

Tess took Zander's hand and squeezed. "Don't call me until after noon if you don't have to." It was unclear who she was talking to.

Poppy looked at me.

"Go," I said. "I'll wipe down."

"Thank you, Janny," my grandfather said, yawning. "Thank you for being young and strong and willing."

I laughed. Kind of.

forty-two

Three days later, the house in Alpine was under contract. I called Nick Pierce and Company to arrange for transport the following Saturday of both the Steinway and the Kawai. Then I let Harry Golding know. He in turn alerted the cook staff that a shindig was underway for that weekend. Then between casketing a WWII vet and checking in a newly deceased woman from Sisters of Charity, I mocked up an invitation on the company computer. When I showed it to Grandy, she smiled.

"So, Saturday night?"

"Yes, but I'll need some help getting Claire out of the way," I said. "Are you free?"

Checking the calendar, she tapped her bottom lip. "Looks like our last service should wrap up by 4:30-ish. How about we plan to take her to dinner?"

"That would be awesome, Grandy. I think Harry is doing up refreshments, so…you know, don't get dessert."

My grandmother came out from behind the desk to sit next to me. When she took my hand, there was a threat of tears in her eyes. "This is a lovely thing you're doing, Janny."

"I'm just giving her back her piano."

"Well, I like this new look on you."

I didn't even pretend not to understand. I knew the last few weeks had changed me, expanded me, and apparently had given me a new look.

I smiled at my grandmother. "It's all good, Grandy."

That night, I sent invitations through cyberspace to my family and Tyson, the staff at Potomac Manor, and Harry. I also sent one to Monica and Jasmine with no expectations whatsoever—I knew Jaz wasn't back in town yet, and it would be a stretch for Monica. I just wanted them to know. I overnighted a hard copy to Oscar, because he's old-school.

Just after 1:00 on Saturday afternoon, Tyson's uncle called to tell me he'd wrapped and loaded the concert grand and was on his way to Potomac Manor. He thought they'd be less than an hour there and then be back to my place with the Kawai no later than 3:00. I called Harry and told him what was happening; he said he'd arranged to have the piano tuner he used look at the Steinway at 4:00.

"You're brilliant, Harry, absolutely brilliant! I didn't even think about that!"

He chuckled. "Well, we can't have an out-of-tune debut, now, can we? And you remember that you will be wowing us tonight, right?"

"That's the plan. What about Mom? You're keeping her out of the gathering room?"

He laughed like a little boy. "I've hung tarps at the common entrances and told the residents that the room is being painted. Most of them know what we're planning and are keeping Claire busy until your grandparents pick her up for dinner. We'll set the room up in recital mode and be ready when they get back."

"That sounds fabulous!"

"And we have éclairs decorated with piano keys." He laughed again.

"Harry, you so rock!"

"I do? Well…" he cleared his throat. "I've slated a 7:00 start time. Will that work?"

"That's perfect. Thanks so much."

"Thank you, Miss January. The unveiling of a Steinway—and your mother—is a very big deal for us. As if you couldn't tell."

***

By the grace of God, there were no bodies delivered on Saturday, but Calvin was on call in case that changed. This meant that Tess was well-rested and a bit less ornery than her usual pregnant self. Grandy had taken Babka to get her hair done first thing this morning, after which they'd gone shopping. When they got home, Babka had a new dress for tonight and Grandy, some new earrings. My day, too, had gone smoothly. I'd had one embalming, which I'd finished by 10:30, and a consult that wrapped up just before noon. That gave me the rest of the day to plan my recital pieces. With no services for a couple of hours, I practiced on the baby grand in the foyer of Duzy House, my phone resting on the music rack so I could watch for Nick Pierce's call. At almost 2:30, I got a text. He had left Potomac Manor and would be to my new address within thirty minutes. So, I went home.

Home. It still felt a bit strange to call the townhouse at Urban Pikewood my home, but every day it felt more real. Especially now that everything had been put away and arranged to my liking. I'd framed pictures, bought plants, and filled a small bookshelf with paperbacks and music as well as the Pulitzers I'd brought back from Chestnut Hill. Tyson had given me a hand-blown vase, tall and oddly shaped—very dramatic. He'd filled it with a few inches of blue marbles, added water and two exotic-looking goldfish. It was the coolest thing in the living room. The last piece of the puzzle was the lovely Kawai.

I met Nick and company—sans Tyson who was in a deposition with a client—in the parking lot of my complex. From there, it was down a small hill and around the corner to my unit. I'd cleared a path in my living room, and the burly team got the dolly through the door and positioned my gleaming new piano against the wall. When they removed the quilted tarps, I nearly lost my mind. It was stunning.

"There ya go, January. Signed, sealed, and delivered," Nick said, grinning. He looked around. "I like your place."

"Thanks. I'm getting used to it." I said as I rifled through my backpack for my wallet. "How much do I owe you?"

Nick shook his head. "Mr. Gold—I think it was Gold—he took care of it."

"Mr. Golding? Harry paid you for…both pianos?"

"He did. He said it was the least he could do." Nick smiled. "That grand piano looks pretty awesome in that fancy room, by the way."

"Oh, I knew it would."

"My nephew told me what you're doing, surprising your mom with her piano. That's nice."

"Well, it belongs in a place like that. And I get…this." I glanced over my shoulder at my new best friend. "I think it worked out great for everybody."

He smiled.

I practiced my selection pieces for the rest of the afternoon, then took a shower. I wasn't quite ready when Tyson rang my doorbell at a quarter to 6:00. He was early, and I answered the door barefoot, holding two different shoes. "Oh, good, you can help me decide," I said, offering up the red stiletto open-toe and the yellow strappy sandal." I was wearing a sleeveless white silk blouse and black tuxedo pants that hit above my ankles, so either one would have been fine. But Tyson did not seem interested in my shoe dilemma. He took me in slowly and shook his head. "Damn, girl. Could you look any better?"

"Awwww, really?" I dropped the shoes and wrapped my arms around his neck. "You clean up pretty good yourself."

After he'd thoroughly kissed me, I pulled him inside and shut the door. "I'll just be a minute," I said, gathering my shoes. In the end I chose some silver flats. It wasn't Carnegie Hall, for heaven's sake; it was Potomac Manor. I slipped on the garnet earrings my grandparents had given me for my graduation from mortuary school and the companion gold chain that again boasted my birthstone. A little more lip gloss and I was good to go.

When I came back into my living room, Tyson was holding a picture of me and my mother. There weren't many, but Grandy had snapped that one of us at Rose's memorial luncheon. It was a random shot, not posed, and had caught Claire's happy reaction to seeing Monica that day. I'm smiling as well at Monica, who is only partially in the photo. I loved the expression on Claire's face—and now the photo had a place of honor on my new piano.

I stepped next to Ty, who was studying the picture intently. And as I looked at it over his shoulder, I suddenly saw it through his eyes, eyes that had never before seen my mother's face. Now I saw plainly the flaws that, after a lifetime of knowing her, went largely unnoticed. I saw the way the left side of her face was sunken, the eye on that side quite obviously artificial, the smile asymmetrical. The scars.

Tyson looked up at me with somber eyes. "This is your mom?"

I nodded.

He swallowed and looked back at the photo.

We'd had many conversations about what had happened the night I was born, but clearly...clearly, I hadn't prepared him. And in an hour, he would meet her. And suddenly, all I could see was Monica turning away from her, unable to get out of that restaurant fast enough, my mother hurt and confused. I felt a tremor start at the base of my spine. What was I thinking?

When Tyson looked back up at me, his eyes were wet. "She's...she's beautiful, January."

I slowly let go of the breath I hadn't realized was caught. "You have no idea," I whispered.

He placed the photo back on my new piano then leaned in and kissed my forehead. Lingered there a moment. "I'm excited to meet her," he said softly.

"She's excited to meet you, too."

forty-three

We got to the care center at just past 6:30, and I didn't see Poppy's car. But the parking lot was unusually full, so I could have missed it. I'd texted Grandy and told her to stall until as close to 7:00 as possible, but I had not heard back from her.

"Wow," Tyson said as he cut the engine. "This is where she lives?"

"Right? Just wait until you see the inside."

We weren't halfway across the parking lot when Harry Golding hurried out of the building to greet us. He was beaming and dressed to kill, his tie and toupee both the tiniest bit askew. I hugged him and introduced Tyson.

"Lovely. Lovely to meet you, son," he said absently, tugging me toward the entrance. "Everything looks wonderful, January, and there are a *lot* of people here."

"People? What people?" I'd sent out fewer than ten invites, and the crowded parking lot had not made the needed impression.

"Oh, uh, well..." he stammered. "We put out the word, and it seems we started a little brushfire. A reporter from the Glen Ridge Weekly is even here. He wants to talk to you."

I looked at Tyson, then back at Harry. "What?" On the most well-attended cultural night Potomac Manor usually just attracted residents, on-shift staff, and a few family members. Brushfire? The Weekly? This was going to overwhelm Claire. "Is Mom here?" I asked nervously.

"Not yet."

Tyson squeezed my hand. "Breathe January," he whispered.

When we got inside, the first thing I noticed was soft music coming from the speakers in the hall. It was strings, very soothing, and it inspired me to relax a little. The next thing I noticed was the soft chatter, and when we followed Harry into the gathering room, I saw the source—rows and rows of chairs, arranged in a horseshoe around the Steinway, most of them filled except for the seats nearest the piano that Harry had evidently reserved for my family. Tyson reacted once more with an awed, "Wow," uttered under his breath.

I don't know what I'd expected, but it wasn't this, and it took me a moment to absorb it.

Mom's beautiful concert grand had been polished to gleaming perfection. Seeing it in this amazing room, blanketed in her awards that I'd dropped off yesterday, was beyond impressive.

"Oh, Harry. It's lovely. Everything."

"Yes," he agreed, a look of pride covering his fleshy face. "I think so, too."

"January?"

I turned to find sweet Oscar Thibodeau approaching. I almost cried as I threw my arms around him. "Oscar! Thank you so much for coming. Look at this place."

He surveyed the crowded room, landed on the piano, and smiled widely. "I wouldn't have missed it. What a lovely tribute you've created for our Claire," he said, looking pleased. "Well done."

"Well, I really didn't…it's kind of taken on a life of its own, I think," I said, glancing at Harry, but he was talking with Zuli, the receptionist, and didn't hear me. "But thank you, Oscar," I went on. "I'm so happy you're here. This is my friend Tyson Pierce. My boyfriend, actually," I clarified, meeting Tyson's eyes.

"I should hope so." Oscar chuckled. "He's got that look about him."

Tyson laughed and squeezed my hand, then let go and took Oscar's. "Nice to meet you, sir. January has told me a lot about you."

I suddenly felt skinny arms slip around me from behind and assumed it was my grandmother, but when I turned around, I yelped. "Jaz! Oh my gosh! You're here!" I cried as we hugged and swayed and gushed. I had not laid eyes on my best friend for nearly four months, but we'd talked and texted almost every day, and she was fully up to speed on my life.

"You look gorgeous," she said to me.

"I was just going to say the same thing to you." I stood back, still clinging to her. She was in a short white skirt and a sleeveless orange tunic with her signature in-your-face-jewelry—this time tiered strands of gigantic baubles in a mix of turquoise, yellow and red. Her dark hair was pulled back in a sleek ponytail. I meant it; she looked fabulous.

She hugged me again, then spotted Tyson over my shoulder. "And you must be him," she sang, letting go of me.

"I might be." Tyson grinned.

She laughed. "Oh, you're definitely him. You're wearing it."

"That's twice now," Tyson said, looking at me then down at himself. "What? What am I wearing?"

Jasmine shook her head. "You are absolutely dripping with that 'I'm with her' look."

"Yeah?" he grinned, taking my hand. "Well, I think I can live with that."

Jaz laughed. "It's a really good look on you."

Tyson's grin broadened. "Thanks. I'm Tyson. I do have a name."

"I'm Jasmine. And believe me, I know your name."

I was about to jump into their banter when Harry Golding shouted for our attention. "Okay, people. Quiet down. Quiet down. They've just pulled up. Take your seats. January, are you ready?"

"For what?" I said, panicked. "What am I doing?"

He shrugged. "I don't know. What do you want to do?"

I had never planned this moment exactly, and I froze. "How about you get things rolling, Harry," I said, anxiously. "Then I'll say something."

His "*It will be my pleasure*," sounded like the opening he'd anticipated all along, which was more than fine with me.

I led Tyson, Jaz, and Oscar to our seats near where the piano had been staged. Harry said something to Zuli, then he walked to center of the room, straightened his tie, and squared his shoulders. He looked over at me and danced his unruly brows. A moment later, my family walked into the gathering room. I saw Grandy's sharp intake of breath. I was vaguely aware that Babi had taken hold of Poppy's arm, because he had stopped in his tracks and Tess's mouth had dropped open. But my gaze was decidedly on my mother.

Claire at first seemed only surprised by the size of the crowd—this was not the usual cultural night draw—but nothing else appeared to make an impression. Until Zuli walked them to where we were sitting. When my mother realized I was there, she broke away from Grandy and made her way to me, arms outstretched. I met her halfway. "Hey, Mom," I said in her ear as my family found their seats.

Zander had apparently been parking the car when everyone else walked in, and when he arrived, I realized we were one seat short. Without missing a beat, Tyson stood up and his presence did not escape Claire. She looked at me, at him, and then back at me. "Mom," I said. "This is Tyson Pierce. Remember, I told you about him."

My mother's shaky hands came to her mouth as she took Tyson in. If she was aware that all this was being played out in front of a room filled with spectators, she did not show it. She simply stepped closer to Tyson and patted his chest.

"It is so nice to finally meet you, Mrs. Duzinski," he said.

Her hand moved to her heart, and she pointed back at him.

Tyson smiled and then indicated his seat. "You'd better sit down, ma'am." He winked at me, then moved to the wall where he still had a clear view. I almost blew him a kiss.

When we were all seated, Harry Golding, who had been waiting patiently, cleared his throat. "Good evening, my friends," he said into the microphone. "It is my great honor to welcome you to Potomac Manor for this very special occasion. You may have noticed that we have something new and grand in our midst—no pun intended." He stepped aside and indicated the Steinway with a flourish and gave those gathered a few seconds to appreciate the sight. "But my friends this is much more than just a grand piano," he said. "Oh, indeed, it is. This magnificent instrument actually has an impressive history all its own. So, before our friend Miss January Duzinski delights us with a performance, she's going to tell us a little about this treasured piano and its owner." He nodded at me. "My dear."

I was suddenly nervous beyond belief and had absolutely no idea what I was going to say. I took a breath to settle my heart and glanced over at Claire where realization had begun to fill her good eye. I kissed her cheek, let go of her hand, and stood up.

I am very much not a public speaker, and the thought of a reporter somewhere in this room taking notes nearly pushed me over the edge.

So, I didn't look out at those gathered as I walked toward the Steinway. Instead, I looked over the sea of awards arranged on top of Claire's massive piano—all evidence of her great talent. I'd seen them, of course, and I knew much of the accomplishments they represented. I'd also been walking around in her life—in her words—for the past two weeks. But suddenly for some reason this moment—*this moment*—felt like a revelation and I got a little light-headed. I had to stop and remind myself to breathe. The picture of Claire receiving the prize for Musical Intelligence and Achievement at Yale caught my eye and calmed me. It was her face, her beautiful, smiling, somewhat shy, very humble, and very young face that settled my nerves. But that is not the award I was looking for. I picked up a smaller framed certificate with an attached ribbon that held considerably more significance and turned to the microphone.

"In 1999 my mom won First place at the Dabrowski Chopin Compendium. In attendance was a tall, kind, smart, dark-haired, Polish mortician. My dad lost his heart that night—but never thought he'd see her again.

"But a few days later there she was watching a parade on Fifth Avenue in New York. A Polish parade. Neither of them really should have been there. She was shopping for a dress. He was there on business. Their paths crossed just long enough for them to find each other. Long enough to make eye contact across a crowded street. Long enough for my mom to be compelled to hold her phone number high above her head, long enough for my dad to write it in his hand before she disappeared.

"The rest, as they say, is history." I put the award back on the piano. "It's been told that my father saved my mother, but I've come to understand that before he did that, she actually saved herself. My mom, Claire Duzinski, I've recently learned, has always been an incredibly strong woman. My dad couldn't help but love her.

"And he loved her like she'd never been loved before, with a love she never imagined existed. And she loved him back the same way. I found out a few days ago that all she ever wanted was to make music and babies with him for the rest of her life." My breath caught as I found Oscar's eyes; they were as wet as mine. I swallowed.

"That dream was shattered twenty-two years ago. That was the night my father died, and my mother was so terribly, terribly hurt.

That was the night I was born." I shook my head. "There is no doubt in my mind that she had a choice that night. I absolutely know that she could have gone with him. She was *that* hurt. I know she wanted to be with my dad. But she stayed. She hung on and delivered me, and then she stayed." I looked over at my mother, whose face was wet with tears, and shook my head.

"How can I ever thank you, Mom? How?" I rasped almost inaudibly. "Thank you for loving me. From the very beginning. And always. And especially when I didn't deserve it. Especially then."

Claire blew me a kiss with both hands, and I blew her one back. Then I just walked over and took her elbow. "Come over here, Mom."

She looked a bit unsure, but she didn't resist me as I led her to the piano. As applause broke out, I saw Monica Fairchild standing, smiling, applauding, near the back row. Even from this distance, I could see the shine of tears in her eyes. I couldn't believe how happy I was to see her.

I was a little concerned that this was overwhelming Claire, but she smiled through the moment even as she squeezed the blood out of my hand. When the room quieted, I put my arm around her and said into the microphone, "Most of you know my mom by her sweet disposition. She's highly agreeable, and she doesn't say much."

There was soft laughter from those who knew her, and I heard a pretty good bark from Harry Golding.

"But inside the sweet and quiet Claire Duzinski was once the phenomenal talent of a true virtuoso who competed and performed all over the world. She won awards everywhere she went, and these are but a sampling." I indicated the piano covered with evidence. "She was the pride of her parents. And though her relationship with them was complicated, they were her most ardent fans. And critics. And they believed in her so much that when she was sixteen, they gave her a piano—but not just any piano, a Steinway. This Steinway." I looked over to see fresh tears streaming down Claire's broken face as she shakily ran her small hand over the smooth ebony. As she did, a tiny moan rattled at the back of her throat. And when she leaned down and touched her lips to the piano, I felt like I had reunited two long-lost friends.

I'm almost sure the applause started with Tyson, but it grew to a standing ovation, and again I was a little worried about Claire. But when I joined in the clapping, and she touched her heart and smiled, I realized there was nothing to worry about.

After that, Harry Golding invited people to visit the dessert buffet as he and Poppy relocated Claire's awards to the fireplace mantle. I wanted to help but Grandy immediately scooped me up and hugged me like I'd won the Nobel Peace Prize. Monica did the same thing and I loved her for it. Tess squeezed my hand and thanked me for ruining her makeup—she did look pretty bad—then kissed my forehead. Then all three of them descended on sweet Claire as Tyson, patiently waiting his turn, just looked at me with watery eyes that said he thought I was amazing. I wanted to kiss him, but Poppy had beckoned him to help lift the lid of the concert grand. It was my chance to check the damage to my own face.

Jaz found me in the restroom freshening my mascara. She looked at me in the mirror and didn't smile.

"You know I have always loved you, January," she said earnestly. "You're my sister in every sense of the word, my keeper of terrible secrets, my knower of embarrassing moments. You're my solid thing, you know?"

"I know. Ditto."

She stepped close and leaned her chin on my shoulder, met my eyes in the mirror. "I didn't think you could get more *more*. But you did. I'm so happy for your mom. And I'm so happy for you…"

I turned around and hugged her. "Please don't make me cry again. I just fixed this mess."

"No promises. I love you. You did good. Finally."

I laughed. "Took me long enough though, right?"

"Yes, it did."

I sniffled. "I'll still share her with you, Jaz," I said. "You're her favorite daughter anyway."

"Oh, I know," Jaz laughed. "She and I just blinked about it."

When I got back, Poppy and Tyson and set the lid halfway and I tested the volume at that position. It was loud, but I didn't think it was too loud for this setting. I tried to get confirmation from Tyson, but he and my mother were in deep conversation with Monica Fairchild. Seeing Monica's arm over Claire's shoulder, my mother leaning in and my boyfriend listening intently to whatever Monica was saying, made me want to weep for its loveliness. I watched them with growing tenderness—Monica so animated, my mother so responsive, Tyson completely at ease. Grandy approached them at one point and hugged Monica again like she was the dear friend she'd once been. And as the three women laughed and caught up, I saw Tyson make his way to the dessert bar and come back with a plate for my mom. Claire touched her heart in thanks, the way she did, and patted his cheek. She liked him, which made me love him more than I had even an hour ago.

I observed all this as I keyed a few chords in preparation for playing some of my mother's favorite pieces. The notes were sheer perfection under my fingertips. The tone was so rich, so flawless, that I was certain I could have made Chopsticks sound Lincoln Center-worthy.

When I was ready, Harry made his way back to the microphone and called for quiet. When he had the attention of those seated, he said, "We all know Miss January here at the Manor. We've heard her play many times over the years. We've watched her grow up and into a formidable talent of her own. Now we know that part of the source of her gift is good genes." He looked over at Claire and bowed to her over prayer hands.

Again, my mother touched her heart.

Harry then looked back at the audience. "So tonight, Claire's lovely daughter will be playing selections that our Claire once performed herself." He then referred to the list I'd given him: "Beethoven's 'Moonlight Sonata,' Debussy's 'Toccata,' 'La Campenella' by Rodriguez, and after that…we'll see." He looked over at me. "Whenever you're ready, my dear."

I let a settling breath flow through me and glanced over at the front row. Babka's little head was resting on Grandy's shoulder—this was late for her. But when I smiled at Babi, she hard-blinked me her "I love you, Kochanie; you can do this." She'd done it every time I'd performed since I was a little girl, and it was my cue to begin.

So, I began.

I'd brought no music…well, almost no music; I knew these notes. But it would not have mattered because, just like when I had first sat down at this piano in my mother's childhood home, the spirit of this instrument was released. It was uncanny, as though it had a memory, had been trained in nuance and perfect phrasing by its owner, a true master. It was an incredible experience to sit where my mom had sat and be the conduit between the ghostly brilliance of preeminent composers and those hearing the beauty of their heart's work here tonight. The more I played, the more my world pared down to only pleasing them with my delivery of their gifts.

And I must have done okay, judging by the audience's reaction when I finally lifted my hands. I stood and bowed my head at the room then glanced at the first row. I did not know which pleased me more—the look on Tyson's face, or the look on Claire's.

It was the Steinway. And it did not disappoint.

I could have walked away then. It had been a good recital. But instead, I spread the only sheet music I'd brought across the rack in front of me. "Fantaisie Impromptu." Since the night Claire had helped me with it, I had played it at least fifty times. It was in my bones now, in my neurons, in my finger memory. I almost didn't need the music. Almost.

The room quieted, and I sat back down. But then I looked over at my mother and had a better thought. I held up a one-moment-please finger and walked over to her. "Will you help me with this last one, Mom?" I whispered in her ear.

Confused, she took my hand, and we walked slowly back to the piano—her piano.

When she saw the sheet music I'd laid out, she purred a little and hugged my arm. But when I asked her to help me start it off, her eye got very wide.

"It's right here, Mom, remember? The G-sharp octave—the all-important beginning." I pointed to the two keys and felt her tremble beside me. Then I waited.

She looked up at me like a little girl, unsure.

"We'll hold them for eight counts," I urged.

She stared at me.

"You can do it, Mom." I pointed. "That's your G-sharp, and I'll take the top one."

Her finger was shaking as it hovered over the key for a long, tense moment, long enough that I was starting to doubt what I'd asked of her. But when it came down with such distinct authority at the exact same moment as mine, I had never in my life heard a more beautiful sound. That single drop of pure melody held my world and made it hard to breathe. It resonated in the room, just as Chopin had intended—preparing, enticing, introducing what was to come.

At precisely the eighth count, my mother lifted her finger at the same time I did, smiled over at me in triumph, and sat back.

Then with my heart pounding, I continued the masterpiece she had begun.

The End